Other Books In This Series

Tesseracts Fifteen

A Case of Quite Curious Tales

Edited by
Julie Czerneda & Susan MacGregor

EDGE SCIENCE FICTION AND FANTASY PUBLISHING
AN IMPRINT OF HADES PUBLICATIONS, INC.
CALGARY

Tesseracts Fifteen: A Case of Quite Curious Tales
Copyright © 2011
All individual contributions copyright
by their respective authors.

EDGE

Edge Science Fiction and Fantasy Publishing
An Imprint of Hades Publications Inc.
P.O. Box 1714, Calgary, Alberta, T2P 2L7, Canada

Edited by Julie Czerneda and Susan MacGregor
Interior design by Janice Blaine
Cover Illustration by Michael O
ISBN: 978-1-894063-58-6

EDGE Science Fiction and Fantasy Publishing and Hades Publications, Inc. acknowledges the ongoing support of the Alberta Foundation for the Arts and the Canada Council for the Arts for our publishing programme.

Library and Archives Canada Cataloguing in Publication

CIP Data on file with the National Library of Canada

ISBN: 978-1-894063-58-6

(e-Book ISBN: 978-1-894817-94-3)

FIRST EDITION
(H-20110621)
Printed in Canada
www.edgewebsite.com

Table Of Contents

Foreword
by Julie Czerneda

The lid of the strange case in the corner creaks open, all by itself. An unseen cell receives a message, giving an intriguing chirp. A breeze from a nearby window wafts the scent of something unexpected past your nose. You pause. You pay attention. You must, you know. Why? Because you're curious.

Curiosity's primal. Our senses scan our surroundings, alerting us most urgently about sudden change. Useful, that. Change can mean opportunity. It can mean danger. Finding lunch or being lunch. We're hard-wired to notice the unexpected, then take action.

That hasn't changed with technology. Curiosity's about having a mind that's interested in, well, everything. A mind like that craves novelty and adventure. It searches for the good stuff.

Here it is. Take a look in the case and you'll find stories that startle. Plots to widen your eyes. Characters who'll dig into your heart when you least expect it. Wonder. Oh yes. That in great amounts.

What I won't promise? That you'll be satisfied.

Curiosity, fed by feats of imagination, can only grow.

Julie Czerneda

Foreword

by Susan MacGregor

When Brian Hades approached me at KeyCon in Winnipeg and asked me to co-edit *Tesseracts Fifteen* with Julie Czerneda, I was honored to be asked, but deep down I figured I was the wrong person to do it. For one thing, I didn't particularly like YA. Whenever we received a YA story at *On Spec*, I usually found the work below par or too young for the magazine. Naturally, I said nothing of this—editing *any* Tesseracts anthology is a huge privilege and I was not about to give that up. I also held my tongue when Julie suggested we ask for stories of "wonder and astonishment" that "engaged the imagination, inspired dreams and left hope in their wake". I had never been a wide-eyed, awe-inspired sort of kid. Instead, I was an old soul who watched the world through narrowed eyes. At six, I discovered that Santa Claus was really Mr. Johnson, the school janitor, dressed up in red. I knew that eating the crusts of my toast would *not* make my hair curly despite adult assurances. I grew up in a time when children were expected to be seen but not heard; I learned this lesson so well that by the time I was sixteen, I was a master at invisibility. My parents neither saw nor heard me come into the house after a night of partying. Uncles drank too much at family reunions, my parents fought when they thought I was asleep, my fourteen-year-old cousin ran away to Vancouver to panhandle with the hippies. My youth was a vivid, furtive time, but gritty rather than wonderful, real rather than sweet.

So it was with a great deal of cynicism that I began to read the slush. I fully expected to be immersed into fluffy forays that celebrated puppies left by Santa, club houses with "No Girls" scrawled on their doors, hockey triumphs and dreamy first loves. How wrong I was. Rather than these sappy sojourns, I was reminded of what it is to be young—*my* kind of young. Yes, there were moments of awe and happiness, but there were even more times of struggle, determination and endurance. As I read, I was often surprised by the honest and bitter-sweet portrayals that the best stories gave me.

A number of common themes emerged as the anthology evolved. Some of the pieces looked at the culture of today and tomorrow's youth—of gaming, of the bombardment of cyber information and the mystique of celebrity, of tagging. Other stories dealt with youthful motivations that are universal, of the need to be "cool", of that peculiar brand of youthful idealism where caution is thrown to the winds in favor of fertilizer and nitro, where the status quo is blown to bits. Some stories won me over because of their voice—their delivery so rushed, impulsive and fresh, that only a middle-schooler could make them, while others offered me vivid characterizations—the players as brash, nervous or practical as any of my childhood friends. Finally, every story I loved had a strong speculative element, a bright and glowing heart that brought the piece to life.

Editing this anthology has changed me in a way I didn't expect. I no longer dismiss YA short fiction as candy-coated prose, a stuffed rabbit held too long in sticky fingers. Excellent writing is excellent writing, in no matter what genre it finds itself. As it did for me, may you find yourself in these pages.

Susan MacGregor

A Safety of Crowds

by E. L. Chen

Jan's phone chimes. She fumbles for it on the bed and brings it up to her face, squinting at the bright display. GPS co-ordinates from London or New York or Vancouver—some city that she will only ever visit from the safety of her house—float on its glassy surface.

Jan scratches at her scarred shoulder blades, phone still cradled in her hand, and sits up. A stripe of sunlight lies across the bed sheets; the curtains have parted a finger's-width in the night. They will betray her in the end, she thinks. Anyone could be watching, even now at six in the morning. Charles could be crouched in the house across the street, clutching binoculars and hoping to add her to his life list.

A video, the message floating on her phone tells her. Would she like to see it? Yes, she would. Jan presses the play button. Bows her head over the phone. Feels unseen eyes raking the scar tissue on her hunched back. On the tiny glass screen, Jenna Crow waves and says hello.

The text message says to meet in front of the Metropolitan Opera at 3:30 p.m. Despite having had an hour's notice, about a hundred Crowheads show up, straggling off the street in threes and fours. They wear Jenna Crow's signifiers like a fairy's glamour: the black pixie shag wig, the blood clot-dark lipstick and Krishna-blue pancake makeup, the stick-on eyebrows, the oil slick feathers that sag off shoulders like an empty knapsack.

Passers-by eye them with mild curiosity, expecting them to break into a dance routine or some other PR stunt-worthy spectacle. But the Crowheads only ripple and murmur, raising their phones and viewing each other with the facial recognition software in their cameras. One of them could be the real Jenna. *Are you Jenna Crow? Are* you *Jenna Crow?* She's played hide-and-seek in a Crowhead flash mob before, first in Cannes last month and then in Tokyo's Harajuku district a week later.

Data whizzes over wireless and satellite networks. Somewhere in New Jersey, a server farm churns through the information like a farmer tilling a field and fires back what it finds. It thinks they are all Jenna Crow because of the hair and makeup. The Crowheads laugh and grumble and check their phones again to see if there are any updates. There aren't. Their phones are blank, save for a push from the Met and the occasional friend suggestion: *Show this message to the box office and get 15% off tickets for this evening's performance. Skatrboi (male, 16, 2 mutual friends) also likes Hellboy comics, Canadian indie bands, and Jenna Crow.* It's 3:45.

At 3:46 someone shrieks and points upward.

As one, the Crowheads turn their heads toward the sky at the hurtling smear of iridescent tar. A hundred phones jiggle and twitch in a hundred outstretched hands, but she's moving too fast for anyone to lock on her.

With a loud *whoomph* her wings unfurl like a great black sail—and she hangs five feet in the air, toes pointed to the ground, as if suspended by wires. She has never landed any other way. Always she falls, never flies.

"We're *all* Jenna Crow," Jenna Crow announces, beaming. The virtual shutters of a hundred cameras click.

On the outskirts of the crowd, the only one not hysterical with joy, Charles Wyn Crowley bites ragged, dirty nails and fails to push his way to the front.

No one knows where Jenna Crow came from or who she was before an NYU student, gazing up from Ground Zero through his phone's camera, saw the superimposed footage of Jenna Crow falling from twin towers that weren't there. A year later and she's a cultural juggernaut, one of the most recognized young women in the world because of her wings. The gossip blogs whisper: are they real or aren't they? Oddly, her Frida Kahlo eyebrows receive as much skepticism as her wings.

She's made appearances, both real and virtual, on every continent. There is even supposed to be a video in Antarctica, although no one has found it yet. Today, however, she's in Miami, being paid a lot of money to DJ a party that never happened.

The club is empty save for her crew and the sleepy-eyed manager who'd let them in. She perches on a barstool while the crew sets up, one petite leg demurely crossed over the other, her wings oozing over her back like motor oil. Her phone dangles in her hand, and occasionally there's the tap-tap-tap of long nails on a touch screen as she posts updates to her stream. Today's plain white T-shirt and innocuous blue jeans are sponsored by Abercrombie & Fitch; she can't remember whose black stilettos she's wearing but she's sure her fans will figure it out with image recognition. The T-shirt is artfully torn to accommodate her wings and publicize Abercrombie & Fitch's new line of distressed tees.

Wendy shows up a half hour later than everyone else, bringing breakfast and a stranger. Jenna freezes when she sees the stocky man with the chunky black-framed glasses. Her feathers shiver. They will give her away in the end, she thinks.

Wendy hands her a coffee and says, "Ivan had to fly back to Portland, his mother's in the hospital." Ivan is their video director. "This is Tim."

Jenna lifts up her phone and views him through the camera. He smiles nervously. On the phone's screen, a carousel of info-bubbles pop up around Tim's head: *Tim McKenzie a.k.a. tim_mc, TimmyMac, The Kenzer. 3 mutual friends. Male, 23, married to Keisha Porter McKenzie. View Tim's profile. View Tim's website. View Tim's stream. View photos of Tim. View videos of Tim. Send Tim a message.*

Wendy *(Wen Yi Lam a.k.a. wendilicious, CrowHandlr. 107 mutual friends)* clamps her hands firmly on Tim's shoulders, perhaps to give him confidence, perhaps to prevent him from running. Jenna never knows how someone will react when meeting her in the flesh. "I've worked with Tim before," Wendy says.

Unable to help himself, Tim reaches out to touch Jenna's wings. She smiles. They can never help themselves. "Nuh-uh," she says. She slaps his hand away. In the viewfinder of her phone, his face turns red.

"Sorry, they look so real," he says.

"They *are* real." She raises one of her famous Frida Kahlo eyebrows behind the phone at Wendy. Wendy shrugs.

Tim flushes again. "Sorry."

"Don't apologize. Everyone thinks they're fake." Jenna puts down the phone and extends her hand. "Welcome to the House of Crow, Timmy Mac. Shall we get started?"

His smile is sheepish, but his handshake is firm and professional. "Thanks," he says. "Er, if you wouldn't mind stepping behind the turntables for a minute, I'm going to check the lighting." Her crew is still setting up the ring of cameras around the club's stage. Jenna hops off the barstool and picks her way over the tangled wires on the dance floor, her wings flickering here and there for balance.

That night, a young man will raise his phone to identify the cute redhead dancing in front of the stage and see Jenna Crow superimposed on the screen, headphones held up to her ear and nodding in time to the music. He'll record a video, geotag it and post it online—and for the next few days the club will be packed with people eager for a glimpse of the ghost-Jenna spinning for a party in a mirror world that only exists in people's phones.

This morning, however, only Tim watches Jenna on the stage, peering through each camera in the ring. Wendy sits at the bar, her laptop open. The club's manager, looking a little less sleepy now that Wendy has doled out the coffee, trundles up to her with an envelope. "Excuse me," he says, "this was taped to the front door. It's addressed to 'J'. I figured it's for Jenna."

Wendy takes it from him and frowns. "Huh," she says. She purses her lips and tears the envelope open.

"Huh," she says again, this time louder. "Jenna, did you post where we are?"

"No. Did you?" Jenna looks down from the stage. Wendy shakes her head. "What is it?"

"Note for you," Wendy says.

"Let me see."

Wendy crosses the dance floor and hands her a single sheet of white paper on which someone has scrawled: *Never forget. Only I know who you really are and can free you. I'll see you soon, angel. -C.*

"Paper," sniffs Jenna, handing the note back down to Wendy. "How old school."

"Do you think it's Charles?" Wendy asks.

"No," Jenna lies.

"What is it?" Tim asks, looking up with alarm.

"Looks like I've got a stalker," Jenna says, trying to keep her voice light.

"Seriously?" Tim says. He looks from Jenna to Wendy and starts to laugh. "But isn't, like, *everyone* stalking you?"

"No one should know where I am right now," Jenna says. Her pulse races. Charles is looking for her after all this time.

He shouldn't know where she is right now. He shouldn't know, and yet he does.

Tim takes the note from Wendy and reads it. "Creepy. I can see why you're scared."

Jenna snorts. "I'm not scared. I have no fears. I'm a *celebrity*. I *am* my fears."

Once a week Jan takes her phone and maps out her world, which is growing increasingly and exponentially smaller. Six months ago she could walk ten blocks in any direction from her house without her phone going off. *Sorry, we could not find any potential friends in this area.* Now she's confined to the little side street the townhouse complex sits on. *Sorry, there is nothing tagged at this location. Be the first to post something here!.*

She yanks the hood of her sweatshirt over her head and peers through the peephole, keys clenched in her hand. She slides the deadbolts; first one, then the other. She opens the door. Slams the door. Locks the door.

She squints at the street. Her sunglasses provide little protection to eyes that rarely see natural light. She hears a noise and spins around, her heart pounding—but her front porch is empty. No one has jumped out behind her, no one has hidden behind a tree, waiting for her to emerge.

She takes a deep breath.

One foot after the other, she reminds herself. She counts her steps. One. Two. Three. She listens for the tell-tale chime from her pocket, the sound of a fork on crystal. She jumps when a man brushes past her, but he ignores the hooded figure walking deliberately, heel-to-toe, down the middle of the sidewalk. Charles isn't here, she tells herself. If she remains anonymous, people will ignore her like the man who just passed her did. She has nothing to fear as long as she's invisible.

Thirty steps. Thirty-one. Thirty-two. *Ding.* Jan pulls out her phone.

You are only 10 minutes away from the nearest Starbucks. There are currently 6 people registered at this location. You could be the 7th! Show this message to the barista and you will all receive free biscotti.

Jan feels shocked and dirty, like she's accidentally stepped on gum. Her back tickles from the sweat beading on the old scars. She hasn't even reached the intersection.

She retraces her path and begins to walk in the other direction from her house. One step. Two. Three. *Ding.*

1-bedroom plus den townhouse condo for rent starting Aug 1. AC, laundry, parking. View photos. Call landlord.

It's for the house next door. She's been painted into a corner. Oddly, Jan feels relieved. Now she can justify staying indoors. There is no point in going outside, anyway. Grocery deliveries, bill payments—they can be managed through her phone. Everything is paid for with electronic money from an account that lives, not in a physical bank vault, but in a space that exists in parallel to the real world. And as long as she too exists in a space parallel to the world, she'll be safe from her past life. Safe from Charles. No one can find her if she doesn't exist.

Jan retreats to her front door. Her mailbox bursts with a week's worth of mail—all junk, none of which is addressed to her. She scoops out a fistful of flyers. Unlocks her door. Opens the door. Slams the door. Locks the door.

A single white envelope falls out, addressed only with the letter *J*. Jan picks the envelope off the floor and tears it open, her heart pounding in her ears. She pulls out a folded sheet of paper. A few short sentences sprawl on its surface: *Never forget. Only I know who you really are and can free you. I'll see you soon, angel. -C.*

The paper flutters to the ground. Jan covers her face with her hands and weeps.

In her pocket, her phone chimes.

Jenna stirs. Her eyes feel swollen and gritty. She's passed out in her makeup again, as if she still needs to be Jenna Crow in her sleep.

Her phone buzzes. She digs it out of the standard anonymous hotel room linen—white sheets and camel-colored blanket. *MartyP (male, 20) is in your area and seeks women aged 18-22 for a relationship. Would you like to meet him?* "Way too early in the morning for this," she says to no one. "It would never work out, Marty."

She closes the message and taps out one of her own: *Livestreaming video in 5 minutes!* She sends it to her stream along with the GPS coordinates of her location.

After checking her hair and makeup, she turns on the phone's front-facing camera. "Morning, kids," she chirps to her mirror image on the screen. "Big day ahead. Tonight's event is going to be epic. But first, I'm going to tour this city. So keep your eyes out for yours truly!" She air-kisses herself and drops the phone back on the bed.

Then she snatches it up again and types: *So where can I get a decent cup of coffee in this town?*

Jenna crosses the room, tears open the heavy curtains, and stares out at—where is she? She checks the coordinates on her phone. Toronto, Canada. She stares out at the skyline. Steel and glass skyscrapers and a spindly tower that looks like set dressing for a '70s sci-fi movie. Everything is grey and cloudy, from the color of the sidewalks to the smoggy horizon. She takes a photo of herself with the CN Tower in the background and sends it to her stream.

She unfurls her wings and lets the feathers lick the window in a sad imitation of flying. They leave oily smudges on the glass. She sighs. Her flightless wings are her punishment, her reward. A constant reminder of her fears that she must wear like a hairshirt. She stretches, first toward the ceiling and then touches her toes. Her wings are a dead weight tugging at her back. She misses her chiropractor.

How did she let it get this far? How did she end up living like this, this artifice of a life like an abandoned snakeskin? Only Charles knows and remembers. He made her what she is, after all. She folds her wings around herself. The feathers are cool and alien against the skin of her arms.

The phone buzzes in her hand. A dozen replies already with recommendations for breakfast. She smiles. As Jenna Crow, she is never alone. She texts Wendy: *Going out. Back after lunch. Will post photos and videos.*

Wendy replies right away: *yes saw ur vid. don't forget mtv interview at 2. bodyguard?*

Jenna considers it. She doesn't feel safe with a bodyguard when she explores cities. It marks her as a tourist instead of part of the scenery. If she's not watched by someone who knows who she is, she can be whomever she wants. She thinks of Charles. *No,* she taps out. *I'll be fine.*

Thankfully Wendy doesn't protest: *cool have fun CU l8tr.*

High-top sneakers today instead of stilettos; she means to walk. In the elevator she checks her phone for the closest group of Crowheads. There are a handful of them only a few blocks away, straggling around the train station.

The train station is a hub for multiple types of trains, including the subway. *There are 54 photos, 26 videos, 6 blog posts and 21 notes associated with this location. Would you like to view them?* No one gives her a second glance as she fights her way through waves of commuters, released by the trains into the city for the day. Jenna wonders if there's a term for multiple crowds, like a *murder* of crows. A safety of crowds, she thinks, weaving and ducking upstream, her wings squeezed tightly against her body. Appropriately, there are only a few letters difference between *crowd* and *crow* and *Crowhead*. A murder of crows. A safety of Crowheads.

She waves cheerily at a pair of Crowheads standing in line at a coffee shop kiosk. They wave back. The open smile and wave is the Jenna Crow not-so-secret handshake.

"Where'd you get your wings?" one of them asks. She can't be more than thirteen, her blotchy cheeks barely camouflaged by a dusting of indigo-blue powder. "They look so real."

"I made them myself," Jenna says, not untruthfully. She pulls out her phone and views the girl through the camera. The girl raises her own phone and gasps.

"Are you Jenna Crow?" she asks.

"We're all Jenna Crow," Jenna says, grinning, showing the girl her phone. It has also identified her and her bored-looking friend as Jenna Crow. She throws an arm around the girl and flicks on the front-facing camera so that they can see themselves on her phone's screen. "Say cheese!" The girl grins, and the photo of the twin Jennas is sent sliding into the space between their eyes and the real world, waiting for the next person to stand in that spot to find.

Jenna buys a large Americano and a croissant—*Sara88 says, "Best chocolate croissants in town!"*—and bids goodbye to the two girls. She steps out of the train station and onto the street. Her phone tells her that the greatest concentration of Crowheads is at a shopping mall some blocks north of where she is now, so she starts ambling toward it, checking her phone periodically for posts that will give her a flavor of the city. *Lost cat last seen here on July 16, view photos. Bryan and Kris kissed at this location for 6 seconds on April 2. Buy tickets here for the Arcade Fire concert on August 14.*

It's the summer, and the city is full of decoys that don't have to be in school. No one bats an eye at the petite blue-faced figure seemingly wearing a black feathered cape. Jenna reaches the mall—*the Eaton Centre was one of the largest shopping malls in North America when it opened in 1977*—but does not enter. A dozen Crowheads stand on the street corner, incongruously in front of a large sporting goods store. She sidles up to the group's fringes and is delighted to find a boy there. Big cities yield male Crowheads; her current favorite, a drag queen named Jenna Faux, is the toast of New York. The boy gives her a small smile but doesn't say anything.

His wings look like part of a child's Halloween costume, the cheap elastic cutting into his shoulders.

The group's alpha members make a decision and they begin to move. Their plan is to camp outside the MTV studio where Jenna is to be interviewed later that day. Jenna lingers at the back, behind the boy who smiled at her. If anyone else notices her, they'll assume that someone else invited her along.

She holds out her phone, livestreaming the view of their backs as the cavalcade of Jenna Crows walks down the street. She wonders how long it will take them to realize that she is among them. She remembers a line from a T. S. Eliot poem. *Who is the third who walks always beside you? When I count, there are only you and I together.* She is the third, existing in the cracks in the world, the ghost in the machine.

After they've walked a few blocks, one of the Crowheads at the front of the procession pulls out his phone and checks the notifications. "Hey, Jenna Crow's streaming video from the city right now," he says. "Looks like she's pretty close."

The others cluster around him, peering down at the phone in his hand. Jenna records them long enough to stream their reactions as they realize they're onscreen—and then bolts, dashing down the sidewalk and then hooking a right onto a side street. "Are you Jenna Crow? Are *you* Jenna Crow?" she hears them jabbering to each other behind her.

"We're *all* Jenna Crow," she says, her shoulders heaving with breathless laughter as she stops to gauge her surroundings. She lifts up her phone and in the viewfinder, a stack of ghost images shuffles over the space before her like a deck of cards.

They all show the same image, although taken at different angles: a pale, slim figure seemingly crucified against a brick wall on a smear of feathery tar, head thrown back in either song or a scream—and then the phone darkens into sleep mode and Jenna sees only the reflection of her face in its screen.

Another mirror of Jenna, although this one is real, as real as a reflection of a simulacrum can be. *I am my fears.* "Damn," Mirror Jenna says. Her battery is dying. She must have forgotten to recharge it the night before.

Jenna shoves the phone back in her jeans pocket and looks around her with naked eyes. She's in an alley beside a row of narrow townhouses, crowded by garbage and recycling bins. She smells the sour milk tang of garbage and remembers blood and terror, brick scraping her raw shoulder blades. She remembers the only person she's ever feared.

Footsteps rasp against the ground, and Jenna realizes that she is not alone.

"Hello, Angel," Charles says.

Jan checks herself in the bathroom mirror: lank, chin-length hair, eyebrows thick and bushy like wings, skin dull and sallow from her self-imposed exile behind closed curtains. An alien face, devoid of gender and personality. It will suffice.

How did she let it get this far? How did she end up living like this, this fragile artifice of a life like an abandoned snakeskin? Only Charles knows and remembers. He made her what she is, after all.

Her phone chimes. Jenna Crow has posted a new video. *Would you like to view it now?* Jan accepts the video. A livestream of Jenna Crow's current location begins to play on the little screen. She appears to be behind a cadre of Crowheads who are oblivious to her. Hiding in plain sight, which is an incredible feat for someone as recognizable as Jenna Crow. Jan shakes her head. She closes the video and slips the phone into her pocket. It's time.

She pulls the hood of the sweatshirt over her head and checks herself again in the mirror. Mirror Jan still has a nondescript face. No distinguishing characteristics. Mirror Jan nods approvingly and turns away.

Jan plods down the stairs where the week's garbage waits by the door. Her heart pounds. This one adherence to social responsibility makes her feel human if only for a little while, and she's not sure if she likes it. Her sunglasses sit on a table by the door. She puts them on and instantly feels safer.

She peers through the peephole, keys clutched in one hand, garbage bag in the other. She slides the deadbolts; first one, then the other. She opens the door. Slams the door. Locks the door. Strides down to the sidewalk, the keys' metal teeth biting into her palm. The heat of the day surprises her; her climate-controlled home makes her lose track of the seasons.

Waste collection for the townhouse complex occurs three doors down, in an alley along the side of the building. An elderly couple shuffles down the sidewalk, and Jan slips behind them, ignoring her phone's insistent chiming. The couple pays her no attention. She remembers a line from a T. S. Eliot poem: *Who is the third who walks always beside you? When I count, there are only you and I together.* She is the third, existing only in the cracks of the world.

She hefts the garbage bag into a dumpster, breath shallow in her chest. The sour milk tang, amplified by the humid summer day, has vivid, visceral associations for her. Blood, dampness, terror. Pavement beneath her raw knees. Charles.

She pulls out her phone, closes the notification that her neighbor's house is for rent and scans the alley through the camera's lens. A carousel of ghost images superimposes themselves over the view on the phone's screen. All the photos are of a girl on her knees, folded to the ground as if praying, taken from different angles. Blood stains the back of her T-shirt. A black, feathery puddle spreads around her. Jan can't see her face. She can never see her face, no matter how many times she fans through the images.

Ding. A message pops up on the screen, obscuring the view of the alley.

Good news, we have found 1 friend for you in this area! charleswyncrowley (male, 21, 0 mutual friends) also likes solitude and Jenna Crow.

Footsteps rasp against pavement, and Jan realizes that someone has entered the alley.

"Hello, Angel," Charles says.

Charles comes closer, and closer still. He holds his phone in front of him at arm's length, watching her on the screen. "Hello, Angel," he says. "I missed you." His voice is kind and without malice. Jenna steps backward nonetheless.

"You've mistaken me for someone else," Jenna Crow lies. Her feathers ruffle as if stroked by an unseen hand.

A trace of a smile appears on Charles's face. "That's not what my phone says." He slips the phone in his jacket pocket without showing her the screen, but she knows it has betrayed her. Without the safety of crowds, she is the one and only Jenna Crow.

"I've been trying so hard to get you alone," he says. Everything about Charles is average: average height, average build, features that are neither too big nor too small, hair and eyes a nondescript brown. It has made him infuriatingly impossible to describe to Wendy and her bodyguards.

"Why? What do you want this time?" Jenna says.

Charles shakes his head. "You really don't remember, do you?"

"Remember what?" she spits. "I remember you. I remember—"

She breaks off and makes a wide gesture with her hands that might have been toward her wings or might have been toward him.

Jenna takes her phone out, praying that there is enough battery power left to call 911 or at least post her location to her stream. She switches it on and holds it up. A ghost video plays on the screen beside Charles *(charleswyncrowley, male, 21)*: a petite figure in a grey hooded sweatshirt backs away from him.

The screen flickers to black and again she sees only her reflection in the glass. "Do you see her?" Charles asks. "Do you *see*?"

"I don't see anything," Jenna says sullenly, slipping the dead phone back in her pocket. "Leave me alone."

"I can't," he says, and his face twists with genuine remorse. "I alone know who you really are, who you were before—"

"Before I was Jenna Crow?" she says, inching away from him, folded wings scraping against a brick wall.

"No," he says. "Even before then."

Jenna tries to remember what happened before the blood and fear and feathers and Charles, but comes up empty. Some of her struggle must appear on her face, for Charles nods and says, "Exactly. You were my—" His voice chokes and he closes his eyes, suddenly silent. When he opens them again, he reaches into his jacket and pulls out a knife. The blade is long and glossy like one of her feathers. "It's time, Angel." He steps toward her.

Fight or flight. Flight is useless in Jenna's case, so her feet remain fixed to the ground. Charles is not large, but he is strong and Jenna is all skin and bones and trembling feathers. He seizes her by the arm and the old terror floods through her and drowns her memory of being Jenna Crow, the woman who has no fears. She forgets how to scream.

He lays the blade on her back and applies gentle pressure. Her feathers twitch helplessly. Blood oozes down her spine like honey.

"I'm sorry," he whispers. "I have to do this." Something wet drips on her bare forearm, and she realizes that he's crying. *But you made me what I am*, she thinks, and then his wrist jerks.

Jenna finally finds her voice and screams. There is a crack and a crash, like a tree tumbling in the woods, and Jenna's left wing collapses onto blood-spattered pavement, twitching.

"I'm so sorry," he says. Jenna screams again. The right wing deflates into an accordion fold of feathers and falls atop the left.

Jenna falls to her knees, her breath fast and shallow in her lungs. A strangled cry carves the air, but it's come from Charles's lips, not hers.

"I don't understand," he says, viewing her through his phone. "I can still see her. The cycle should've been broken. You should have become one—"

Charles's head snaps up at the sound of feet scuffing pavement. He swears and tucks the bloodied knife back into his jacket. "This isn't over, Angel," he says and dashes away in the opposite direction of the footsteps.

Two men and a woman round the corner, phones clutched in their hands. The woman says, "Is everything okay? We heard screaming—"

She gasps. "Are you…are you Jenna Crow?" She and her friends view Jenna through their phones. Virtual shutters click.

"We're all Jenna Crow," Jenna whispers, and only then does she look up.

"Can I have your jacket?" she asks one of the men.

"What?" he says, stepping back.

"Can I have your jacket?"

The woman makes an impatient gesture at him and he says, "Yeah, sure." He takes it off and hands it to Jenna.

The denim is warm and soft. Jenna wraps it around her shoulders and staggers to her feet. "Thank you," she says and then she runs.

Back at the hotel, she sits under the shower with her clothes still on, watching blood and blue makeup swirl down the drain. Beyond the hammering of the water she can hear a faint pounding on her door; it's probably Wendy, but she doesn't want to talk to her. She doesn't want to talk to anyone. In her mind, she is still running.

Charles holds out his phone before him, viewing Jan through its lens. "Hello, Angel," he says.

He comes closer and closer still. He is a man of average height, build and face, but the scar tissue on Jan's back tingles at the sight of him, nonetheless. She feels the itch beneath her skin; her body remembers him well even if she doesn't.

"I'm not an angel," Jan croaks. Her tongue is a wedge of dried meat sitting in a mouth as dry and brittle as onion skin. She can't remember the last time she spoke out loud.

Charles reaches out and tugs the hood of her sweatshirt off of her head and then plucks off her sunglasses. "That's not what my phone says," he says in a gentle tone as if reprimanding a child. He tucks the phone in his jacket pocket without showing her the screen.

"Leave me alone," she says. "You got what you came for last time."

"I can't," he says, and his face pinches with genuine regret. Jan inches backward until she finds herself pressed against brick. The sour smell from the garbage cans chokes her, or maybe it is her own fear. "Oh, Angel, you've forgotten so much. And I messed it up last time."

Jan lifts up her phone and views him on the screen: *Charles Wyn Crowley a.k.a. charleswyncrowley, male, 21*. No other information pops up in the carousel. Beside him, however, she sees the ghost footage of a pretty young Crowhead staring at him, backing away with a phone in her hand, stark horror and confusion on her pixie-like face. Her wings cascade from her shoulders, feathers fluttering in an unseen wind.

"Is that—" she says.

Charles grabs her wrist, and she cries out in pain and surprise. No one has touched her for a long time. "Do you see her?" Charles urges. "Do you *see*?"

The ghost video flickers and disappears as his anguished face fills the viewfinder of her phone. "I—I don't know," she says.

"You have to remember. You have to remember who you were before, when you were my—" His voice breaks off. Jan tries to remember how she came to this point in her life, but all she remembers is blood and fear and feathers and Charles. "I'm here to make it right," he babbles. "I'm here to make you whole again."

But you made me what I am, Jan wants to say. She steps back, hands outstretched, until she feels jagged brick scrape her shoulder blades. He seizes her by the arm. Her phone drops. The glass screen shatters.

Terror builds inside Jan's chest but has no place to grow; her pounding heart is already as taut as a drum. The skin on her back feels as if it's on fire. She has forgotten how to scream, but she screams anyway. The surface tension breaks, releasing every nightmare that has haunted her since the last time Charles stole her memories.

He recoils in horror, releasing her arm as if it were a live snake. "No!" he says, his eyes wide. "Not again!"

Feathers as thick as tongues burst from Jan's upper back, licking the torn skin like flame and slicing through the layers of T-shirt and sweatshirt. Something hot trickles down her back; at first she thinks it's sweat, and then she sees crimson droplets on the ground. Her wings snap out like a switchblade, wet and downy like a newborn chick, and Jan realizes that her feet are dangling above the ground.

Charles turns his wide eyes from her to the sound of running footsteps. "It wasn't supposed to happen like this, again," he says with despair.

Two young men and a woman round the corner, phones in their hands, the woman saying, "Is everything all right? We heard—" They stop in their tracks. "Oh my God," one of the men breathes. They raise their phones, and photos of the angel Jan slide into the space between one's eye and the real world.

Jen's phone chimes. She squints at the lit-up display. Scratches at her scarred shoulder blades. A video, the message floating on her phone tells her. From London or New York or Vancouver. Jen presses the play button.

On the tiny glass screen, Janna Crow waves and says hello.

By day, **E. L. Chen** pushes pixels at an interactive agency in downtown Toronto. By night...she sleeps. Most of "A Safety of Crowds" (as well as this bio) was written during her lunch hour, appropriately on an iPhone accessing the cloud. Elaine has been previously published in anthologies *The Dragon and the Stars*, *Tesseracts Twelve*, and *Tesseracts Nine*, and in magazines such as *On Spec*, *Ideomancer*, and *Strange Horizons*. She lives in Toronto with a very nice husband, two lagomorphs, and, at the time of writing this, a (currently) unborn fetus. An early version of "A Safety of Crowds" cast Jenna Crow as a frequently-televised rock star, which goes to show you how much has changed in the past few years.

Fragile Things
by Amanda Sun

There are only two news crews this morning, so after I turn out the workhorses and feed the unicorn, I might actually make it to the bus before it pulls away. Maybe.

I take a bite out of the stale bagel Dad's left out on the counter and slug down my glass of orange juice. It makes a sticky ring on the table when I clank the glass down and hoist my backpack over one shoulder.

I stand in front of the chipped green door a moment, catching my breath before I have to go out there.

"Two cups of bran!" Dad hollers down the stairs. His voice is slurred, but I can't tell if it's from sleep or booze.

You think he'd know by now that I know how much to feed the friggen' Frankengoat.

I squelch the ugly door inward and press on the hinges of the screen. I head for the barn, keeping my head down so I don't make eye contact with the reporters out front. The more aggressive ones used to follow me from house to barn, but since Dad put out the NO TRESPASSING and BEWARE OF DOG signs, the reporters have lost their nerve. Too bad they don't realize the dog is a ten-inch high Chihuahua named Paris. Dad's girlfriend has a dumb sense of humor.

My fingers slip into my pocket for the key to the side door of the barn. I jiggle the padlock on the door, listening for any fancy-loafered footsteps that might thunder up the dirt path. But they don't and I pull the rusty lock open, slipping into the musty darkness of the stable.

The Clydesdales whinny in the stuffy air and once my eyes adjust, I see Bill's velvet snout sticking out above the grimy stall door, his nostrils huge and sniffing. I want to reach out and feel the greasy silkiness of his muzzle, but I'm late enough as it is, and I can't miss another English class or Ms. Jung will seriously murder me.

I climb the ladder up to the loft and pull down two flakes of hay, the jagged ends sticking my fingers like sharp needles. I toss them into the other stalls and listen to the sounds of munching. I have to go into the storeroom for the lead, and I reach above Bill's door and clip it onto the halter ring, but not before his big-arse workhorse muzzle reaches out and slimes the arm of my jacket.

"Agh!" I stare at him with fury in my eyes, but he just keeps blowing his warm breath all over me. "Dumb horse."

I check my watch. There's no way I'm gonna make it now.

I shovel two scoops of bran into a black rubber pail and carry it to the stall at the very end where the unicorn is practically gleaming in the dust and woodchips.

He lifts his head to look at me briefly, his vacant eyes staring at mine, and when he sees the little cloud of dust as the grain pours into his bucket, he figures it's worth walking across the stall for.

It's not like I hate him. I'm just sick of the attention a defective horse gets. It's like those puppies born with three heads—you wouldn't think that's a real Cerberus, so what the heck makes the unicorn more than a deformed horse with a goat antler twisting out of its head?

He looks like the dog from *The Grinch Who Stole Christmas*.

I check my watch again. *Frig*. I head for the door, locking the padlock behind me and shoving the key deep into my pocket. I shoulder my backpack and look down.

Always look down. That way, you won't feel like crap for not answering them.

I hear the feet pounding in the dirt as I push toward the street. They're coming now. They're not going to hold back.

"Alex, can you tell us how the unicorn is doing today?"

I hate when they call me by name. Like they know me or something.

"Have you received any calls today regarding this week's miracles? Can you fill us in?"

No one ever believes me about the Frankengoat. There aren't any miracles, but Dad says it's better for business if no one knows that. So we just keep our mouths shut and people keep making stuff up.

"Alex," and this time it's a woman's voice, and I know she's that pushy reporter that got her pumps stuck in the mud last week. "Has the unicorn healed anyone today? Is it true you're trying to breed him?"

I snort a little at that one. I can't help it. Like we'd want double the attention. Although we're pretty sure he's sterile, anyway. Mules usually are.

"Mr. Wheeler, can you make a statement about the Wiccan priestess visiting the premises this coming weekend? Are you expecting any unusual results?"

Bunch of morons. Do they really believe this crap, or does it just make good news?

I can hear the engine of the school bus. My eyes flick up from the ground, from my scruffy red-and-white sneakers to the long black trousers the crews are wearing. A couple of men hoist heavy black cameras on their shoulders while the reporters shove microphones at my throat. Through them all I can see the mustard-yellow school bus rumbling from side to side as it snorts forward.

Crap.

I push my way past the news crews, squeezing my backpack straps with both hands as I race after the bus.

"Mr. Wheeler!"

The school bus isn't stopping, so I run up alongside it and bang on the side of the bus.

"Mr. Wheeler, could you let us in to take photos of the unicorn?"

I slap the metal with my palms over and over until the bus screeches and jumps back on its lousy brakes. The little flashing stop sign stretches out to the side, and I run to the door opening wide to swallow me in.

The reporters rush right up behind me, and the doors close in front of their microphones. The bus jerks forward and I climb up the steps to the driver.

I watch the news crews drift away through the cloudy glass windows.

"That stuff's crap, man," says Riley, lifting a cigarette to his lips. We're standing a foot off school grounds so the teachers can watch us smoke but can't do a thing about it. "How can you stand it?"

I shrug and flick my lighter until the end of the cigarette flares red.

I didn't ask for the unicorn, but before it was born Dad and I were gonna get evicted. Since then we've been getting by, so who cares what people think? We've got a roof over our heads, even if it leaks when it rains. Maybe that's the one miracle the dumb mule ever managed for us.

"Hey," Riley says. "She's looking at you again."

I look over at the school parking lot and she's there, Lily Thomson, wearing a light purple crocheted cap over her pale blond hair. I catch her eye and she looks away, clutching her books to her chest and pretending to talk with her friends.

"What's she see in you?" Riley says, and I smack him in the arm while he laughs, but really, he's right, because what could she see in a slacking loser like me with dried horse snot down his jacket sleeve? She's frail as a china doll, her once-curvy legs now skeleton-thin and her face so pale you'd wonder if she has a pulse. She coughed through half of English class before Ms. Jung finally asked her to go to the nurse's office, which pissed me off—like she doesn't get juggled enough between doctors who can't figure out what the heck is wrong with her.

I look back at Riley and take a drag from the cigarette.

"She wants you."

"Shut up, Riley," I say and flick the ash at him. But when I look back at the girls, she's looking over again, and just seeing her green eyes makes my skin go all hot and itchy.

"Hi."

She talks to me. She friggen' talks to me, like this is some sort of normal conversation. Like girls from her side of town talk to drugged-out farm boys like me. She's holding the violin case from her music class, and I'm walking past to Chemistry 'cause I wouldn't touch music with a ten foot pole. I stop, my back almost pressed against the rusty peach lockers lining the hallway, the heat spreading down the back of my neck.

She's still wearing that crocheted cap, a pink flower unfurling on the side of it. I wonder if she made it herself, or if her mom bought it for her at the Loghouse. She stands there looking so delicate, like if I reach out and touch her arm, it might break off.

I just stare at her, so she tries again.

"Alex Wheeler." And the sound of my name on her tongue gives me goose bumps, but I try to look like I don't care, so I kind of shrug and lean back into the lockers.

"Lily Thomson," I say, hoping she'll think I'm making fun of her, hoping she won't hear the way my voice wavered when I said her name. And then she smiles, this tiny little afraid smile that makes me wonder how she could have made it this far in life and still smile like that. I bet her dad's never slapped her around in his life.

"I saw your mom on the news," she says.

"She's not my mom," I snap and as the smile fades from her unsure lips, I kick and scream inside my head because of course she thought it was my mom. It's not her fault, so why am I getting all worked up about it? But I want to look like I don't care, so I keep staring her down to see if she'll leave.

She doesn't.

"Is it true the Pope is coming to see it?"

That one makes me laugh, and I shake my head, running a nervous hand through my close-cut hair. Why is my hand friggen' shaking? She looks so fragile, like she's gonna spook the way horses do. One loud sound and I might scare her off.

"The Pope's not coming," I say, "but we did have a busload of Tibetan monks last week." She smiles and it feels like it spreads through me too, the warmth of it tingling in the pads of my fingers and the back of my neck.

She's silent for a minute, squeezing the handle of her violin case tighter between her pale fingers.

"Do you think I can come see him?" she whispers, eyes down to the floor.

No friggen' way—does she believe in that stuff? Does she really think he's a unicorn?

And then she looks up at me with those green eyes with flecks of brown that gleam under the buzzing hallway lights, those eyes that look like miniature forests you could just as easily get lost in....

"Whatever," I shrug, while my heart pounds in my chest. "But it'll have to be after six." After the visiting hours finish up for the day, after the news crews pack up and rumble away in their white glossy vans.

"Okay," she smiles, and she only makes it halfway down the hall before she has one of her coughing fits, and some of Riley's friends are crowding me in the hallway and calling me awful things for talking to her, shouting gross names until I punch one of them in the arm and he falls over laughing, but who cares?

Lily Thomson is coming to my house.

Lily fumbles with the rusty handle and I have to kick the door from the inside to make it open. Her face is pinker than I've ever seen—she's always pale as china—so I hear the apologies flooding out of my mouth before I can stop them.

"Everyone has trouble with that handle," I say. Which is kind of true. They just don't need me to kick out the truck door.

She's still wearing the same crocheted hat and a long jean skirt that looks too old to be in fashion, but the curves fit her in all the right places, and I have to stare at the road for a while until I can think of something else.

We used to let anyone come to see the unicorn for free, but with our money issues, Dad decided to start charging. And then one time some medieval nutcase decked out in full regalia jumped the fence. Her skirt billowing in the wind scared the crap out of the unicorn, but the wacko kept chasing him until Dad tackled her, while the news crews filmed everything. Since then we've had to restrict visiting times and pre-screen guests, at least until we can get the new secured paddock installed for next summer. It's like living at a friggen' zoo.

It's dark out now, and the vigil of New Agers snuffed their candles and left about half an hour ago. I don't want my dad to know Lily's visiting, because I don't know if she'd ever talk to me again after stepping foot in my house. It's not like things are that bad, but I can only imagine that Lily lives in some kind of castle compared to the grimy, cluttered home we try to exist in. So after we park I take her straight to the barn which looks like it suits her just fine.

I fumble with the padlock and yank it open with more force than I need to. I'm trying to show off, but instead I pull a weird muscle in my arm and the pain sears through me like crazy. I don't want to show her it hurts, so I just sort of shake my arm a bit and curse a little. I swear she giggles before she breaks out coughing.

I say nothing but open the door wide so she can step in. She's got her frail fingers cupped around her mouth as she coughs, but she ducks into the dark mustiness of the stable.

I flick on more lights and she stops coughing for a bit.

"You have other horses?" she says and I nod.

"A pair of horses for driving," I say, "and a couple studs."

She looks in the stalls, but all we can see are velvet noses munching in the darkness.

"Cute," she says, looking in Bill's stall. Her hair curls around her shoulders and looks as thin as the rest of her, and I wonder if she'll talk to me again after this, if she'll look my way again or if it's a one-time curiosity. I wonder if I'll see the same fear in her eyes as the time I flicked my lighter over and over at the back of English class.

The last stall around the corner is the unicorn's, and she moves toward it slowly, full of anticipation. I want to tell her it's just the Frankengoat, that it's just a mule with a birth defect. But there's so much reverence in her wide green eyes that I keep my mouth shut. Her life's been all about losing things, about hopes being destroyed. Maybe this once I can make it more than it is. Maybe I can make it real for her.

She presses her thin fingers between the bars of the stall door, lifting onto her toes to look into the darkness. I stand close beside her, rising up on the balls of my feet to help her search.

"Ain't there," I say. "Must be in the paddock."

"The paddock?" she says, and as we crane our necks to stare into the empty stall, I feel the warmth from her hand as it presses against me, like the heat shoots from her skin straight into mine.

"We can't put him in the front paddock at night," I say. "Not safe. So we turn him out in the back paddock if his legs need a stretch." I rock back on my heels and lead her down the hall, pull on the big metal bolts and slide the door back into the frame of the wall. "At night we have to turn on the security cameras," I tell her, and she wraps her jacket tighter around herself. I feel like I should give her my jacket or something, but when I look down I can still see the patches of horse snot smeared up the sleeves.

But she's not looking at me, anyway. Her eyes are far away, far from the hay bales stacked against the side of the barn. Far from me or my dirty jacket, far from anything familiar.

He's gleaming in the darkness, the whiteness of his coat somehow radiating like the stars. He's always been spooky like that, lit from inside somehow in a way our other horses aren't. But tonight he practically glows, his white mane tumbling down his neck as he shakes his head from side to side, searching the ground with his big velvet muzzle.

His antler hits against the fence of the paddock as he bobs his head up and down over a patch of grass. *Tak, tak, tak.*

Lily walks toward him like she doesn't own her own feet anymore, like she's compelled to be closer to him. I don't blame her—lots of people react that way, but I usually roll my eyes. With her, I can't take my eyes off them. The hem of her skirt glows just a little, the way the unicorn does, and they look like such a pair I can't believe it.

And then Lily starts coughing, harder and harder, and she lifts her hands to her mouth and hunches over. The unicorn lifts his head so quickly to see what's going on that his antler hits three planks like a wooden xylophone.

And the coughing pisses me off, because why can't the doctors figure out what it is already and help her?

"You okay?" I say, moving toward her in the darkness. I can hear the unicorn snorting through his big nostrils.

She stops coughing and nods, all the color drained from her face. I want to reach out and tuck her hair behind her ear, warm up her icy cheek with my hand, but instead I step back like a friggen' coward.

She wraps her fingers around the fence and the unicorn comes right up to sniff them. "Sorry I frightened you," she says quietly, but I don't know if she's talking to me or the mule.

The unicorn gets bored when we don't shove carrots and apples at him, so he takes off down the paddock to the water bucket. I can see Lily's face fall as he steps away and suddenly I'm so angry the heat feels like it's radiating from my skin.

Because what the heck? Both of them are so beautiful but there's something seriously wrong with them.

And I start to think maybe they can help each other, maybe I can fix things for her, just for one night....

"Want to pet him?" I say and Lily looks at me with those green eyes that tense every muscle in my body.

"Can I?" she says. I nod and grab the fence with my hands, pulling myself over the planks. I know it's going to set off the security cameras, but this is more important than Dad's rules.

I reach for Lily's hand and help her climb the fence. I can't let her in through the gate because it's closed with a special padlock, and the key's in the house. Anyway, lifting her over the fence makes me look strong, like I could take on the whole world for her.

Her feet land in the soft dirt of the paddock and I jump down beside her. We probably only have a few minutes before my dad figures out what I'm up to, but somehow I don't want to rush her.

The unicorn perks up at the sound and peers at us, his head held high. Steam rises off his back in the darkness, and he's still gleaming from ear to hoof. Lily steps toward him slowly, carefully, and he stands there, his ears flipping back and forth as he watches her with his big brown eyes.

She's stepping toward him, and he's standing there watching her, and everything in my world seems right for a minute.

And then the unicorn lets out this really loud whinny like I've never heard before because he never makes a peep, and the sound startles the crap out of me. Lily goes all rigid, and suddenly he's galloping at her and my throat tightens up because if she doesn't move, he's going to plow her down.

I stumble forward, the dirt squelching as it sticks to my sneakers.

I'm not going to make it, I'm not going to—

And right in front of Lily, the unicorn digs in his front hoofs and his whole body ripples with the effort to stop, and then he's lifting above her, rearing and flailing his legs near her face....

And she's screaming—

And I'm screaming—

And then he bends his nose toward his belly, and his antler goes straight into her chest with a terrible sucking sound, and she's not screaming anymore—

I run toward her, shouting her name, and I give the unicorn a hard shove and he bolts away. I press my hand against the red trickling down Lily's shirt but she's passed out, and then the lights flick on in the barn and I know Dad is coming, cell phone pressed to his ear.

And for the first time in a long time, tears streaking my vision all blurry, my dad can't come to my side soon enough.

She's sitting up in the bed when they finally let me in, and there's a pale smile on her lips, tinged with the same blue as the hospital robe. I want to ask how she's feeling but I'm burning up 'cause they wouldn't let me stay with her when we got here, just wheeled her away and left me in the waiting room. Like I wasn't broken, too.

There are five news crews outside the hospital and more arriving but I want Lily to feel better, so I try to look like I haven't been flipping out, like I'm not scared what's going to happen if the reporters show up outside her house.

"Are you okay?" she says to me.

To *me*.

"What about you?" I say. "Does it hurt?"

She shakes her head from side to side.

"A bunch of stitches, but I'm fine."

I want to say I'm sorry, that I was stupid to put her in the paddock with a mutated Frankengoat, but the words stick in my throat.

He nearly killed her. That's what I heard her parents whispering with the doctor. If he'd hit any closer to her heart—

But he didn't. And she's okay.

And the hate in me wells up, buzzes in my ears, and I'm glad Dad promised Mr. Thomson that the unicorn's gonna be destroyed...

And then Lily's smile fades and we both realize something. Because she isn't coughing. Not at all.

"Lily," I say, and she touches her chest, taking breaths so deep the bed sheets crinkle up and down.

"I can breathe," she says, her eyes those forests of green. I touch her hand and it's warm, not icy, but warm.

She presses the call button and starts babbling to the first nurse who comes in, who gets a doctor, who gets another doctor...

And my head is swimming, because I've been in here half an hour now, and she ain't coughing.

And she looks at me, and I look at her, and we know it somehow. The unicorn was trying to save her.

I stumble outside and press my phone to my ear, wait for my dad's voice to pick up.

"You ready to come home?" he says.

"Dad," I say. "We can't destroy the unicorn."

He hesitates. "Alex—"

"She can breathe, Dad. He was helping her. He's real!"

"Alex, I'm coming to pick you up now. It's late."

Tears are burning in my eyes, my pulse drumming in my ears. "You're not listening. You have to—"

"Look," he says. "The unicorn is already in the trailer, and Max is picking him up in an hour. The press won't leave us alone, and if Mr. Thomson sues we can't...." And my ears buzz so loudly I can't hear him, because no matter what I say he isn't. Friggen'. Listening.

I snap the phone shut and go back to Lily who's sitting there not coughing. Her cheeks are actually pink when I go in.

She reaches for my hand, her warm fingers wrapping around mine, her eyes wide and damp.

And we both know what I have to do.

The truck stinks of saddle soap and leather, and my hands are shaking so much I can barely slip the key into the ignition. As soon as I turn the key, Dad's going to hear. He'll come stomping out and it'll all be over.

The press is camping out at the end of the street, talking to protesters in medieval dress, so it's my one chance to slip out the back path onto Wylie Road. A breath shudders through me, every inch of my skin prickling, and then I turn the key.

I release the brake handle and step on the gas slowly, pulling the trailer behind me as we rumble through the dirt. I can barely see in the moonlight, but there's no way I'm going to put the headlights on. I want to bolt but it'll be too obvious, so I creep out of the back driveway like a snail, my mind screaming that I'll be caught any minute.

But then I'm at the end of the path and no one's run up to me yet. I turn onto the road and after the bump from dirt to gravel, suddenly everything is smooth, and we're traveling away from the barn, away from the candlelit New Age protest and Max driving up in his black pick-up.

And I don't know where the unicorn and I are going, but I know it's somehow toward life.

I drive until my legs ache, until the twang of country voices on the radio make my eyes heavy with sleep. I drive deep into forest, letting the branches tangle around the trailer, letting them claw at the windshield.

And when the truck can't go any farther down the narrow path, I turn the key and the rumble of the engine dies away.

I pull out the pin on the loading ramp and it slumps down into the ground. The unicorn's inside, gleaming in the darkness like a lantern. He stumbles backward down the ramp, tossing his head as he goes.

"Easy, boy," I say against the clank of hoof stomping on metal.

I reach my hands around his halter and unclip it, lifting it over the tufts of his ears.

And it's time, and tears well up in my eyes before I blink them back.

Because farm boys like me don't cry. And I'm darn well not going to start now.

And the unicorn's staring at me like a big, doe-eyed idiot.

"Go on," I say, lifting the loading ramp and sliding the thick pin back through the door.

He blinks at me.

And I think about Lily, knowing that he saved her life somehow. He's not defective. He's not broken.

But I kind of feel maybe I am.

"Go," I say again, but instead he reaches his big muzzle at me and blows hot breaths in my face until I press my fingers into the velvet of them.

And he's still standing there, and they're going to follow my tracks and find him and then....

"Get lost!" I shout at him and I snap off a branch and smack him on the flank.

He bolts into the trees, and at first I can see the gleam of moonlight off his backside, and then he's gone.

And I'm glad he's gone.

And I fall to my knees in the damp grass, and I cry until my body aches, until I cry so much that I cough and cough and can't stop.

And when I finally stand up, I can breathe.

Amanda Sun grew up in Deep River, Ontario, where she learned to ride horses on the same Wylie Road as in "Fragile Things." Sadly no unicorns there, but they could be quite possibly roaming Algonquin Park.

When Sun isn't writing into the wee hours while her daughter sleeps, she's knitting, gaming, and sewing costumes. Her love of cultures has led her to study Japanese, French, Ojibwe, Latin, and Middle Egyptian hieroglyphic—and to complete a degree in Classical and Near Eastern Archaeology.

Sun won the 2007 *Room Magazine* Fiction Contest, and was also published by Drollerie Press in the anthology *Playthings of the Gods,* where she cast Icarus as a mutated teen trapped in a dystopian labyrinth. She's currently hard at work on her YA Fantasy novel set in Japan.

Sun interns at Harlequin TEEN, where she gets to work with fabulous YA books—and booklovers—all day.

Just Dance
by Erika Holt

A shrill keening burst into Marie-Lunie's head as the power needles she'd pressed into the ground around her house warned of an intruder.

"Uuuh!" she growled to no one. Reluctantly she set aside her father's dusty notebook before extinguishing the array of lanterns. Whoever was here had likely already seen the candles flickering through the tower's stained-glass windows, but she wasn't going to make things any easier for them.

Looking out with her left eye—her regular eye—she scanned the garden below. No shadowy figures lurked. But the overgrown caragana, honeysuckle, and cotoneasters offered many hiding places, and there could be *other* things about, things not visible to her left eye. She flipped up the patch over her right socket, now filled with the crimson glass orb she'd found six months earlier on a tiny tripod hidden behind her father's books.

Why she'd thought to try the thing as a surrogate eye, she didn't know. Intuition maybe, or an inherited sense of curiosity. It'd taken some doing to insert the delicate thing into her tight socket, empty since birth, but she'd managed. When the first new images had popped into view, Marie wondered why her father hadn't said anything, hadn't offered this wondrous bulb to give her back full sight. Then she'd looked outside and understood.

Peering outside now, the world seemed to throb and stretch, as though through a web of living blood—the Otherrealm, a place that existed both within and apart from reality. But nothing unnatural stirred, no ghouls seemed to be about at the moment. She flipped the patch down.

So, who was here? The house was at the end of the road on the outskirts of town, not on anyone's way anywhere. It'd been at least three months since an RCMP officer or Concerned Teacher had ventured near the place, and she'd added five more needles to the perimeter since then, imbuing them with strong *stay away* urgings that had, so far, worked. Whoever it was that crept through her garden must've come here *specifically*, with a steely determination to make it past her defenses.

Tip-toeing through clutter on the floor, Marie-Lunie settled into her father's oversized armchair and curled in her limbs like a spider. She listened.

The doorbell gonged, bouncing around the dusty house like a racquet ball. Light knocking followed. A pause, and then a loud creak as the heavy front door opened. Gutsy. If the intruder said anything, their voice was lost somewhere in the two floors between.

Marie-Lunie reached for her father's slingshot and wedged it in the cushion crack, then tugged on a tattered top hat over her mass of frizzy black hair and slipped into fingerless gloves. Though she doubted very much it was a ghoul—ghouls didn't respect social niceties such as doorbells—she fastened her silver listening trumpet onto her right ear.

Several moments of quiet before a bang and thud, as someone tripped in the darkness. Marie huffed and removed the trumpet. Ghouls didn't trip.

A slow clomp, clomp, clomp, as the intruder mounted the stairs.

Then, "Hello? Marie? I know you're here."

A female voice, young and vaguely familiar.

"Are you up there? Ow!"

It sounded like she'd kicked something. Hard. Marie's lips twitched.

Finally the footsteps, now limping, arrived just outside the tower door.

An LED flashlight swung around the octagonal room and pinned Marie, blinding her good eye.

"Oh! There you are! What are you doing?"

"Who, me?" Marie-Lunie replied, squinting. "Why, I'm just in the swimming leg of an iron-man triathlon, thanks for asking. Now get that light out of my face and get lost."

The girl fumbled to flick the flashlight off.

It finally struck Marie who the owner of the voice was: Kelbee Worth, the ringletty-haired treasurer of the high school yearbook committee. One of Alice Eastwood's giggling followers who used to laugh when Alice had called her "patchwork," mocking both Marie's old patch and that its standard-issue skin coloring was so much lighter than her own. Marie hadn't seen Kelbee in the year since Marie had ditched out on school and hadn't talked to her for perhaps three years before that. Good riddance, she'd thought.

She was tempted to ask what Kelbee wanted but resisted the urge, letting the girl squirm in the silence. Marie was used to silence.

"Can we turn on some lights or something? You're creeping me out."

When Marie didn't stir, Kelbee hunted around for the switch. A single, wooden elephant lamp buzzed into illumination, casting a wan glow over the large, tangled tower room.

"So, you're a hoarder now?" Kelbee wrinkled her nose as she surveyed teetering piles of books, papers and drawings, garbage bags spilling clothes and shoes, various knick-knacks and gadgets either collected on exotic trips or crafted by hand—all of Marie's father's things pillaged from the rest of the house and gathered in the tower room where she'd, for the most part, holed-up.

"How can you stand all this junk? It smells musty." The pretty nose wrinkled further.

"Shut. Up. And get out."

The edge in Marie's tone was enough to wipe the smug judgment from Kelbee's face. But the girl's gummy pink lip gloss and shiny metal braces still made Marie want to kick her in the shin. Hard.

"I said OUT." Marie slowly raised the slingshot and stretched the band back. Of course, she wouldn't shoot, but Kelbee didn`t know that.

Kelbee stumbled backward, fell. The impact cracked her eggshell veneer and she burst into tears. "My dad's gone, Marie! You have to help me!"

Marie studied the sling while listening to Kelbee sniffle and whimper. Finally she said, "What about your mom?" Marie hadn't had a mom to rely on when her dad went missing. The mysterious woman had left when she was just an infant.

"That's really mean, Marie, even for you." Kelbee was sitting now, blue mascara streaking her pale cheeks. An improvement in Marie's books. Kinda gothic.

"My mom died in grade eight, remember? Uterine cancer. She was in the hospital for, like, seven months."

Marie hadn't remembered. "Oh," she said. "Suck."

She kicked at the floor with her scuffed boot. Finally, she lowered her weapon and offered Kelbee a hand up. The girl's skin was soft and warm. It'd been a long time since she'd touched anyone.

Kelbee inhaled a couple more shaky breaths and wiped her eyes. Marie cleared a leather bean-bag chair and stomped back to her seat, resigned to hearing the sniveling girl out.

"My dad, he—he went out and never came back. That was almost two days ago. It's not like him. I'm worried."

"Um, pro-tip: there are people who get paid to solve just these sorts of mysteries. They're called cops."

"This isn't funny! He could be d—I have to find him before someone notices he's gone."

"So, what do you want me to do?" She resisted pointing out that neither she nor the useless cops had been able to find her own dad.

"Well," Kelbee fiddled with the band on her pink leather watch, "people say that you're a...I don't know. You keep people away. I want to do that, too. Until I find my dad."

Marie hardly heard anything after "people say." Dangerous territory. Talk sometimes led to action. "What people?"

"Oh, just some of us. Not teachers, adults. It's like...It's like to them you don't exist anymore."

Marie released lungfuls of air. Kids she could handle.

"I just don't understand where he could've gone," Kelbee continued, oblivious to all but her own problems. "He said he was going to catch a show and never came home."

"So, that's it?" Marie cut in. "He went to a movie?"

Kelbee nodded then added, "Oh, and my overdue library books were gone from the counter. I guess he must've returned them."

Marie's skin prickled. "Which library?"

"Central Memorial."

"Um, what's his...name? Your dad?"

"Robert. Most people call him Bob. Why?"

Marie jumped up and went to the desk, shoving papers aside until she found her moon calendar. One day until the new moon. Not. Good. She tugged on her hair, hard, and considered what to do.

This girl didn't deserve her help. Kelbee was a prissy snot who wouldn't give Marie the time of day unless she needed something. And Marie was loath to part with any of her needles, not to mention taking the time to teach the girl how to use them. She had more important things to do—reading her father's notebooks, for one. In their yellowed pages she was learning things—about gadgets he'd invented, scientific discoveries he'd made and things *not* explainable by science—lessons Marie was putting to use, like with the eye and the needles. Why *should* she help?

Because she knew what it felt like to lose someone. Wouldn't wish it on anyone, not even Kelbee Worth.

"I know I'm going to regret this," she said finally, "but I'm going to try to find your dad. So you'll stop bugging me."

Marie grabbed her pack and moved expertly around the cluttered room gathering supplies. She pressed her listening trumpet back into her ear and packed a small pouch containing the pin cushion with her remaining power needles. A traveling token was a necessity, as was a pair of one-lensed spectacles she'd crafted from the glass of a strange red mirror that allowed her to see the Otherrealm with her good eye.

But the most important item, a short black cape hanging on the coat rack in the corner, she stared at a long while before reluctantly swinging it around her shoulders.

"Let's go."

Kelbee watched Marie with a half alarmed, half bemused expression. "Where...why? Okay, you look like a cross between a kid wearing her dad's magician clothes and the Wicked Witch of the West!" Her giggle sounded like a complaining donkey.

Marie glared. Her hat *had* held a bunny or two and she *was* wearing her dad's clothes—a white dress shirt and black pants, rolled up at her wrists and knees. And she supposed her holey, striped tights *did* rather resemble the legs poking from beneath Dorothy's tornado tossed house. But she knew when she was being made fun of. She debated throwing something. Instead she flipped up her black studded eye patch.

Kelbee screamed.

"Like my new eye? It helps me see things. And shoot lasers at idiots who annoy me." A lie, but Kelbee's jaw dropped in the most satisfying manner.

"Now, if there's any chance of getting your father back *alive*, we have to go now. I'm pretty sure he's being held captive in the library. By ghouls."

They wound down creaking flights of stairs and Kelbee mostly stayed quiet, for which Marie was grateful. But it wasn't long before another pesky voice piped up, as Marie had known it would.

"Oooh! An outing! I *love* outings!"

Kelbee screamed again. Marie flinched, the sound magnified by the trumpet in her ear.

"You're going to have to stop doing that."

"Where's that voice coming from?"

Marie didn't answer but instead muttered under her breath, "If you *must* talk, use your *inside* voice. Inside my head, that is."

As usual, the voice had ideas of its own. "I'm Ervin," it said aloud. "Pleased to make your acquaintance. I'm afraid Loony Marie is somewhat lacking in manners."

"One of these days, I'm going to set you on fire."

"I fear things would turn out badly. For you. But it would be *such* fun if you tried!"

Kelbee grabbed Marie's elbow and spun her around. "Who're you talking to? I can't see anyone!"

"Why, I am right here! Just—"

"Shut up, you useless hunk of moth-eaten cloth!" Then to Kelbee, Marie said, "It's the cape. Just ignore him."

Of course Kelbee ignored Marie, saying, "Oh, cool! A magic cape!"

"At your service, my lady," replied Ervin, swishing a little as Marie ground her teeth.

Kelbee and Ervin gabbed all the way across the garden. Though Marie tuned out their banter, she thought maybe it wasn't so bad having another massive ego along to distract Ervin from his own goodly self-opinion.

Before exiting the circle of needles, she stopped. "Put these on and keep them on." She handed the one-eyed spectacles to Kelbee. "Things are going to look weird. Trust me and just do what I say."

Kelbee held the frames as one would a sweaty gym sock then proffered them back. "I'm not wearing these. I'll look like a dork."

Marie shrugged. "Have fun trying to follow me, then. It'll be like walking blind through a fun-house. You'll fall, won't be able to see ghouls coming, and might just disappear through a hole. But whatever."

Kelbee's eyes widened and she hurriedly placed the crooked wire frames on her nose. She *did* look like a dork. But to her credit, she didn't make a peep about the swirling red world Marie knew she was now seeing. Marie pushed open the rickety metal gate and stepped outside the relative safety of her front yard.

The house and other real world things faded to barely visible. Even with one eye anchored in reality, the Otherrealm dominated, clouding everything with misty blankness. Still, the faint reality was disorienting to Marie as normally she would have *both* eyes fixed on Otherness.

"How do you know where you're going? And what *is* this place? Why can't we just take the bus like normal people?" Kelbee's voice quavered only a little.

"With my new eye I am visible to Otherrealm creatures. I figure it's best to see them coming. Anyway, no talking. It'll attract ghouls."

Marie enjoyed a split second of silence.

"She's lying," Ervin piped up helpfully. "Ghouls care nothing for our chit-chat. And trust me—I *love* chit chat!"

Marie crumpled a corner of the cape into a ball but the fabric sprang back with nary a wrinkle.

"Ooh, that tickles! Do it again!"

But for all his bravado, the further they strayed from Marie's house, the quieter Ervin got. She'd never asked him why, but got the feeling he was listening—on guard. He'd saved her bacon more than a few times. Once he'd transformed into a chain mail doublet just as some flying creature's talons had raked across her back, saving her from vicious wounds. Though he was beyond annoying, Marie had to admit he'd proven himself more useful than your average oversized hankie.

The air was thick with familiar, yet strangely out of place smells. It was as though Otherrealm was a collector of human aromas, plucking them from homes and malls and industrial yards and then tossing them in a mixing pot like so many spices: cotton-candy, burning rubber tires and shampoo one minute, new carpet, paint, and sweet-peas the next.

"Ew, gross!" Kelbee said at regular intervals as though Marie might not have noticed or could do something about it.

The undulating ground over which they moved bore no resemblance to the neighborhood street, sometimes provoking the uncomfortable sensation of walking perpendicular to the ground or even upside-down. Marie had learned to ignore the pesky faux-gravity, but several times Kelbee stopped, crouching to cling to the insubstantial surface. Only Marie's threats to leave her behind prodded the girl on.

Avoiding holes was trickier, especially with only one eye, but Marie steered them straight (or in loops as needed). Once Ervin coughed, bringing her attention to a deep crack she hadn't noticed and nearly plunged into. She whispered a grudging, "Thanks."

Occasionally, real world sounds broke through: sirens, yelling and fragments of house party music, but mostly through her trumpet Marie heard just jungle noise: hoots, growls, screeches, and a strange, chittery clacking made by some creature Marie had never seen.

They'd been traveling for a while when posts and a wooden bridge appeared, arched over nothing in particular—certainly not water. Her neighbor's ceramic garden donkey seemed to balance on an ear tip on the railing, but Marie knew this was just a bit of real world peeking through.

Marie stopped but Kelbee kept on, seeking the security of the seemingly solid structure. Marie grabbed the girl's collar, near-choking her but preventing her upraised foot from falling on the bridge.

"Trolls get angry if you cross without permission," Marie said.

"Um, *trolls*?" Kelbee sounded at once skeptical and on the verge of panic.

"Oh, trolls aren't that bad. It's ghouls we have to worry about. *They'll* devour our souls, trapping us in here forever."

Kelbee squeaked.

"But we still have to wait or we'll get ripped to shreds." Marie leaned against a post and adjusted her hat.

And wait they did for what seemed like fifteen minutes but might've been thirty or only two. Then a shuffling and stream of expletives emerged from beneath the bridge as a beast hauled itself out from the shadowy depths.

The first time this had happened to Marie, and given the volume and deep timbre of the voice, she'd expected a huge monster. But trolls were actually rather short, about waist-height and ugly, with mashed up features and a left-in-the-fridge-for-a-month, rotten vegetable reek. But they had razor claws and were speedy—at least, so said her father's books. Marie had never tested the theory, abiding instead by the simple advice to bring a gift.

"Who goes?" rasped the hideous creature, face twisted 45 degrees off center.

"It's me, Marie-Lunie. I brought you a present." Marie proffered the token, a gold-colored rook.

"Oooh! Shiny!" The troll snatched the chess piece and skipped in wobbly circles, eyeing its treasure and sniffing as though it had a smell. Maybe it did.

"May we cross?"

"Yep yep!" Still, its eyes did not leave the item clutched in its knob-knuckled hand.

The two girls clomped over the bridge which disappeared behind them the moment they stepped off.

"Um, how are we going to get back? Do you really know what you're doing?" Kelbee's voice rose in pitch until only dogs could hear.

"Aaannnddd, cue meltdown." This time Ervin kept his voice down.

Kelbee's lip quivered and she clung to Marie, breaking into sobs.

Marie stood frozen, hands at her sides while keenly aware of her dampening shoulder and the choking sounds in her ear.

Subtle strains of "Try a Little Tenderness" began to radiate from the cape.

"Not now, Ervin!" hissed Marie.

She raised a tentative hand to pat Kelbee's back, accidentally brushing a bra strap before snatching her fingers back.

"Come on." Marie gently pushed the girl away. "We're almost at the library. If your dad's around, Darren will know where he is."

"D—Darren?" Kelbee sniffled. "Darren who?"

"Fodey."

"Oh, that geek?"

All soft feelings for the girl evaporated. "Darren's my friend." She started off again, not particularly caring if Kelbee followed.

A second bridge appeared moments later, and a spindly troll with enormous ears gave them back the very same rook while gleefully extolling its virtues. Marie made a show of admiring it and thanked him profusely.

They crossed three more bridges guarded by three more trolls, one with a single eye on its cheek, one with horns protruding from all over its body, and one with three feet, and the back-and-forth exchange of the rook continued. Thankfully, Kelbee didn't even bother asking how it was possible.

Yet...something niggled at Marie. She hadn't yet heard any ghouls; a sound not unlike the whining of a remote-control car only louder and infinitely more frightening, coming as it did from a long-limbed creature with no features aside from a gaping mouth. Their absence was worrying. Suggested they were busy with something else. And Marie had ideas about what. Or whom.

"Library ho!" Ervin announced.

"You can take off the glasses now." Marie flipped her patch down, and the old brick library jumped into focus. She glanced at the sky, noting only the slimmest sliver of moon.

Bounding up three steps, Marie rapped a code on the front door. After a minute the entrance swung open to reveal Darren, wide awake, dressed and with his own set of Otherrealm glasses perched on his head as though recently in use.

"Hey, dude." Marie bumped knuckles with her friend.

"Dooooooood!" echoed Ervin.

"Hey, Marie. Hey, Ervin. I'm so glad you guys came. Something's up. Wait...what's *she* doing here?"

"Um," replied Kelbee, "*you're* the one still dorking out at the library at one in the morning. Just *saying*."

"He lives here," Marie interrupted, "and I suggest you shut it if you want his help." She turned her attention back to Darren. "Something's up?"

"Yeah. You should see it for yourself." He paused. "Is she, er, cool?"

"Most definitely not, but she's coming anyway."

The trio moved through the cold stone foyer, past rows of mildewed stacks and down the spiral staircase into the basement. They paused before a worn wooden door with a sign that read: NO ENTRANCE—HAUNTED.

"So, yesterday, I was cleaning up puke down here...man, you should've seen it. Bright. Orange. Can you say 'Too many Doritos'?" Darren guffawed.

"And?" Marie prodded.

"Anyway, I thought I heard something. I cupped my hands to listen at the door, like you taught me and, well, there's definitely ghouls in there." Darren's acne-dotted forehead bunched seriously, and he wiped his plump palms against his cargo pants.

"Yeah," Marie sighed. "I think they have her dad."

"Why would you think that, anyway?" Kelbee interrupted. "I mean...tons of stuff could've happened to him. Normal stuff." She pulled at a snag in her sweater, unraveling a daisy.

"Simple. Your dad came here, to a ghoul hive, a couple nights before a new moon—the time when their power in our world is at its greatest."

Darren nodded as though this were elementary information.

"And his shortened name starts with a 'B,'" Marie added. "Ghouls love to eat the souls of people with 'B' names. It's like a delicacy to them or something." Marie shrugged.

Kelbee paled beneath her makeup.

Tugging on the brim of her hat Marie asked, "So, you guys ready?"

Darren swallowed audibly. "For, um, what?"

"Glasses on!" Marie commanded as she turned the key in the lock.

"Wait," said Ervin. "Give me to Kelbee." His *inside* voice, finally. "She needs me. More than you."

Marie glanced at the girl. She was huddled in on herself, looking sick, and hadn't even seen a ghoul yet. She'd be toast without Ervin.

The cape slipped easily off Marie's shoulders and settled around Kelbee. Marie fastened it at her neck. She offered a slight smile, though she wasn't exactly brimming with confidence herself. Their eyes met and for the first time, Marie thought she caught a glimpse of the real person behind all the powder and eyeliner, an insecure girl, not so different from her. But there was no time for bonding or other mushy crap.

High-pitched whining assaulted Marie's trumpet, staggering her. Darren was right—ghouls. Lots of them. *All* of them, maybe. In the center of what should be the storage room, but now was only red-blackness smelling vaguely of cheeseburgers and nail polish remover, she could see a swirling vortex of stuff: books mostly, as well as dismembered doll parts, plastic playpen balls, a hockey stick, and scraps of yarn. The flying clutter formed a nest and Marie had no doubt about what was at its center.

An eerie green circle swung in their direction. An open mouth. Ghouls always had their jaws open, and the insides of their mouths glowed, lit by radiant green teeth. The circle fixated on the trio, and a horrible, raking howl rose above the general din. More green mouths turned outwards.

"So, uh, what's the plan, Marie?" Darren asked.

"I…." She watched a stack of books tumble, knocked over by a ghoul edging closer. It seemed reluctant to leave its treasure, but tempted. "Oh! The needles! If I can somehow stick them, I can keep them at bay long enough to get Bob out!"

"Decent plan," Ervin chimed in, "but you'll need a distraction. Darren?"

Darren shook his head slowly, backing toward the door.

"Come on, Darren," urged Marie. Bravery wasn't her friend's strong suit. "You can do it. Just pretend it's a Wii game."

If Darren gulped or swallowed or swore, the sound was drowned out by the growing shrieks of over-excited ghouls. Finally, he waved his arms and shouted, "Here!"

A ghoul pulled free and charged, long arms reaching. Marie was ready. With its attention focused on Darren, she stabbed a needle in its side and thought *Stop!* as hard as she could. The creature halted as though it had smashed into a brick wall.

"Do it again, Darren! It's working!"

Darren hopped from side to side, arms flailing. More ghouls noticed and left the swarm.

"Give me a few needles, Marie! I can help!" Kelbee grabbed her elbow, and Marie shoved the pin cushion in her direction. The girl plucked a handful.

Darren huffed and panted, running around like a rodeo clown. The girls kept their movements as low and slow as possible, so as not to attract the ghouls' attention.

Long toes grasped Marie's ankle and she fell hard. Her focus shattered. The pinned creatures shook off her influence and reached again for Darren. She thought *Stop!* while scraping along the ground, dragged by her bootlaces. Her hat came off, knocking her eye patch down.

The Otherrealm disappeared. Everything was black, the storage room unlit. But she felt her laces pull tight as the creature continued to haul her away.

"Darren, help!"

After a second, the grip on her ankle loosened and she kicked free, flipping her patch. She saw it had been Kelbee, not Darren, who had rescued her. The girl stood between her and the ghoul, out of needles but fists balled as though ready to fight. Marie threw herself into a forward roll and stabbed the ghoul behind the knee as its jaws snapped just centimeters from Kelbee's face.

The two girls exchanged shaky grins.

Marie needled creatures wherever she could—a hand, a toe, an elbow. A ghoul grabbed Kelbee's shoulder but a corner of her cape shot out and wrapped itself around its thin finger, twisting. The ghoul screeched and let go—leaving its twitching finger behind—and Marie drove a needle through the top of its foot.

About a dozen ghouls stood limp but even more were taking notice.

Marie struggled to maintain her thought-command. The pinned ghouls began to twitch, heads swinging toward Marie as if they now understood that it was her, not Darren, who was their real target.

"Not sure how much…longer I can…hold them." Shouting and thinking at the same time was a struggle.

Kelbee grabbed the pin cushion and stabbed a couple more creatures while Marie strained to maintain focus. She sank to her knees with her head in her hands. Ghoul noise pressed at the edges of her consciousness. They were fighting back psychically now and threatened to overwhelm her mind. That, she hadn't counted on.

Kelbee stumbled past her and with effort Marie looked up to see her moving jerkily to stand among the ghouls. Her face showed pure panic, as if she'd lost control of her body and had no idea what she was doing.

No longer a black cape, Ervin appeared now as a red leather jacket with exaggerated shoulders, black stripes and raised fins. Synthesizer music suddenly blared.

Kelbee's head snapped down and up, from side to side. Her body began to twitch to the music in a herky-jerky dance as though she were a zombie. Her terrified expression—teeth bared, eyes wide—added to this impression.

"Think *follow*!" Ervin yelled.

Follow, follow, follow! thought Marie as hard as she could.

At once the pinned ghouls relaxed and turned to Kelbee. They studied her and slowly began copying, moving in unison, hesitant at first, then with more confidence, as though performing a choreographed piece; stomp, stomp, shuffle, shuffle, marching from side to side with arms swinging. More and more ghouls joined, even *free* ghouls, who neither girl had needled.

Marie was flabbergasted but not about to waste the opportunity. "Darren! Let's get Bob!"

Marie continued to think *follow* while dragging her large friend toward the center of the nest. She dodged a flying copy of *The Black Cauldron* and grabbed the hockey stick to fend off other debris. Finally they spotted a man in a plaid shirt curled on the ground. Unconscious, but alive.

Darren hefted him over his shoulders, and he and Marie fought their way back through turbulent winds and flying junk.

All of the creatures were caught up in the dance, now. Kelbee's movements were fluid, her expression calm.

Marie watched the scene through squinted eyes. She *swore* the ghouls looked almost…happy. They performed with more gusto than necessary, jerking their bony shoulders and tapping their long feet. The corners of their toothy maws were even turned up in what could be…smiles.

Darren leaned over to whisper in her ear, "Is that, um, *Thriller*?"

Marie paused then nodded incredulously.

With a grand flourish and loud creepy laughter, Kelbee's dance came to an end. The Otherrealm filled with the chittery clacking sound Marie had often heard, but never identified. Until now. *Laughter.* Ghoul laughter, she was sure of it. Who woulda thought?

"What now, Ervin?" she asked quietly, not wanting to disrupt the moment.

"Oh, we should be able to go. If there's one thing ghouls like better than feasting on a human soul during the darkness of a new moon, it's a spot of fun. They won't hurt us. At least, not for a while."

"Um, that might've been something to tell me sooner. Like, say, all the other times we've been in the Otherrealm." Marie ground her teeth.

"Oh," replied Ervin casually, "it wouldn't have worked. I've *seen* you trying to play *Dance Dance Revolution.*"

Marie punched him, eliciting a cry from Kelbee who rubbed her shoulder then ran over to grab her dad's limp arm.

"You've *really* gotta update your music selection," Marie said to Ervin, back at the house about two weeks later. If she heard Lionel Richie's *Dancing on the Ceiling* one more time, she was going to scream.

Ervin responded with *Oops, I Did it Again* and Marie growled, slamming the tower door behind her as she sought somewhere in the huge house where she wouldn't be subject to Ervin's attempts at comedy.

But outside the tower room was hardly any better.

Fourteen ghouls now lived in her home—the fourteen she and Kelbee had pinned.

She hadn't noticed them trailing behind until arriving back at her house. Too late, she realized she hadn't revoked her "follow" command. They'd pushed past her and settled in, some on couches and chairs, others on tables and bookcases, one even winding itself through the rungs on the staircase.

Ervin told her it would be too dangerous to remove the pins or order them away, urging her instead to think happy thoughts, claiming ghouls were really joyful creatures at heart. Whether this was true or Ervin simply enjoyed her annoyance when they played hopscotch *loudly* outside her room, or dressed-up in sheets and jumped out from behind doors to startle her, Marie didn't know. Anyway, their mouths *did* make excellent nightlights.

And after Kelbee had settled back in with her dad (and suggested he go by "Rob" from now on), she dropped by a couple of times a week. She told Marie it was for dance practice with Ervin, but usually she'd end up in Marie's tower and the two girls would talk for hours. Sometimes Darren even joined them, and the three would play *Clue* until late into the evening. Whether Kelbee told Alice or any of her other school friends about her visits, Marie doubted but, to her surprise, she found she didn't really care. Turned out Kelbee wasn't too bad to hang out with. And sometimes, in the quiet just before she fell asleep, Marie had to admit to herself that they were becoming...friends.

Now, if only she could find her own dad, things would be pretty good.

When not writing or editing fiction, **Erika Holt** likes to snuggle her dog, paint her toenails strange colors, and, of course, dance (ballet mostly, though she's taken jazz, tap, and Bollywood classes, as well). She reads slush for *Scape*, the e-zine of Young Adult speculative fiction, and has stories forthcoming in *Shelter of Daylight* and *Evolve Two: Vampire Stories of the Future Undead.* Her story "Just Dance" was inspired by her littlest nephew's habit of calling eyes "eye bulbs."

Adaptation
by Francine P. Lewis

i.
from your origin, find your way
along the x-axis
eyes down
to divine the processes of earth

ii.
getting from here to there
is all that counts
in life

do the number of steps matter
across the Plains of the Serengeti

iii.
from your origin, find your way
along the y-axis
eyes up
to divine the processes on the horizon

iv.
footsteps preserved in wet mud
marching up through the strata
as one aeon supplants the next,

the beauty of Descartes

v.
the beauty of Descartes

as one aeon supplants the next
marching up through the stratosphere
footsteps preserved in lunar dust

vi.
to divine the processes along the continuum perpendicular
    to here and there
rise up
along the z-axis
from your origin, find your way

vii.
across the Sea of Tranquility
the number of steps do not matter

in evolution
all that counts
is getting from there to here

viii.
to divine the processes of all
soar upon
the winds of dreams
and from your origin, find your way

Francine P. Lewis writes—not that many people read what she writes, judging from the number of rejection letters she collects, but she continues to write—poetry, short stories, novellas, and novels. And she reads. She likes to read a lot...almost as much as she likes to write. Francine has had poems published in local magazines and short stories in science fiction anthologies. She has written one science fiction novel—which is still searching for a home—and is currently working on another novel, a novella, and a collection of poetry. Her first poetry chapbook, *Eurydice Dreams*, Conch Pearl Press, was launched in 2009. She is also a member of the team that brings the Art Bar, Canada's longest running poetry-only reading series, to a Toronto stage each week.

Saving the Dead, or The Diary of an Undertaker's Apprentice

by Jennifer Greylyn

Saturday, April 20, 1912
12:45 p.m. Three days out from Halifax and we're nearly there. I can feel it. The tremors have become constant and I can almost hear voices. I told Uncle John and he wanted to tell Captain Larnder, but praise God, George intervened. He hasn't lost all his sense in the excitement. Then the point became moot as we received a wireless message from another steamer in the vicinity, reporting three bergs and many bodies northeast of our position.

We'll arrive by nightfall, the captain predicts. My older relations both smile. They don't seem to notice (Uncle John) or care (my second cousin George) how that causes the crew to give us uneasy looks.

Rough men in their heavy scarves and oilskins, stubbly faces hardened and fissured by the bitter winds and cold fogs of the North Atlantic, they're still unnerved by what we're going to encounter. They don't understand how Uncle John can be so joyful, striding on deck freshly shaven and beaming every morning. Nor do they like that George, who began the trip as solemn as the headstones he carves when he's not lending a hand at Grandfather's funeral home, now has an anticipatory gleam in his eye.

As for me, they deplore my youth and physical condition. They shake their heads and mutter, "It ain't right. 'Tis no place for a boy. Especially one who's sickly." They conveniently ignore two facts: some of them are only a little older than my fifteen years and, had they met me in other circumstances, they'd think me perfectly sound. One might hope they'd at least recognize my pallor and dark-circled eyes as signs of how seriously I take this enterprise. But no, their disapproval is almost palpable, as strong as my mother's was.

The crew, at least, should understand that we are simply doing our duty as men. The *Mackay-Bennett* is ordinarily a cable ship, laying and repairing the undersea telegraph cables that connect the New World with the Old. But did she hesitate when an agent for the White Star Line wanted to hire her to investigate the site of the disaster, now six days past?

Of course not. Captain Larnder and all his men knew it was their Christian duty. Just as I knew it was mine when Uncle John asked me to accompany him and George. It was an opportunity everyone else in the family business was clamoring for. I couldn't refuse, although I hardly consider it the height of my career, as Uncle John does, or my chance at immortality, as George believes.

I don't need the world to remember my name. The dead already know who I am. They've been calling to me for almost a week now. I must help them. I must.

8:00 p.m. We've arrived and it's worse than I imagined. I'm bundled up in three wool sweaters and an overcoat, but I'm still quaking so hard I can barely sit up in my bunk. George keeps stealing concerned glances at me while he and Uncle John play cards, but neither of them feels what I do.

There are just so many! One reads the numbers bandied about by the newspapers—maybe over 1500 dead—and one can't conceive of it. But to be here where it happened...

I force my hand to be steady with the other. My words are still no better than a scrawl. But I need to record this. The family needs to know what I'm experiencing.

A manifestation of our banshee blood, Uncle John insists, believing that old story about why we're all so drawn to death. Mother's more modern. She's studied spiritualism and thinks it's to do with our souls. Something about etheric vibrations. I wonder if she'll have forgiven me by the time we get back...

Dear Lord, I thought I was ready for this. I've known the victims of fire. Murder even. But it wasn't like this. My skin is throbbing. My skull is about to crack. They don't understand that Captain Larnder won't allow the recovery effort to begin until daybreak and we can see.

For now, even to me looking through our little window, they're just broken glimpses in the cloudy moonlight. Tiny dark shapes appearing and then disappearing among the equally dark but bigger shapes of debris and the glinting islands of ice. But they don't know that. They only know their own need.

How will I ever make it through the night?

Sunday, April 21

10:30 a.m. My head aches, but I welcome it. It blurs their whispers and gives me an excuse Uncle John will accept to take a break. After listening to me moan and thrash in my bunk above him last night, George kindly offered to switch places with me. "We can't have you falling and killing yourself," he whispered with his typical mordant humor. "We've enough bodies already to deal with."

My burst of frenzied laughter drew a troubled frown from George and woke Uncle John across our small room. Instantly alert, he took one look at my haggard face in the orange flicker of the kerosene lamp we'd turned low on the table between the two sets of bunks and sent George to beg some laudanum from the doctor.

Any other time, I'd have bristled at his high-handedness. We'd already had words about this. Uncle John knew Mother had given me the bitter, powerful soporific when I was a child and my gift first appeared. I'd told him I didn't need it anymore, but that was back in Halifax. When George returned with a familiar brown-glass bottle, I took a long swig from it without waiting for a spoon. It succeeded in putting me to sleep, but I still dreamed.

I relived our treacherous passage through the ice yesterday, dodging growlers and bergies as the sun sank in the sky. Three times, a huge iceberg loomed, each bigger than the one before. The last was the size of a mountain, streaked with the fires of sunset. I quailed before its terrible beauty, unable to escape, the voices filling me with their fear and confusion.

It was a relief to wake to George's hand on my shoulder and hear Uncle John whistling as he scrubbed his face. Our little ship was clearly still intact. It echoed with the booted footfalls of the crew, already about their duties even though it remained dark outside. I wondered if, on some level, they were infected by the restlessness of the dead too, or if they simply wanted to get on with our grim task.

Dressed but unable to face the breakfast my two relations enjoyed, I went out on deck, clung to the rail and fought the tremors. Anyone watching would think I was still not accustomed to the frequent rolling of the ship. That was true, but the tremors made my lack of equilibrium worse. Today, though, there was a different quality to them. I felt like the sky, filling with light as dawn finally came. Filling with hope and anticipation.

But there was no warmth. My breath whitened the brightening air before the wind scattered it. The cruel, leaden ocean slapped the sides of the ship. I exchanged nods with many of the crew, but no one said "Good morning". It wasn't a day for that. Uncle John and George joined me as the first boat was being lowered and I felt urgent tugs in a dozen different directions.

Soon, it was possible to see the nearest bodies bobbing head-up amid the grey swells, a fact remarked upon by Captain Larnder when he paused beside us in his habitual pacing. "Astonishing," was his opening comment, a weathered hand rubbing his gaunt, bearded cheeks. "I can't believe they're still afloat. They must be waterlogged, but they wait for us as peaceful as sleepers."

He lapsed into pensive silence, as if to invite a reply, but none of us offered one. I kept my eyes fixed on the boat, as though fascinated by the way three of the men braced themselves against one side and kept the vessel balanced while the other two leaned far over the other side and fished out a body with a long boathook. I winced to think of its sharp point piercing flesh but felt instead a profound sigh gust through me as the body was dragged aboard.

I must have made some noise of my own because Larnder glanced at me, then at George who was studiously blank-faced and lastly at Uncle John who wore a strange, satisfied expression. The captain shook his head and muttered. "It must be the lifebelts. As far as I can tell, they're all wearing one. Not that it did them any good, poor blighters. Good day, gentlemen."

Barely had he left us when Uncle John exclaimed, "I knew I was right to bring you, lad. They *are* waiting for something, aren't they? They're waiting for you."

I flinched and George shot a wary look in Larnder's direction. Fortunately, he was out of earshot, deep in conversation with the men about to drop a second boat. George admonished my uncle "Careful, John", but Uncle John wasn't listening.

"We'll show those so-called experts in the papers," he opined with relish. "They were sure there'd be almost no bodies to recover. Sucked down with the ship, they said, or tangled in the wreckage. But those poor people deserve a decent burial. We'll see that they get one."

Nodding decisively to himself, Uncle John turned away from us and shouted orders at the nearest crewmen to clear space on the deck so he could begin his vital work. There was a sardonic slant to George's mouth at my uncle's autocratic single-mindedness, but he too, moved to obey. Until he noticed I wasn't and looped a muscular arm around my shoulders and forcibly led me away from the rail.

There's a knock at the cabin door. Uncle John's sent a crewman for me. Although there's more I want to record, I go back to my duty gladly.

Monday, April 22
11:15 a.m. So much has happened. So much to write. My hand shakes again but not with the ship's motion or their need this time. Rather with their fury and my own. I make myself breathe. Slow, calming breaths. But, as I push back the heat of anger, panic invades, cold and creeping like the fog obscuring the window.

They feel betrayed and so do I. They waited for us, their rescuers. We didn't arrive in time in life, but we could save them in death. If only they held on, the ocean would not have their bodies. We'd take them back to land, maybe reunite them with their families.

Instead...

I rub my frigid hands and pick up my pen again. It started off so well yesterday. Uncle John got his makeshift embalming table set up and I concentrated on assembling his supplies. The tremors actually eased as the first bodies were removed from the boats. George went to oversee that. I didn't need to be there, too. They were quiet when they came aboard, content and trusting.

Most were in remarkably fine condition, well-preserved by the cold water. Now that their nightmare was ending, I could see that Captain Larnder's description of them as peaceful sleepers was apt. A lot of them were in their pajamas, with a coat or dressing gown thrown on over top for warmth. They'd clearly been roused from their beds and had been expecting to return.

Now, they would go to a bed of earth, but at least, they would be at peace. I clasped tight that thought whenever natural human sadness threatened to overcome me. It was especially hard when I saw the child, no more than two or three, chubby and fair-haired—

My boy! My little boy! Where is he? I lost him…

His mother. We haven't found her yet, but we will. She's one of the clearest voices, although that's not quite right. It's more tone and emotion than words. She's loudest when I think of her young son. Her sorrow chimes with my own. Support for Mother's theory. Harmonic resonance between their souls and mine.

No, I won't let myself be distracted! No matter how much I long to blot the horror from my mind, I can only expunge it by finding a solution. So I must write and remember, although it pains me. Write and breathe.

I was talking of George. He took it upon himself to stand witness while Mr. Barnstead, the Deputy Registrar of Death from Halifax, examined each body. Mr. Barnstead would attach a piece of canvas with a number to show the order in which the body had been pulled from the water. Then, with George's help, he'd strip the body and search it for distinguishing marks. He'd record the physical features along with the items on the body—clothes, jewelry, money and so on—in a ledger next to the appropriate number. It was a system he invented to help with identification.

Occasionally, some whisper would start me shaking and I'd be drawn to a particular body. I'd discreetly pass along to George whatever impressions I had, no matter how incoherent. We don't know what details might be important. He'd put them in his own ledger, which he told Mr. Barnstead was a copy for the funeral home.

In total, fifty-one bodies were rescued yesterday before Captain Larnder had the boats hoisted at sunset. Uncle John and I embalmed twenty bodies, all of whom Mr. Barnstead and George had determined were first-class passengers. We then had them sealed in pine coffins we'd brought from Halifax.

I presumed the rest of the bodies—second and third-class passengers along with crew—were being kept on the hill of ice we'd also brought in the *Mackey-Bennett's* hold until Uncle John and I had time to attend to them. It was a sad irony considering how they'd met their end, but it was a practical solution. I suspected nothing amiss when I heard the ship's bell peal, summoning us all to the forecastle deck where Canon Hind, the Anglican minister who'd come with us to bless the bodies, was to hold divine services.

Although my heart was lighter for beginning the rescue, I still felt heavy with exhaustion and the demanding whispers of the dead yet to be saved. I was accustomed to going to church on Sunday and was looking forward to a little spiritual comfort. But, standing between Uncle John and George, I froze when I saw the long rough sacks stacked like cordwood on the deck, maybe two dozen in all.

"No," I moaned, a low guttural protest, understanding right away. My knowledge of what was about to occur somehow communicated itself to the dead because I felt them stir, baffled and uncertain. I swayed and George caught my arm.

Meeting his dark gaze, I just knew that, instead of transporting all the bodies to the hold, he'd sewn some into canvas shrouds and weighted them with scrap iron. "How could you?" I began to accuse him, but he clamped a hand over my mouth. Then, after he and Uncle John shared a look, the two of them hauled me into our cabin at the stern.

The bell rang distantly just as they released me. I couldn't hear Canon Hind say, "For as it hath pleased God, we therefore commit this body to the deep." Nor was the splash that must have followed audible. But I felt the dead man's shock as he struck the water he'd so recently been rescued from, followed by his scream as he sank into its lightless depths.

I screamed too, over and over. I don't remember much after that. Only George's fist flying out and everything going dark for me, as well.

I woke just a little while ago, laid out on my bed like one of Uncle John's cadavers. I don't know what's going on. The door's locked. I pounded and shouted, but no one came to release me.

They've picked up more bodies though, I can tell. New voices blow through me. Frightened and angry. They don't know what's happening to them, either.

12:30 p.m. I can't believe I ever trusted Uncle John and George. I believed them when they said they wanted to help. But they betrayed the dead and they betrayed me. I have to set things right.

They arrived not long after I finished my last entry. Uncle John unlocked the door and stepped into our cabin, a relieved smile banishing the uncharacteristically wary expression he'd initially worn. "Good to see you're recovered, lad. I can use your help."

I glared at him, but the worst of my temper was reserved for George, who entered behind my uncle, carrying a tray with a steaming bowl of soup and a half loaf of bread on it. My stomach pinched at the smell of the food and reminded me how long it had been since I'd eaten. But I ignored it and finished the accusation I hadn't been able to make yesterday. "How could you?"

George, setting the tray down on our little table, misunderstood and flushed a deep, mortified red. I'd never seen him show so much emotion. "I'm sorry I hit you, Jamie. I overreacted. I didn't know what else to do. You were raving."

I shook my head impatiently, making the bruise on my temple throb. "I don't care about that. I mean the sea burials. How could you let that happen?" Then I realized George would never have made such a decision on his own. I rounded on my other relation. "How could *you*?"

Uncle John had claimed our sole chair, positioned it in front of the table and left George to perch on the edge of the other lower bunk. Unperturbed by my furious tone, my uncle turned calm eyes toward me. "It has to be done, lad. We don't have nearly enough embalming fluid for all the bodies. Besides, some of them are too far gone or battered to be saved. We can't take them back to port like that. It's a public health issue."

He sounded very reasonable, disappointed yet accepting, but I wasn't placated. My voice rose in pitch, fuelled by the emotions of the dead. "But we came here to save them! That's why you brought me, isn't it? Or was it just to make sure you could do your job? It would have been embarrassing for you if there'd been no bodies, wouldn't it?"

I knew I'd gone too far when Uncle John's back and face grew very stiff and George winced. "Enough, James," my uncle said with cold finality. He was a hard man to argue with at the best of times and this was far from the best of times. He hated to be questioned, but I felt I had no choice. Trying for a softer tone, I ventured, "Isn't there any other way? We could send a message for more supplies…"

Uncle John responded with an abrupt headshake, his offended dignity poorly disguised. "It'd take too long. Some of the bodies we've pulled out so far today are in a very bad state. I understand how you feel, but the most important thing is they've been found. They'll be remembered. Their families will be notified. We'll see to that."

Inwardly raging, I struggled not to show it and dropped my eyes. He couldn't understand how I felt. No one could. Except maybe Mother. But her gift was different from mine. She sometimes foresaw death, but she hadn't this time. She'd wondered if her soul had been too distracted by the way everyone else's souls had seemed to ring in the excited clamor the press had made over the ship itself. The *Titanic*. Grand in name. Grand in design. Grand in the awe it had inspired.

The failure of her foresight must be eating away at her. Just like my inability to help was now clawing at my innards. Strange I should feel sympathy for her when she'd protested my coming and we'd parted in anger.

When I glanced up again, George broke off a long stare with Uncle John, and my uncle visibly collected himself. Gentling his voice, he asked me, "Will you help them, lad?" but what he really meant was, "Will you help me?" He was still focused on himself.

I clenched my jaw and nodded because I knew it was the only way I'd get out of our cabin. Both my relations smiled at me, Uncle John pleased and George with relief. "Excellent," pronounced my uncle. "We'll leave you to finish your meal in peace. Join us when you're ready."

As they walked out, George made sure to leave the door ajar so I'd know I wasn't locked in again. He threw me another apologetic look, but I pretended to be too intent on slurping my soup to notice. My appetite had fled, though, as I wondered what I could do to truly help the dead.

Writing this down has given me an idea. What would people think if they knew all the bodies weren't being brought back? If I could get a message to Mother, she'd make sure the papers found out. She'll be as horrified as I am.

I know where the wireless room is. Captain Larnder showed it to us when he gave us a tour the first day we came aboard. He made a point of telling us an operator would be on duty at all times. He wasn't going to miss any messages like the captain of our sunken ship had. And, surely, the operator wouldn't mind sending a message to a sick boy's mother.

Tuesday, April 23

Don't know the time. Locked in, again. Oh, Lord, it took everything I had to rise and stumble to check the door. Now I can hardly keep my eyes open. Hardly hold the pen. But the dead are reaching out to me. Their need so strong. Their voices like hooks. Pulling me out of the darkness. Giving me no respite. What do you want? What do you want?

"Dear God, Ida, why did you wait for me? Why didn't you get into that lifeboat? You could have lived!"

"My sons! Where are you? Are you alive? I'm so sorry I took you from your mother. This is God's judgment. Please, dear Lord, don't punish them for my mistake."

"Someone is going to pay. I paid a fortune to be on that ship and I expect to be compensated. Do you know who I am?"

Barely know who I am. Adrift in terrible dreams, caught by their voices. A bitter taste in my mouth. Not just their misery, their fear, their anger. Uncle John dosed me again. Pressed the bottle against my mouth. George held my arms. More bruises as I struggled.

"How could you, James? Captain Larnder found out about your message and he's incensed. All messages are supposed to be cleared by him first."

"John, don't blame him. He's clearly not in his right mind."

"Maybe he'll think more clearly after a good long sleep. Pass me the laudanum, George. Don't fight us, lad. This is for your own good."

No! No. I didn't want to sleep. Don't want to sleep. I dream of the ocean. A vast, dangerous creature, breathing in swells, endlessly hungry. Icebergs are its cold, merciless teeth. They strike and it swallows. None of us are safe. I'm sorry. I'm sorry. I wish I could help you. I wish I could give you what you need. But the dark is devouring—

Wednesday, April 24

9:30 p.m. I'm worn to the bone, but I can't sleep. Not after what I've seen tonight. Uncle John and George are both pretending to. It's easier than talking about it, I suppose. Maybe they hope it'll fade like a dream with the morning.

I hope it doesn't. Not after how they disappointed me and the dead. But they know better now. The dead have a way of making us pay attention. My relations have discovered that for themselves. The first I knew about it was their voices penetrating my darkness. Hushed but hissing.

"He must be responsible! Who else could it be?" Uncle John, his chill tone cracking with ill-concealed panic.

"We shouldn't have given him so much. Not after his…injury." George, hesitant and guilty, then stronger with rage. "Look at him!"

A pause, then a throat-clearing. "Nevertheless, you know what we saw. He must be connected to it. Help me get him up." Uncle John much less imperious than usual, almost pleading.

Silence from George, then a mutter of agreement.

They lifted me from my bunk and draped one of my arms over each of their necks. Moving sideways, they dragged me through our doorway and out another door. A blast of freezing air struck my face. I blinked but couldn't clear my eyes. Thick fog again. We were on deck and then we were inside once more, descending.

I could feel the throb of the engines. We were moving toward the engine room along a corridor lit by dim electric bulbs. But I felt something else too. Tremendous pressure in my head. So much constrained emotion. It was enough to force my eyes all the way open. Everywhere I looked, there were bodies.

I remembered what the papers called the *Mackay-Bennett* before we left— "the Death Ship." I'd thought that was foolish. It's what they should have called the other ship, the one that sank despite everyone saying it was unsinkable.

Now, though, I reconsidered. Bodies were piled along the walls, all the way up to the ceiling. Dozens of them. So much naked flesh, all ghastly grey and blue. Uncle John and George must have run out of coffins, even run out of space on the ice in the hold. But, for so much decaying flesh, there was almost no smell. Only the smell of cold, cold water.

There was one body slumped against the door to the engine room at the far end of the corridor. I presumed the pitching of the ship must have dislodged it, but then it turned its head toward us.

Uncle John and George both tensed. I felt it in their arms. I didn't. Somehow, it wasn't a shock. There was a link between us. More than its voice, a rumble of anger. *Someone is going to pay...someone is going to pay...*a deeper link. I could feel its limbs almost like my own. Like my energy was running through them.

It lurched to its feet. I felt even more drained but closer to it in understanding. *He* lurched to *his* feet. Unclothed and discolored, he nonetheless stared at Uncle John and then at George, unblinking, defiant. I twisted my head from side to side, the same look in my eyes.

Uncle John began, "We've done all we can—" But his eloquence failed this time. I shook with the force of my anger, *his* anger, *their* anger. The dead man shuffled toward us. The bodies along the walls began to tremble.

Energy poured from me. They sucked it in. Other bodies began to rise. The dead man took a few steps closer, less halting, more purposeful.

Uncle John gaped, wordless for once. George gasped, "Jamie, do something!" I narrowed my eyes at him and then at my uncle.

"*Save them*," I whispered, barely audible, but the words were echoed by dozens of throats, an exhalation down the corridor. *Save them...save them...* to where *he* was standing just a few feet away, eyes accusing slits just like mine.

"Yes! *Yes!*" promised Uncle John and George was saying, "We'll do whatever we can! *Please* believe us!" I heard the truth in their voices and nodded. That took the last of my energy.

I slumped in their arms and the dead man drooped, too. The rest of the bodies went still. I vaguely noticed several wan faces pressed against the glass window in the door to the engine room. Their eyes were huge and incredulous. But Uncle John and George didn't stick around to explain.

They hastily carried me back to our room and talked about setting the chair under the door handle to bar entry to anyone or thing. But, before they turned in for the night, I made them keep their word. I sent them to talk to the captain. I confess I smiled just a little at how reluctant they were to leave our cabin.

Thursday, April 25
Captain Larnder is still intent on continuing the sea burials, George tells me. Although some of his crew saw the moving bodies too, the captain didn't and he doesn't believe what happened. I want to talk to him myself, but the doctor won't allow it. He says I'm dangerously weak. I'm confined to my bunk, but the door stays open.

George also tells me another ship, the *Minia*, is coming to help with the recovery effort and bringing us more supplies of embalming fluid and canvas. We picked up eighty-seven more bodies today. None were buried, though. Uncle John stood up to Larnder and insisted it wouldn't be proper without shrouds for them. It's only a delay, but it's a start.

Friday, April 26
George just gave me the news. Captain Larnder got a message to stop the sea burials. It seems someone leaked the story to the papers and the public is outraged. We're ordered back to Halifax. Out of the three hundred and six bodies we rescued, we're taking one hundred and ninety home with us. Thank you, Mother. I look forward to saying that to you in person.

Now I can finally rest, but I'm smiling too much to sleep.

Jennifer Greylyn has been writing for most of her life, mainly because her characters discovered early on that they could drive her crazy if she didn't. (They wouldn't necessarily mean to, but they could be quite insistent.) She started publishing her stories about three years ago, and they have appeared in markets as diverse as the magazines *Abyss and Apex, Beneath Ceaseless Skies,* and *Neo-opsis* to numerous print collections, most notably another EDGE anthology *Evolve: Vampire Stories of the New Undead*. She has several writing projects on the go, again due to the demands of her characters who like the idea of seeing their stories reach a wider audience. She has tried to persuade them she could get more done if they'd let her concentrate on one project at a time, but they don't seem inclined to cooperate. Talks are ongoing.

Feral
by Nicole Luiken

Half-hidden in the trees, a werewolf paced her.

A hot ball of shame and anger lodged in Chloe's throat as she ran along the dirt track through the forest. Bad enough Coach Wharton had tried to excuse her from training on the grounds that she couldn't keep up with the others, but now he'd assigned her a baby-sitter?

Humiliated, she put her head down and increased her pace until her feet flew down the trail, crunching on bright yellow leaves, until her lungs heaved and a bright stitch of pain appeared in her side. But she neither lost her shadow nor caught up with the rest of the Pack. Still she kept running, pushing her body to the limits. Werewolf limits. Chloe had all the extra werewolf strength and agility, her senses were keener than her townie classmates and she'd had no difficulty qualifying for Track. But her fifteenth and sixteenth birthdays had passed, and she still had not Changed.

All the other teens in her age group had. Even Judy, the smallest and most nervous of them all, had Changed three full moons ago.

Chloe couldn't decide which was worse, the sympathy in Judy's eyes or the veiled contempt in Coach Wharton's. Both rubbed her ego raw. Chloe was used to being the leader of their little pack and now everyone was Dominant to her. Last week she'd heard Coach Wharton tell Dean she might never Change because she was too afraid of the pain. Her! Who'd never so much as whimpered during one of Coach's brutal three-hour training hikes.

And now that contempt had spread to the other kids. They closed their shoulders against her when she came up, as if she were a townie.

Tears burned in Chloe's eyes, blurring the trail. She misstepped on a root and twisted her ankle. The anger raging inside her made her want to keep running through the pain, but that was stupid. She stopped and sat on a fallen log at the side of the trail and drank some of the water in her squeeze bottle. Her ankle would be fine in a moment. Werewolves healed fast. So fast it took something big to kill them, like the fiery plane wreck that had killed the Jennings family.

How could she have all the werewolf gifts and not the ability to Change? Her mom kept telling her to be patient, that there were records of werewolves who hadn't had their first Change until they were nineteen, but Chloe could smell the acrid scent of worry masking her words. Because there were also records of Duds, werewolves by heritage who were unable to Change.

Chloe's fists clenched. She was not a Dud. Glaring, she looked up—and caught the yellow eyes of a wolf staring out at her from some underbrush.

In a second, Chloe was on her feet, temper pumping through her. "Cut it out. I can see you, you know. I'm not blind." Was this some kind of test? Did they think they could scare her? She'd grown up in the Pack.

The wolf faded back into the brush and she sat back down, feeling satisfied. But in five minutes when she resumed her run, the wolf started tailing her again. Chloe pretended not to notice, waiting until her pursuer got a little too close, then suddenly she reversed direction and cut left into the trees.

A thick stand of pine kept the wolf from retreating. He hunched his shoulders and growled at her. Chloe stopped in surprise as she got a good look at the wolf's coloring: creamy chest and under-belly, salt and pepper gray back and tail. Who was it? She knew all the wolves in their Pack and no one had coloring like this one.

The wolf couldn't be wild. Natural wolves stayed far, far away from Pack territory unless they were sick, and this one was just standing there, staring at her. Chloe sniffed hard—instead of the usual Pack scent, the wolf smelled of wildness, musk and a hint of iron—but she didn't catch the distinctive scent of disease. All the Pack kids got rabies shots as a matter of course, but Chloe's dad had made sure she could recognize distemper and other canine ills.

The werewolf's pelt lacked the shine of a healthy wolf, and she could see its ribs. It was skinny and not full-grown. A rush of anger filled Chloe. "That better not be you, Gail," she threatened. Judy's sister was thirteen, a not unheard of age for the Change, but...

She took a step forward. The wolf snapped its teeth at her and broke left past her into the trees.

Instinct had her give chase, but she stopped after a few steps because—hello?—four legs were always going to be faster than two.

"Chloe, what's bothering you?" her mom asked.

Chloe slouched down in her chair and sighed. She might as well tell her; her mom was like a pit bull when in pursuit of a secret. "Coach says I can't Change because I'm a coward."

"Oh, did he?" her mother said in sudden cold fury.

"What's that?" her dad asked, wandering into the kitchen.

"Conrad Wharton, in his infinite wisdom and experience, thinks Chloe's delay in Changing is due to cowardice," her mother said. From the look in her eye, she and Coach Wharton would be having a little chat soon. Chloe's mom Changed into a small brown wolf and Wharton outweighed her by at least a hundred pounds and ranked third in Pack hierarchy, but Chloe would bet on her mom. Chloe had long suspected her mom could have ranked much higher if she'd cared enough to assert herself.

Her dad snorted. "Our Chloe?" He ruffled her hair before snagging a cookie. "If anything, she has the opposite problem. She's not scared enough."

A warm feeling grew in Chloe's chest. She'd been getting more and more anxious about the Change as the months dragged on, but she'd never been afraid of Changing itself. Something inside her relaxed at the realization.

She ate a cookie and her mind circled back to the other thing that had been bothering her. "Dad, are there any werewolves visiting from other Packs right now?"

Except for a certain number of matings to keep their Pack from getting too inbred, the other Packs didn't have much to do with each other. Packs were territorial. The nearest Pack Chloe knew about was three hundred kilometers away in British Columbia.

"No. Why?"

"Oh, I thought I saw a strange wolf this afternoon. I was probably just mistaken." Chloe deliberately made it sound as if she'd merely glimpsed a strange wolf in the distance.

To her surprise her dad frowned. "I'll phone around and find out if any alerts have been issued. I don't know if they ever found Paul Riebel."

Chloe remembered hearing about Paul Riebel. The Ontario werewolf had caught his wife in bed with another man and had gone berserk, Changing and killing them both. He'd run off into the woods afterward, and they thought he'd gone feral. Wild wolves were shy of humans. Feral werewolves, who'd rejected their humanity and given in to their wolf, were dangerous.

Chloe had seen pictures of Paul Riebel. He'd been a big man and so had his wolf. The strange wolf she'd seen had looked nothing like him.

At midnight Chloe slipped out the door.

She'd been thinking all evening about her problem. If she took it as a given that she *wasn't* a coward, then maybe what she needed to spur the Change was to connect with her wolf nature. Like a run outdoors in the moonlight.

She inhaled the crisp autumn air and began at a slow jog to allow her night vision time to adjust. Even though the darkness held no danger—werewolf scent kept away all big predators, she had a GPS in her pocket and she could heal any accidental injuries—something about being abroad at night made her blood run a little faster. Her already-acute senses sharpened. She heard the hoot of an owl, the dry rub of branches and smelled the rich loamy scent of the forest.

Just to make things perfect, the white orb of the moon shone through the treetops. Her dad insisted it was nonsense, but Pack lore was full of stories of werewolves Changing for the first time beneath the full moon.

Maybe tonight it would be her turn.

Shivering with excitement, Chloe increased her pace. Without thinking about it, she returned to the same part of the woods where she'd encountered the wolf last time. A true wild wolf would have stayed far away, but Chloe only had to jog about a quarter mile before she heard rustling noises off to the side of the path again. *Gotcha.* Not wanting to spook the wolf, she kept her eyes forward and kept running.

Her strategy worked. The strange werewolf grew bolder and began to run beside her, only a few paces away.

She tried to blank out all thought, to be wild, to be a wolf....

She felt a sense of joy and companionship, but though she willed it as hard as she could she didn't Change. Disappointment crept in and her pace slowed.

She would *not* cry.

To distract herself, Chloe sneaked glances at the feral from the corner of her eye, still trying to place the werewolf's coloring and failed. After a moment she realized he was male. Definitely not Gail then. And the next youngest after Gail was only eleven, a flat-out impossibility. Chloe's brow knit as she went over all the teenage boys in the Pack. Dean, Brian, Kyle...and then a big gap before her cousin Jayson, a gap which used to be filled by the Jennings kids before the crash.

Chills cruised down Chloe's spine. Her eyes widened and her steps slowed. It couldn't be. "Marcus?" she whispered.

The wolf paused when she did, tongue lolling. His yellow eyes seemed to ask why she'd stopped.

She took a step forward. "Marcus, is that you?"

It seemed to her that he hesitated. And then a branch cracked from farther up the trail, and he broke and ran.

Chloe sank to her knees on the path, trying to get her breath back and to think.

Holy crap. Marcus was or had been ten months younger than her. At the time of the plane crash he hadn't had his first Change yet. This could be Marcus. If he'd somehow survived the crash.... Well, werewolves could heal almost anything, but they burned a lot of energy doing it. The Jennings' plane had gone down in the Northwest Territories over a year ago, almost two thousand kilometers from the Hollow. Chloe supposed a wolf could have traveled all that distance, maybe, but...why do it as a wolf instead of Changing into human form and using the telephone? Her dad would have hopped a plane in a flash and brought him home.

The answer came at once: *because he can't Change.*

"Oh, no, no, no..." Chloe breathed. All Pack kids were warned, over and over, of the dangers of remaining in wolf form for days on end. Stay too long and the werewolf went feral. Wild. Dangerous.

The feral trotted back up the path then slowed when he saw her kneeling. He crept forward, his belly hanging low on the path, as if trying to make himself smaller to show he was no threat.

Chloe held out her hand.

Whining, the feral came closer and bumped her fingers with his head. Tears pricked Chloe's eyes. "Marcus? Is it really you?"

Another whine. Chloe settled her hand on his head, petting
him. Soon, the cream and gray wolf was snuggled up against
her side. Chloe kept stroking him, near tears, as she thought of
how far he'd come, of what he'd been through.

Chloe hated to ask, but she had to know. "Did anyone else
survive?"

The wolf whined and the pain in his yellow eyes was far too
human.

Now the next question. "Can you Change back? Try, Marcus,"
she urged, holding his head between her hands. She knew that
he hadn't gone feral, not if he let her this close, but no one would
take the word of a Dud.

The wolf closed its eyes and hunched its shoulders. Chloe held
her breath—but nothing happened. Just like nothing happened
every time Chloe stood in the moonlight and tried to Change.
She laughed bitterly. "Well, aren't we a pair?"

The SUV's windshield wipers ceaseless motion hypnotized Chloe.
She yawned. Last night's excursion had left her tired, a little
sore and impatient for the day to be over so she could go back
to the woods.

There had to be a way she could help Marcus. If it was Marcus.
"Mom, can the Change be triggered by adrenaline? Would a
'traumatic event—' (like a plane crash) trigger it?"

Her mom glanced over at her in alarm. "Possibly. But, Chloe,
promise me you won't put yourself in danger on purpose. Your
Change will come in its own time."

"I'm not stupid," Chloe said sharply. "I won't drive the car
into a tree or anything."

"Glad to hear it," her mom said.

Chloe continued to think out loud. "So, if adrenaline can
trigger the Change from human to wolf, do you need to be extra
calm to Change back?"

Her mom pursed her lips. "It helps. When I first Changed
back, I did it while I was asleep. It took me awhile to master the
trick consciously."

Chloe felt disappointed. If Changing back were as easy as
falling asleep, Marcus would have done it on his own already.

Determination filled her. Marcus had traveled two thousand
kilometers to get home. She was not going to let him be branded
as a feral and run off, or worse, be killed.

"Why weren't you at practice today?" Judy asked after letting a wet and dripping Chloe into her house. "Are you quitting Track?"

Coach would probably be happy if she did. Chloe ignored the question. "Do you still have that stuffed bear that used to belong to Ilona Jennings?"

Judy had showed it to her last year. Her mom had let her keep it after they'd cleaned out the Jennings' house. "Yes, why?" She blocked Chloe's way. Since Judy was now technically Dominant to her, Chloe was supposed to bow and scrape and ask permission.

Screw it. She didn't have time for dominance games.

The bear had been in Judy's room, sitting on a shelf over the bed, Chloe recalled. She removed her shoes and simply pushed past Judy down the hall. "I need to borrow it. I want to make a memorial for the Jennings," Chloe lied.

Judy looked puzzled, but Chloe's behavior had thrown her off enough that she didn't protest when Chloe took down the bear, a plush Gund with a red ribbon.

"Thanks." Chloe headed back for the door, Judy trailing after her. She paused after putting her wet sneakers back on. "Hey, Judy, do you know if Marcus ever had a girlfriend?" A girlfriend could give Marcus a reason to Change back.

Judy snorted. "He had a major crush on an older girl."

"Who?"

"That would be you."

Chloe held the stuffed bear out for the werewolf to sniff. She held her breath, hoping for a reaction—and got the wrong kind.

Marcus threw his head back and howled. Crap! This wasn't reminding him of why he should turn human; it was reminding him of his grief, of why he wanted to remain a wolf and live in the present.

Chloe tossed the bear aside and put her arms around Marcus's furry neck. He shuddered in her arms, keening.

After a moment she started talking, trying to dredge up better memories. "Hey, do you remember that time my mittens got soaked and my fingers were freezing? I sat between you and Dean so I could stick one hand in your jacket pockets. The seat wasn't big enough, and you had to sit half in the aisle. Every time we went around a corner you almost fell off." At the time, Chloe had mostly been interested in snuggling up to Dean; now she wondered if Marcus had already had a crush on her then. She should have paid more attention.

Under her hands Marcus stiffened, his snout lifting to sniff the air.

"What is it?" Chloe asked, getting to her feet.

The feral's lips peeled back, his shoulder tensing. Deep growls ripped from his throat.

Dean came around a bend in the path. "Has Little Chloe finally Cha—" he broke off.

Crap.

Dean sniffed. "Who's that? He's not Pack." Dean bared his teeth.

Though Dean had at least twenty pounds on the feral, he didn't retreat. Any second now, Dean would Change and the two werewolves would tear into each other.

"Out of the way, Chloe."

"No. Leave him alone." Chloe moved forward between the two werewolves. If her dad had been there he would have blistered Chloe's hide—only an Alpha could get away with that kind of move—but she didn't know what else to do.

The feral didn't like that. He growled again and circled in front of her. Did he think Chloe was part of his Pack?

Dean sneered back, a hair away from Changing.

"Stop it!" Chloe yelled, but neither wolf listened. It was for situations like this that Coach Wharton trained them; otherwise wolf instinct took over thought. And Dean had only been a wolf for eleven months. Chloe wished desperately that she could Change.

An itchy prickle ran over her skin but no fur came.

The feral feinted left, snapping his teeth.

Dean danced back out of the way.

Chloe pushed between them, shoving the feral away. "Stop it! Just stop it!"

The feral looked confused. He backed up and whined. Dean growled at him. Chloe stepped forward, blocking him. The feral loped off, but he stopped at the top of the hill and looked down at her in—confusion? disappointment?—before vanishing out of sight.

Dean got right in her face, trying to glare her down. "What were you thinking? Never get between two wolves in a fight. You know that, Chloe."

Chloe suppressed the instinct to cringe before a Dominant wolf. She did know it, but— "It worked, okay?"

Dean stared at her, disbelief written on his square face. "That wasn't me and Kyle tussling, that was a feral werewolf. You could have been mauled. What were you doing with the wolf in the first place?"

Chloe shut down her expression.

Dean's countenance turned to one of disgust. "Only you would try to make a pet of a feral. I bet you're just doing this to get attention. Everyone knows how much you've missed being teacher's pet."

Teacher's pet? Indignation fizzed in Chloe's veins. She opened her mouth to protest then stopped. Because two years ago she had been a bit of a teacher's pet. In Coach's eyes she could do no wrong—just like Dean couldn't now. Had she been this arrogant then? Well, if she had, she'd been more than punished for it these last fourteen months.

"You're lucky it hasn't ripped your throat out."

"He wouldn't do that."

Dean raised his eyebrows. "He won't get the chance, because as soon as I get home I'm going to tell my dad, and he and the others will drive off your little feral." He turned away.

Chloe caught his arm. "He isn't feral," she ground out. "He's Pack. It's Marcus Jennings."

Dean's eyes widened. "What? Marcus is dead!"

"All they found in the wreckage were burned bones," Chloe said stubbornly. "He could have escaped."

Dean made a scoffing noise. "No way is that Marcus. The Jennings are dead. If he'd survived he would have shown himself when your dad flew up there to see the plane crash."

Chloe shrugged. "Maybe he was wounded or crazy with grief." *Because his whole family died.* Just the thought of something happening to her mom and dad made her throat tight.

"You're delusional," Dean declared. "And even if that was Marcus, he's still feral. He needs to be driven away before he hurts someone. Coach will shoot his ass."

"*No.*" Chloe grabbed his arm again, voice fierce. "You can't tell Coach."

"Says Chloe the Dud. Why would I listen to you?" Dean asked.

Chloe felt a flush of rage, but this time the feeling wasn't followed with shame. So what if she hadn't Changed yet? Last year she would never have let him get away with talking to her like this, and she wasn't going to anymore, either. She looked him dead in the eye. "Because if you don't, I'll tell your dad you've been sneaking around to see Marcia Brown." Who was not only a townie—dating townies was discouraged, but not forbidden—but the daughter of the local RCMP officer. She could cause a lot of trouble for the Pack if she developed a grudge against Dean.

Dean's mouth hung open for a moment. "Have you been spying on me?"

Chloe raised an eyebrow. "As if I have the least interest in who you date." Last year she'd thought Dean was pretty cool, now, not so much.

"You wouldn't dare tell." He stepped close, trying to dominate her again, but she locked her knees and didn't budge.

"Try me."

Dean looked uncertain.

Pebbles hit Chloe's window, causing her to look up from her homework. Who—? Could Marcus have Changed?

But when she rushed over to the window she saw Dean's younger brother, Kyle, standing on the lawn below. He motioned furiously and then faded back into the shadows of the elm.

Chloe told her mom she was going out for a walk, then grabbed her shoes and jacket and whipped outside.

"Is it true?" Kyle demanded. "Dean said you think Marcus is alive." He looked torn between hope and anger.

Kyle and Marcus had been best friends, Chloe remembered. She should have recruited him days ago.

"Yes, but he's feral—" Chloe started.

Kyle grabbed her jacket and pulled her along. "Hurry. We have to find him before Coach and Dean do. They're out looking for the feral right now and Coach has his rifle."

Chloe followed him into the woods, feeling as if she'd been hit in the stomach. "Dean told Coach?"

"Coach got on his case about him and Marcia. Dean started yelling back about how you were the one who was really endangering the Pack by harboring a feral, who could be Paul Riebel for all you knew."

Chloe bared her teeth. "Dean saw the feral; he knows darn well he's not big enough to be Paul Riebel."

"If you're so sure it's Marcus, why didn't you tell me?"

"Gee, let me think. Could it be because every time I've seen you for the last five months you coughed 'Dud' into your fist?"

Kyle flushed. "Sorry," he mumbled.

Chloe slowed her steps as they reached the stand of pine where she usually met up with the feral. She looked but couldn't see him. "Marcus?" she called softly. "Maybe you should give me some space—"

A rifle shot cracked out.

Chloe was running before the echo died. No warm-up, just flat-out effort, legs and arms pumping, head tucked down, barreling down the path. A branch scratched down her cheek, but she didn't slow down, desperate to get to Marcus, to save him.

A small red wolf dashed past her; Kyle, Changed. Frustration bit into her. She was too slow—

A wolf howled, the noise followed by a second gunshot.

She might already be too late. Not much could kill a werewolf, but a bullet through the brain could. And Coach Wharton was an excellent shot.

Adrenaline stormed her body, taking it over. Fur prickled her skin, and Chloe's back bowed on a wave of pain as she collapsed on the path. Changed—

Wolf sight stung her eyes. Wolf smell exploded in her nose like a bomb. She saw/heard/smelt her Pack under attack.

She had to help Marcus. Clothing constricted her front legs. Unbearable. She ripped at the cloth with her jaws, squirmed free of her jeans and hoodie. She raced on and within moments burst into a small copse of poplars.

She took in the scene at a glance: Marcus, bleeding from the shoulder, Kyle, whining, cowed by a Dominant, Coach moving forward in man-form, a long-stick in his hands.

Growling, Chloe threw herself in between Coach and Marcus. Mine! Stay away!

"Chloe?" Coach smelled as if he were surprised for a moment, then he sighed and made noises without meaning. He raised the long-stick to his eye, pointing it at Marcus.

No. Not a stick. *A gun.*

Chloe charged. She hit his thighs with her whole weight, bowling him over. He snarled, threw the long-stick away and Changed so fast even her wolf eyes could only pick out a few random details: Coach's nose pushing forward into a snout, the sudden rash of black fur on his back, the silent snarl of pain on his now-black lips, tail sprouting, bones popping and rearranging themselves... and it was done. A black wolf twice as heavy as Chloe faced her.

He arrogantly stalked forward, expecting her, the lesser wolf, to get out of his way.

Chloe blocked him, growling.

He snapped his teeth in warning but she stood her ground. Marcus was still healing; she would protect her Pack.

He attacked, drawing blood with his fangs. Her shoulder burned with pain, but she didn't roll over, didn't back down. Growled her defiance.

Again he tried to go around her, again she blocked. His smell changed from impatience to puzzlement. He loomed over her, growling, but this wasn't about being bigger or even stronger. Dominance was about will.

Maybe if her Change had come easily two years ago she wouldn't have been able to do it. Maybe those months of being called a Dud, of persevering, had all led up to this moment, or maybe she'd been born an Alpha, but Chloe stared him down.

And then Marcus stood at her shoulder, his movements still stiff, but rapidly healing. He yowled his own defiance. Mine!

Mine! She howled back.

And then the two of them ran into the forest, paws hitting the earth, hearts beating as one. They were Pack!

The smell of apple pie drifted into the forest.

Chloe's wolf self didn't think much of the smell, but it brought forth strong memories of home and warmth and love. Marcus nudged her, puzzled, but she turned and trotted toward the smell.

The house was full of smells and so was the woman who stood in front of it, another werewolf in human shape. The house and the woman and the smells both drew Chloe and made her uneasy. She hung back at the end of the driveway.

The woman's voice was low. Chloe discerned meaning in the sounds she made. "It's time to Change back, Chloe."

Change back? But she'd only just found her wolf form. Chloe wanted to run some more. She wanted to roll in the fall leaves and hunt squirrels and howl at the moon with Marcus. But her Alpha had spoken so, reluctantly, she hunkered down and tried to Change. Her fur rippled.

Marcus whined. He looked morose.

Afterward, Chloe's dad theorized about hormones causing the Change and how it wasn't *adrenaline* teenage boys were known for overproducing, but at the time Chloe acted sheerly on instinct. Wolf instinct.

She flirted her tail over Marcus's nose, giving him her scent, then Changed.

And he mirrored her, Changing from wolf to boy. Pulled along by a mating instinct much stronger than the call of the wild.

They lay panting together in the bracken, almost nose-to-nose. And then mouth-to-mouth, lips and tongues meeting in a flurry of wildness.

When her mom rushed up, Chloe let her wrap them both in blankets, but she kept hold of his hand, smiling triumphantly.

He didn't speak, and his eyes shone feral, but those were problems for another day. Marcus was home at last. They were both part of the Pack again, accepted.

Nicole Luiken wrote her first book at age thirteen and was published while still in high school. She is the author of eight Young Adult novels. Her most recent titles are *Frost, Dreamfire,* and *Dreamline.*

Dreamfire won the Gold-medal Moonbeam in 2010 and *Frost* was both a Red Maple Honour Book and the winner of the Golden Eagle Children's Choice Award. Nicole lives in Edmonton with her husband and three children. It is physically impossible for her to go without writing for more than three days in a row.

A+ Brain
by Katrina Nicholson

I'm really looking forward to college. From my brother's Facebook posts, I can tell that there are more parties to go to than he can keep up with. The problem is my grades. It's the end of September in my senior year, and I still haven't earned better than a C- in anything. My dad says if I want to go to college, I have two options:
1. work harder,
2. brain replacement surgery.
I choose the surgery.

I'm feeling very understimulated, David.

I hear the stern voice inside my head and I almost drop my controller. On screen, the Master Chief freezes in mid-charge and gets owned by some noob.

The doctor had said to expect some disorientation, but he'd never mentioned hearing voices.

I stop to listen. It doesn't come back.

I decide that it was a side effect of the pain left over from the surgery.

The pain is an angry line that stretches across my forehead, over my ears, and meets at the back of my skull. It's from where they lifted the top of my head off to take out my crappy C-brain and replace it with a brand new A+ brain. It's satisfaction guaranteed by Instant Intellectuals of America Inc.

I think I'm unsatisfied. My new brain won't leave me alone.

Your spatial perception is adequately developed, my new brain insists as I play Xbox. *It's time to abandon visual entertainments and move on to more challenging and academically relevant endeavors.*

"Adequate?"

"Relevant?"

"Endeavors?"

It's really weird when your own brain uses words you don't understand.

Of course, as soon as I think that, my new brain explains: *I mean you've played enough video games. It's time to do homework.*

I thought the point of having a fancy new brain was that you didn't have to do homework anymore.

I ignore my brain and start a new game.

I end up doing homework anyway.

My brain was nagging me constantly while I played. It was driving me crazy. I started looking around the room for something I could hit it with and my eyes landed on my math textbook.

And my brain went silent.

As long as I'm looking at the book, my brain is quiet.

So I'm spending my weekend on algebra instead of playing paintball with my friends.

I want my parents' money back.

It's impossible to have fun online anymore. Every time I log onto the computer, I end up on the wrong website:

www.facebook.com becomes the Harvard Political Review,

www.youtube.com becomes NASA's Hubble Telescope Page,

www.twitter.com becomes National Public Radio.

It's annoying, but it's even more annoying to listen to my brain say things like: *This is shallow, topical material, David. You can do better,* every time I try to watch a video of a guy getting smashed in the nuts with a wrecking ball.

Too bad. I really wanted to see that video.

In their Facebook statuses, my friends are complaining about how the upcoming math quiz is getting in the way of their Facebook time. I don't comment.

I'm too busy actually studying.

My parents beam at me when I bring them the results of the math quiz.

B. I'm improving.

Well, my grades are improving anyway. With no *Halo* and no Facebook and no YouTube, I'm pretty much miserable. I can't even watch TV anymore. At least not anything good. The only channels my brain approves of are the ones that show documentaries. And the worst part is how excited my brain gets whenever I see a book.

I hate reading.

I do a lot of reading now, even outside of my school work. It's the only way to get my new brain to shut up. It's easier just to do what it wants than to listen to it nag.

Did you know that some types of frogs can change sexes if they can't find anyone to mate with? Or that Alpha Centauri is the closest star to Earth apart from the sun? Or that impressionist paintings are more about capturing the feeling of something than just how it looks? Or that guys my age in the 1940s had to shoot real Nazis? Because I do, now.

My friends don't really understand. They've stopped texting "whr r u? prty @ joez. b their" because I only message them back to correct their grammar. They've stopped sitting with me at lunch because I keep asking them things like what they think about the debates last night on C-SPAN or whether they want to go see the local theater company's performance of *A Streetcar Named Desire*.

I can't help it. My brain thinks Tennessee Williams and his writings are more important than Jenny Williams and her date for the prom.

There's nothing left in the house to read. I've read all my dad's computer books, all my mom's detective novels, even the manuals for the television remote and the microwave and the printer that hasn't worked for two years. It's like I'm hungry and there's nothing to eat. I mean, it's like my brain is.

My dad just about falls over when I ask for a subscription to *National Geographic* for my birthday. The paper version. My mom suspects it's because there might be topless natives in it. But I tell them it's because we're woefully undereducated about the anthropogenic effects on the biosphere. That's something my brain said one time while it was switching the TV away from *Jersey Shore* and onto *Daily Planet*.

My parents just blink at me. I don't think they know what anthropogenic means.

A couple months ago, it would have taken me a whole month to read an issue of *National Geographic*. But I read much faster now. Maybe it's my new brain. Maybe it's because I get a lot more practice. I blew through the issue in a single day, and now I don't know what to do. But of course my brain does. I lurch like a zombie out of the house and down the street. I've never been up this way before. I round the corner, and there it is: the library. I beg my brain to think of another way.

Only nerds go to the library.

I love the library. But only because it keeps my brain so quiet, of course.

It's always quiet in the library. So quiet that I bring my books there to study for my Biology quiz. It's much easier to concentrate here than at home, where my mom is always clanking pots together in the kitchen, and my dad is always yelling at sports on TV.

I write the quiz and bring it home to my parents. On the front, there's a letter A in a circle of red ink.

"Well done! We're so proud of you, David!" they say.

Funny. That's the same thing my brain said to me when the teacher handed me back my quiz.

I thought the books at the library would keep my brain happy, but they aren't. I spend almost all my time there, reading. I haven't seen an episode of *Jackass* in two months. My Xbox is gathering dust. My friends no longer speak to me. All I do is read. But still I can feel a pressure building up in my skull. Like there's something that needs to get out.

We're not meeting our full potential, David, my brain says. *We need to share, David.*

That's not very specific. What do I have to share?

Is this what happens when your immune system rejects your new brain? I've read that it happens to people who have organ transplants—hearts, lungs, kidneys. And the brain is an organ, too.

I worry that my head will burst open and my brain will splatter across the classroom. Thanks to my new brain and its love for math, I can guess where most of the drops will land. My classmates aren't going to like it.

I wonder if I'll have to take my old brain back?

My dad brings me back to the clinic.

He asks the woman behind the counter about my old brain. It's gone. It was only a C- brain. No one wanted it, so they threw it away.

She lets us in to see the doctor, even though it's late and we don't have an appointment.

The doctor listens to me describe the problem: the pressure, the swirls of thoughts clogging my brain, the feelings of dissatisfaction.

He takes out a pad of paper and a pen. I think he's going to write me a prescription, perhaps for a dumber brain. Maybe I just can't handle an A+ brain. Maybe I should never have tried anything higher than a B.

But he doesn't write a prescription. He hands the pad and paper to me.

Even though I have an A+ brain, it's not until I get home that I figure it out. The pad and pen *are* my prescription. I sit at my desk and put the pen to the paper. All those extra thoughts in my brain come pouring through my arm, down the pen and onto the paper.

I write a five thousand word opinion piece about the parallels between frogs that change sex when they can't find a mate and people who change their minds when they read other people's comments on their Facebook status.

And afterward, I feel much better.

I hand the piece in to the English teacher at my school, even though we didn't have any assignments due.

She loves it.

It turns out that she's also the faculty advisor for the school newspaper. She asks me to boil it down to four hundred words so she can print it.

I do.

It appears in the very next issue.

My old friends didn't read the school newspaper, so I assumed no one read the school newspaper. I was wrong. Several students came up to me in the hallway to tell me they liked my piece. Some of them want to be writers, but others want to be artists or scientists or politicians. They all have A+ brains, too.

They were born with them, of course.

We form a study group.

It turns out that the cathartic effect I got from writing the opinion piece also works on lab reports, art projects, history essays and English papers.

The average on my midterm report card is A+.

I'm really looking forward to college. From my review of his transcripts, it seems like there's much more to learn there than my brother can keep up with.

I'm not sure what I want to major in, yet. I think it may be everything. I want to scour the jungle in search of rare frogs. I want to promote environmental practices among my peers. I want to read everything Charles Dickens ever wrote.

I'm no longer concerned by the disembodied voice in my cranium. I've learned to recognize it for what it is.

Me.

Katrina Nicholson's brain is a natural one somewhere in the B- to A range (depending on how much sugar is in it). She and her brain started making up stories together when they were really young and got published for the first time when they were eight years old. As grown-ups, they studied history and writing for film and television before eventually becoming blogging, screenwriting, freelancing, library clerking authors. They like science fiction best, but they'll write pretty much anything. You can find their other stories, "Improbable Mission Force" and "The Wild Helicopters of the Australian Outback" in the anthologies *Undercurrents* and *Airborne* by Third Person Press.

The Road of Good Intentions
by Cat McDonald

Lee was too young to know why they called it the Road of Good Intentions and quite nearly too human to walk it. Three-quarters human, which is a lot. But, regardless, he found himself walking, one foot directly and precisely in front of the other, on the thin balance-beam chain of hatred.

A million such chains, perhaps more, hung in every direction all around him, further below, above and to all sides of him than he could possibly see. They slung in easy catenaries from one "core" to the other—from one human heart to another—in a rattling network of ill-will. Lee didn't know what the cores looked like; he could never see them through the tangle of connecting chains.

No one had ever seen the end of the Road, although they speculated about what was at its very bottom. As for Lee, he was beginning to think that it didn't have a bottom at all. If not for the fact that the falling lights always came from above, he wouldn't even be sure that the Road had an "up" or a "down". He couldn't see any colors anywhere but a mottled shade of streaky orange-gray, a forest of chains so infinite that they became everything.

Here, for once, he looked too human. In the real world, his pupils were always too wide even in midday glare, but at least he had pupils at all. Outside the Road, his skin was a gray tan almost too ashen to be human, but at least he had skin. It covered his whole body, too, and that was something. Outside, his fine movements were too quick and jerky; he had to slowly, patiently flick open his lighter, carefully retrieve his cigarettes. People didn't like to see his hand jump and twitch too fast to follow but luckily, down here, that kind of thing was expected.

From every chain, from every direction, he could hear voices: howling voices, shrieking voices, whispering voices, nothing but the voices of the Travelers. Ordinarily, he liked the sound.

His foot settled unevenly over a round link in the chain. His heart dropped and lifted like a bird in a hurricane as his body stumbled and, somehow, found its footing again.

If he fell, he'd have to find out what was down there, or else risk materializing in some completely random place in the real world which was, acre for acre, mostly barren ocean. He was on a clock, an important one, so he didn't have time to get lost even if he didn't drown.

Lee had walked much larger, thicker chains than this. Almost all the chains he walked were as wide as a sidewalk, some even as thick as a highway; whoever had spun this chain, it wasn't personal. That was a start. So, Marcel was probably right; it was probably a hired man. Lee had never seen chains this careless and casual between people who genuinely hated each other.

At one end of the chain, far into a distance that swallowed every Traveler's scream of rage, was the Summoner who had called this down on them. At the other end, about fifteen minutes behind—maybe more, if time existed on the Road—was his friend lying in bed, pale and hollow. Luckily for Lee, there was still time. Regardless of what novice Summoners believe, Travelers never killed the targets; they waited for the targets to kill themselves.

Marcel had a large family: six brothers and two sisters. A lot of fuel for the nightmares that had been eating him alive for a week before he and Lee finally realized what was going on. Lee didn't envy him the nightmares that locked him in a gravestone sleep, unable to wake up or even cry out for help. Eventually, they would completely devour him.

As soon as they had guessed what was responsible, Lee unraveled himself, tore himself open at the seams, dissolved into air and found himself sewn back together to the right pattern on the chains of the Road of Good Intentions. He listened to the howling and tried to isolate the particular sound of a Traveler he had probably never even met.

Without anything to hold on to, the way became difficult. How did anyone expect him to walk along such a weak, narrow hatred?

It sagged under his feet the further he got from his friend, more like a tightrope now than a balance beam. Ballroom dance had given him good enough balance for a beam, but he had never been a circus acrobat. No amount of Tango would prepare him for a balance beam that wasn't even stiff enough to keep still under his footsteps.

In the real world, or the solid world, or however he wanted to think of the world he normally inhabited as compared to the Road, there wasn't much time left. If he had known a hit would be this hard to trace, he would have tried to trace the hate-chain that bound Marcel and the man who had hired the Summoner in the first place. From there, he could have just done things the easy way: cut the answer out of someone, found the Summoner, solved the problem. But they had only the vaguest idea at the time that it hadn't been personal. Lee had expected just to be able to run along a nice wide chain to the other core, re-materialize next to someone who hated his friend enough to summon a creature to drive him to suicide and solve the problem. With a knife, if need be—Lee completely expected that need. Having to solve his problems with blades was really nothing new.

Beneath Lee, the chain started to shudder. At first, he could barely feel it, a twitching under the soles of his feet that could have been anything, including the links of the chain grating against each other, so he kept walking, one foot in front of the other. But the shuddering worsened, grew into a tremble that sent the links clicking and ringing all down the line into the distance.

Marcel had a large family, including two older sisters. The older of the two, a Necromancer, was a strange, unsociable lady with a threatening presence. Lee barely knew her even though he and Marcel had been friends since childhood; all he could remember was that she kept a number of hallucinogens in her garden.

Estelle, the younger of the two, had hated Lee for as long as he could remember. They never spoke, and Marcel knew better than to keep his not-entirely-human best friend and his demon-hunting sister in the same room.

"Oh no, Marcel, no. Please no," Lee murmured, as quietly as he could to keep his voice buried deep in the din of the Road. If Marcel knew that he was being attacked from here, would he go and speak with Estelle? Would she have him sleep in a protective chalk circle to lock out the world's many evil spirits?

Did she know what those things did on the Road?

A light shone over his shoulder from behind, from the place where he had been sewn back together, the brilliant blue light of the Circle of Solace. Lee had to drop to the chain and hold on.

The chain was ice-cold against the skin of his face. He wrapped his arms around it, pulled it in close to his chest and wrapped his legs around it to try and weather the storm the Circle of Solace would send down the line. It began to shake, began to ripple, sent waves into the distance, raising Lee and dropping him again, fighting to shake him off. At the bottom of the each swing, he had to clutch at his own forearms, holding his head in close to his chest and locking his legs together, however invasive the chill of hate felt against his body. This close, he could feel the trembling of something twisted in the chain's core, sense its violent rage at the intrusion. Of course, there was an influence acting through the hate chain; Lee hadn't met a Traveler at the chain's beginning, but Marcel had been attacked. Whoever was causing the nightmares hadn't arrived yet; these nightmares were just premonitions.

Which meant things were going to get worse.

Farther down the line, he heard a bellow of rage. It was close.

Nine times the chain rose, and nine times it fell. Each time, Lee felt the chain bruise his upper arms and the insides of his legs, and each time, he found it harder to resist the force of the wave's very bottom.

Each time, the roar down the line came back even louder.

After the ninth roar, the chain quieted and tightened. Lee was left hanging upside-down, clutching at his wrists, squinting away the glare of the Circle of Solace whose blue light had grown to completely envelop the beginning of the chain. And to think, in the real world all that pretty chalk picture did was give Lee a little headache.

He managed, pulling tight every still-functioning muscle in his battered core, to pull himself back upright, push himself to his feet and resume his walk along the chain which was once again taut enough to allow it. If he wanted to go back, to walk back to the beginning of the chain and stitch himself back together by his friend's bedside, the light would prove impenetrable. Beyond the Circle of Solace, the chain didn't even exist anymore.

So there was nowhere to go but forward.

A new chain arced over his head, wandering the void in search of an anchor that wasn't there. The other end snaked off in search of the core that was that damned meddling Estelle.

"I greet you, Fellow Traveler!" groaned a voice further down the line, a low rumble like the wind howling through desolate places, like a house at its breaking point, droning, flat and featureless. Its owner lumbered into view, a Traveler many times larger than Lee. In the light of the Circle of Solace, every detail of its body was visible.

This Traveler didn't look human but like a pile of ash-gray meat and skin propped up on armatures in a human shape, rolling on a platform attached to the chain. Tight, too-tight bands of rusting metal bound its flesh into the rough shapes of arms, of legs, of a neck and drew black blood along their orange-gray edges. Rods of metal jutted out of its chest, its back, its shoulders, bent and battered, scabbed into the flesh with thick blackish cement. Its face was sagging and lifeless, half-shadowed by a twisted chunk of scrap that had been caught under the band that shaped its neck. The Traveler's yellow eyes glowed slightly within that shadow, as all eyes did on the Road. The burnt meat and brimstone stench of a Contract lingered around it, although Lee wasn't close enough to smell the particular clauses.

So began the Ritual.

"And I you, Fellow Traveler," Lee said in return. He would begin the next stage. "I ask your name."

It paused, the significant ritual pause before the Exchange of Aliases.

"I am One Who Knows Better," it replied, its lips flapping limply outside its words. "I ask yours in return."

"I am One Who Makes His Contracts. I ask you, Who Knows Better, your purpose on the chain we both walk."

This pause was not part of the Exchange of Purposes; it had to raise its hand to shield its face from the blue light.

"I walk to pursue my Contract. I ask you, Who Makes His Contracts, your purpose on the chain we both walk."

"I walk to pursue my Contract. I have now met you, Who Knows Better."

"And I have now met you, Who Makes His Contracts."

They both advanced, meeting somewhere between them. This chain was not thick enough for them to pass one another, so they stood face-to-face a moment. Lee could see his shadow blacken into focus against the Traveler's scarred stomach, see the Traveler's yellow eyes dim as it squinted against the light of the circle. Lee hadn't planned on dealing with the Traveler, or rather, he had hoped not to. He wasn't strong enough to solve the problem on a knife's edge, not against a creature like that. Even here on the Road of Good Intentions, he was material enough to be torn apart, and the Travelers were strong enough to do it.

He just wanted to hurry to the other side. He had hunting to do.

"How did you do that, Who Makes His Contracts?" Armatures squealed in pain and terror as it lifted its pendulously sagging arm-flesh to point at the chain still following above Lee's head. It had already latched onto Estelle, but wouldn't find its other anchor until Lee had left the Road.

"Come, sit with me." Lee sat down on the chain, pushing his hands into the links on either side of his hips, letting his bruised, exhausted legs hang over a gray-streaked abyss. Travelers couldn't be hurried.

The Traveler did the same, seeming to melt onto its platform.

"The chain appeared because I realized my hate."

Its already-slack jaw sagged even further, opening a cavernous, shapeless mouth within which Lee could see a glimmer of skittering movement. "You…have the power to create chains. Then, you are…you are a Descendant. It is as I thought."

This was how Travelers referred to humans, like Lee, who could count a Traveler among their family tree's twisted branches. Lee himself had only ever met one other, but creatures with Eternity to consider would have seen enough to name them. Lee just called himself a man and let the matter drop there.

"Yes."

They sat in the silence, Lee inhaling the odor of the Contract. He could pick out the clauses now, smell the standard lines in the standard ritual, the Line of Torment, the Vow of Safety. Maybe there was something he could do here rather than slinking along this slack balance-beam to the other core.

"You say you have a Contract," it said, and a little of that skittering movement fought its way nearly to its lips before being crushed by a heavy, thick tongue. "I do not smell it. This is a Contract of the Disputed Land—a Contract of Paper and Whispers."

It was a good term for the real world, "Disputed Land". To the Travelers, it was always a struggle to weigh the place down with chains, lest other forces, ones Lee had never seen, wrest it away from them. It sounded better to Lee than "Real World."

Lee didn't argue with it about the Contract. How could he explain to a Traveler the concept of his childhood friend? It was a Contract, one into which they had both willingly entered but which they had never signed.

A nearby chain shook with footsteps. That chain was the size of a highway, broad enough for an army to march along. At least, Lee thought it might be; he couldn't tell how far away it was and couldn't accurately guess its scale. It trembled and rippled as a Traveler ran along it, striding with triple-joined legs, chased by a streak of white cobweb hair, wailing and tearing strips from its own body, scattering the flesh into the abyss below. Its arms were bleached bone, exposed where the mourning Traveler had torn the flesh off and thrown it to whatever "bottom" the Road had.

It screamed for its brother.

"You stayed! Why did you stay!?" it shrieked into the endless Road. There were no bounds for the sound to reflect from; the sound fell dead into eternity without echoing. The mourner, too, ran into the distance, absorbed by the gray, endless Road of Good Intentions.

"They have abandoned us!" cried Lee and Who Knows Better in near-unison. It was the only appropriate ceremonial response to those still mourning Those Who Stayed Behind.

"I am surprised that you know the response. Descendants are... too young to remember them," rumbled Who Knows Better, its voice almost too low to be intelligible. "I was once a mourner."

"I do not remember them, but I know the ways of the Road." There had been in some indescribably distant history—before mankind was even created some of the Travelers said—only one family where, now, there were two. The Travelers had lived with Those Who Stayed Behind in harmony until the war. From what Lee had heard of the war, it was a failed revolution, a crushed rebellion that left the Travelers wandering this half-rusted abyss. When asking Travelers about it, the best Lee usually got was vaguely-coherent gibbering of names too big for Lee's too-human mouth.

"I see. Many Descendants do not."

"Many did not bother to learn. Tell me, Who Knows Better, about your contract. I can smell the Line of Torment. You have been charged with the death of the one at the other end of this chain, am I right?"

"I have. Your Contract takes you in the opposite direction, Who Makes His Contracts. Are our purposes at odds?"

"They are." Lee felt a trembling in his body, the anxious need for a cigarette, but he clutched the chain and left the little cardboard packet in his pocket. Cigarette smoke would dull the scent of the Contract. "I have come here to prevent harm to the one on the other end of this chain. What are we to do?" The formal diction still felt foreign between Lee's lips; he would much rather curse, clip his words, make euphemisms and jokes, speak in riddles, offer to "take out a package" for the right price, but Travelers were too old and their dignity too rigid for them to respond to his reality. Lee had no choice.

The deep rumbling thickened to a tremor in the Traveler's rubbery chest. "I am bound. I cannot break the Contract."

Lee took another breath. The Line of Torment was thick and heavy in the scent, all but masking the cold smell of the Vow of Safety. Almost all Travelers were forbidden by this line to harm the one who had summoned them. Anyone who summoned one without insisting on his own safety was quickly found torn apart.

Their dignity was too rigid for them to suffer servitude.

"I wish to propose a deal, Who Knows Better," Lee finally said, letting the scent scour his lungs, pretending he could taste cigarette smoke somewhere under the brimstone and blood. It would do until he could re-materialize. "If I can free you from your Contract, will you abandon it?"

"If the Contract is dissolved..." The creature squeezed out a reply from between flabby, lifeless lips caked with something deep and warm in color. In the light of the Circle of Solace, almost everything looked blue and violet. "If the Contract is dissolved, and if you explain to me the nature of your Contract of Paper and Whispers, I will abandon it."

"In exchange for your abandonment of the task, I offer my aid in dissolving the contract and in understanding mine. This is our deal."

"So let it be honored."

"So let it be honored."

As soon as the ritual was complete, another bond appeared. A slit opened up in Lee's rust-smeared palm and a smoky ribbon, like a searching snake, wound around and through before finding another ribbon like it from somewhere behind Who Knows Better's head. The ribbons tied themselves together, and the deal was official.

Lee took a deep breath. "Men are not really bound by Contracts of Paper and Whispers. They just believe themselves to be. If a man believes that he is bound to do something, then he will do it as surely as if he is bound by a true Contract. Real Contracts are unnecessary with creatures like that."

"I see. Knowing this, you have entered into one. Why?"

Lee didn't know why. Because they had been friends, forever. Because, to Lee, who had always had trouble with people more than three-quarters human, the concept was strange and precious. Because his dearest friend was lying in a bed somewhere, imagining acts no man should ever happen to witness, happening to himself, to his family. Some Travelers took the faces of family members and loved ones for the torment. Maybe he dreamt it was Estelle who was hurting him. Eventually, the lack of rest, no matter how deeply he slept, and the terror would drive him to kill himself.

In the distance, one of the lights fell. From somewhere above them and far in the distance, a white streak plummeted from the infinite grayness above to the infinite grayness below.

"Welcome, brother!" shouted Lee, Who Knows Better, and a near-infinite chorus of Travelers whose voices sounded like everything but human voices. Voices like fire, voices like metal, voices like death rattles, voices like scorpions, all of them welcoming a new Traveler. A Following One.

And then Lee knew.

"You remember the time Before the Road, do you not?" he asked. "I hear stories about it. Stories about how the Travelers and the Ones Who Stayed Behind were one family. Loved one another. Before the Travelers were led here."

Who Knows Better's voice was a strained rumble, as though the breaking house Lee had heard when they first met had finally collapsed; Lee could practically smell the debris in the air. "I remember that time."

"Mortals...still have times like those. This person and I... are like you were back then. So I must protect him from harm."

"I see. It is not a Contract, but...but it is a bond. Now, my own Contract."

Lee took another deep breath, and the scent of burning flesh tried to completely choke him, grabbed fistfuls of his windpipe and twisted it. He could smell most of the clauses now. The Line of Torment and the Vow of Safety, of course, but the Contract Name too, delicate and sharp, underneath them. Somewhere in the mist that rose from the bound Traveler, Lee could even smell a Method Line. The Summoner had specified how the deed was to be done. It smelled like torture with a hint of terror. Like suicide.

But, this scent was too simple.

"It's missing something," Lee said. His sense of smell wasn't what it used to be, not since he had taken up smoking. For any other cause, he would have said it was worth it.

"Find my answer," Who Knows Better groaned, desperation percolating somewhere within the mountain of its flesh. Lee could understand it; he was starting to get desperate, too. When he set out, he had forgotten how seriously Travelers took their work; just killing the Summoner might not even have worked.

He searched for the scents he knew and he found them: the brimstone, the meat, the burning wood, the incense, the Summoner's blood. Everything seemed to be in order. Everything seemed to be there. The Imperative Clause had been added, so they weren't dealing with a total amateur. He at least knew well enough to specify that the Traveler—who had Eternity to consider—complete the request in a timely fashion.

The Contract couldn't be perfect. It was woven by a human being, or else there would be no need for the Vow of Safety. Humans made mistakes. This one had too.

Lee himself was three-quarters human, so he knew better than anyone.

"There is no Duration clause," Lee said, searching the aroma for the weak, fleeting scent of the clause. "Normal Contracts specify that the contract ends when the task is complete. He forgot it."

"So my Contract is permanent?"

"No, no. It only lasts until one party dies. A contract written in blood will never outlive its signatories. There's an Imperative Clause, so it's not like you can wait until he withers."

"I cannot kill him. I am bound by the Vow of Safety. You cannot help me." Who Knows Better stood, its metal frame shrieking under the strain of all that useless flesh, returning to its feet to squint into the light of the Circle of Solace. The scent of the Contract rose like pyre smoke from its body, its eyes aflame with a purpose that had been hammered into it.

Luckily for Lee, the Circle of Solace would prevent the Traveler from reaching his friend. Although it was just chalk in the real world, on the Road it was an impenetrable wall. Even if Lee failed, Estelle would protect his friend.

The chain above Lee's head dwindled and disappeared.

"No. It appears that I cannot. Not yet."

Who Knows Better lumbered along, rolling on the underside of the chain as though there was no top or bottom, around Lee, and leaving the blackness of his shadow. The ribbons connecting the two of them stretched apart, pulling on the skin of Lee's open palm, but it was all right. Lee would do things the hard way. As long as Marcel stayed with his sister, there would be time to search for the Summoner at the other end of the chain, re-materialize, cut the Summoner's name out of the first person he saw and solve the problem. Even if those ribbons stretched to opposite sides of the Road first, it was possible. He didn't have to race against the Imperative Clause.

As Who Knows Better moved toward the light, the chain started to move.

"No, no, no," Lee said to himself, struggling to stand on the moving chain. "No, Marcel, just stay in one place for once!"

The end of the chain drifted to the left, slowly leaving the Circle of Solace. His friend had left his sister's care and the Traveler drew nearer.

"Wait!" Lee ran along the chain, trying to remember the meticulous steps that had got him so far away from his friend in the first place and forgetting his cool planning. "Wait, Fellow Traveler! I can help! The deal shall be honored!"

Lee had no idea whether or not he was telling the truth. He was, after all, one-quarter Traveler. More important than truth or lies, however, was the burnt-herb scent of the Imperative Clause.

Who Knows Better stopped and turned. It was a mountain of shadows with its back to that blinding light, nothing but a shapeless blackness with a pair of glowing yellow eyes surrounded by a halo of cold blue that constantly drifted to the right like a setting sun. They were still tied together.

"So let it be honored."

Lee took another breath of the Contract. There had to be another mistake. A bigger mistake. Some loophole through which he could thrust his arm and choke the Summoner to death. The chain drifted ever leftward, and soon the core that was his friend's heart would be out in the open.

There was a gap in the scents. Lee had not noticed it before, because he had smelled the lack of Duration and thought that the entire gap was one clause. But there were two clauses, usually right next to one another, whose combined absence formed that gap. There was supposed to be something sweet and dusty in there, something like an old woman's china cabinet.

"The Vow of Silence. It's not in there."

Who Knows Better glared down at him, leaning over amidst the screaming of its body. The metal bands pressed even tighter into its flesh, drawing a trickle of black blood that ran down its scarred stomach.

"The Vow of Silence?"

That was all Lee needed. As the Circle of Solace completely left the core, Lee's heart finally caught hold of a steady surface and began to recover.

"You are forbidden to harm your Summoner. But, he never forbade you from telling another who he is and where he is."

Lee was only three-quarters human and he had slit throats before. That part would be easy.

Cat McDonald is a freelancer living near Edmonton, Alberta, with more hobbies than she has fingers. She's a cook, a game designer, a 25-year-old, a tea enthusiast, a connoisseur of fine web comics, and a member of the Big Lake Environmental Support Society. Moving at age eleven from the lush St. Lawrence River valley made an impact on her, and her new home may have held a little inspiration for the landscape in "The Road of Good Intentions." If she could be an animal, she would be a seal, a cheerful critter who can always manage to work and play at the same time.

The Windup Heiress
by Leslie Brown

When Aliantha Mercit was betrothed to Hasaidi Odi, no one actually consulted Aliantha on the matter. When she questioned her father, she received a blank look.

"The House of Odi supplies all the crystal circuitry for our windups. Who else would I ally us with?"

Aliantha's mother was slightly more sympathetic but just as obdurate.

"It's the way things are done, my dear."

Since Echo had only been settled for one hundred and fifty years, any traditions were arbitrary creations of the wealthy people who lived there, and Aliantha did not care for a custom that had her marrying at the tender age of seventeen. She sequestered herself in her lab and tinkered with the genetic makeup of dormice for eight hours until her parents had the lock blasted off her door.

"All the arrangements have been made," Aliantha's mother said as she walked beside her daughter as she was dragged by two windup servitors. "Your father has some wonderful wedding presents for you and all that remains, is to hire a companion from the Spaceport labor pool to escort you to the Odi Estate."

"Why can't you just send me with a servitor?" Aliantha muttered and then repeated her mother's answer along with her:

"It's tradition."

Aliantha's mother gave her the same gift her own mother had given her: a strip of filter paper with three drops of her mother's blood on it, DNA proof that Aliantha came from an unbroken matrimonial line originating with the first colonists of Echo. Aliantha jammed it impatiently into the carry pouch around her neck.

The Mercit family's sole human servant, known only as The Butler, went to the Spaceport and hired a companion, a young woman of Aliantha's age. Tiza came with a stony expression and an indeterminate figure concealed by a shapeless Mercit jumpsuit. However, The Butler, whom everyone in the Mercit family trusted implicitly, seemed very satisfied with his hire. On the marble floor of the House foyer were three travel cases. One was the symbolic overnight bag that Aliantha was to carry to the doors of the Odi mansion; the other two were her father's gifts. He came out of hiding to bid farewell to her.

"My dear," he said, not meeting Aliantha's gaze, "I've designed a new type of windup for you as a wedding present." He pushed a button on each case, and the small boxes expanded and blossomed into two windup horses, one white and one black.

"This is yours," her father said, tapping the white horse on its forehead. The eyes blinked and swiveled toward Aliantha.

"Good afternoon, Miss Aliantha," it said in a mild voice. "My designation is Falada."

"Charming," Aliantha told her father. "Just what I need: a horse."

"It's still a prototype," her father said twitching nervously.

"And the black one?"

"Less sophisticated, with no verbal interaction chip, but something for your handmaid to ride."

Since both her parents were devout agoraphobics, it was a given that neither would be attending her wedding or even be capable of watching a live broadcast. Aliantha allowed herself to be packed up with Tiza and transported to the magneto-rail station at the edge of Mercit Island. Glumly, she watched the train approach along the viaduct that stretched out over the inland sea. The Butler placed Tiza and the bags into their private coach and bid them farewell.

"Well, that's that," Aliantha huffed as she flung herself into a luxurious seat opposite her handmaiden.

"You don't seem pleased," remarked Tiza. Aliantha was startled that a servitor had spoken without being asked a direct question until she remembered Tiza was human.

"I'm not. This marriage is pointless. The House of Odi will always sell circuitry to the House of Mercit whether their children are allied or not. I can only hope this Hasaidi Odi is as sexless as the rest of his generation and will leave me alone after a few children."

"Is there no love in Family marriages, then?" asked Tiza.

"Occasionally, but it is discouraged."

"Have you even met this man?"

"No. We don't even know what each other looks like. It's traditional."

"Do you want me to get you anything to eat?" Tiza asked, suddenly helpful.

"A protein bar would be nice," replied Aliantha. "Use this credit band. It's handy for small purchases." Tiza was back shortly with several packages of protein bars. They chewed in silence.

Later, a soft chime woke them from their naps.

"We're at Odi Island," Aliantha said, her voice hoarse from sleep. "Grab those bags and I'll lead us."

Tiza picked up the two windup horse suitcases and looked pointedly at Aliantha's small bag. Aliantha looked blankly back.

"I've got my hands full. You'll have to carry that bag," Tiza told her.

"I'm not to carry my own luggage. That's what a handmaid is for."

Tiza gave a violent sigh and summoned a servitor porter. Aliantha was increasingly offended by Tiza's attitude, and she vowed to send the girl back to the Spaceport labor pool as soon as possible.

"Where's your welcoming committee?" asked Tiza.

Aliantha hesitated deliberately before deigning to answer.

"I will be greeted when I reach their gate. This is where we use father's windup horses." She pushed the buttons on the cases and the two horses sprang into shape on the platform.

After an hour of riding up the winding path, every muscle in Aliantha's body ached. She was also terribly thirsty. She stopped Falada.

"Tiza," she demanded, "fetch me some water from that stream."

"Get it yourself."

Aliantha stared in shock at her handmaid. "How dare you refuse an order! Do you want to be sent back to the Spaceport immediately?"

"You're going to do that anyway, so why should I humiliate myself any further?"

Aliantha was at a loss for words. Servitors never spoke back, were never snippy. The stream's happy tinkle spoke of cool relief. She slid off Falada's back and hobbled over to the water. She glared at Tiza as she passed her and scooped water into her mouth with cupped hands. When she turned back to the windups, Tiza was sitting on Falada. Aliantha reached up to pull her off.

"I think not," said Tiza.

"I beg your pardon?"

"I'll be riding this windup the last bit of the way to the House. You'll ride the black."

"What on earth are you talking about?"

Tiza held out her hand displaying a large gaudy ring with a purple stone. "Do you know what this ring is for?"

"No."

"It's a governor controller."

"I still don't know what it's for."

"A governor is a small device that is fed to a person. It lodges in the throat next to the vocal cords and extends small microfilaments into them. When it is switched on, like so, you are unable to speak." Tiza tapped the ring's purple stone and Aliantha clutched at her throat in alarm. She snatched for the ring and was neatly kicked under the chin. Horrified, she climbed back to her feet.

"I'm skilled at self-defense, Miss Mercit," Tiza told her. "The lessons you should learn are to never eat anything offered by a stranger and never offer physical violence unless you are sure of winning. Now, pay attention. The controller has a second feature in that if I squeeze the outer band three times, the governor will explode, tearing your throat out. Very messy. Shall I demonstrate?" Tiza raised the ring.

Aliantha shook her head violently.

"I won't if you co-operate," Tiza said. "We are to switch places. I will be Aliantha and you will be Tiza. I will marry Hasaidi Odi. You will be a servant of the estate as long as you please me. I see you are fumbling for your little filter paper sample. I took it from you when you were sleeping on the train. Now, mount up." Tiza tugged on Falada's reins.

"You are not my mistress," the windup said.

"Do you understand the conversation I just had with your mistress?" Tiza asked it.

"I understand that you mean my mistress harm."

"And what is the best course of action to prevent me from harming her?"

There was a pause while Falada's neural net pondered the question.

"Remain silent?"

"Correct. Good horsie."

They continued on with Tiza in the lead and a fuming Aliantha bringing up the rear. The fear Aliantha felt was an entirely new emotion. Tiza was stronger and faster and had planned this out with great care. Aliantha needed time to come up with a solution. The white walls of the Odi House appeared before them.

"What do we do now?" Tiza asked softly, her finger pressing the ring lightly. Aliantha could speak again and she drew a breath to shout.

"Ah, ah, ah!" Tiza's finger descended toward the ring and Aliantha let her air out reluctantly.

"Press the intercom button beside the gate and announce yourself," she told Tiza sullenly.

"Any particular way?"

"Say you are Aliantha Mercit, daughter of Kaitlinda and Ovidiah Mercit. You are here to join the House of Mercit to the House of Odi. That's it for formalities. The wedding will be tomorrow after you've presented the stolen filter paper."

"Thank you for your advice, Tiza." Tiza touched the ring to silence Aliantha and then pushed the intercom button. She announced herself, and immediately the gate opened and a flock of Odis emerged, swarming the windup horse and engulfing Tiza in a happy, chattering crowd. Aliantha looked on, perplexed and uncomfortable at the presence of so many real people. The throng gradually cleared, revealing a young man who was gazing in awe at Tiza. He took her hand and raised it to his lips. Someone touched Aliantha's arm and she looked down at the face of an elderly human servant.

"You must be Miss Mercit's handmaid. Please dismount and take some refreshment after your long trip."

Aliantha glanced over at Tiza and caught a hard stare. Quickly, she bowed her head to the human servant, unsure of how to communicate that she couldn't speak. He helped her dismount and handed her a drink with an umbrella in it.

"My name is Conrad. Now, you are not to worry. Miss Aliantha has just explained your problem to us. We have a perfect job for you and a lovely cottage for you to live in. Nothing too demanding since Miss Aliantha tells us you get upset when you are stressed."

Aliantha gaped at him. He thought she was a simpleton. Numbly, she followed Conrad into the compound. The Odi mansion was perched on top of a hill and was ornamented with a great number of pagodas, reflecting their Japanese heritage. In a horrible mix of architectural themes, there were a dozen alpine cottages on the grounds below the mansion, arranged as a village. Conrad led her to a cottage with an attached shed. A sign over the front veranda said "Happy Dreams Cottage."

"You'll be living here and sharing accommodations with Vanessa, the shepherdess," Conrad told her, holding the door open for her.

"Shepherdess?" Aliantha mouthed at him carefully as she stepped into the cottage.

"Yes, she tends the windup sheep. You will be our goose girl and look after our windup geese."

Aliantha cocked her head in obvious question. As soon as she could get a stylus and compad, she would ask Conrad for help.

"You are to herd them," he told her.

Aliantha, in the process of opening the cupboards in the small kitchen looking for writing materials, stopped to stare at Conrad.

"The Odis like their estate to have a bucolic setting, that is, like a farm."

Aliantha rolled her eyes. *I know what bucolic means.*

"I must caution you, Tiza, about your attitude. Criticism of our employers is not to be tolerated."

Conrad's lined and pleasant face was now creased in a frown. Aliantha felt uneasy and then realized it was because no one, with the sole exception of her mother, had ever expressed disapproval of her before.

She ducked her head and produced an apologetic grimace. She was surprised at how well it worked. Conrad was all smiles again.

"I understand that you are unsettled right now, Tiza. You'll feel better once you are in a routine. Vanessa will be home shortly and she will explain the geese to you. Your work day tomorrow will be short because of the wedding. A festive peasant outfit will be provided."

Aliantha manufactured a delighted smile but it must have been too artificial because a small frown wrinkled his forehead.

"If there is any trouble, Tiza, we are instructed to send you back to the Spaceport."

Aliantha shuddered. The Spaceport was too rough a place for a mute with no identification papers. She mimed writing.

"Miss Mercit has told us not to provide you with writing materials because you can't help but write offensive things. She doesn't want the Odis upset. I am amazed at how fond she is of you. Most employers would not tolerate such a dysfunctional servant."

Stymied, Aliantha watched him trudge back up to the House. Tiza had blocked her at every turn. Her hand crept up to her throat. What was to stop Tiza from activating the explosive? She must know that she couldn't keep Aliantha under control forever. The new, unaccustomed feeling of fear slithered around in Aliantha's stomach until Vanessa's arrival distracted her.

Vanessa was a blonde chatterbox, full of excitement at having a room-mate and at the prospect of a wedding feast the next day. She remembered to show Aliantha the fifty geese, lined up on shelves in the shed, and warned her to set them outside first before broadcasting the "on" signal. They were programmed with random behavior that required room to move.

Aliantha flipped open the cover of the circuit pad controller and mimed punching in a program. When Vanessa stared at her blankly, Aliantha took two geese and programmed them to walk in a figure eight.

Vanessa was astounded. "How did you know how to do that? But you aren't allowed to alter them or even switch them off to have a break. One of those sharp-eyed great aunties will see that they aren't behaving like normal geese and complain. You have to herd them, like I do the sheep and Conrad does the cattle. At least Conrad has a windup dog to help him. I've been asking for a nice border collie for ages but that would look too Scottish or something. I really have no idea what the problem is."

Aliantha tried to tune Vanessa's non-stop talking out. The shepherdess made them hot chocolate before bed and lent Aliantha one of her nighties. Each had a bedroom of her own, so finally Aliantha could shut a door on the girl's chatter. She had learned more of the situation at the Odi estate, and it did nothing to put her mind at ease. Hasaidi Odi had been infatuated with his bride before he had even met her. He had written a song for her that all the human servants were going to have to sing at the wedding. Hasaidi's mother was long dead but his father, Benatu, would be at the wedding.

Aliantha waited until she could hear Vanessa snoring, then slipped out of bed and got dressed. She needed to find a communication panel and call The Butler.

She crept to the door of the cottage and glided silently out into the damp night. Vanessa had mentioned a community hall designated for servants. There must be a com panel there. She stepped off the porch.

"Back to bed, Tiza." Conrad emerged from the shadows. "Miss Aliantha told me you were a wanderer. I was just coming to lock you to your bed."

Aliantha gaped at the leg restraint he had in his hand and shook her head violently.

"Wear it or pack for the Spaceport."

Left with no choice, Aliantha watched as Conrad attached the soft restraint to her ankle and locked the other end to the steel bed frame.

"Good night." Conrad left, shutting the door quietly behind him. Aliantha stared in despair at the wooden ceiling above her and squeezed out a few tears. Then a hard determination came over her. No Spaceport schemer would get the best of a Mercit. Tiza would rue the day she tried to take Aliantha's place.

The next morning, Vanessa let her out of her leg restraint, Conrad having left a key and a note. The geese herding was a nightmare. The windups honked, waddled, and shat very realistic green poop that she slipped in several times. To add insult to injury, Aliantha had to feed them the pellets that made the poop. She was close to tears after an hour of trying to get the geese out of the cottage yard and down to the large ornamental lake that was the centerpiece of the estate.

"Tiza!" Vanessa called to her from the cottage. "Bring the geese back. It's time to get ready for the wedding."

I just got them going in the right direction, Aliantha groaned to herself. She turned the flock back toward the cottage.

Their festive outfits had arrived, and they were just more elaborate versions of the shepherdess and goose girl costumes they were already wearing. When they arrived at the House, they were each given a bag of rose petals to throw. A pagoda arch had been erected on the green lawn. Beneath it stood the groom in a blue, embroidered kimono. With him were a religious official and a stocky man in a blue suit with close-cropped gray hair.

"Benatu Odi," Vanesa said in a loud stage whisper. There was scattered applause to greet Tiza's entrance. She was dressed in a scarlet bridal kimono and Aliantha had to admit she looked stunning. The sullen laborer had become a cool dark-haired beauty. The ceremony was brief and then the rose petals were thrown in the air over the couple by the cheering staff who then sang Hasaidi's composition. The wedding party formed a reception line. When she reached Tiza, Aliantha glowered at her.

"Buck up, Sweetie," Tiza whispered to her. "Cat got your tongue?"

Aliantha's eyes went involuntarily to the rings on Tiza's hands before she stepped sideways to greet the groom. He was slack jawed with delight. His father pressed a credit band into Aliantha's hand.

"A gift from the Family to commemorate this day. Tiza, isn't it?"

Aliantha nodded and bowed, making way for the next person in line. It was done. Tiza was married to Aliantha's intended. She helped herself to food from the lavish buffet and then slipped away around the side of the house. She wondered if she could get inside and find a com panel.

"Oh, Miss Aliantha, if your mother could see you now."

Aliantha spun around. There was a pile of what appeared to be scrap metal behind a bench, and Aliantha saw it was composed of disassembled horse windups. Falada's head was on top, still attached to part of the arched neck, and the eyes swiveled whitely.

Aliantha bent to examine it. There was no sign of the circuit panel. She had hoped to punch in commands directly so Falada could understand her.

"I have been feigning complete deactivation in the hope I can be of assistance to you, Miss Aliantha."

Aliantha tossed her plate away and picked up the head. There was a door into the House nearby with two large potted plants on either side. Aliantha hid the head behind one of the pots. The door was unlocked and she walked in. With most of the staff at the wedding reception, she did not run into anyone before she found a com station in an office. She wrote "I need help!!!!" on a compad and dialed the Mercit House's address. The Butler appeared on the screen and Aliantha held up the compad with a relieved smile.

"I think not, Miss Tiza."

Aliantha gaped at him.

"You are not to make any trouble for Miss Aliantha. Do you understand me?"

Aliantha felt tears sliding down her cheeks and her hands started to tremble.

"Everything will be fine if you keep silent, Tiza. You are my cousin and I have promised to look after you. Once Miss Aliantha is expecting a child, you can come home."

It only took a few moments for Aliantha to puzzle it out. Tiza had been inserted by him into the Odi family. Once she was pregnant, her status as mother of the Odi heir would protect her despite her non-Mercitness. It was silly but it was the law on Echo. The Butler did not mean Aliantha any harm as long as she didn't try and hurt Tiza's chances. Then he went and ruined everything.

"Just remember, I'm here looking after Aliantha's parents, keeping them safe. It would be terrible if the House caught fire. Her parents wouldn't be able to run outside. An awful thing, these phobias."

Aliantha started to cry in earnest. With a disparaging shake of his head, The Butler signed off. She threw the compad into a waste chute.

"There you are, Tiza." Conrad's voice startled her and she jumped.

"You've gotten yourself lost and upset," he said kindly. Vanessa was behind him, peering over his shoulder worriedly. He held out a hand to Aliantha who had no choice but to take it. As they emerged from the mansion, Aliantha shook free and darted over to Falada's head, hugging it protectively to her chest.

"All right, Tiza, you can keep it for now. Madam Odi has told us to keep an eye on you and put you in the cottage for a nap so you don't get overtired. Go with Vanessa."

Aliantha gritted her teeth as Vanessa led her back to the cottage. It was a clear message: if she went where she wasn't supposed to, she'd be tied to her bed. She lay down keeping a tight grip on Falada. Vanessa tied her to the bed and puzzled briefly as to what she should do about the head, but the lure of the wedding reception won out and she left it in Aliantha's arms. As soon as Vanessa was gone, Falada's eyes swiveled to Aliantha's face.

"Oh, Miss Aliantha, if only your mother could see you now."

Aliantha gave the horse a sharp flick with her finger between the eyes to reset it. Its lips fluttered violently for a brief moment.

"Your pardon, Miss Aliantha, I am not myself."

Aliantha sat up and held the horse's mouth against the restraint band. Obediently the windup started chewing until the band separated with a painful snap. Aliantha fetched eleven geese from the shed. With a metal nail file of Vanessa's and odds and ends from around the cottage, she gutted goose eleven and grafted its innards onto the wires in Falada's neck. Through hand signals, she was able to convey commands to Falada's head that were, in turn, relayed to the other ten geese, rewired by her to obey eleven's transponder. She hid the gutted goose under some straw and practiced commands with the remaining ten.

Everything was back in place a few hours later when Vanessa stumbled tipsily into the cottage. She had a plate loaded with food.

"I got you some dinner, Tiza. Oh, what happened to your strap?"

Aliantha, lying on her bed, shrugged carelessly. Vanessa frowned in concentration then hiccupped.

"Oh, never mind. Here's your food."

Aliantha took the plate, touched that the shepherdess had remembered her. Vanessa was soon snoring in her bed. Aliantha got one of the programmed geese out and signaled to Falada to send it toward the now-quiet Odi mansion. The head gave her a running commentary of what it could see through the eyes of the goose.

"Oh good, a cat door. Left or right from the kitchen, Miss? Oops, stairs. We can't seem to get up them, our legs are too short and I can't figure out how to flap our wings. I think we need more geese, so they can make ramps with their bodies."

Aliantha signaled Falada to call back the goose. This might take a while and she didn't want Tiza to get any inkling of what they were up to. She tucked the goose away with the others and put Falada in a corner, facing away from her. She didn't like the idea of those reproachful eyes glowing at her in the dark.

The next day she took her flock to the lake. It was much easier than the day before because she had programmed the ten geese to subtly help herd the others. Someone was sitting on a rock by the water and as she approached, she saw it was Benatu Odi. She couldn't veer off at this point so she brought her charges down next to him and turned them loose to splash in the shallows and pretend to eat the duckweed.

"Don't mind me, Tiza. I came down here for some peace and quiet. That Mercit girl has gotten my son whipped into a frenzy of subservience, and it makes me a bit queasy to watch. Still, the boy seems to be quite fond of her already. Strange, given her reputation."

Aliantha cocked her head questioningly.

"I had heard that Aliantha Mercit was as cold and emotionless as the windups that raised her. However, my son's wife is passionate and full of opinions."

Aliantha quickly glanced down so that he would not see her outraged expression.

"I'm sorry, Tiza. I know you don't understand half of what I'm saying." He ran his hands tiredly over his short hair. "It's just that I feel old right now and pushed aside."

Aliantha's curiosity was piqued by his melancholy. She mimed tears flowing down her cheeks.

Benatu thought for a moment. "Sad? I wouldn't call what I feel that, but I do feel pointless. My father started the nanocircuitry business, and I made all the improvements I could. There's nothing more to do. Maybe I should just let myself fade away or take up geese herding."

Be my guest, thought Aliantha. How could a man at the peak of his career, with all these resources at his fingertips, find his life pointless? Put her in his place and she could keep herself busy for fifty, a hundred years. She sat, nodding occasionally, as Benatu mused aloud. A goose wandered over to Benatu and tried to eat his shoelace. He laughed and picked it up. It struggled briefly and then nestled in his arms.

"I admire Mercit for what he does with his windups. I make my own pets, but they are alive, not windups. I've recreated creatures of legend such as the basilisk and the gryphon. It was a fun hobby, but I've taken it as far as it can go."

Aliantha raised her eyebrows, impressed at genetic tinkering on such a scale.

"You like that, do you, Tiza? Shall I show you someday?"

Aliantha nodded enthusiastically and then stopped when Benatu laughed. She realized it made her seem even more the simpleton.

"Ah, there's the lunch bell. Some other time, perhaps."

Aliantha was disappointed. There wasn't going to be another time. Tonight, the commando geese were going to complete their mission.

That night, Aliantha decided to practice the stair climbing technique on the back steps of the cottage. Any mistakes in the House could result in the geese being discovered prematurely. It took most of the night but finally the geese were able to flatten themselves on the steps so that the others could climb up on their backs to the next level. By the time she was done to her satisfaction it was too late to try for the House.

That day, Benatu showed her his lab. The creatures he had engineered were very impressive and surprisingly docile for all their fearsomeness. She was consumed with envy when she saw his state-of-the-art micromanipulator and nanotech geneslicer. There was so much marketing potential here, she could not begin to calculate the wealth it would generate for the Odi clan, yet Benatu saw it as just a hobby.

Aliantha delayed her plan a few days more. The geese needed to be perfect before she launched them on the House. Each day she spent hours down by the lake being talked at by Benatu. She was not used to conversing with real people but it was easy to sit and listen. He talked more to her than her father ever had. At the thought of her father, she suddenly sobered. What was she doing dallying when her parents could be in danger?

That night she sent the geese to the house. They performed flawlessly, clambering over each other's fat bodies up the grand staircase to the second floor. They waddled down the corridor to the bedroom where Tiza and Hasaidi slept. They formed a tottering pyramid so that the top goose could press the button to open the door. They flowed across the expensive carpet to Tiza's side of the bed.

"Oh Mistress, the ring, it's on her finger! She wears it to bed."

Aliantha spun Falada's head to face her. She was sitting in a deck chair on the back porch of the cottage in the dark. The infrared receptors in Falada's eyes could pick up her every gesture. She hesitated. It was grotesque but her parents were in danger. She mimed biting and swallowing. Falada's lips quivered; Aliantha felt them moving against her palm.

"It's done," the windup whispered. A shrill scream echoed from the mansion. Aliantha beckoned madly to the horse head. *Bring the geese home to me.*

Other shouts joined Tiza's screaming. Rising above the racket were excited honks. Ten geese swarmed up on the porch, and Aliantha clapped her hands to turn on the light. One goose had a bib of scarlet. She held out her hand imperiously before it and it obediently horked up the finger with the ring still on it into her palm.

"A bit drastic, don't you think?" A pale Tiza stood at the bottom of the steps with her hand wrapped in a small towel.

"You can speak, you know. The microfilaments dissolved a day or so ago."

"Er," said Aliantha, testing. "That makes me feel rather foolish."

"I'm the foolish one, underestimating you. I've paid for it with a finger." Tiza grimaced.

"You seem rather calm about your plan falling apart." Aliantha felt a tremor of fear. What had she overlooked?

"I didn't think it could last forever. Do what you like but please read this before the others get here." She handed Aliantha a folded note.

My Dear Aliantha,

By the time you read this, I will have left your parents' service and will be very hard to find. As for my reasons, I watched you grow from a sad and lonely child into a sad and lonely young woman. I do not think that this marriage is what you need, so I provided an alternative. I hope you've made the most of it. I leave Tiza in your merciful hands. Try to understand that she was only trying to better her situation, something I wanted for both of you, the daughter of my body and the daughter of my heart.

Yours truly,

Gerard Sims, Butler

Aliantha reread the letter again. Should she believe him after the way he had hurt her when she had come to him for help? All she knew was that she had no intention of fighting for the right to marry Hasaidi. She looked up at Tiza. "You love Hasaidi? Are you carrying his child?"

"Probably yes, and most likely, no."

Hasaidi, Benatu, and Conrad thundered up to the cottage.

"Here she is," panted Hasaidi. "My darling, are you bleeding?"

"Yes," Aliantha said quickly, "and it's my fault."

"What do you mean?" asked Benatu sharply, "And how is it you can speak?"

"I had this foolish plan to impress you enough that you would take me on as an apprentice. Aliantha kindly agreed to help me by hiring me on as her handmaiden," said Aliantha, nodding at Tiza. "I programmed the geese to sneak into the house and form a funny tableau for you to see in the morning but something went wrong and Aliantha got hurt. I feel awful." Aliantha proffered the missing digit to Conrad who took it with distaste.

"Conrad, call the city for a medsquad to put that back on," said Benatu. "Apprentice yourself to me? Whatever for?"

"Sir, I'd heard about your biomanipulations and wanted to study them. I have extensive windup experience, and I think there would be many financially rewarding possibilities if we worked together."

"Father, I want this woman arrested! She hurt my Aliantha!" Hasaidi was trying to cradle Tiza to him and look indignant at the same time.

"Later, boy. Tell me about these possibilities, Tiza. I'm intrigued."

"With pleasure, Sir." *Hah, I'll be running this place in six months,* thought Tiza Sims as she bent to rescue Falada's head from the milling geese.

Leslie Brown makes her home in Ottawa, Ontario. By day, she is a research technician in a laboratory studying Alzheimer's disease. By night, she tries to stay away from television and computer games to write science fiction, fantasy, and horror stories, much to the disapproval of her Welsh Cardigan Corgi who wants belly rubs. This story was based on the fairy tale "The Goose Girl," In the original, the counterfeit princess pays for her sins by being rolled down a hill in a barrel studded with nails (pointing inwards, of course). Tiza gets off much more lightly in Leslie's story.

The Bridge Builder
by Kevin Cockle

This was cool.

Hundreds of people wandered through the aisles of the vendor section of the Calgary Gaming and Comic convention. Mike stayed close on Donnie's right side, using him as a crowd-break as they slanted through the throng.

"Dude." Donnie slapped Mike's arm, nodding to a line of celebrities signing autographs along the western wall of the convention center. "Stacy Keibler. Told ya."

Mike stared, star-struck. Sure enough, Stacy Keibler sat behind a table, smiling cheerily up at a fan. She was promoting some new wrestling/combat game which Mike already knew to be garbage, but which he suddenly felt compelled to purchase at all costs.

Donnie laughed at his spellbound friend. "Dream on!" He scoffed.

They shuffled along at a gallery pace. Crowd noise was deafening—hundreds of voices, thousands of footfalls multiplying in the cavernous room. Booths hawked games of all sorts: video games and board games, role playing games and gambling games, card games, dice games, scale-miniature and shared-world games. It was amazing stuff for Mike—well worth the effort it had taken to scrounge up the cost of a day pass.

Some actress in an elf costume approached on Mike's right flank. He knew she was a hired professional because, although there were tons of people dressed up for this thing, *none* of them looked like this girl. The memory of Stacy Keibler, so vivid just a moment ago, disappeared as the elf drew near. Her costume was a classic wood-elf look: a short cape draped over her right shoulder with a brown, belted tunic over forest-green tights, finished with knee-high buckskin moccasins. She wore her Keibler-esque blonde hair long and loose about her shoulders and down her back. The tips of convincing pointed ears poked through on either side. Her face was perfect. Whoever had hired her had really known their stuff. She was all high cheekbones and delicate, arching brows. Her amber eyes looked like liquid honey. And as she passed, she turned those amber eyes on Mike and smiled.

Mike froze as though she'd slapped him. The girl passed by without saying a word.

"Dude," Mike gasped, stopping and turning to watch those long, be-legginged legs stride away. "Did you see that? She totally smiled at me!"

"You need to learn to distinguish between a grimace and a smile. She was in agony, Mikey. One look at you—cramps."

"No, but did you see?"

"Yeah, I saw a chick about to throw up on a hobbit...hold on now." Donnie's attention had been snagged by a vendor selling mail shirts and a variety of edged weapons. "Come on!" he said and led the way.

Mike followed. Donnie and his weapons. Sure, Mike thought weapons were neat, who didn't? But Donnie...Donnie had a real fixation. And, Mike recalled, it was a weapon that had forged their friendship in the first place.

It had been two winters ago, after school, and sure enough, Mike was in a shakedown yet again, three against one—the three all older and bigger than the one. Mike struggled to keep his glasses on his nose as he kept his head down, fearing to look the predators in the eyes...but when they started shoving him one to the other, it was kind of difficult. They were expensive prescriptions, those glasses. Mike had had rare cataract surgery shortly after being born and had weak eyesight ever since. But that wasn't the half of it.

He'd had half a dozen surgical procedures before his first birthday: heart, spine, left foot correction, left pinky finger separated from its neighbor, kidney, hernia. Once, when he was five, a doctor at a walk-in clinic had told him he'd be blind before he was twenty; his mom freaked out and got other, less dire, opinions. But the idea of the near-term due date—or doom date—lingered, a weight upon Mike's spirit, an ever-present shadow or a cloud. The shade of that doom date imposed a ceiling on the number of times he could smile in a day; put a brake on how loud he would laugh. Sometimes, he thought that if the bullies knew how fragile he was and had always been, they'd go easy on him.

But then reality set in and everything boiled down to keeping his glasses in one piece.

"Hey, Brainiac," one of them kept saying. "Brainiac gonna think your way outta this? C'mon, Brainiac!" Mike had advanced a couple of grades to be in grade six well before his body should have been there: the nick-name "Brainiac" was a foregone conclusion. He hadn't wanted to accelerate, but his mom had explained to him that if he did, the government would pay to get him in a better school and that it was SO important to do so. Well, the school may have been better, but the kids weren't. They had proven to be pretty much the same knuckleheads as poor kids… maybe even worse.

One of the kids punched Mike in the back, just above the hip. Pain spread out from the impact in shockwaves and Mike bit back on tears. Start crying now, and it would be over. They might not stop until there was blood.

"Leave the kid alone," the voice had said, the voice that would turn out to belong to Donnie Kane. He was twelve to Mike's nine at that point, but he wasn't much bigger than Mike, and more importantly, he wasn't as big as the trio of thugs in charge. Still…his voice had carried a chill. He hadn't shouted or done anything dramatic, but he'd managed to convey real menace in a conversational tone. The bullies stopped their pushing, sniffing the wind for fresh blood. Seeing the size of the new kid, they responded with the appropriate jackal-grins.

"Brainiac's buddy," one of them said, to obligatory sniggers. "You want some?"

Donnie stepped forward. He had no toque to cover his unruly mass of long black hair. His slender body was bulked up by a long green military surplus coat, and his jeans were stuffed into hiking boots with the laces undone. His pale face was thin, angular, and his blue eyes were that washed-out shade you'd see in some Husky dogs. He crimped his lips and then answered, "The question is, do *you* want some?"

And Donnie withdrew his left hand, brandishing the first and only switchblade Mike had ever seen in real life. With a deft thumb-press, the blade snicked open, shining deadly in the dull grey light of the winter sun.

The three bullies blanched. The sight of the knife had stripped away their pretensions. They were little boys now, struggling to keep their disguises intact. They didn't want to run, but they backed off. When they were far enough away, they turned and stalked off, voices raised in fresh bravado, leaving Mike alone with the psycho.

Donnie closed the knife and put it back in his pocket. "Jerks."

Mike said nothing.

"Hey, man...relax," Donnie said, recognizing the fear in Mike's eyes. "Seriously, I knew they wouldn't do nothin'. You live around here?"

Mike nodded. "Up over the hill. I'm in Briar." Briar was the other side of the Crowchild Trail and a whole world away from the roomy mansions and giant lawns of the Heights.

"Me too," Donnie said. "You wanna walk?"

A burst of synthesized electro-pop music from a nearby game-console display wrenched Mike's attention back to the present. Donnie turned from the weapons smith's display counter with a mail shirt of intricate, finely wrought links, holding it up against his chest and giving bug-eyed looks while going. "Eh? Uh? Yeah, baby!"

Mike smirked—goofball. Ever since that first day, Donnie would usually show up at Mike's school and walk him home. The thugs would shout their insults, but they'd do it from a safe distance, behind the schoolyard fence. Nobody wanted to mess with Donnie, no matter how big they were.

Mike remembered bringing Donnie in one afternoon while his mom was out working and thinking how much crap he'd catch if she found out. A) No strangers in the house—that had been a stone-cold rule ever since Donnie could remember. And B) though not a rule as such but probably implicit in the no strangers' rule was: no switchblade-wielding strangers. But when Donnie had seen Mike's game laid out on the kitchen table, all traces of the lethal tough-guy seemed to fade away, replaced by typical twelve-year-old wonder.

"Holy crap!" Donnie had said, stepping to the table and staring at the dice, miniature figurines and monsters, hexagonal sheets, pads of paper with Mike's scribbled notes, and of course—the drawings. Donnie picked up an 8"X11" black dragon Mike had been working on and whistled. The drawing was easily the equal of anything on a comics' stand and Mike knew it. "Did you draw this?" Donnie wanted to know.

"Yep," Mike said, grinning.

"Kid's got skillz!" Donnie marveled.

Mike joined him at the table. "It's something I've been working on. It's a...I'm a game designer. I'm building my own role-playing simulation system."

"No way," Donnie said, holding up a picture of a cloth-encased ninja assassin in mid-leap.

"Way," Mike said, earning a laugh from Donnie.

"Why don't you just buy D&D or something?"

"Too expensive. Mom said no. Besides, it's fun to figure out the rules yourself."

"If you say so. How old you say you were, again?"

"Nine."

"What're you—some kind of genius?"

Mike winced. He had heard the word used from time to time, at school or at the children's hospital, in meetings his mom would have with teachers or doctors. It was the adult word for Brainiac and he didn't want it to ruin things with Donnie. "Everyone's smart at something," Mike shrugged, deflecting the question with his stock response.

"Well...can I play this?"

Mike chewed his lip, thinking. It wasn't a completed system yet. He had a Critical Results Table set for standard combat which could be extended to missile combat, but he was still sketching out the rules for unarmed fighting. Campaign stuff, he could figure out as they went along, but he only had a couple of character-types fully detailed. Still...he'd been itching to try the system, to beta-test it like the real pros. Even though there'd be hell to pay with Mom, he couldn't let this opportunity pass.

"Sure!" Mike said. "I'll teach you."

And that was that. They'd been playing ever since. After early suspicions, Mike's mother had come to enjoy the idea of Donnie being there with Mike until she got home, especially on nights she had to be late. Of course, they kept the weaponry on the down-low. No mom was *that* cool.

Back at the vendor's table, Donnie had picked up a rapier and Mike could see his friend was falling in love. Wandering conventioneers shouldered their way between Mike and Donnie, and Mike stepped back to get out of the way. He was looking for a good place to stand when he saw the elf girl down the aisle, staring at him.

She's not staring at you, Mike self corrected. *She's looking for somebody.*

But when the girl smiled and briskly motioned with her hand for him to come over, Mike had to assign a high probability to the idea that it *was* him she'd been looking at, after all.

Holy crap!

Mike swallowed, glanced at Donnie who was totally enraptured by his sword, then began angling his way toward the elf.

Mike's heart galloped. To his chagrin, his heart was thudding in exactly the same way it would as if he were being bullied at school. Like his body didn't know the difference between talking to a girl outside of school for the first time ever...a beautiful girl dressed up like an elf...and getting the tar beat out of him.

As he closed, he wondered just exactly what "first base" was, and if this was it. And if it was, then reaching first base at eleven years old *had* to be some kind of a record!

"Hey," he said. All of a sudden, he felt the weight of his glasses and wished he wasn't so damn small, so goggle-eyed. She was a full head-and-a-half taller but didn't look to be too much older; it was hard to tell actually, but he felt like he needed to be a full-fledged teen for a stunt like this.

"Hey," she smiled. Her voice was breathy, sweet—like she could probably sing well if she wanted to. She glanced once up the aisle, then fixed her amber gaze on Mike once again. He felt heat rushing to his cheeks and knew it was too late to make a good impression. *I'm eleven years old*, Mike despaired. It wasn't going to matter to her how smart he was.

"C'mon," she said, threading her left arm in his right and coaxing him forward. "You want to go somewhere and talk? Let's go somewhere. What's your name?"

"Mike," Mike said. "Mike," he affirmed, just in case.

"Mike. I'm Cynara."

"Whew," Mike said. "For a second there I thought you were Stacy Keibler."

Cynara laughed in spite of herself, surprised at the attempted wit. Mike had only intended to be conversational, not funny, so he counted himself lucky in the exchange.

She led them through the milling crowd, in a winding path up and down the aisles until Mike was good and turned around.

He knew he'd left Donnie somewhere behind him, but wouldn't be able to find the weapons smith on purpose. It made Mike a little apprehensive: he never would have come all the way down to the Stampede grounds by himself. His mom had taken to calling Donnie his "big brother", and it was understood that if Mike went downtown or someplace far, that Donnie would go with him. Suddenly separated, Mike realized for the first time just how big this place was.

And if he was apprehensive before, then he was doubly reluctant when Cynara pushed through a door marked "NO EXIT" and attempted to pull him through. For the first time, he balked and stuttered. "Umm...I don't think we're supposed to...I mean, the sign says..."

She looked at him with those arched brows, a look that said, "What're you, eleven?" and it was enough. Swallowing hard, Mike went through, following her down whitewashed concrete steps.

This part of the grounds was old. The heavily over painted cement floors and cinderblock walls made Mike think of World War II buildings. The clunkiness of construction and the smell reminded him of some of the older hospitals he'd been in—all such buildings seemed to be of an era. His footsteps echoed in the empty stairwell as he slid his hand along a steel rail painted black. Cynara's footsteps made virtually no sound, her suede moccasins whispering as she skipped the steps ahead of him.

Two flights of broad stairs, one long hallway with ancient-looking fluorescents in long rectangular housings above. Now Mike was nervous.

"Hey," he said, stopping at last. "I need to get back."

Cynara glanced up the hallway, then fixed him with her gaze again. When she stared right into his eyes, Mike felt woozy. His skin tingled as if he were cold, though in fact, he was overly warm from the quick-march in his winter coat.

"It's not safe here, Michael," she said at last, after carefully considering her words.

"What do you mean?"

"I mean, I had hoped to get you out of here."

Mike took a step back in alarm. "Nervous" upgraded to "afraid" in three skidding heartbeats.

Cynara raised her palms. "No, Michael, it's...I had hoped to explain this to you."

There was a sound from the far end of the hallway, back at the stairway. Mike turned and saw that the stairway lights had gone out.

They could hear patient footsteps descending within that darkness and the whining skirl of metal being scraped against concrete.

"Get behind me, Michael," Cynara said, her voice quiet and cold. Mike turned to see her holding a long, slender rapier in her left hand. If he squinted, he could see a faint blue nimbus glowing about the blade.

A bank of lights went out at the end of the hall. Mike gulped, and skirting wide around Cynara, took up a position behind her. Now he was terrified for his choices seemed to be stay and maybe die, or run and be alone. He couldn't choose between those awful outcomes. He stood rooted to the spot but poised for flight, his mouth slightly ajar.

It was at times like these—and also in the bad times at school— that Michael most wanted his dad. His mother had told him that daddy had "gone missing in Afghanistan when you were just a baby" but as years went on, sometimes the country was "Iraq", and on one occasion, "missing" had been transposed with "killed." Mikey was a smart kid; everyone had always said so. These inconsistencies in narrative were bothersome to him. He also watched and understood the news, and knew that Iraq was an unlikely deployment for a Canadian soldier. And eventually, he knew without being told that mommies sometimes lied to little kids in the false hope of protecting them, and that little kids pretended to believe to protect their mommies in turn. So he knew his dad probably wasn't a soldier, but sometimes, Mike really wanted him to be.

Another bank of lights went out. The footsteps and the metal-scraping noise drew closer.

Cynara slid her left foot back, picking the heel up off the floor, pushing her weight onto the ball of her right foot. She waited in her stance, the sword tip angled toward the floor. In a moment of thunderclap clarity, ridiculous under the circumstances, Mike realized that her pointed ears were real.

"Mi-keeeey," a voice called out from the darkness. Donnie's voice. "I thought you were supposed to stick close. Bro's before ho's, man."

Donnie emerged into the light, but darkness clung to him like smoke, rolling off his shoulders in sensuous rills. His washed-out eyes, always unsettling but especially so when he was angry, were blazing. He was as furious as Mike had ever seen him, because he was as calm as Mike had ever seen him. In his left hand he held a rapier, though whether it was the one from the vendor's table or not, Mike couldn't say. Whatever it was, it too, glowed a pale blue, as though Cynara and Donnie were living batteries of some kind.

Donnie's face had changed, still recognizably Donnie, but different in bone structure. And his ears were pointed.

"Hey, Cyn," Donnie drawled. "Long time, no see. Sorry for the snub upstairs. Didn't recognize the shape you'd taken—that, and I didn't think you'd be so obvious. It's funny, when I'm human, I only seem to see what I expect to see, you know?"

"This does not have to happen," Cynara growled. "Especially in front of the child."

"Oh, no? What was your plan then? Take the bridge builder to his house, make him send me back? I can't even begin to tell you how much that's *not* going to happen." When Donnie had said "bridge builder" he'd nodded directly at Mike. Mike had no clue what it meant.

"You are going back, Yrrl. You must. One way, or the other."

"Let's make it the other, shall we?" And with that, Donnie lunged.

He leapt forward, dragging his left foot behind him as he raised the sword from the floor, aiming the point for Cynara's liver. Cynara parried, pivoted left. Donnie circled so that they cut the hallway in half, facing each other. And then all hell broke loose.

They were at each other like lightning bolts. Donnie would drive Cynara's back to the wall, Cynara would raise her right foot and front-kick Donnie in the body, shunting him backward. Cynara would attack with wide left-hand sword strokes punctuated by swift, straight right hand punches. Donnie would parry, block and counter in kind. Mike was familiar with a wide variety of martial arts, he had to be for his hobby, but he'd never seen this combination of southpaw techniques before. Both combatants used sword/right hand in combination: lead right foot for front kicks, the back left foot for swinging round kicks. The idea of keeping the left foot back didn't make sense from a traditional fencing standpoint—it kept the sword farther back for left handed fighters—but as Mike watched the lethal ballet unfold, he began to get a sense of the form as a whole.

Their swords crossed: Donnie triggered a short right hook, turning Cynara's chin to the side, buckling her knees. Pushing sword on sword, he hurled the girl back to the wall where she hit with a flat slap of flesh on stone. She'd hit the back of her head in the bargain—Mike could see she was stunned—and Donnie hopped in, driving the point of his sword into her right hip as she turned in the nick of time to take away her belly.

Cynara cried out as Donnie cackled. He regrouped, pulling back in his stance; Cynara fell to her right knee. Donnie lunged—and Cynara twisted on the spot, driving her rapier's tip up under Donnie's ribcage. Deep into his torso.

Donnie gasped, eyes wide.

Mike cried out: shock, grief, terror.

Donnie dropped to his knees, and slowly, slowly faded from sight, the lights down the hall coming on again in his passing.

Cynara groaned, collapsing back to a seat against the wall. She dropped her sword to the side, crossing her arms against her body.

Mike swallowed, felt his tongue dry against his teeth. His hands clenched and unclenched at his sides.

"Are you...." Mike began, his voice catching in his throat. "Are you okay?"

"I need a moment, Michael," Cynara said. He could hear the pain in her voice; she sounded much older to him now. He looked, but could see no blood. None had come from Donnie either.

"Come," Cynara whispered, her eyes closed. "Sit with me."

Mike came and sat cross-legged, facing her left side. He suddenly noticed that her sword had disappeared.

She looked at him then, gave him a sad smile. "I'm sorry Michael. I know he was your friend. I know you thought of him as a friend."

"What...what *was* he? What are you?"

"The game, Michael. Your game. You have a very...unique imagination. You've worked so hard at that game for years now. Taught yourself to draw just so you could decorate it: On weekends, sometimes you stay up all night, don't you? Balancing probabilities, sketching out encounters, thinking how best to represent reality. You've committed your nervous system, brain and all, to the game's realization.

"We believe that in designing your simulations, a bridge was opened. That happens, when special people focus intensely enough, for long enough. You did not create Donnie as you knew him, but you created the context for him to exist here, gave him a shape, parameters. It...it is hard for me to explain to you. When we create, if we do it well, the things we create take on lives of their own and in so doing, cease to be our creations...do you understand? You pulled Yrrl—Donnie—through, but he was dependent upon you. Playing the game with you made him more real on this side, made him stronger. Soon, he would have been able to build his own bridge. And Yrrl's creations would not have been pleasant."

Mike's mind reeled. He thought of Donnie's way of simply being there when he got out of school: he didn't attend the school himself. When he'd asked about Donnie's home, Donnie had always given him a rueful little smile and said, "Trust me, you wouldn't want to know." Donnie's penchant for army-surplus clothes, Donnie's lack of other friends or acquaintances. On and on, the more Mike thought it through, the more it all made sense. There was no Donnie without Mike. Not really. There was only Mike's playmate, Mike's protector, Mike's soldier.

"I just wanted someone to play with," Mike said in a small voice. He almost never sounded like a kid when he spoke. He sounded like a kid, now.

Cynara's eyes welled with sympathy. She placed her long-fingered hand on Mike's knee, giving him a reassuring squeeze.

"Michael, I need you to promise me something," Cynara said, focusing on him again, making his skin tingle. "Not just any kind of promise, though. I need you to make a promise like you would if your mom was crying, and keeping your word was the only thing in the world that would make her better. Don't promise me if it can't be that kind of promise."

Mike swallowed hard, staring back at Cynara in silence. She'd hit the nail on the head, all right. If he made a promise like that, he'd keep it or die trying. "Okay," he whispered.

"I need you to go home and gather up your game. There's no point in destroying it," she smiled, "but its material nature, it's thingy-ness, all the drawing you've done, all the tables and notes, are still important. What I want you to do is put it way deep in your closet or up on a high shelf somewhere, someplace where it will be out of sight. And then, just leave it for a while. Things, and even thoughts, have a way of gathering dust and getting misplaced over time. Maybe you'll move someday and the game will be lost, or, who knows? Maybe you'll have other games to play. Or, at least, if you do take it out and look at it again, think about it again, it would be good if you were older. Someone like you, whose creations are so real that he can't control them, needs to have a bit more stuff-of-life in him before dabbling in such things."

Mike nodded. He didn't fully understand, but he knew if the game he'd created was helping to create other things, then he wanted no part of it. In retrospect, he felt lucky that it was only Donnie who had come through. Could've been much, much worse.

Cynara took a deep breath and smiled. "Help me up?" Mike stood, gave her a hand. She was remarkably light. She dusted off her leggings, obviously feeling stronger. He could see the hole in her clothes where Donnie's blade had penetrated, but no blood or entrails, which was a very good thing.

"Come on." She extended a hand, now more herself, or at least, what Mike had come to think of as herself. She led him down the hallway and up the stairs, back into the main convention floor and through the milling masses. At the far side of the room was another stairway—going up this time, and public access (much to Mike's relief). On the second floor, large gaming tables had been spread around, sponsored by many of the bigger gaming companies with the space provided free for one and all.

It was marvelous stuff. Some of the tables were covered with military models and fortifications with themes running the gamut from fantasy to World War II. Starships on galactic grid maps were pushed with long shuffle-board thingies. Tanks and mammoths and gargoyles and dragons posed and menaced. Kids and adults alike played, rolled dice, hooted in triumph or bellowed in alarm. It was chaos, but it was thrilling and fun chaos...not the other kind. More than a few of the players looked up from their games when Cynara passed, and Mike was painfully conscious of holding her hand. He had no idea what it looked like—maybe they thought she was his sister? If they only knew!

At the far side of the room, they came at last to an unkempt, circular table of three players and one game-master. All were screaming and arguing: no playing was getting done, only negotiations on finer points of law. The game-master was a girl, probably just a little older than Mike, with the stout, sturdy features of one of those corn-fed American gymnasts Mike had seen on TV. A shock of teal dye colored her otherwise brown hair along the left side of her head. He couldn't help but stare for a moment. Girl game-masters were as exotic in their own way as wood-elves. She sat there with a tight-lipped, annoyed expression, shaking her head and saying "no" at intervals while a chubby kid to her right insisted something should be "yes."

Cynara stood for a moment, then cleared her voice. All eyes turned and all voices stopped. The boys at the table, all a few years older, but not acting that way, gawked as though Stacy Keibler herself now addressed them.

"Guys?" Cynara said with a smile. "I'm wondering if you could use another player. This is Mike, and I'm here to tell you, that Mike plays magic-using characters like no one else you've ever met. Do you think he could sit in?"

The boys at the table stared at the female elf. The game-master looked at Mike with a sour expression, then pointed her pencil at him and said, "Do you whine and moan about every little rule in the book?"

"Nope," Mike said. Far as he knew, he'd never whined and moaned about anything in his life.

"You're in. Roll up a guy."

Mike blinked, a stunned, half-smile on his face. He looked up at Cynara, who smiled down and squeezed him behind the neck. "Sit down. Have fun. I'll have a cab paid up and waiting for you at six: do *not* stay down here after dark."

"Okay!" Mike stuttered. And with that, Cynara turned and sauntered back into the crowd as though she had been paid to put in an appearance.

Mike joined the table. The game-master helped him roll up a character and he caught on quick. Eventually, play did get under way and dungeons were explored, monsters slain and treasure horded. The game itself was simplistic by Mike's standards, but he couldn't recall ever having more fun. Once, he even laughed so hard that he forgot about his doom-date for a second. Being at that table made it seem like he didn't have to be in such a hurry all the time, that he didn't have to try to fit everything in before something bad happened. When he was at that table, with those kids, it felt like there would be enough time after all.

And Mike came out of the experience with the phone numbers, twitter-accounts, emails and social-network invites of four new friends who didn't ask him how old he was, didn't care about his glasses or bug him about how small his hands were.

On the cab ride home (the driver had been holding a sign with Mike's name on it—just like in the movies!) Mike stared through the backseat window at gently falling snow. He thought over all he had witnessed and vowed to keep his promise to Cynara. He'd put the game on the top shelf of his sweater closet where he couldn't reach it without a chair. When, and if, he ever did reach it without a chair, maybe he'd be old enough to use it, or possibly too old to make it work at all.

He thought about Donnie and how it had been fun to have a friend and a soldier like that, but he also realized that Donnie had been keeping him alone on purpose, using him to get that bridge built strong to the other side. There had been no chance to really connect with kids at school—not with Donnie waiting outside every day. And if Donnie had still been around, Mike never would have met these three new guys and a girl game-master. Whose name was Melissa: "Call me 'Mel' if you like, but if you call me 'Missy', we're gonna tangle, and you won't ever be that unhappy, again."

And lastly, he thought of Cynara and he suspected that if Donnie was in some sense his creation, maybe she was, too. He'd needed a Donnie to get through a rough patch at school after jumping grades...but what had he needed Cynara for, except perhaps, to get away from Donnie?

He shook his head, the thoughts finally too heavy, even for him. Wherever she was, whatever she was, Mike hoped Cynara would be all right on her own.

"The Bridge Builder" represents something of an artistic departure for **Kevin Cockle**. As a frequent contributor to *On Spec* magazine, Kevin's stories often deal with adult themes and explicit language which might not be suitable material for all readers. As a sports journalist, Kevin followed professional boxing and became conversant with what is often an unapologetically brutal business. Kevin's story in the Stoker Award nominated *Evolve* (vampire) anthology was characterized by one reviewer as "the most disturbing" in the collection, while the author himself acknowledged an "appalling" level of violence when asked to describe the piece at a book reading event. It is with some irony then, given such credentials, that the story Kevin has contributed to *Tesseracts Fifteen*, a Young Adult anthology, may be the most mature piece of fiction he has yet produced.

My Name is Tommy
by Mike Rimar

"Commander Paul won't ever let me be the *Plymouth Rock's* captain," I said. "He says I'm not smart enough."

"Really?" Mom buttoned up my pajama shirt. "Commander Paul said that, huh?"

"Yeah." I breathed in the strawberry smell in her hair. "I know I'm different. Other moms and dads think eighteen is too old to play with their kids. Is eighteen too old?"

Mom said something but I was too busy staring at the fluffy clouds on my bed sheets. They looked just like the clouds in the old Earth vids. That planet must've been magical because those clouds looked ginormous and floated in the sky like they were weightless.

"Tommy, are you listening?"

I tried to remember what she'd said then shook my head and smiled.

She smiled back and I saw lines in her face where it used to be smooth. Every day she seemed skinnier and skinnier, and her face looked tired all the time. Sometimes I worried it was my fault. Taking care of me must be hard, especially without help.

Mom reached for her reading pallet. "I've got a new manual to read tonight."

My shoulders sagged. Last year, Mom took me to the ship's ice cream factory on Ring B to see how ice cream was made. It was cool. Get it? Ice cream is cool. When I told Mom that one, she laughed real hard. Then, she explained why it was so funny. Now, it's one of my best jokes.

Tour Guide Sam showed us a big vat where the milk and sugar mixed together. "Wow," I said. "A thousand liters."

"I was just going to say that," said Tour Guide Sam and gave me an odd look. Later, at the end of the tour, I got a free ice cream cone.

"Tommy," Mom said while I licked melted chocolate off my hand. "Did someone tell you that was a thousand liter vat?"

Air filled my cheeks. I wanted to tell her how the vat turned into a cartoon in my head. It started out flat then stretched out, spinning around, numbers filling the spaces until everything stopped, but saying everything turned into a cartoon sounded made up. I blew the air out. "Yeah, someone told me."

Mom nodded slowly then ruffled my hair. "Eat your ice cream."

Ever since then, she traded my good bedtime stories with tech manuals. As I crawled into bed, I scowled at the reader, wishing for more of that ice cream.

Mom looked about to say something. She looked very small in her uniform, and her lips moved very slowly into a smile. Mom did everything slow now, like her bones and muscles hurt to move. She didn't eat much, and her skin had turned kind of yellow. She always seemed to have a cold because she coughed all the time.

Finding herself, she began to read about security protocols.

"Please read me *The Three Little Pigs*," I said.

"Tomorrow night. Tonight, we read about security protocols."

I slapped the crispy-clean sheets. "I'm sick of how security works, or how the engines work, or how navigation works. Why do I have to know this stuff, anyway?"

Mom sighed. "All right, Tommy. You win. We'll read *The Three Little Pigs*."

Smiling, I settled in for a real story. *The Three Little Pigs* was one of my favorites.

"Tommy." Mom put down the reader when she finished. "Do you tell anyone what we're reading about?"

"That's not funny." I gripped a handful of blanket. "You know no one talks to me."

Mom kissed my forehead. "I'm sorry, Tommy, dear. The others are so cruel. Maybe they were right. Maybe I should have..." She straightened suddenly and wiped her eyes with the back of her hand.

"It's okay, Mom," I said.

She meant *abortion*.

One day I heard some of the crew use that word. They looked right at me so I knew they were talking about me. I said the word inside my head until I got home to get a definition. When I was a kid I used to write strange words down but usually spelled them wrong. Mom taught me how to use the computer on her desk. It had voice *rek-ug-ni-shun*, which means it understood what I said. Finding definitions was much easier after that.

When I *definitioned* abortion I cried all day.

"We have to keep our bedtime stories secret, Tommy." Mom kissed my cheek. "Don't tell anyone, promise?"

"Promise." I crossed my heart to show I meant it. The abortion word got me thinking. "Mom, who did you have sex with to get me?"

She laughed until she coughed so much I had to slap her back a few times.

"You mean, who is your father?" she managed to say. "I can't answer that, my love. I made a promise to him."

"Why doesn't he want me to know? Is it because I'm stupid? Didn't he want me?" I sucked in air. "Did you want me?"

"Don't ever say that." Her arms were around me before I took another breath. "I always wanted you. You're the most precious thing to me—and you are not *stupid*."

"I know I'm supposed to act more like a grown up." I squeezed her back, but not too hard. I didn't want to break her bones. "My brain just doesn't work that way."

"No." She sighed. "You're not like the others. You see, with only so many people, well, our forefathers gave us tests to check babies when they were still eggs. If we found something wrong—"

"You have an abortion," I finished.

"Yes." She held me at arm's length. "As captain I had so many responsibilities, and I might have waited too long to have children. When the tests came back, I wasn't surprised with the result, but I wanted a baby so badly, and I knew this old body couldn't go through another pregnancy."

She paused long enough to give me a quick kiss and hug. Then she drank from her teacup as if it was some magic strength potion. "But rank has its privileges and I carried you to term. That means the full nine months. My decision didn't sit well with the others. Some have forgiven me, but many still harbor ill feelings. You've been paying the price all your life, and for that I'm so very sorry."

I looked at her for a long time. "If you had an abortion I would not be here, right?"

She nodded, tears bubbling in her eyes.

"Then don't be sorry."

She hugged me so hard it hurt, but I didn't stop her. I just held my breath 'till it was over. Our talk made me happy. I learned many things I hadn't known. One more question still bugged me. "Mom, do I have to make a baby with someone?"

She turned away. "Tommy, you can't make babies."

"Oh." I was glad she couldn't see the smile on my face. Babies are hard work.

"When do you think she'll go?" Ensign Will whispered to Commander Paul but I heard him.

The Command Center was a five-sided room. Each side controlled some part of the *Plymouth Rock*. In the middle of the ComCen was the captain's terminal where Mom usually was, but she'd been called out. Mom left me at the navigation terminal which was always empty because the *Plymouth Rock* always went where it wanted.

I never minded. The terminal had an excellent 3-D generator for things like planets and star charts, and I'd pretend to float within the universe. Sometimes, Mom would set little projects for me like find this planet or search that solar system. She told me she was looking for a secret planet and I couldn't tell anyone what I was doing.

"I don't know." Commander Paul didn't try to whisper. "She's getting thinner every day, but her mind is sharp as ever."

"What about him?" Ensign Will nodded toward me. "You think he knows anything?"

Commander Paul snorted. "He barely knows his own name, never mind that his mother is dying."

I spun in my chair. "Mom is dying?"

"Eavesdropping is a bad habit, Tommy," said Commander Paul.

"I'm sorry." His scolding was unexpected. "But, you said my mom was dying?"

"See what I mean?" He frowned. "We could have meant anyone."

For some reason I felt better. Someone was dying, which was bad, but it wasn't Mom. "I'm sorry, Commander Paul," I repeated and turned back to the star chart.

"What are you doing there?" Commander Paul put two thick hands on my shoulders. "Look here. I know this part of space. We passed through it just a year ago."

"Five hundred million, nine hundred and sixty-five thousand, five hundred and twenty kilometers," I said, overcome with a need to impress Commander Paul.

"What?"

"That's how far away we are from where you put your finger."

"Really?" Commander Paul leaned forward and typed something into the console. He smelled like limes.

The exact same number flashed on the screen and I swelled with pride.

Commander Paul brought up another map and touched a planet. Not Mom's secret planet, though. I couldn't talk about that.

"How far are we from there?"

"I don't know," I said. "What's the scale?"

Commander Paul grunted and touched a key. "There."

Numbers whirled in my brain. Space between a cartoon planet and *Plymouth Rock* folded like paper then spread out again. It was a very big number and I concentrated hard. "It's 239,893,393,756 kilometers away."

He double-checked with the computer. "How did you do that?"

I wanted to tell him about the cartoons but then I saw his eyes, cold and gray as metal. I shrugged instead.

"Savant," he said under his breath. Just then Mom entered the ComCen and Commander Paul shuffled away with a casual, "Carry on."

Savant. The word kept repeating in my mind. Or was it servant, and I just heard wrong? I didn't serve anyone, so why would he say that? Concentrating on star charts was impossible, and I asked to be excused.

"Hello, *Plymouth Rock* computer," I said when I got home. "What does savant mean?"

"Hello, Tommy. A savant is one with detailed knowledge in a specialized field. A wise one."

A wise one. I liked that answer.

"Reference Idiot Savant," said the computer then *definitioned* that meaning of savant.

That definition made more sense. That definition made me cry.

"Want to know a secret, Tommy?" Mom peered over her reader. She looked more tired every day.

"What?" I whispered even though we were alone in my bedroom.

She leaned in close and I smelled liquor on her breath. "No one knows why we're here."

"In my room?"

"No, silly, here on the *Plymouth Rock*. You see, many years ago, even before your Great-great-grandma Deloris was born, there was a fire. It damaged the ship's main memory core and wiped out a lot of essential information, such as why so many people chose to live on a space ship, and where we were going in the first place. Since then, we've recreated most of our history in stories and songs, but the captain of the time had the forethought to make a copy of our original manifesto."

"Mani-what-so?"

"Manifesto. A declaration of our true purpose. That copy has been passed down from Smith to Smith since Captain Bill."

"Captain Bill? Wow!" Of all the Smiths, he had the most great-greats in front of his name. "But why don't we tell anyone? Why is it a secret?"

Mom tucked my blanket under my legs. "Because the Captain Smith of the time believed the fire wasn't an accident but an attempt to hide our true purpose. Time proved him right. Our songs and stories have distorted the truth to fit what people want to hear."

"Like the one where a giant lizard ate the earth and everyone stays on the *Plymouth Rock* because the lizard only eats planets?"

"Yes." Mom smiled. "Like that one. Most believe the *Plymouth Rock* is where we belong and we've no need to go anywhere else.

"The truth is we are a ship lost in the galaxy. Only luck has kept us alive, but I fear luck is running out.

"The engineering faction has been reporting more mechanical failures. Our factories are unable to make new parts because of dwindling resources. We have food to feed us, but if the ship fails, all the food in the five rings won't save us.

"The ship is dying.

"Commander Paul and others like him don't want to see the truth. Their faith is in the *Plymouth Rock*. Faith is good but useless if misplaced."

Mom gave my hand a quick squeeze. "I'm working on a plan. We have to keep this between you and me. You know how the others are. They might not like what I have in mind. Tommy, when the time comes, I'm going to give you the manifesto."

My toes tingled with excitement. This wasn't just a secret; it was a *big* secret.

"I know what you're up to, Mallory." Commander Paul blocked our way like a bulkhead.

"Move, Paul." Mom's soft tone surprised me. I knew what *in-sub-ord-nishun* was, and Commander Paul was doing it. No one ever used Mom's first name. Until I was five, I thought her first name was Captain.

Commander Paul stayed where he was. "I see him sneaking around the old navigation terminal. Why is he looking at star charts, and how does he know how to calculate distances like that? Oh, yeah, he showed me that little trick."

"It's a gift." Mom put an arm around my shoulder.

The corner of Commander Paul's mouth curled. "Thought you might say something like that, so I did a little looking myself. Something I should have done eighteen years ago. Damn it, Mallory, why did you have him? You knew he was damaged. Look at him, eighteen years old and can barely dress himself."

"Tommy is standing right here." Mom's voice took on a hard edge. "Stop talking as if he wasn't."

"That's the thing," Commander Paul growled. "He shouldn't be here. You saw the tests." He stepped closer, hands open at his sides. "Mal, we could have tried again. All you had to do was abort."

"No," said Mom. "I told you in the beginning I would never do that. I wanted Tommy."

"*You* wanted him? What about what I wanted? One child, Mal. That's all I'm allowed. One! And this is what I get because of what you *wanted*. This—this retard!"

Commander Paul's sneer hurt like a slap in the face.

Mom held me closer. "Stop it, Paul. You're scaring Tommy."

"What were you thinking, Mal? What did you really want that you risked playing God? A little puppy to pet and hug when you came home at night? Because that's about all he's good for, and barely housebroken, too."

"Shut up, Paul." Mom was so mad, I actually felt her get warmer. I tried to step away, but her arm held me close like a magnet.

"Are you happy with our son, Mallory?" Commander Paul pressed his attack, unaware of his danger. "Because, I'm not!"

Mom finally released me. Hands clasped behind her back, she straightened to her full height. Her face was empty of any emotion.

I knew that look and stepped way back.

"Commander. Either get out of our way or mutiny."

That took Commander Paul by surprise because his mouth clamped shut and he moved aside standing at rigid attention. When we passed him, he saluted, raising his hand so fast I felt the breeze on my cheek.

Mom didn't return the salute.

As we passed, I braved a look back at Commander Paul, seeing his gray eyes differently, comparing the forehead, the thin lips, the square chin.

That's how I learned who my dad was.

The insistent knocking stopped and the door opened. Someone must have found the command override, something I learned from all those tech manuals.

Commander Paul entered first, followed by Doctor Marcie who touched Mom's neck and wrist, then slowly clasped her hand around mine. "Tommy," she said, quiet and low. "You're going to have to let go."

I held Mom's hand tighter, trying to squeeze warmth back into the cold stiffness. "No. I want to be here when she wakes up. Maybe she'll make bacon and eggs or pancakes. They're our favorite."

"Tommy," said Doctor Marcie. "Your mother has been sick for a long time. Surely, you've noticed?"

I looked quickly at Mom's pale, still face. "She got real skinny and lost her hair."

"Yes, after-effects of her treatment. She had a disease called cancer, but I'm afraid the treatment didn't work. She's gone, Tommy."

"Gone?" My throat ached. "But she's right here."

"Be straight with him," Commander Paul snapped. "Your mother is dead."

I matched his hard stare with my own. Words caught in my throat. She couldn't be dead. She wouldn't leave me—alone.

Moaning softly, I buried my face in Doctor Marcie's shoulder so my dad wouldn't see me cry. I didn't have to worry. When I looked up again, he was gone.

The funeral was the next day. The *Plymouth Rock's* flag—an old sailing ship bumping against a large rock—draped over my mom's casket like a tablecloth. People I had never seen before crowded into the launch bay.

Dr. Marcie and other officers said nice things about Mom. Sometimes, I laughed but most times I cried. When no else had anything to say, two ensigns folded the flag into a tight triangle. The huge bay door rumbled open and Commander Paul wordlessly handed me the folded flag.

I barely reacted to his presence as the casket atop a wheeled truck pushed through the pressure field and into space. The coffin lifted, turning slowly. The bay doors closed with a boom that shook my bones, and I knew my mom was really dead.

Almost everyone shook my hand. Commander Paul didn't. He hadn't said a word for my mom, and he was among the first to leave when the big doors closed. I didn't care, not about him or about anything.

Doctor Marcie gave me a quick hug followed by a peck on the cheek. "Come on, Tommy," she said. "Let's get you home."

I never heard the *Plymouth Rock's* passageways so quiet, like everyone went to sleep after the funeral. The only sound was our footfalls. They were a lonely sound.

"Tommy." Dr. Marcie placed a hand on my shoulder. "When you have limited living space, perfection is ill advised. We have to allow certain illnesses and diseases as a natural way to keep our population under control. Other times, we have to take steps to weed out aspects that might be seen as unfruitful to our society."

"Okay," I said, unsure what she meant.

"I just want you to understand, Tommy, you never should have been born. Tests showed you would have had severe brain and organ damage. Your mother knew this, but used her position—no, that's not exactly true. She thought she forced me, but I could have denied her. She wanted you so badly and the likelihood she could conceive again was so remote."

Dr. Marcie brushed back a lock of hair as gray as the walls in the industrial ring.

"You were barely more than an egg when I operated, hoping to repair what damage I could. Truth is, I had no idea what I was doing, checking ancient textbooks every step of the way. All these years, I thought I had failed.

"But your mother never saw you that way. Mallory carried you to term and gave you life. She made you a success. I should have told her that. Now that's too late, so I'm telling you, instead. Tommy, you are a success." She hugged me and I hugged her back because I thought that's what she wanted, even though her perfume made me kind of sick.

Dr. Marcie kissed my forehead and walked away. When the passageway was empty again, I clutched my mother's flag to my chest and entered my silent home. I put the flag atop the kitchen table and stared. My mom was dead and all I had to remember her was a giant satin napkin. What was I going to do?

Like a flash of light in my brain, I knew. I was a success, and I was a Smith. I rushed out the door, positive I was doing the right thing, the smart thing. By the time I reached the Command Center, I convinced myself that everyone waited for me, standing at attention and saluting. With head held high, I stepped through the doorway.

No one saluted.

Commander Paul, dressed in utility coveralls, glanced at me. "Scan for any debris fields that might damage the hull." He smiled a cold smile at his order. A captain's order. And everyone obeyed.

I cried all the way home. By the time I arrived, I was tired and empty. "I'm sorry, Mom," I said to the holo-picture on her desk. "I tried to be the captain, but they were right. I'm just a...a retard."

The picture hovered within a silver frame. Mom and I, cheek to cheek, stared out, forever happy. She was much better then, her face rounder, all the lines gone, her hair brown and wavy. The tears came again. Mourning, it was called. I *definitioned* it. I didn't like mourning.

A small red light at the bottom corner of Mom's computer flashed on and off. There was a message waiting for her. Everyone knew Mom was dead. Someone was playing a dirty trick and I jabbed an angry finger at the playback button.

"Hello, Tommy."

It was Mom's voice. I jumped and hid behind the chair.

"If you're hearing this, then I'm dead. I arranged to have this message automatically sent to you when someone struck my name from the active roster. First, I'm so sorry I didn't tell you I was sick. When I first found out, I was sure I could beat the cancer. Then, when the chemotherapy didn't work, I was just afraid. Most of all I didn't want you to worry. I don't know if that was right or wrong. If I hurt you, please forgive me."

"I forgive you, Mom!" I rushed around the chair. Mom was on the computer monitor, sitting in her leather chair. My heart hurt in my chest and my whole body shook. I placed my hand on the empty seat, wishing so bad that she was there to hold me and ruffle my hair.

"Tommy, I have something important for you to do. Something I couldn't do myself. Being captain means you have to do things even though you know they're wrong, but you—" She coughed as though her lungs clapped together. When she finished she looked up and gave me a sad smile. "Look at you now, tall and strong. I did my best to give you a normal life when others thought you shouldn't have one at all. It's too late to ask your forgiveness for that now."

Mom touched her nearly bald scalp with a shaky hand. "Tommy, I'm not sure how, or why, but you can do calculations in your head like a computer. We're going to put that gift to work. Remember all that studying we did, all those tech manuals we read together?"

I listened to every word she said, pinching my leg when I felt myself wandering. What Mom said was important, but mostly it was her voice I wanted to hear. Then the message ended.

"I won't let you down, Mom," I said to her fading image.

Not much had changed when I returned to the ComCen. Everyone still ignored me, only this time I didn't mind as I shuffled over to the empty navigation terminal. When no one watched, I pulled out the small notebook from the satchel slung over my shoulder.

My fingers brushed the cover like it was sacred. Whatever she wrote must have been really important because she used real paper. Taped to the notebook's back cover was a wafer-thin data sleeve. The *Plymouth Rock's* manifesto.

I reread the notebook's first page and removed a small candlestick from the satchel. Mom called it a flare and that I could find one in any of the emergency utility rooms spaced around the ship. The flare fit snug in a tight space between the computer and the floor. Checking my notes, I flicked the flare's trigger, counted to three, then hurried for the nearest alarm button.

Smoke and red sparks filled the ComCen. The emergency klaxon was the loudest thing I had ever heard, but I managed to yell "Fire! Fire! Fire!" above the noise as thick smoke filled the ComCen.

"Everyone out," Commander Paul shouted. "Let Fire Control take care of it."

I joined the crowd heading for the door but never quite got outside. Commander Paul stood in the corridor looking back at me. "Get out there, you retard."

"No." I smiled at him. "And my name is Tommy, you retard." I pushed the button to close the door, then another to lock it.

"Hello, *Plymouth Rock* Computer," I read from the notebook. "Temporary lock on Command Center access. Protocol 234235, Smith, Tommy, Captain."

The door had just begun to slide open when it slid back shut with angry shouts from the other side. "Change Command Center access code. Protocol 234235, Smith, Tommy, Captain. Code is now 02-5468+85744*85453. Confirm 02-5468+85744*85453."

"Hello, Tommy," said the computer. "Confirmed, Captain."

"Good," I said, whistling air through my teeth. No wonder Mom looked so tired all the time. She'd been busy. When the computer removed her from the active roster, it triggered all kinds of little programs she'd written. The best one so far made me the captain of the *Plymouth Rock,* at least for a while.

With a small fire extinguisher from my satchel, I doused the flare and coughed. The emergency *vent-late-shun* pumped most of the smoke out, but the air still smelled like dirty socks.

When Mom first told me to look at the old star charts, she wanted me to look for a special planet with water and air to breathe. And I found it too, the very first day I looked, but star charts were so fun, I didn't tell Mom.

It was a pretty blue planet with greens, and browns, and whites and two small moons that chased each other round and round.

Mom's planet trailed blue like a comet as I switched star charts.

A loud boom at the door made me jump. "This is the Captain. Open the door, Tommy!"

"Not by the hair of my chinny-chin-chin," I whispered and turned back to the star chart. I touched the planet. "Hello, *Plymouth Rock* computer," I read from the notebook. "Lock coordinates on new destination."

"Unable to comply, Tommy. Access has been denied."

Wow, I thought, *that was fast.* Mom once said Commander Paul was an ass, but not a dumb ass.

I'd always laughed at that one, but not now. My fingers trembled as I typed in the words and numbers Mom had written in the notebook; codes that allowed manual access of the navigation computer. Again, I brought up the star charts. The space between Mom's planet and the *Plymouth Rock* folded together then stretched out again. I typed in the numbers floating in my head, then made the computer search using those numbers until it found a planet that matched that distance. At first it found a giant gas planet, so I told it to keep looking.

A loud pop came from the door, and a thin blue spike of fire poked through the metal. Commander Paul was trying to cut his way in with a torch. Sweat stung my eyes as I waited. Then Mom's special planet came into view and I typed the command to make that our new destination.

Next, I inserted the data-sleeve into the computer and transferred the file so anyone could look up the manifesto to learn new stories and new songs.

I tore up Mom's notebook, stuffing the bits into a nearby recycle chute. All I had to do was wait for Commander Paul. He was gonna be real mad, but what could he do? He was the captain and I was just a retard, but like it or not, the crew followed my one and only order.

With nothing better to do, I went back to the navigation station and played.

The facts are these: **Mike Rimar** lives in Whitby, Ontario. He lives with his wife, Kat, and two young daughters.

Beyond that, he is a man of mystery, even to himself. That he writes at all is most baffling since he can barely spell and grammar makes his head hurt. And science fiction! A taco puzzle wrapped in an enigma tortilla shell: only an average student in school, science was far from his best subject. He does like a good cooking show and has been observed staring at non-stick frying pans too long to be healthy.

Exactly when he got the foolish notion of becoming a writer is open to conjecture, but somehow he did and has been published in *Writers of the Future XXI*, Orson Scott Card's *Intergalactic Medicine Show*, online e-zines and other anthologies, as well as *Tesseracts Fifteen: A Case of Quite Curious Tales*.

Darwin's Vampire
by Elise Moser

Carola was washing dishes, singing along with the radio, and didn't see the vampire until it had landed on her wrist, but then it was too late; she'd already felt the sting. She smacked at the vamp with her other hand and suds flew everywhere. She peered around but it must have flown off. There were two bright red dots of blood beginning to well up in the center of the pinkish welt just beside her wrist bone. "Damn it," she muttered.

She held her wrist up while with the other hand, she pulled open the kitchen junk drawer and rummaged for the VampStop. There was masking tape, a Baggie full of twist-ties, a plastic fork. Where was it? She heard a faint buzzing, but her hand was starting to throb and she knew she didn't have time to look around—she needed to apply the VampStop within a minute or it would have no effect. She started tossing things onto the counter: a pencil with a broken end, the warranty from the coffee machine...she expelled a quick breath. There it was. The trademark blood-red applicator, there, at the back. It had been a while since there'd been a vampire around here. In the winter they usually liked to go south.

Carola pulled the tube out, and the cap fell off and rolled under the counter. Damn it, Greg never closed things properly. The spongy end of the applicator was bone dry. She frantically dabbed it at her puffed-up hand, but there was no moisture left at all. She hurled it onto the kitchen floor and ran to the bathroom, throwing open the medicine cabinet and sweeping everything

from the shelf into the sink. There had to be another VampStop
in here. Greg said that vampires were once as big as humans,
but it seemed so unlikely. "Darwin's finches," he said with that
superior scientific air of his. There used to be a VampStop in
here, Carola was sure of it. Her breath was starting to come in
short gasps, close to sobs. She threw two lipsticks and a bottle
of cough syrup into the bathtub. Where was it?

"Don't panic, don't panic," she chanted under her breath.
Last summer, when they were packing to go camping, she'd
asked Greg to buy a fresh one for the trip, but he packed the
one from the bathroom instead. *Damn it.* She fled to the front
hallway. She had a mini in her purse. Why hadn't she just gone
for that one, right away? Her bitten hand was bright pink now
and radiating heat. She tore open her purse and upended it.
There, right there—she grabbed it and tore the cap off with
her teeth. She couldn't bend the fingers of her other hand at all
now. She viciously jabbed the spongy end of the applicator at
the wound, jabbing and jabbing until the mini VampStop was
empty. Then she watched in horror as the liquid on her hand
turned blue. *Too late.*

Carola sat on the floor in the hallway, slumped against the wall-
paper, the contents of her purse strewn around her. Her brain
was foggy and her bones felt weirdly compressed. It was uncomfortable.

She'd miss Greg and his science stories. His favorite was
about the finches on the Galapagos Islands. Carola remembered
how, when they first fell in love, she and Greg used to sit in the
dark and look at the pictures on his computer. The finches had
all evolved different beaks—a large one for eating hard seeds,
a short one for eating insects, a long, slender one for feeding
on cactus pulp. They developed so quickly that scientists could
track the changes from generation to generation.

Carola's face was damp and itchy from dried tears, and her
skin felt tight all over. She suddenly thought of the poster they
used to have up in her grade five classroom, an old-fashioned
sign from the time of the Eradication, during her mum's childhood. It was a photograph of a grinning hunter holding the
small head of a vamp which he'd presumably just chopped off.
The body, about the size of a cat, lay at his feet, stumpy wings
crushed against its back.

Carola's mum used to tell them stories about when the vamps started flying in through the windows. By the time she was in high school, she said, they were as small as sparrows, and the Eradication almost ground to a halt because they were so hard to hunt. Then someone invented the electricity-field nets. The only vamps that survived were those small enough to pass through them. "That," Greg used to say at parties, "was an evolutionary leap." Carola sighed wistfully; he loved to lecture. "Devastating for the population," he'd drone, rocking back on his heels, "but an evolutionary leap." Then he'd go on about insect robotics and aerospace engineering based on mosquito flight dynamics.

Carola noticed that the hall light fixture seemed very high up, the ceiling cavernous. The sound of passing traffic vibrated dully against the walls. She wondered if she should try to leave a note for Greg to tell him what happened, but everything was so far away. The prospect of finding a pen defeated her. She imagined herself carrying a ballpoint as tall as a log, and it just made her feel tired. There were two spots on her shoulder blades that felt hot and sore and nubby. She wondered if she'd hurt herself somehow without knowing it, maybe while she was flinging the contents of her bathroom around.

The cool dimness of the hallway was soothing. It occurred to her that her cell phone must be on the floor somewhere...she could call Greg. She forced herself to crawl through the large detritus from her handbag to look for it, but when she found it, it was a huge thing, the size of a rowboat. She reached up and tried to press the button to unlock the keypad, but it wouldn't move. She thought she might be able to jump on it. She surprised herself by opening her stiff new wings, and with a startling feeling of strength, lifted herself onto the phone, landing lightly on the asterisk key.

Now that she was here, she found that she didn't want to phone Greg, anymore. She was trying to remember why she'd wanted to before, when she heard a distant buzzing from the direction of the kitchen. Maybe it was that vamp again. She turned quickly, in time to see a dark spot flitting through the lighted doorway. As he flew closer, Carola could make out his clean, sharp features. He approached and the sound got clearer; she sensed it resonating in the vast space. Suddenly she realized that she could understand it in a whole new way. It wasn't buzzing at all—he was singing!

The vamp flew over and landed on the screen of Carola's cell phone, and the two of them stood and looked at each other for a moment. She found herself thinking that she would like to see Greg again, after all. He'd always had a sort of meaty smell. She'd like to bite him.

Elise Moser has published twenty-five stories in various genres as well as a novel, *Because I Have Loved and Hidden It*. She had a story in *Fantasy: the Best of the Year 2007* as well as a number of honorable mentions in several Year's Best collections. She recently finished two and a half years as Literary Editor of the *Rover*, a Montreal-based online arts and culture magazine, and she is currently president of the Quebec Writers' Federation. She has accumulated three cats, one of whom is the size of a small tank but much fluffier. She and les trois chats live in Montreal, Quebec. She avoids the eating and wearing of animals.

Costumes
by Shen Braun

I opened my sister's yearbook to the page I'd marked last night and tapped the picture with one finger. "See? I told you," I said to McKenna.

"Wow," was all she managed.

"Yeah, no kidding. That guy has absolutely no shame."

"We already knew *that*," McKenna said. She couldn't take her eyes off the picture, and I couldn't blame her. I hadn't believed it at first either, but there it was, in full color, taking up a quarter of the entire page. "Is he wearing a mask, too? His face is different. It's all wrinkly and kind of saggy. Are you sure it's him?"

"I'm sure. Look at the caption. This is how I knew that he dyes his hair...it's all gray there, see?"

"Oh, yeah." She laughed a little. "Maybe he got a face-lift, too, to get rid of all those wrinkles."

"Maybe," I said, "but if he did, they pay teachers way too much."

"It was worth it. He's hot."

"That's creepy," I said. "He's crazy old, McKenna, like older than your dad." But I had to admit that she had a point. Old or not, Mr. Billings was sort of cute, especially for a teacher.

"He doesn't look it," McKenna argued. The bell rang then and we both leaped up, eager for the day to begin.

This was the first day that I'd actually looked forward to History class. To any class, really. School wasn't so bad. It was pretty easy when you got right down to it, but it wasn't usually a whole lot of *fun*, either. I could say the same about History, too, except you never knew what Mr. Billings was going to do. There was a sick fascination in wondering about, and then watching, the show. And he did put on a show, that's for sure.

I'd been warned about Mr. Billings by my sister, so he didn't manage to freak me out the way he did everyone else, but there was no doubt he was the weirdest teacher we had. Not bad, exactly, just very, very weird. For example, at least once a day he'd just start singing—sometimes words, but more often just strange, lilting melodies none of us recognized. Jordan had asked him once, sourly, why he wasn't a music teacher if he liked singing so much.

"The emanations of juvenile instrumentalists are hazardous to the aural functions of the truly sensitive, I'm afraid," Mr. Billings had replied. "I would not be able to stand them."

That was the way he talked most of the time. And he was lazy, too. Instead of just teaching us History like he was supposed to do, he would make *us* teach *him*.

"Miss Delaney," he'd say, "tell me, if you will, what a house-wife's typical day might have entailed, circa 1200."

He'd nailed me with that one, once. Then when you couldn't answer him, bang, you got yourself an assignment to do. Not cool.

Everything he did was just off the grid, even compared to the rest of the teachers who weren't all that normal to begin with. But when we filed into class and saw him in his full Halloween outfit, even I had to struggle not to laugh. Becky had been right: he wore the exact same costume every single year, probably since the dawn of time as far as we could tell. It had been nine years since Becky had been in high school and from her descriptions, not one thing had changed. I hope he was at least having that thing dry-cleaned every so often.

A few people stopped and stared. I slid into my usual seat at the desk I shared with McKenna and pretended not to pay any attention. Secretly I watched Mr. Billings out of the corner of my eye. He was a sight, that's for sure. The yearbook picture did not do him justice.

The first thing you noticed was his long cloak, so red it almost burned the retinas. All of the colors were really vibrant, bright as new cloth never-washed. He had a shirt of deep forest green with loose sleeves and long triangular tails both in front and back. Over that, there was a yellow vest, though I bet he'd have called it "gold." Silver thread made interwoven patterns of leaves on his vest and the leather belt around his waist. His boots matched the belt and looked like suede to me. It was a bold guy who would wear boots like that. Heck, who would wear *anything* from that outfit. Say what you would about Mr. Billings, he never got embarrassed, even when maybe he should have.

Dressed to match that old picture, it was even more obvious that he had done some serious improvements to himself between then and now. Ten years ago, he'd almost been paunchy, and now there wasn't a hint of a gut. His hair was jet black without a trace of the old gray. Any girl would envy his skin: smooth, totally without blemishes and it didn't have that plastic look you saw on movie stars who had gone under the knife one too many times. He'd managed to shave off at least twenty years by the look of him. Not bad at all. I could understand why McKenna had a crush on him.

Of course, it was Jordan who challenged him. Big shock. Someone needed to cut his testosterone dose by about half. "What are you supposed to be?" The big goon eyed Mr. Billings up and down.

"Welcome, class," Mr. Billings said to us all in his typically cheery way. He was always happy and it was enough to drive you nuts, especially first thing in the morning before your coffee had had a chance to work. He spread his arms wide to give us all a better look at his costume before answering Jordan. "Good sir, I am an elf."

"An elf?" Jordan repeated dubiously. Maybe he didn't understand what that meant. With Jordan, anything was possible. "If you're an elf, where are your ears?" Guess he got it, after all.

"Yeah, good question," Brooke piped up.

I rolled my eyes at McKenna and she agreed with me: Brooke thought everything Jordan said was a "good question" or a "good answer" no matter how stupid it was. The girl had it bad. One time in Science class, Jordan had seriously suggested that after gases and liquids, the third state of matter was "people." Brooke had blindly backed him up. Good answer, Jordan, that makes sense. Give me a break.

"Actually, elves don't have pointed ears," Nathan piped up in that I-can't-believe-you-don't-know-better voice of his. "It's a common misconception, but the myths and tales surrounding the origins of the elves refer to them only as 'magical beings of

great beauty'. Even when they assumed diminutive stature during
Roman times, no mention was ever made of their ears possessing
a deformity that set them apart from humans. Tolkien never put
pointed ears on his elves, either. The movies got that wrong." He
stopped and the room was momentarily quiet. Into the silence
he added, "Hobbits were never specifically mentioned as having
large feet, either, only hairy and tough."

There were a hundred things to say to that, but if I'd learned
anything from sharing a class with Nathan it was that arguing
with him only extended the length of your suffering. Mr. Billings
swooped in to save him before anyone could get started.

"Thank you, Nathan, that's entirely correct. Besides, when I
wear my pointed ears, people always think I'm dressed up as
Mr. Spock." He winked at us, then turned toward his desk with a
flourish of his cloak. In bold letters, he wrote HALLOWEEN across
the top of the whiteboard before facing us again.

"Today, we're going to examine the history of Halloween, an
appropriate and timely endeavor, wouldn't you say? Tonight the
streets will be filled with goblins and vampires, rock stars and
great literary characters, and it pains me to think that so very few
of them will know why they do it."

"Uh, for candy?" Dillon said and we cracked up.

"Quite right," Mr. Billings agreed. He scrawled "candy" under
HALLOWEEN. "The 'treat' portion of the old moniker. But why?
How did it begin? Why does it have such a hold over us that
we should dress up with reckless abandon once every year? You
started us off, Mister Adams. Pray carry us forward and answer
any of my questions, please."

Dillon never batted an eye. It would take more than a Mr.
Billings to rattle him. "Well, gee, Mr. Billings," he said with mock
innocence, "it doesn't look like it has a hold on *all* of us." He
scanned the room deliberately. Less than half of the students had
any sort of costume on, and none of them were anywhere near
as extravagant as Mr. Billings's. "At least, not as much as it does
you," he added and got the laughter he wanted.

"Touché," Mr. Billings said, smiling. "But you still haven't
answered me, young man. I await your response with eager
anticipation."

I needed a picture of that outfit. If the day ended and I didn't
have a shot, I'd definitely kick myself: it was just too humiliating
not to have some sort of permanent record. The yearbook picture

just wasn't as versatile as a good digital copy. While Dillon tried to put together something coherent rather than just clever, I slipped my cell phone out of my pocket and turned it on. Carefully I angled it so that it had Mr. Billings the Elf dead center in the screen.

"Miss Delaney!" Mr. Billings turned from Dillon to me in a flash, startling me so badly I fumbled and almost dropped my phone. Hurriedly I tried to tuck it away, but it was too late.

"Place the device on your desk, please," Mr. Billings said crisply. He came over and snatched it up. "You are far too intelligent a young woman to be ignorant of this academy's policy in regards to these pernicious devices. Therefore you leave me no choice but to confiscate this artifact. Ah! No arguments, if you please Miss Delaney. It will be safely returned to you at the conclusion of this day's lesson.

"You have managed to save poor Mister Adams, however, by placing the spotlight clearly on yourself, and I'm certain he appreciates it greatly."

Dillon smirked at me, silently laughing. Jerk. At least I'd gotten the picture.

Mr. Billings went back to the front of the class. He picked up one of the markers and looked at me expectantly.

"Tell us all, please, why is it you choose not to participate in this annual custom? Since you dress as a student every day, one can hardly claim you have embraced today's opportunity to change."

I glanced down. I was part of the majority that was dressed normally—no costume for me, thanks. "I don't know," I said, shrugging. The whole class was looking at me. Mr. Billings was good at making you squirm, but it was a lot more fun to watch than to experience.

"Two months you have been one of my pupils," Mr. Billings said. "Certainly you know by now that I am unlikely to be content with such a paltry non-response." He stood with his marker poised over the whiteboard as though he was willing to wait all day.

I gave in and took a shot of my own at Mr. Billings's expense. "Trying to be a little more mature, I guess. It just seems pretty babyish to still be dressing up and begging for candy from strangers."

He wrote "maturity" on the board. "An interesting argument, Miss Delaney, thank you." If he was bothered by my calling him a baby, he didn't show it. Some of the kids wearing costumes didn't look so happy, though: I'd forgotten about them. Oops. I was out of the spotlight, at least, because Mr. Billings turned to the whole class now.

"Can anyone speak to that specific point, in relation to historical purposes of festivals and carnivals? Anyone at all? Yes, no reason to raise your hand, Mister Lewis."

Nathan was dressed up like some bearded old man, and I must have ticked him off too, because he threw me a superior look before he cleared his throat and spoke.

"Festivals and holidays were intended to be days when *mature* people could have a break and stop being *mature* for a little while. If someone doesn't need to take some time off, maybe they aren't really being all that *mature* during the rest of the year, I would think."

Now he'd got the other half of the class, those of us dressed normally, mad at him in a sad effort to get back at me. Mr. Billings stepped in before it got worse; he was always saving Nathan from himself.

"Thank you, Mister Lewis, well done, although you may keep your editorial comments to yourself, next time." He paced back and forth in front of us, clearly enjoying the way his cloak swept around with each turn.

"Why costumes?" he asked then answered himself. "Imitation is often considered a form of flattery. Assuming a particular guise could be viewed as homage to a king or queen, or another beloved figure. Yet many chosen costumes are generic, referring to no specific individual. Ninjas and pirates are examples of this. Others have a supernatural influence. Devils and witches, for instance."

"Or elves," Dillon muttered, just quietly enough that Mr. Billings could ignore him.

He was on a roll, anyway. Mr. Billings did this every so often, just preach and lecture with hardly a pause for breath, normally about something he was really passionate about. Once he really got going, you could pretty much do anything without fear of being suddenly called upon.

"In a superstitious world, dressing as a spirit was an attempt to placate or even fool the dark forces that existed. Of course, wearing costumes did not begin with Halloween." Mr. Billings was starting to wander. Soon it would be safe to zone out. "From the very earliest days of pre-history, humans have worn costumes. You have, of course, been told many times that you can be anything you wish in life. This is not a new idea. Ancient hunters believed that it was possible to gain the power of an animal, for example, by wearing their skins…a sort of primitive and grisly costume, if you will."

"Talk about stupid," Jordan said, bringing Mr. Billings back to reality. I could have kicked him.

"Why do you say that, Mister Thomas?" Mr. Billings looked interested to hear the response, even though he had to know it wasn't going to be very smart.

Jordan stalled like a gear was skipping somewhere then finally came out with, "Because it doesn't work like that."

"Good point," Brooke chirped. "That's true."

"It would certainly appear to be the case," Mr. Billings agreed. "Otherwise every Halloween we would see a new crop of real villains and superheroes. The same idea would have occurred to those ancient hunters, as well. It must not have taken them long to see that simply donning an animal hide did not automatically and instantly confer great strength or speed. Undoubtedly some refused to participate, perhaps feeling the tradition was a trifle immature, as Miss Delaney has suggested. Others, however, might have concluded that perseverance would be essential. Rather than simply giving up, they would have worn their lion skins for years, perhaps even decades." He began to gesture broadly as he delved into more detail and a collective sigh of relief went up from the room. Mr. Billings, for all intents and purposes, was gone.

"He almost blew it," I whispered to McKenna, indicating Jordan.

"Yeah, no kidding," she whispered back. "I've still got my phone. Here, we can share."

We spent the rest of the hour working together at really hard Sudoku puzzles. Mr. Billings blithely carried on until the bell rang. In a surge, everyone grabbed their books and headed for the door.

"Enjoy your Halloween, everyone!" he called to us as we filed out. "Gather great quantities of booty!"

A few of us giggled at that one. We were halfway to the Science lab when I remembered.

"My phone," I said to McKenna.

"Right. I forgot, too. Go on, I'll tell Mrs. Hunt why you're late."

I nodded and darted back. If I hurried, I wouldn't be late at all. In a rush, I burst through the door.

"Mr. Billings, you still—" I froze.

A pair of whiteboard erasers moved in steady circles over the board, wiping the words beneath them out of existence with a complete lack of concern over the fact that *no one was holding them,* no one at all. The only person in the room was Mr. Billings, writing at his desk with his back to the possessed erasers, seemingly completely unaware that objects were levitating *right behind him.*

He started up in wide-eyed surprise at my entrance. The erasers fell, clattering loudly to the floor. There was no sign that Mr. Billings heard them at all.

"You startled me, Miss Delaney," he said, his face calming. He looked at me without guile. "Is there something I can do for you?"

"Uh…"

Had I really seen what I had seen? Objects don't move by themselves, they just don't. I rubbed at my eyes. Mr. Billings watched me patiently.

"Miss Delaney?" he prompted.

I shook myself and managed to speak a whole sentence. "You… uh…you still have my cell phone." My lips and tongue felt numb, though my voice somehow managed to sound pretty normal.

Immediately, he opened a drawer and pulled out my phone. He came across the room to offer it to me. "You have my apologies for my poor memory. Hopefully we won't have to do this again." In front of me he paused, looking at me more closely. "Are you feeling all right? Forgive me for saying, but you look pale."

Just going crazy, don't mind me, I felt like saying. If Mr. Billings had noticed anything weird happening, he was putting on a good act. His blue eyes, bright as a clear summer sky, regarded me with honest concern. I stared at his dark hair, his smooth unlined face. Did he just *look* younger, or was he *actually* younger? Had a plastic surgeon's scalpel taken away his wrinkles? Or something else? My gaze drifted down and over the brilliant colors of his costume, worn time after time.

I am an elf. His earlier words floated into my mind, trying to explain the impossible. *Perseverance would be essential.*

"I'm okay," I heard myself say, as if from a distance. "I'd better get to class."

"An excellent plan, Miss Delaney. Until tomorrow, then." He sat back down at his desk and continued with whatever work he'd been doing.

Halfway out of the door, I paused. "Mr. Billings?"

"Yes, Miss Delaney?" He looked up from his papers.

Feeling sheepish, I felt myself blush. "I think I might just try wearing a costume next year."

He beamed with sincere approval. "I'm delighted and look forward to seeing it. It's always a pleasure when a lesson resonates with a student."

Then he winked at me. Just for a moment, a crystal clear white radiance shone from his eyes, lighting up his entire face, the entire room. Then the gleam faded and was gone, but it had definitely been there. I was sure of it.

The bell rang and I was off, the memory of magical light illuminating a single question in my mind: out of everything in imagination, what was *I* going to be?

Shen Braun has been writing since he was old enough to grip a crayon and has the towering stack of mostly finished stories to prove it. He eventually escaped from a small town and an enormous horde of relatives to go through years of university followed by numerous careers involving neckties and business lunches. Now, he's a stay-at-home dad in Brandon, Manitoba—his favorite job by far because he gets to focus on raising his family (when he's not ignoring them in order to get some typing done). This is the first time Shen's work has been published, and he couldn't be happier to see it happen.

Civility
by J. J. Steinfeld

What startled me most
was the ability to know
my words and fears
though our lips never moved
not that the space alien
had lips or that my lips
were anything to write home about
wherever home might be
especially if you believe in
innumerable galaxies.

The space alien
was amazingly polite
offering me a warming hand
but the worrying luminosity
made me hesitate.

Should I be rude
and merely nod
in acknowledgement
a cold morning hello?

I want to say I dislike
handshaking, you know,
the spread of germs
and the world is
full of germs.

Still, the expression
on the space alien's face
made me forego apology
and take the extended hand.

No words, no common philosophy,
certainly no shared world view,
yet a common fear of germs
and we both seem to smile
at least in our own
otherworldly ways.

J. J. Steinfeld has been writing poems, stories, and plays since
he was a young adult, when dinosaurs roamed the Earth. In
fact, he had his first poem published at fifteen in a community
newspaper. An eon later, over 200 of his short stories and nearly 500 poems have appeared in anthologies and periodicals in
every Canadian province and internationally, and over forty of
his one-act plays and a handful of full-length plays have been
performed in Canada and the United States. J. J. lives on Prince
Edward Island, where he is waiting patiently for Godot's arrival and a phone call from Kafka, along with the return of the
space alien that appears in his poem "Civility." While waiting, he
has also published fourteen books—ten short story collections,
two novels, two poetry collections—the most recent ones being
Misshapenness (Poetry, Ekstasis Editions, 2009) and *A Glass Shard
and Memory* (*Stories*, Recliner Books, 2010).

Take My Waking Slow
by Michele Ann Jenkins

I wake to sleep, and take my waking slow.
I feel my fate in what I cannot fear.
I learn by going where I have to go.
—Theodore Roethke

"Who the null gave you access?"

You're not supposed to verbalize obscenities like that in the nursery Simulation, but I know they don't belong in this program the instant I see them flickering in the doorway. I can tell right off there's no Mind behind either of them, they're just Code. Creating Code that even tries to look and act like people is totally against Specifications.

"What library are you part of?" I try again.

They just stand there not blinking, the sky-blue background visible through their pale faces. They're close enough Simulations that none of the little kids milling around the matrix table realize there's anything wrong. I try to view their source but I can't get to anything. It's like they're just overlaid on the background, but not actually here.

I'm the oldest one active in the nursery—usually there are a few Middlers here to interact with the Minors. We're supposed to stimulate their synaptic paths to create normal sociological connections, even though their physical brains are miles below us in cold storage along with everyone else. Today it's just me, working overtime, again.

I try tabbing out into someplace else: home, the root directory, anything. But I'm stuck. I can feel the Sim increasing my heart rate, sending the unpleasant sensation of cold sweat trickling down my back (I should remember to hack out that subroutine as soon as I have access again). I step between them and the children.

"You're not following the rules," I say. If I can get them to communicate, I'll have a better chance of accessing and maybe disabling their program. "Who made you? Because they are going to be in *so* much trouble. Hacking into the kids' place is totally uncool." I'm still expecting a guilty adult or sheepish kid to show up and zap this program out of existence, but there's nothing.

"We can take her out, too," says the boy. His voice sounds like it's pieced together from corrupt audio files.

"She is too old," says the girl. "Her neurology is permanently altered."

"What?" They're talking about me. "My neurology is none of your business."

"We're here to take you out," says the girl, speaking past me to the children. They're all quiet and wide-eyed, trying to decide if they should be afraid or play along. Everything is kept lucid and linear in the nursery, so they're going to figure out this isn't right, pretty quick.

They look at each other, sharing some un-verbalized communication. Finally, the girl nods. The boy walks around to the far side of the table so the kids and I are between them. They both hold out their arms, fingers spread wide. An arc of light leaps between their hands, encircling us.

"Hey!" I just have time to holler. And then everything is dark.

There's a blurry, piercing light. From far away comes a deep thrumming and the squeal of metal shrieking across my cortex. I'm definitely not in the form I had in the nursery. Everything is off. The body feels heavy and slow and somehow liquid at the same time. The senses are inputting strangely, too.

After a few false starts, I manage to blink the eyes. Visual shapes start to form out of the lemony light. Or maybe the lemon was a smell. I try to sort the sensory data into streams but nothing happens. I try to access the source for this scene; nothing happens. There's a hole in my mind where I should be able to get at the Code. I'm locked out.

The body twitches like one of those goose-stepped-on-your-grave shivers you get in horror Sims, only strong enough to shake the table. There's no sound except raspy breathing, no input except the muted feeling of fabric, the press of the table and my own lonely thoughts. I make the body take a deep breath, hoping I can trigger a subroutine to lower the heart rate—I'm on the verge of a panic feedback loop.

I can feel the movement of air down the back of the throat, the lungs expanding. Whoever designed this Sim totally gets an "A" for realistic physical sensation, but they have the pain threshold turned down way too low and the sensory input up too high. Maybe some sort of artistic statement? Not comfortable at all.

I try to pull up a low-level terminal. Even if everything else is fragged, I should be able to send a textual ping to an Admin. No one bothers with orthographic communication any more, but it's still part of the system and I can use it to scream bloody murder. Someone is going to get scoped over this. I don't care if it's art or experiment; I didn't sign up for either. I'm waiting for the black box to swim up across my visual cortex, but there's nothing there, either.

Total segfault; this sucks.

I hear a click—the sound grates on my cerebrum. Again with the crappy raw data! A figure looms across the line-of-sight. The visual input goes all streaks and star-bursts, and I feel wetness on the cheeks. A teardrop rolls into the ear. *They thought of everything.*

I'm able to parse the visual, now. Short black hair cut blunt across the eyes, some sort of drapey gray robe, a young man— really a boy—with a cold, serious face. He looks like people—but so did those kids-that-weren't.

I try to hold still; maybe he doesn't know I'm active here. Of course, there's another twitch. The feet banging nosily against the table, like a bird slamming against a window not understanding there's no way through.

"You clearly sustained less trauma during the evacuation than previous groups." I must be getting used to the input levels, because hearing his voice doesn't hurt so much. "I am called Aderic."

"Croak." I can't access the verbal subroutine. I try exhaling and moving the mouth, lips and tongue all at the same time to form the air into words. "Waah...ell...diiii."

I try again. "What the hell did you...where...?" That's all I can manage.

It takes a huge amount of mental effort to make the body respond. *Data loss.* The thought rises up on a bubble of panic. What if there's been some sort of data loss, what if I've been damaged? There are always rumors of someone n-degrees from your network who hit a bad memory block and suddenly lost a chunk of cognitive control. I always thought it was just to scare kids from hacking outside their access level.

"My adjustments to the algorithms were as successful as the projections predicted." He speaks in a monotone stream of words, not waiting to see if I understand or respond. He must represent some sort of low-level subroutine, no personality protocols to speak of. "Your data access patterns suggest you did not integrate large amounts of scientific, economic or sociological data. But you are coping well within parameters."

I try to shake my head "no" but can barely move it to one side. His mouth is pinched and drawn. He turns away and there's a cranking noise. Music fills the room. But it's not a data stream, it's just there, sound waves in the room.

"Where are the others—the kids?" I try to look around, but all I get is coppery metal walls ribboned with pipes and wires. Everything is rough and warped, almost more organically grown than designed. Just like this body, it's outrageously detailed but all wrong. *Who would Code a place like this?* Only a madman.

"They have adapted much more rapidly than you. Their neural networks are more flexible. They quickly adjusted to their bodies and are now engaged in free-form socializing and repetitive exercises—playing." Aderic bends over and I can see his shoulders working and hear the rattle of gears. The table tilts until I'm almost standing upright, though the body is still held by wide leather straps.

"The ambient music will help with the transition. It provides the illusion of a background to focus on when you're synaptic networks require more input. It will be several hundred hours before you adjust."

He unbuckles the straps and helps me step down. I sway on my feet but the body doesn't fall. Out of reflex, I try to change the music with a simple Code patch; I get nothing but a dull burn for my effort. I reach a hand up to the head to touch the throbbing dark place. The hand feels huge and puffy, wet and dry at the same time, but it looks within the usual design specs for a human-form Simulation.

"I require you to respond to a series of questions to determine if your memory engrams are complete."

"Why the 'fault, should I talk to you?" Words are coming easier now and I plan on using them.

He blinks for a few seconds, trying to process my response.

"I am attempting to aid you," he says finally.

"Aid me? You—or your programmer, anyway—hacked me right out of the nursery, a protected Sim, and non-consensually transferred me into this freak-show form, in this clearly illegal Simulation. I don't even know how many rules you're breaking..." I can't finish, the body is caught in a loop, gasping for air.

He looks at the ground, processing different response-patterns, or maybe waiting for feedback from another function. His left hand is shaking until he balls it up into a tight fist. I've never seen that sort of detail in a program like this. Who would build a human-perfect form with emotional tremors and use it to load a utility program?

"I am not a program." I must have been wrong about the personality, because he's sure communicating something like sadness and regret now. "Nor are you, any more. And this is not a Simulation. You are Outside, in the real world and in your real body." His eyes catch mine, and it's as if he's staring through the form into me.

"That's *the* most ridiculous thing I've ever heard." I move the body back a few steps. This isn't just illegal, it's deranged. "Everyone knows there's nothing Outside any more—just an empty shell of a planet, toxic dirt and ruins. No one can go Outside the program."

"That was true. For hundreds of years, it was true," he says, his voice flat and clipped again. "But not everyone chose to escape into a virtual world. Some remained hidden under the surface in self-sufficient habitats. Now parameters have fallen within the range suitable for human habitation. People must return to corporeal forms and to the planet's surface."

I look down at the hands, the fingers all uncreased and new. *Was it possible?* No. This couldn't be what's real—the pain, the lumbering weight of everything, the smells and sounds pressing down from all sides, and no control, no escape. How could anyone live like this? If this was what was waiting for us Outside...

"You're lying! Your logic's screwed!" I'm almost yelling now, gulping air into the lungs. "For one thing, there's no way it's been hundreds of years. I was born Outside the program just like all the other kids. I'm fifteen years old." Actually, not for another six weeks, but he didn't need to know that. "The youngest kids are barely over ten. You seriously need to run some diagnostics."

"How do you know how many times the Earth has completed its orbit since you were uploaded? You have existed in a virtual world; it is equally trivial to alter the color of the sky, the shape of your form or your perception of time. With sufficient processing power, you could experience decades while, in reality, less than a minute would elapse. To shrink decades into years is even easier."

The head was shaking back-and-forth, making the room swirl. I wasn't even telling it what to do now, it was responding directly to unconscious thoughts. The hands came up, trying to block out Aderic and his crazy theory. I didn't want to think about what he was saying, I didn't want to analyze it, I just wanted to get away. Enough of this.

I flex the toes, the calves, the thighs, everything responds instantly. Aderic turns away to consult a dial on the wall. I bolt for the door. For a second, I'm not sure I've got the balance right—I'm going to slam face-first into the door. There's a small wheel, like on a submarine, instead of a door knob. I use the force of my fall to spin it and push at the same time. The hatch creaks open, and I throw the body through the opening expecting to feel a hand on the shoulders any second. Then I'm out, slamming the hatch. Either his program isn't equipped to deal with the scenario or he's just not fast enough.

I'm in a narrow corridor, more like an overgrown pipe than a hallway. I turn left because I know it doesn't matter which way I go: it's a program, just like every other place I've ever been. Programs don't have an end; if you move beyond the edge of what the designer thought of, it all just repeats itself. But maybe there's someone else in here, someone sane, someone who can get me out and give me access again. It's like being paralyzed, not being able to manipulate the Code, to change the world with a thought.

I'm just starting to think I've stumbled into one of those endless loops when I come around a corner and nearly run smack into a tree trunk. I stop too quickly, the knees give out and I'm on ground at the foot of the tree. It goes up and up as far as I can see. I can just make out in the leaves above, sunlight as it streams in through a huge glass dome.

The ground is cool and damp. Blades of grass tickle the cheeks, the back of the neck. I see the veins of leaves, smell rot and dirt and growing. The body is sending a rush of conflicting signals—the lungs burn, there's a vague, pulling pain on the lower left side, but somehow it feels good, too. I can feel the heart pumping blood, the hands and feet tingle with it, almost hear it. I can't even imagine the amount of Code, the processing power, it would take to create and sustain a Simulation like this.

But it can't be real. Because, if it's real, everything else has to be real, too. The game is over; the real world needs us back again. I'm going to have to live like this for the rest of my life: no Code, no Network, just one broken planet, everything we thought we left behind. How is it that this place doesn't collapse under the terrible weight of it all? Reality itself should come crashing through the great glass dome.

"Mira!" a tiny voice pipes. A little face, then another appears—the kids are here. They found me.

I roll to one side and push the body upright.

"Are you okay?" I look from one to the next, expecting fear and confusion but see only smiles.

"You have grass in your hair!"

"We're having a picnic!"

"Come on! Come on!"

A dozen little hands pull and push me up.

"Do you want a strawberry?" The littlest girl holds out a berry the size of her palm. It's misshapen, sort of crumpled on one side and still whitish-green on the top. "They taste funny. Funny-good."

I can only nod and let her push the fruit into my mouth. It's bitter and rough with clusters of seeds. It doesn't taste like any strawberry I've had before. *Because I've never tasted one. I've never tasted anything. Not for real.* I've only had lines of Code stimulate my rostral insula and adjoining frontal operculum. Taste, texture, even temperature, all simulated. Skies that are always blue. Strawberries that are always ripe. Fear and dread and sorrow only in measured amounts.

"Come, look out the window! It's outside—outside the Outside!" She giggles and takes my hand.

Michele Ann Jenkins was born and raised in California, just north of the Golden Gate Bridge, but has spent most of her post-University life living and travelling abroad. She was drawn to computer programming because of her love of science fiction and now writes science fiction when she needs a break from computer programming. Recently, it dawned on her that writing elegant code has a lot in common with composing functional stories. She lives in Montreal with her husband, two children, two cats, and too many books.

The Weirdo Adventures
of Steve Rand
by Claude Lalumière

Surrounded by five Hellscorpions, the Weirdo draws his ropegun and laughs maniacally while the disembodied voice of Madman Mastermind issues yet another death threat. The Hellscorpions spit toward the young adventurer, but the Weirdo easily evades the missiles of burning spittle, pirouetting in the air, firing his ropegun, and lassoing the monstrous quintet. The instant the Weirdo lands he's knocked to the ground by the force of the Powerful Pachyderm running into him at full speed. Before the Weirdo can catch his breath, the extendable arms of Professor Kraken grab him and hold him tight. Have all his foes teamed up against him? Madman Mastermind materializes, facing the stunned teenager and pulls off his arch-enemy's mask, revealing that the Weirdo is in reality—

Steve Rand, sitting at the kitchen table, drops his spoon into his cereal bowl, splashing milk and flakes on the table and on himself. He gasps for air, as if surfacing, desperate for oxygen. His mother scolds him, but he pays no attention to her. He pulls at his face, thankful to be himself again. Much too soon, that ichorous light appears again and swallows him up—

The Weirdo can hear, smell, and taste the dreams of the city's sleeping residents. Night after night, the sounds are getting more strident, the odors more toxic, the flavors more repellent. For weeks now, the dreams of the innocent have been getting darker and more violent. Using the beacon function of his dreamwatch, he's finally located the source of the nightmare infestation: the thirtieth floor of an abandoned office building in the ghost town that was once a thriving financial district. Getting inside the building was no problem. His dreamwatch guides him to a windowless door. Behind this door is the source of what's been plaguing the city. He knows he should be wary of what might lurk inside that room, but it's not in his nature to balk in the face of unknown dangers. With his blastgun, the Weirdo destroys the door. He hurls a weirdbomb into the room and runs inside, announcing himself with the trademark laughter that has been terrorizing criminals and supervillains since he has taken on this identity. The weirdgas dissipates, and the Weirdo sees that the room is empty. Thick steel walls fall from the ceiling and clang down to the floor. It's a trap! Ghostly forms surround him, all speaking in one voice. the Malignancy! That monstrous hive mind that seeks to infect and enslave the entire planet. Many times has the Weirdo foiled their schemes. "Your ceaseless obstruction ends this night, Weirdo." Their synchronized voices echo metallically with an otherworldly crackle. Whips snap from their insubstantial bodies, lacerating and entangling the trapped vigilante. One of the whips encircles his neck, choking him. Another tears off his mask, "This is the end for both the Weirdo and—"

Steve Rand cries out, more in shock than in pain, when his mother slaps his cheek. She yells, too close to his ear, "Wake up! I've told you before not to stay up all night. Reading those comic books. I know that's what you were doing again. That's why you can't stay awake, now. Why can't you just do what I tell you? You have to learn to listen. And to focus on your homework. Or it's boarding school for you."

But Steve ignores her. That's twice in one morning. They've never happened so close together before. Barely minutes apart.

"There's milk all over your clothes! Go change now! And don't you be late for school again!"

He stands up, still woozy from the shift, and staggers toward his bedroom. But that gooey, disgusting light appears again, enfolding his entire body—

Police sirens fill the night. Searchlights pierce the darkness of the cityscape. The Weirdo is wanted for murder. And the whole city is after him. No one will believe that he was impersonated and framed by the extraterrestrial Agent Metamorph. No one knows of the planned invasion or even the aliens' existence. Only he can save the world—if they let him. He has spent the entire night dodging police bullets. The Weirdo is exhausted. He must somehow make it home undetected. Once he sheds his costume, he'll be safe to plan his next move. No one knows his real identity. He's only three blocks away from his home. It's time to active his shadowcloak; he has five minutes before its charge runs out and he becomes visible again. He collapses in his bed just as the shadowcloak effect wears off. His bedroom door crashes open. The police! Officers aim their guns at him, and a detective says, "It's over, Weirdo, we know you're really—"

Steve Rand, fourteen-year-old boy, fallen down on the floor in the hall, just outside his bedroom door, his face lying in a pool of his saliva, his mother shouting his name. He can hear her, but he can't find the strength to respond or even to move or react in the slightest.

Steve wakes up in a hospital bed. Briefly, he thinks it might be the Weirdo and not Steve himself who's in the hospital. But no. This is happening to him. Or really happening. Or whatever. He dimly remembers being brought here in a stretcher. He remembers a nurse taking off his clothes and slipping him into a hospital gown. He had been too detached from his body to be embarrassed about it then, but now he cringes at the memory.

He has vague recollections of a string of brief dreams about the Weirdo, each one of them ending in disaster for the adventurer. And then, a long period of blissful oblivion.

For the first time in months, Steve feels rested and at peace. Maybe it won't happen again, he hopes. Why does he suffer these hallucinations?

Why and how did he ever dream up the Weirdo? He doesn't crave adventure. Smiles, let alone laughter, do not come easily to him. He is nothing like the teen vigilante, nor does he aspire to be like him. And yet, he has now lived through hundreds of dangerous episodes where he becomes—or, at least, it feels as if he becomes—the Weirdo, always in the thick of deadly combat with grotesque villains.

Getting through high school without getting noticed and coping with his overworked, lonely, bitter mom is hard enough as it is. He doesn't need or want any of this strangeness.

And yet, every day for more than a year now, he has zoned out of real life and segued into this fantasy life. But that morning he collapsed had been the most intense ever. Three episodes, back to back. And not ordinary episodes, either. In all three, a different incarnation of the Weirdo had been trapped by some of his worst enemies. Maybe to the death. Followed, later, by dream images of more versions of the Weirdo being defeated time and again.

Could it be over? Had his subconscious finally gotten the message that he didn't want to experience this craziness? Had he dreamed the conclusion to his serial hallucinations?

Steve hasn't hallucinated once since being released from the hospital eight days ago. But the absence of his hallucinations has not afforded him the relief he had hoped for. He hasn't slept a wink since.

Earlier, he stole some of his mother's sleeping pills. He gulps down four of them and slides into bed. Hours go by, and he doesn't even doze. He's both restless and exhausted. His mom doesn't know about the sleeping problem, but at one point he's going to get so tired that she'll be bound to notice. He has to solve this by himself, and soon. She'll panic and blame him, and it'll be a waking nightmare. The less she notices him, the better.

The night is interminable. When the morning light starts to seep through the drapes he gets up and decides to take a bath before breakfast.

The bath is soothing. Calming. Steve is using his mom's aroma-therapy oils. They smell girly, but the effect is nice. This almost feels like being asleep. The hot water, the steamy air, the dim lighting…

…And he wakes up with his head underwater, drowning. Something's holding him down. But he can't see anyone or anything. Nevertheless, abrasive, scaly invisible fingers dig into his flesh and prevent him from surfacing.

Scaly? He remembers this sensation. He's being held down by Doc Croc, one of the Weirdo's most vicious enemies. As soon as he realizes this, Steve is no longer in the bathtub but in the sewers, beneath the city, wearing the Weirdo's psychedelic costume. Doc Croc is drowning him, killing him.

And there's another figure behind him, one he can't quite make out. He can hear his voice, though, and it sounds vaguely familiar, but it's too distorted by the water for the Weirdo to identify it. "After this, there's only one left. The most pathetic one."

The Weirdo dies, and Steve springs up in the bathtub and starts spewing water, emptying his lungs. He coughs; and it's painful, like sandpaper. He tries to get out of the bath, but he's weak and trembling. He leans over the side of the bath and projectile-vomits the entire contents of his stomach on the floor.

The retching seems to go on forever. Finally, after he brings up only bile for three times in a row, it stops. He can't remember ever feeling so weak and drained. The smell is so disgusting.

Steve coughs uncontrollably, each cough grinding against his insides. He starts to cry—from pain, from despair, from humiliation. He tries to keep the noise down, so as to not wake his mother, but he can hear the coughing reverberate though the apartment.

His mother, of course, bursts into the bathroom.

But, to his surprise, she doesn't yell at him. There's a combination of fragility and resolve in her glance that he has never seen before. "My baby..." she repeats over and over as she steps barefoot through the sludge of vomit, bile, and water on the bathroom floor, to reach her crying, coughing, and trembling son, who's holding on to the side of the tub with what little strength he has left.

She kisses his forehead. She gently rubs his bare back. Then she rests his head against her chest, and for the first time since he was a little boy he remembers that he loves his mother.

Doctor Parnum is an idiot and a dork. It's been weeks since Steve has told him anything even resembling the truth. Steve hates coming here, being forced to smell the therapist's aftershave and the tobacco odor that wafts from his tacky clothes. His lapels are so wide they reach back into the 1970s.

After months of medical testing he did not want to undergo, after countless ineffective prescriptions, it was determined that Steve's insomnia was purely psychological.

Again, with the constant prodding about his childhood. Steve doesn't even bother to keep track of the lies he tells the therapist. He repeats stuff from TV or from movies. Steals the anecdotes of other kids at schools. Mixes it all up. This entire process is so irrelevant. As if he would ever reveal anything intimate to this man.

Now, Steve can only fall asleep from utter exhaustion, managing to sleep on average two or three times a week. And even then he rarely stays asleep for more than three or four hours at a stretch. He has no control over when he falls asleep. At any moment, his body may decide that it can no longer withstand being awake, and he sinks into sleep with no warning. On the bus. In class. In therapy. Anywhere. And, once he's asleep, nothing can wake him up. He loves it when it happens in therapy.

He's tried sleeping pills, exercise, masturbation, reading—nothing succeeds in putting him to sleep. The dark circles and wrinkles around his eyes make him look twenty years older. His grades have nosedived. His mother is constantly, cloyingly concerned. At first, he loved her devoted attention. She was so focused on his well-being—without being judgmental, without always trying to tell him what to do. She'd really rallied when he desperately needed her to. He felt close to her. Like they were a real family and not the broken dysfunctional twosome they had been for too long. But it's become too much. She suffocates him now.

Steve stares at the certificates on the wall behind Doctor Parnum. The writing is too small for him to make out. He glances at the framed photos of trees and mountains and lakes.

Wait—what's the doctor saying?

"...I know who you really are. I'm surprised that you haven't figured out yet that I am controlling this lame-brained puppet. I have no fear of telling you. I want to gloat. To savor these moments with you, knowing that you know that you are trapped! Here, with me. You can't get out of coming here. You're by far the weakest of all your multiversal incarnations. And I've got you in my clutches, Weirdo. The last one of you. I traveled from reality to reality to engineer your downfall in all parallel histories. Your mind is mine! And soon the world—all worlds—will be rid of you. I've traveled to this mundane world to get my final revenge! You're under the power of...Madman Mastermind!"

"How do you know those names? I've never told you about any of this. I've never told anyone!"

"What are you talking about, Steve? What names? I was asking you if we could change days next week..."

In a panic, Steve springs up out of the big leather chair. He grabs his bag and runs out of the doctor's office without another word.

By the time Steve gets home, his mother is there, even though she should be at work. Immediately, Steve understands that Parnum called her and told her about the way he fled his office. What can he tell her to get her on his side? He can't see that jerk anymore. Steve must have babbled about the Weirdo one of the times he fell asleep in the doctor's office, and now Parnum's playing some sick game with him...

His mother says, "Come sit with me, baby." Steve sighs and joins her on the couch.

She takes his hand. He hates it when she gets too touchy-feely with him, but he lets her. He needs an ally.

"You're smart enough to know that the doctor called me."

Steve nods.

"Tell me your side of it, Stevie."

Ugh. He loathes that baby name. But he doesn't object, glad at this opportunity.

"Thanks, Mom. But can I get up and get a glass of water first?" He needs to stall, to figure out what to tell her.

"Sure. You stay here. I'll get it."

She comes back, sits down, and hands him the glass. He gulps it all down.

Steve's worked out what to say. "He's just creepy, Mom. And he smells bad. I don't trust him. There's something kind of pervy about him. I don't want to see him anymore. I'll see another doctor if you want me to. And I won't make a fuss. I'll cooperate. I promise. Just don't make me see him again. Please."

"Are you scared of him?"

Steve pauses, then nods. "Yeah, I guess I am. I hadn't thought of it that way. But that's it. You've got it."

"That's what he said when he called. That you were growing scared of him because the therapy was getting somewhere. You're getting close to the heart of the problem. It's not the doctor you're scared of, baby, it's whatever happened to you in the past to make you like this."

"What do you mean, 'like this?'"

"Well, your problems. A new doctor's not a good idea, baby. You'd be starting from scratch, and you're getting so close. You just need a little more—" The doorbell rings. She squeezes his hand again, and he can see in her face that she's holding back tears. She gets up to answer. "Just sit here, Stevie. I'll be right back."

She opens the front door, and three big men in white suits come in, followed by Doctor Parnum.

Steve's mother is crying now. "This'll be good for you, my baby. I'm sorry. But you need to get better. Trust the doctor, Stevie. He's a good man."

Diagnosed as violently delusional and self-destructive, Steve is kept strapped to his bed in the sanatorium.

As he does every night, Doctor Parnum comes by to gloat. "This is simply too delicious. Seeing you so helpless. Really, I should just be done and have this idiot I'm mind-controlling kill you."

Steve strains against his bonds. But it's no use. He swears at the doctor.

"That's it. Keep it up. Sound and behave like the violent lunatic I want them to believe you are. It'll make killing you all the easier."

"Aren't the cameras recording you, too? I don't understand. Why are you pretending to be Madman Mastermind? Why are you doing this to me?"

"Silly boy. Only you can hear this. The cameras are picking up some psychiatric mumbo-jumbo I'm having the doctor say. I'm not pretending anything. You're the last surviving iteration of my arch-enemy, Steve Rand, alias the Weirdo. But I got to you just as your powers started manifesting, before you'd learned to master them. You're the easiest of them all. The others were all hard work."

"What are you talking about, you lunatic? I don't have any superpowers. Besides, I haven't hallucinated or dreamt about the Weirdo in months. Why do you keep bringing up that crap? Let me go back home!"

"Why do you think drugs can't affect you? You're quite the topic of conversation around here, you know. I should probably finish you off before they decide you're too interesting. Every Weirdo is different. I'll admit, I'm a bit curious as to what your full range of powers would be, but not so curious as to jeopardize my mission. Enjoy your last sleepless night, Weirdo. Tomorrow, you die. I've scheduled a private therapy session. But you'll be in restraints. I'll have this body strangle you, with no one around to stop it. And then I'll leave the doctor behind to take the blame for your murder. The useful fool won't remember any of this, of course. Then, I can continue with my plans, unopposed."

"What plans? Why do you want to kill me? I'm just a kid. I don't care what you do. Please let me go back to my mom. Please."

"My plans? Oh, the usual. Mass murder. Random mayhem. Slavery and subjugation. Absolute power."

"You're insane!"

"Of course! I don't call myself Madman Mastermind for nothing."

Steve Rand is brought into the doctor's office in a straightjacket. He's been screaming that the doctor wants to murder him, but no one believes him. They all think Steve's crazy. He's screaming even louder now, faced with Doctor Parnum himself.

One of the orderlies asks, "Should we gag him, sir?"

"It won't be necessary. But do stand outside and make sure we're not disturbed. He's liable to shout about his delusions. Begging to be 'rescued'—but don't interrupt us unless I call for you."

"Yes, sir." The orderlies leave them alone. The doctor locks the door behind them.

"Well, now," gloats Doctor Parnum. "Isn't this cozy? Only a few minutes of life left, and then you'll never interfere with my plans again."

Steve is silent now. Glaring. *Maybe I should play along. Maybe that's what he wants. If I play along, he'll stop all this nonsense. Stop scaring the shit out of me.*

"You'll never get away with it, Madman Mastermind."

"Oh, please. Stop with the clichés. They're so beneath you. You, my greatest foe. Well, the most pathetic incarnation of my greatest foe. I saved you for last because you were the least dangerous."

"How do you know that? You admitted you didn't know the full extent of my powers. Maybe I've been playing possum. Only pretending to be trapped."

I should do the laugh, thinks Steve. *The Weirdo's maniac laugh, which always seems to scare his enemies. I've never tried it in real life, but I've hallucinated it enough times. I should be able to do it.*

Steve laughs. And the doctor falters. Fear flashes across his face.

Steve laughs even more. He becomes the laughter. And that's when he knows. The laughter is the key. It unlocks the Weirdo. He really is the Weirdo, after all. And he knows what his particular power is: he can channel the abilities and memories of all the other Weirdos who have ever existed across the multiverse.

His hallucinations weren't hallucinations at all; they were growing pains. His body and consciousness adapting to his burgeoning powers. And the lack of sleep was due to an energy imbalance because he hadn't used his powers yet.

Steve Rand slips out of the straightjacket with practiced ease. His hospital gown vanishes, replaced by the garish uniform of the Weirdo. His guns appear in his holsters. His weapons belt is filled with weirdbombs and other gadgets. His shadowcloak is fully charged. His dreamwatch is searching for the location of Madman Mastermind's real body; not this puppet he's been mind-controlling.

Inside Doctor Parnum's body, the essence of Madman Mastermind cowers.

"You realize your mistake now, Madman Mastermind. You should have killed me while you had the chance. I'm the most dangerous Weirdo you've ever faced."

The Weirdo laughs again. His dreamwatch has found Madman Mastermind's secret lair. The hunt for evil is on.

The Weirdo's laughter echoes throughout the sanatorium.

If you enjoyed **Claude Lalumière**'s "The Weirdo Adventures of Steve Rand", you might want to explore his collection *Objects of Worship,* which includes a number of strange superhero stories. Claude is also the author of *The Door to Lost Pages,* the dark odyssey of a young runaway who finds a new home in a reality-hopping bookshop and is thrown in the middle of a war among ancient gods and monsters. Claude had stories appear in three previous *Tesseracts* anthologies (Nine, Eleven, and Fourteen) and he edited volume Twelve: *New Novellas of Canadian Fantastic Fiction.* With Rupert Bottenberg, Claude is the co-creator of "Lost Myths," which is both a live show and an online archive of cryptomythological fiction, comics, games, art, performances, and more.

Every You, Every Me
by Virginia Modugno

"If everybody is thinking alike, then someone isn't thinking."
—*George S. Patton*

Locker Room, Level 1
Passchendaele High School
Present Day, 08:45 hrs

No matter how many times I blink, she still won't disappear. The hair, the clothes, the shoes, the backpack they all scream "stuck up" like it's going out of style: the hair band that sits like a crown just before the peak of her manicured hair, the blouse that's blindingly white, ironed crisp and suctioned in by a corset-like sweater vest, the regulation-length kilt that skirts her calves, the Mary Janes polished to such perfection that you could literally watch the other students mill by on her glassy toes, the knee socks that seem glued on. The knee socks!

She has a smile for everyone, not too wide, not too sweet, and makes eye contact with anyone who crosses her path from the Slurpie-guzzling mathletes to B-ballers so tall, they could slam-dunk her. She walks down the busy halls with the poise of a life-size Barbie. She doesn't dump her bag into her locker, then slam the door so hard it makes the whole row bucket back and forth like I do. She doesn't sneer at Edwin Banks, the first-year emo wannabe who follows her around like a groupie at an MGMT gig like I do. Instead, she gingerly plucks the photo collage off the inside door of the locker—my locker!—to make room for her magnet mirror which she carefully manoeuvres until it is dead center, framing her tastefully made-up face. After reaching into the front pouch of her backpack, she unfurls a single tube of blush-colored lipstick and daintily coats her lips. She presses them together, then smiles winningly at herself, a pre-packaged starlet recast as a humble high-schooler in an update of *The Prince and the Pauper.*

As she weaves through the halls to her first class, there's no mistaking it—people are *loving* her. Or at least, the scene she creates. Mean girl glares go from glacial to predatory. Geek squad sprout instant wood. Even the slackers wake up long enough to notice something's happening. Cells are snapping pics in a frenzy to rival the paparazzi, thumbs are pounding, handsets are erupting, alerts are beeping, statuses are being updated by the second. She's a perfect storm of the scandalous and the spectacular on the 24/7 gossip circuit.

The worst of it is—she's me.

A new and improved me, now with less angst. A me with a flawless outer shell—all sparkly teacher-bait—but with no guts, no grit, no grunge. She's a Mac, and I'm like the least PC person, ever. Analog. Practically Luddite. Wouldn't even glance at a pair of Mary Janes, let alone wear them. As I watch her prance into first period, I barely suppress the urge to charge up to her and wring her prissy little neck, but those rumor-junkies would love that even more—a title bout between Versions 1 and 2.0, right there in the main hall—an easy million hits on YouTube if ever there was. I throw up a little bit in my mouth at the thought of my personal hell being exposed to the cheesy poof-scarfing masses, then a lot more once I retreat to the girls' bathroom. It's not every day you come to school to find that your photo-double has somehow taken over your life.

My first thought, after chugging the last of my Red Bull to kill the puke fumes: Android. My second: Who ordered the upgrade? My third: Where is Sam?

Basement Lair
Sparks Residence
08:00 hrs
It was the high note at the end of the Jimi version of *Star-Spangled Banner* that finally got me to crawl out from under my ginormous fleece comforter. The ringtone was Sam's idea, personalized the last time he swiped my phone.

My BFF Samson is the poster boy for "Don't Ask, Don't Tell," a red-blooded, US-born weekend cadet squad leader who plays fullback, bench-presses two-fifty, and plans to enlist the second he turns eighteen. He's also a card-carrying Friend of Dorothy, who moons over his WWE Superstars Calendar and stealthily prowls the guys' locker room after practice. We let everyone think he's a serial horndog who's slumming it by hooking up with me. Once upon a time, Samson was just as gaunt and mascara'd as I am, but now that he's found the Corps, he's the size of a tank.

I hadn't really planned on moving before 1:00, hence the hiding out in my brother's room, but a text from Sam this early had to be some sort of 911. I'd been avoiding school in general for most of the week, preferring to perfect my guitar fingering and work on my graphics portfolio, which translates to playing *Rock Band* 'till I get early-onset arthritis. The glare of the screen is harsh, but when my eyes focus I manage to make the message out:

```
WTBleep, Rayns?
Since when did u
go Sharpay on me?
```

I stare for a bit, then shrug, then slump back under the covers until Jimi wails at me again. "What now?" I muffle-bark, angling the top of the wedge near the center of my ear.

All I hear is: "Holy."

"Please don't tell me that I am conscious before 12:00 hrs because Street Jackson dropped his towel in front of you again. You practice every day. You shower together. Every day. You should be—"

"Rayna, where...where are you right now?"

"At home, Brain Trust. Duh."

He clams up, but I can hear him wheezing on the line, fast and sharp, like he's being strangled. He clears his throat—once, twice—then sucks in a deep breath.

"No, you're not. You're just...not."

"Sam, make sense."

"You better get down here, quick. Serious. There's a...you're not gonna believe this, but there's a *you* walking around. Another you, I mean. Just..."

"If this is part of your upstanding citizens' initiative, I swear..."

"Rayns, it's not. Straight up. We have what I can only describe as a FUBAR situation here."

Jeez, a girl can't even play hooky anymore without being called out to baby-sit.

I sigh, then groan. Even the thought of cracking open my cocoon exhausts me, let alone the idea of dressing, walking to school, actually attending class...but something's weird in Sam's voice, and not the normal kind of weird. I better go see what's up, if only so I can keep him away from the school nurse long enough for whatever he's taken to wear off. Probably another bad reaction to his allergy meds.

"Fine, I'm coming. Watch your six. Sparks out."

"Will do. Colbert out."

Room 307, Level 1
Passchendaele High School
11:35 hrs

Hours later, I still can't believe my eyes. I stare and stare at her through the square of glass in the center of the door, like a future Alice peering through the TV screen at a Wonderland version of herself. Except in my case it's more like a window into my own personal Bizarro World, though no mirror I've ever gazed into has hit home the 4-D totality of what it's like to watch myself in action. As much as I want to call her bluff when third period lets out—consequences, schmonsequences—the last three hours have been like the trippiest makeover show ever, one made just for my ironic viewing displeasure.

Of course, I'm not the only one goggle-eyed at her shtick. Mr. Bueller's History class is usually a primo opportunity to catch some pre-lunch Z's; today, you'd think he was giving a lecture on the signature styles of David Beckham by the way almost everyone is straight-backed, leaning slightly forward toward the faux-me sitting at the front of the class. The craftier ones have even deployed heavy duty tactics: angling their compacts for a side view, sitting on books to add height, and the classic "whoops, my pen" from the guy who managed to score a seat beside her. Even Bueller can't seem to take his eyes off her, not that she'd give him a chance. Her hand flies up so often I'm surprised she hasn't dislocated her shoulder.

Only Brix Overstreet, half-pint hack, is head down, thumbs to his hidden keypad with such fury that even his Blackberry's fuming. There's no doubt in my mind that this is just the "local color" story he's looking for to end that day's homeroom broadcast. Worst thing is, I'm semi-curious to see how she reacts.

"Psst!" Sam slides out from behind a row of lockers, crouching down to run their length before landing at my side. He straightens then follows my stare. "Whoa. Bogey at twelve o'clock."

"You're telling me," I exhale blinking, brain still not computing the fact of her existence. "BTW, where in the name of the red, white and blue have you been? I've been on watch for three hours!"

"That's need-to-know, only."

"Well, I need to know!" I exclaim, so loud that we have to duck down. "Tell me you didn't go to class at a time like this."

"Negative. Spent my time in the nurse's office, establishing an air-tight cover story for why I might have to suddenly sprint out of class."

"Which is?"

"Possible upset stomach due to over consumption of jalapeno-flavored Doritos past their sell-by date. Ate a whole bag after morning practice. Don't feel so good."

"For real?"

"Yeah, but it's cool. I lied about the date part. And the fact that my mom forgot to put the acai berries in my protein shake. Tasted like fertilizer."

"Still better than Army grub."

"Too right," he nods. "So, what's the game plan?"

"No clue."

"Bell's gonna ring in ten. Better think of something. And, you know, retreat to a secure location. Only thing worse than not knowing what's up is not knowing what's up while half the school is watching the two of you give each other the stink eye."

"True words," I agree. "Supply closet?"

"Are you asking to get caught?"

"Right. Auditorium?"

"Already checked. Mr. C's rigging his DVR to one of the monitors."

"Ugh," I groan, then slump against the cranky aluminum side of a locker. "Maybe I should just have it out with her. Pistols at dawn, that kind of thing. Find out what she's made of. Literally."

"I don't know," Sam cautions. "She's already trending way higher than you on PeerTutor.net. You might have to face a few too many inconvenient truths."

"Yeah," I sigh. "Not exactly a newsflash, but still. I guess there's only one foxhole the enemy won't patrol."

"If it makes you feel better," Sam grins in that All-American way of his, "I swiped a jar of Mentholatum from the First Aid shelf."

I smile, possibly for the first time that year. "Colbert, you're a prince among men."

Garbage Depot, Basement Level
Passchendaele High School
11:55 hrs

By the time we skulk up to the vault-like steel door at the far end of the cafeteria, the sulphuric stench is worse than that time Laney Bryce's homemade science fair volcano exploded all over the Chem lab. As a die-hard social outcast, lunchtimes usually find me hunched over the back corner table, aptly nicknamed "Siberia," which is how I discovered that the door to the garbage depot provides easy, unlocked access to the great outdoors. It's the perfect escape route from the withering stares of the diva contingent, and has probably saved me more than a few ambulance rides. The only downside is you have to hang with the grody-to-the-max stench—oily ooze and tampon stink—until the caf' clears or the G-men come to collect.

As Sam smears a Mentholatum 'stache across my upper lip, I rev into full-on panic attack mode: breath gulping, palms spewing, gut spazzing, not to mention that I can't stop my teeth from chattering even though the caf's like a furnace from all the broiling and stewing behind the lunch counter. I'm yanked into the depot before my fight or flight kicks in. I'm about to go all *Jennifer's Body* on him when I stop short beside Sam, who's already scraping his jaw off the floor.

It's just a truck, really, although this one looks like an alternate universe NASA one, where man didn't stop when he reached the moon. The back door is cracked open and farting dry ice like a '70's disco, such that you can't really see inside. It's the green antennae headlights and rocket-launcher spoilers that sell the effect, explaining a little too much about where all that mystery meat we're served comes from.

"Soylent Green *is* people," Sam mutters under his breath.

I consider heading back to my basement, my ginormous comforter, my obliviousness; instead, I clunk down to my knees and start to whimper.

Sam drops down next to me, puts a hand on my shoulder. "Rayns, it's probably just a meat locker. Company tricked out their ride to get an edge on the competition. Economy got deep-sixed. You know the drill."

"It's not just that," I bleat, feeling crushed by the hugeness of it all. "What the hell is happening, Sam? What am I going to do? There's another fricking *me* out there, stealing my thunder, harshing my buzz, living my life for me! Even if tomorrow she just poofs away again, I'm still left to clean up her sick."

"Roger that," he replies, with a curt nod. "And it sucks, don't get me wrong. But are you really gonna let this stand? Let that... I-don't-know-what take over?" He thinks about it for a while, then adds, "or maybe this is the best thing that ever happened to you. How many times have you talked about ditching your parents and hitching a ride to New York when you hit eighteen? Well, adulthood just came a few years early."

"Oh, man, my parents!" I exclaim, freaking out even more. "Do you think she'll try to infiltrate my HQ after school?"

This horror-flick scenario just went from bad to apocalyptic. School's a fight I've already lost, but the battle is still raging on the home front and I don't want anything to make it worse. Unless, of course, it's something I come up with.

"Affirmative," says Sam. "Also, wow. That's intense. What are you gonna do?"

"What I have to," I declare, newly locked and loaded. "Wait out the school day. Stalk her. Poach her. End her."

Sam's eyes bug out at this.

"Whoa, Rayns. What do you mean, 'end her?' You don't even know what her game is or where..."

"Her reign, not her life. Unless, you know, she really is an android."

Sam thinks about this for a minute, then laughs. "Don't even wanna know where her kill-switch is."

"Thanks for that mental image."

"Think she's a clone? Like a backup disc your parents dug out when you looked like you were about to crash?"

"Huh. Wouldn't surprise me. They've tried pretty much every-thing else to get me to do what they want."

"See what I mean? This could be your chance, Rayns. Your plan is solid, sure, but when you meet up with her, don't be afraid to improvise. Find out what this is all about before you turn her in. For all you know, could be a blessing in disguise. This situation is workable."

"Right," I nod, ready to hurry up and wait.

"Also," Sam adds, "you might want to consider letting your hair grow out. Your natural color is *lush*, girl. Just saying."

"Go," I command with a snort. "On the double. Text me in fifth. I want intel, and I want it yesterday."

"Got it. Stay frosty."

Northwest Hall, Level 3
Passchendaele High School
14:07 hrs

Once Sam skedaddles, there's only me, the bins and that freaky truck. I'm not very good at keeping still at the best of times, but the wait for the final bell is almost lethal. I just can't shake the feeling that I'm like a mouse who doesn't know it already has one foot in the trap. Maybe it's just the stink of congealed cheese.

Once the bell for fifth period rings, I put my hoodie to good use and sneak out the garage door, then up the back fire escape to the third floor. As the furthest hall from the teacher's lounge, it's notorious for being a ghost town in the afternoon. This is the domain of my crush-du-jour, Thurber, a stretch of ultra-fluorescent hallway that sits behind the auditorium's control center and ends with the AV room, which he runs for extra credit. Thurber's a technocrat who's repeating his senior year for flunking all his liberal arts classes (deliberately), which he sees as pointless in a world where all menial tasks will soon be done by robots, and the only truly practical field of study is Computer Science. He was on my radar long before the latest crisis, though for very different reasons. In my world, a social-activist hacker with a laptop bag full of multicolored pills is even better than Prince Charming.

True to form, he's swishing around his console on his wheelie stool, Bluetooth hooked in like an overgrown earring, zipping between touch screens with the magnetic grace of the call center drones of the future. I veer toward the far end of the counter so as not to spook him, but he's too in the zone to even notice me. I wait a beat before dinging the bell, hoping he'll spin around for a spare part or something, during which I take in the full effect of the new look he's sporting. The best way to describe it is Suburban Time Lord, or maybe Hipster Caddy. Gone are the sarcastic T-shirts hidden under his school whites, the tracksuit detailing on his trousers, the vintage Converse, the streak of electric blue on the underside of his forelock. Instead, he looks freeze-packed into his uniform, Mr. Rogers cardigan in full effect.

Don't get me wrong, he's still teched-out enough to headline my dreams. If he keeps this up, though, he might have to share top billing with Matthew Gray Gubler.

"Ding-dong, the witch is back!" I announce, then slap my palm down on the bell.

This sets off a sound and lights show a theme park would envy. It's only then that I realize a thin sheet of glass has been mounted in the service window, probably sound-proofing the AV room. Thurber barely glances in my direction. Instead, his voice rumbles out of the above speakers in a dry monotone.

"State your name, grade, and class, affiliation, ID number, and request."

It's a recording. I decide to play along.

"Rayna Sparks, 4C, Society for the Prevention of Cruelty to Lab Frogs, 90210, and your full attention, please."

"Received," the speakers acknowledge. "Your request will be processed by the end of the day. You will receive confirmation of your booking and further instructions by text. If for some reason the materials you requested are not available, a secondary time and location will be determined."

With a grunt, I smack the bell again, then curse when the message repeats.

"Thurbs!" I yell, banging on the glass with my fist. "It's me! Open up!"

When this doesn't catch his attention, I try the door, first knocking, then pounding, then shoving into it with my side. Seriously, what gives? Did Mr. Snidely key into his side gig and lock him in? I half expect some kind of siren to start blaring, but the door holds, gray and immovable, like the back of an armored truck. I move back over to the window and press my face against the glass, hoping he'll get that tingly feeling on the back of his neck if I stare at him long enough. Nothing. He just slides between his consoles, the maestro of mecha, oblivious.

That's when it starts brewing, in the pit of my stomach, as if I'd swallowed a gallon of Coke and a whole bag of Pop Rocks. The feeling of a prank turned deadly, of a trick gone all kinds of wrong. For a while, it was okay. Exciting, even. A weird, freaky adventure that I'd figure out, eventually. But this roller coaster's taken one turn too many, and I'm officially ready to get off the ride. Needs to stop, like right now. Never thought I'd say this, much less think it, but I want my crappy life back.

My cell trills in the nick of time, before I can do something really destructive like hurl it into the plate glass. A text from Sam:

```
OMG, entir periodic
tabl recitd by heart!
Def. android! Watch out
4 alienz! U thnk shes
a lizard like in V?
```

That's it. My terror tank has reached "full." Time to bail.

Outer Perimeter
Sparks Residence
17:38 hrs
At first I think she's not going to show.

After doing doughnuts on my skateboard around the mall parking lot for two hours, trying my best to let the flow of my body on the breeze work its tabula rasa hoo-doo on my mind, I give up and head for home. Once I swerve into the half-circle that's my street, I lose all my Zen, not to mention my cool, since there are two cars parked in the driveway and the house is lit up. My parents are home early—like pink-slip early—and have obviously been in honeybee mode for a while. The house is so alive with activity it's practically buzzing. I can see Dad power vacuuming in the upstairs hall, while Mom pops between the kitchen and the dining room like a groundhog who can't decide whether or not winter's ending.

I crouch down on my board, pretending to carve an epic arc around the circle, but instead turn sharply just before the end of the driveway and slip in under the family SUV's back bumper. I cool my heels under the car, waiting for a glimpse of those Mary Janes. Like any sniper worth her salt, I've got both entrances covered. I'm within earshot of my primary location, and I'm decked out in the color of my surroundings, black on black. My cell's on vibrate, but I haven't gotten a text in ages and Sam's not answering. Maybe she gave him the slip.

Still no joy at 17:45 hrs, and I'm not the only one peeved. Both my nervy parents are now permanently stationed behind the bay window, their brows lifting expectantly at every passing car, as if waiting to meet their first grandchild. A false alarm has them scurrying back and forth to the door like chipmunks, but it's only my brother, Nate, stopping in for a snack before judo. Just as I'm afraid I'll doze off, that telltale clicky-clack pounds the pavement behind me. Those glossy navy blues all but skip up the drive, then break into a trot when she spots my parents, who have burst out the front door to greet her.

Every hug they give her is like a vise tightening around my chest. Every coo and pet they lavish on her makes my skin crawl. I rest my cheek on the cold, oil-stained pavement as they whisk her into the house, feeling like road kill. Except that my guts aren't smooshed all over the front drive, they're still inside me, aching in a way even I don't really understand. Ever since I can remember—or at least since sophomore year—I'd have done anything to be out of here, on my own, like those emancipated rich kids you see in cheesy TV movies of the week. Now, the dice have been rolled for me, I've earned my Get Out of Jail Free card, and I'd give anything to be able to buy a few houses for my pathetic little Marvin Gardens lot. Maybe even a hotel.

That might have been my cue to run as far and as fast as I can, but I just can't let it go. I have to watch the whole travesty play out like a rubbernecker at a car crash. I peel myself out from under the car and stash my board, then sneak around back. I've never been so thankful that my dad never got around to dismantling the tree house in the sturdy maple out back. It gives me the perfect vantage from which to watch the Disney-fied version of my life unfold. I don't even need sound to know what's being said by the cheery faces behind the glass. Heck, I don't even have to see their lips to know they're smiling.

"How was your day, dear?"

"More brussels sprouts, darling?"

"I was thinking of going out for the cheerleading squad."

"Mrs. Brady was wondering if you could baby-sit Saturday night."

It's enough to make you spit.

Once I've overdosed on domestic bliss, I hunker down on the creaky, probably bug-infested mattress and consider my options. Knifing her in her sleep jumps immediately to mind, but that's not a very Girl Scout move. Honestly, I don't even know if I want to stick around and solve the Case of the Picture-Perfect

Double. My knee-jerk has always been "screw it", and I can't say I'm feeling any different about this situation. I wish I'd never crawled out from under Nate's comforter. I wish I'd never set foot in that school. But most of all, I wish my mom would look across the table and start to scream bloody murder until my dad calls the cops on 2.0, or orders her out of the house, or whomps her on the head with a frying pan.

But, as five-star General Dwight D. Eisenhower once said, "Neither a wise man nor a brave man lies down on the tracks of history to wait for the train of the future to run over him." I need a plan and a good one, if I'm ever going to get out of this. Also, the "escape fund" I've been squirreling away for months, hidden in the roof access panel at the top of my closet. Time for some cloak and dagger.

Second Floor Bedroom
Sparks Residence
20:17 hrs
Sneaking in and out of the house might have been harder if I hadn't done it so many times before. I may not end up getting my GED, but I could definitely teach a master class in how to avoid being seen by your parents. Not being detected by my doppelganger could be way trickier, though, especially since I don't know whether she's animal, mineral or cyborg. There's really no telling what kind of advanced tech or alien capabilities are under her hood; for all I know, she might already have picked up my heat signature on the whiz-bang surveillance system in her left elbow or something. Not even lightning bolts zapping out of her eyes would surprise me at this point.

After I'm certain all the family units have retired to their usual night time haunts—my dad to his workroom, my brother to his video games, my mom to her knitting, and me-bot to, drum roll, her homework!—I make a B-line for the side door to the garage. Once in, I tiptoe across the cement floor, then ease open the inside door. I wait for alarms to blare, flood lights to spin, 2.0's head to start revolving 360 degrees, but *nada*. The house is so quiet I can hear the steamy exhale of the dishwasher as it changes cycles. It's a hop, skip, and a jump to my room from there, where the light has handily been left on. I guess environmental concerns aren't part of new-me's programming.

As soon as I get a glimpse of my former lair, I realize there's no chance of my parents copping a plea to this crime. The place has been whitewashed—or, rather, magenta-washed—to suit the Rachel Berry-on-crack stylings of their new addition. Even if I had wanted to pack an away bag, there's nothing left to pilfer. I flop down on the end of my old bed and spare a moment of silence for my stuff: the skull and crossbones lampshades I picked up at my friend Annabelle's garage sale, the collection of Jeff Buckley bootlegs I "borrowed" from Nate, the vintage issues of *Thrasher* I scored on our trip to California, my autographed poster of Hrithik Roshan from the Bollywood Nights festival Sam took me to last month...if the thought of them being trash compacted into oblivion enrages me, knowing that my mom gleefully got rid of everything she always hated about the "me" part of me makes me mental.

I race over to the closet, fling the door back, wrench the color-coded selection of preppy clothes apart, then jam a desk chair into the neat stacks of shoe boxes lining the floor. Leaping up, I punch open the ceiling panel, then search around for the old fuse box where I keep my cash reserve. I nab it and drag it down, hugging it to my chest like a rusty shield, the better to deflect any phaser beams or death ray fire a certain someone might shoot at me. I break for the door, ready to blast out of there, when She stops me cold.

She hovers in the door frame, eyes wide, mouth a perfect "O," like Snow White tempted by the poisoned apple. She plays the innocent act to the hilt, taking an instinctive step back, then quickly charges forward to force me further into the room. Careful not to get too close, she slowly circles me, taking in every thread of my clothes, every pore of my skin. Every sprig, every freckle. I can't help it, either—she's as fascinating as she is terrifying to me.

Finally, she stops, smirks. I want to pummel her, but I'm scared to touch her. She lifts a dainty hand and pageant-queen waves at me. Bye-bye. Then, she starts shrieking at the top of her lungs.

Back Alley
Dunkin' Donuts
03:20 hrs

Who do you call when your life's been taken over by an evil twin, your best friend's gone MIA, and you've got $700, a cell phone, and a shoulder bag to your name?

I feel like I'm stuck on loop. I keep going over everything in my head, reading Sam's last text over and over, trying to find some clue I missed, some hint that I overlooked. In my mind's eye, I keep seeing everyone's reactions in close-up—my classmates, my parents, Sam, Thurber, Nate, as I bolted out the door—like the end of an Agatha Christie movie just before the murderer's name is revealed. I have an endless list of suspects, but no one really to blame.

Except, of course, the obvious.

On a whim, I dig out my cell and pound the redial button, praying that this time Sam will answer. I listen to his voice mail greeting as I huddle under the tattered sleeping bag I fished out of the goodwill bin at the back of the mall, the sound of his clipped, stern message the closest thing to a lullaby I'm going to get. I end the call before the sound of the beep.

Locker Room, Level 1
Passchendaele High School
Next Day, 08:30 hrs

No matter how many times I blink, he still won't disappear.

I had to come. I had to know. Even though two bus tickets to New York City are burning a hole in my pocket. Even though I watched that creepy truck back into the garbage depot just before I walked in. Even though I saw it in my brother's sad, sad eyes last night, seconds before I dashed out the front door. I have to know the truth. If not about myself, then at least about Sam.

Posed in a classic jock lean over both Trina Desmond and her open locker, he stares into her eyes, chancing the occasional flick down at her cleavage, with the kind of sincere intensity that went out in the 1950's. At first glance, there isn't that much different about him. He's still quietly flaunting the letters on his varsity jacket. He still stands in a way that suctions his crisply pressed pants around his muscular thighs. His buzz cut still screams of his military ambitions to anyone passing by. He still glances in Street Jackson's direction as he struts down the hall, but he doesn't check out his ass. That's just not my Sam.

Suddenly, he glances in my direction, giving me the once-over before turning back to Trina's baby blues. Not a flicker. Not a glint. The smell of dry ice fills the air. A hand falls on my left shoulder, then another on my right.

I don't bother to turn around.

A self-employed writer and subtitle editor, **Virginia Modugno** is grateful that watching all those episodes of *Twilight Zone* and *iCarly* has finally paid off. After completing her Master's degree in Media Arts from the University of London, she worked in both adult and children's television, most notably writing an episode of TV Ontario's *Fun Food Frenzy*. A member of the Quebec Writer's Federation, it was through a workshop that she discovered YA fiction. She is currently at work on her first novel at home in Montreal, her wee corgi serving as both foot-warmer and in-house critic.

The Oak Girl
by Helen Marshall

She would watch him as he worked,
the thin spirals of wood falling in ringlets
to rest carelessly
or scatter when he moved.
Her half-lidded eyes traced the sweep
of the knife,
dreaming it when she slept
in the warm crook of the chair.

Once, his eyes flicked up,
caught her gaze
like a saw fumbling in a knot of wood.
He knew the shape of her
with a glance.

Watching in the midnight silence
(but for the whssssk of the blade)
she often wondered
who was trapped
beneath the layers of bark

waiting for the knife to finish.
As the last furl
fluttered to the floor,
she stared at the smooth, streaked limbs
of the other,

her finger tracing
the blue vein in her hand
over the scar
where he had cut too close.

Helen Marshall really does spend most of her time searching through dusty manuscripts for arcane lore—just ask her Ph. D supervisor! Her poetry has been published in *ChiZine, NFG,* and the *Ontarion Arts Supplement.* "Mist and Shadows" published originally in *Star*Line,* appeared in *The 2006 Rhysling Anthology: The Best Science Fiction, Fantasy and Horror Poetry of 2005.* She is the Managing Editor for *ChiZine Publications,* and the Co-organizer of the Chiaroscuro Reading Series. Some day she hopes to discover five words to make a man fall in love, the truth about artichokes, and the secret language of cats.

Edge of Moonglow
by Ed Greenwood

My hands were shaking so hard I almost dropped the pry bar. Hissing something unprintable, I grabbed it hard in both hands, *just* before it could whirl down and be lost in the darkness, and squeezed it as hard as I could—as if somehow melting it could make me calm.

I was as nervous as all get out.

Small wonder; I'd never broken into a building before.

Yet even here, clinging to a second-floor window frame of this oldest wing of Northwood College—sorry, no ivy-covered walls around me, just dirty red brick—only a thickness of old glass away from Professor Darrback's darkened and deserted Biology lab, I wasn't as scared as I'd been on the other side of the glass this afternoon.

Old Franklin "Frankenstein" Darrback had outdone himself this time...and if he succeeded, I was doomed.

We called him Frankenstein because he loved electricity. Crackling arcs of snarling lightning bolts, like in Frankenstein movies. He even chortled as he played with his flashing, dancing currents, a deep, crazy giggling that creeped us all out. Some of the gals in class literally sank down behind the giant fish tanks when he laughed like that.

Like them, I couldn't decide if I hated him more than I feared him or the other way around. Until his big announcement this afternoon, that is. Now I knew I was more afraid of him than I'd ever feared anyone or anything in my life before. With the flick of a switch, he could end my life.

If you believed Frankenstein Darrback—and I did, boy I did— he had perfected a way of replicating moonlight precisely with artificial lighting.

He'd waved a thick sheaf of notes at us and then proudly used them to point at his "prototype installation," a tube on a tripod that looked more like a cheap amateur telescope than a light bulb.

He wanted us all—three classes of students, mine and the two that had followed mine in that lab class, I'd heard—to help him in "extensive research" for the rest of the term; research involving his artificial moonlight. The moment he could get them built, his moonlight bulbs would be all over the lab, and we'd be hard at work.

And the moment the rays of one of his lamps touched me, without stronger real sunlight also bathing me, I'd start to Turn, and the whole world would discover that the skinniest Sci sophomore in Northwood College was a werewolf.

There wouldn't be a thing I could do to stop myself. The "wolf blood" came down through the female side of my family. My mother and grandmother and aunts all had ways of resisting The Turn that had to do with womanly cycles and strange concoctions they mixed and drank that smelled of cinnamon and burned my nose and lips just sniffing at them, but as a guy, I had…nothing.

Which is why the males of my family had tended to die young and often back in the days of the settlers, and the surviving womenfolk had moved often.

So, I'd sat there this afternoon literally sweating and feeling as cold as ice, both at once. Staring across the lab and seeing it suddenly as a prison cell. Until I realized who I was staring at out of sheer chance and looked away—Murelle Benson, who sneered at me whenever she looked at me, had a tongue that she used on most of the guys, me especially, like a whip, and was way too beautiful for a skinny guy with glasses to have any hope of ever even befriending. Even though I was, of course, helplessly in love with her. Not that she'd ever been the slightest bit nice, or even polite, to me. "Spiteful b..." was a mild way of describing her everyday manner, and toward me "actively malicious" would have been closer...yet, I couldn't help myself. One of the things about being a werewolf was being really good at smelling things, and I was crazy about the way she smelled.

That was, of course, something I couldn't ever see myself being able to tell her without results that'd be anything short of disastrous, but that didn't stop me smelling, and dreaming and...

Well, and that was a heck of a road to be letting my thoughts run down now, while I was out here clinging to a window frame in the night, with a cold breeze rising and the night passing.

The odd thing, though, this afternoon, while Frankenstein pranced about the room rubbing his hands and waving his notes and chortling, was Murelle's face. She'd looked as scared—as utterly trapped—as I'd felt.

Hah! As I'd *be*, if I didn't get a move on! I'd only have one chance at this, to steal and destroy the prototype and the prof's notes now, before he set us to work making duplicates of the damned thing. If the Science department photocopier hadn't been on the fritz, he'd already have dozens of copies of his notes carefully stashed away; I knew him well enough to be cold certain about that. Oh, he'd have his originals at home; I'd only be delaying him—but tonight was my best chance to slow him down, and just maybe stall the whole thing once the Dean and the senior faculty council found out *why* there'd been a break-in and started to wonder just *when* Darrback was going to teach us what he was supposed to be covering this term, what with all this moonlight stuff, I was sure he hadn't told them a thing about.

Scared as I was, tonight was the best night. After this bold try—if I *managed* a bold try—the moonlight lamps and the notes would be locked away or guarded, or both, and students shivering outside windows with pry bars wouldn't stand much of a chance of derailing Frankenstein's grand promenade into scientific greatness...and the doom of all werewolves in the vicinity.

Just in case, I was wearing sneakers and old, loose clothes I'd found in the lockers at the back of Anderson's repair shop after it closed down, last fall. The Turn was hard on clothes and even harder on me wherever they were tight. If I went "were," I'd probably end up naked, which was why I'd hidden a bag of old, not-mine clothes up in a tree across the road from the college, in the trees around one of the big old houses whose owners didn't have dogs.

All the lab windows were white, grubby painted metal—a projecting lip or ledge along the bottom like the one I was standing on, then a metal panel up to waist height, then above that, swing-out windows about two feet tall and six wide to let fresh air into the classrooms if they were opened (which of course, they never were for long...all the profs seemed to hate fresh air), then a cross-frame, and then big, flat fixed panes of glass above up to another projecting lip at the top. Birds loved those ledges, which meant the college maintenance staff hated them, but it also meant they had safety belts they could hook onto massive metal eye-bolts that had been welded onto the windows some years back. I was using one of those belts right now and was working on the end window—the one I'd contrived to open just half an inch this afternoon.

Just enough for the pry bar edge to slip inside. Well, I wasn't going to get any calmer, but the night would run out on me if I just stood here waiting, so...

The window squealed a bit as I pulled it out and open, giving me a good whiff of the warm, stale air of the lab. This wasn't some television spy show or science fiction series, so there were no electric-eye beams or alarms inside. Just a grubby lab with a worn checkerboard linoleum floor, lots of burns and stains on those tiles and the fixed lab desks, a row of faint glows from the giant aquarium tanks that had dim night lights in their hoods, faint light from the distant streetlights reflecting back off the row of terraria full of snakes and plants and pond scum...and that chilling white telescope-thing on its tripod at the front of the class, Frankenstein's proud invention.

The moonlight lamp.

I clambered through the window, both my shirt and my pants catching and ripping and being dragged half-off. I caught them before they could fall into the night and carried them with me to cover my hands or wipe away fingerprints. The sneakers made faint squeaking sounds, and I kicked them off and stalked barefoot down the aisle. Quick and quiet, quick and quiet and out...

I reached for the lamp, and—*CRASH*. KA-KLANG, ALANG, CRASH.

I'd kicked over lots of tin cans down on the floor. Empty cans, all strung together. Who knows where they'd come from, they certainly hadn't been there when—

I'd already snatched the lamp, and was turning and running, running back to—

The lab light switch clacked on behind me, and the room was flooded with light.

"Going somewhere, Mister Traskin?"

Frankenstein's voice was coldly triumphant. Gleeful, even.

I'd frozen for a moment but didn't bother to turn around, just ran for the window as fast as I could.

I got three steps before I almost cut my hands on wire as it stretched tight and dragged me to a stop. There were bare copper wires attached to the moonlight lamp, now running straight back behind me, and—

EEEAAAAGH!

Frankenstein chortled like a madman as I sobbed, fighting just to breathe as the electricity danced through me and played along my fingers.

"I suspected someone would try to steal my masterpiece. Students are *so* predictable. Almost as reliable as this electric cattle prod. Enjoying it, Mister Traskin? Oh, go ahead. Batter that lamp to proverbial smithereens on the floor. It's not real. Just a prop, part of my little thief-trap. *This* one is real."

There came the snap of another switch, and a bluer, paler light flooded past me. A moment later, the main lights went out, and Frankenstein giggled and started to sing a popular song, mangling its words to apply to me.

"Dance, little thief, dance in the moonlight..."

I was already on the floor, helpless, twisting and crying in my boxers, flooded by the snapping, crawling little lightnings of Frankenstein's plug-in cattle prod. Now I felt The Turn starting, that flesh-creeping feeling of the fur reaching up out of my skin, the muscles starting to shift and swell...

Behind me, Frankenstein stopped singing and cursed in astonishment.

And then in fear.

The light was changing, which meant my eyes were Turning, and I was...I was roaring now, not crying. Jeez a-please, the *PAIN*.

Through it, I heard the prof's voice rise in terror and get a lot closer. And then he was hitting me.

Hard and often, with a chair that splintered and fell apart, though he just kept at it. Bashing me with the cattle prod in his other hand, too, bringing them down again and again. I couldn't breathe, couldn't get up off the floor, couldn't control my arms and legs with all the lightnings surging through me...

Twisting desperately, I managed to roll, trying to get away from him. But the lab desks were in the way, and I ended up backed against one of them, blinking up at him through tears I couldn't stop as he clobbered me, the chair down to one spear-like leg now. If he thought of stabbing me with it...

Then something loomed up above and behind Darrback as it arrived atop a lab desk in one lithe spring.

Something large, sleek, and furry. Another werewolf!

Frankenstein must have heard or felt its arrival, because he started to turn—in time to meet snarling jaws driven by a body at full spring, a body too long-limbed to be a real wolf, too—

My mad Biology professor staggered back helplessly, cattle prod sparking from end to end as he tried desperately to use it. He glanced off the edge of a desk, lost his footing, and crashed—right *through* the biggest aquarium tank, cattle prod first.

Sparks burst everywhere. He didn't even have time to scream.

The werewolf skidded past him and the tank, fetched up against a desk, sprang atop another and raced down the room, gathering speed.

The moonglow lamp didn't stand a chance.

In the wake of its terrific crash, its glow faded and I started to Turn again.

I could hear faint smashings in Frankenstein's back office where the other werewolf had gone, and then a soft curse. A moment later, the snaps of metal latches opening.

The first aid kit!

I staggered to my feet, feeling horrible. I was up in time to see someone come back out of the office, holding up a freshly-bandaged hand and wriggling her fingers to see if anything bled.

Yes, *her*. I could see that clearly, even in the faint glow of the streetlights through the windows. It's not hard to tell you're looking at a girl when she's naked.

I barely looked at her lovely spots, though. I was too busy staring at her face and dropping my jaw to somewhere around my ankles.

I was staring at Murelle Benson.

Oh boy. Time for brilliant, manly repartee.

"Uh, Murelle! You're—uh—"

"Smarter than you are," she told me with a smile. "Unless you manage to wipe away *all* your fingerprints, everywhere in this room, find any other moonglow notes Darrback has here, get out before anyone finds you—and still manage to catch up with me."

She turned away, giving me a smile and a wink that was a clear invitation over her shoulder. The last thing I saw was Frankenstein's notes bandage-taped to her other thigh.

Then she was gone, light and silent on her bare feet, out through the lab door into Northwood's darker depths whence she'd come.

Leaving me blinking at the dimness where she'd been, and wondering how in the world I'd ever catch up to Murelle Benson. Now, when I wanted to, more than I'd ever wanted anything in my life before.

Ed is an award-winning Canadian writer and game designer best known for creating the *Forgotten Realms*® fantasy world. He's also a New York Times bestselling author whose 140-plus books have sold millions of copies worldwide in more than thirty languages. Ed has also published more than seventy short stories (from SF and fantasy to horror, pulp adventure and mysteries), hundreds of magazine articles and columns, poetry, and scripts for comic books, radio plays and screenplays.

In real life, Ed is a well padded, white-bearded librarian often mistaken for Santa Claus. A Ryerson journalism grad, he was once hailed as "the Canadian author of the great American novel." When not working in a library, he shares an old farmhouse with his wife, a reigning cat, and more than 80,000 books.

Ed's most recent novels include *Falconfar* from Solaris Books and *Bury Elminster Deep!* from Wizards of the Coast.

Split Decision
by Robert Runté

So Mr. Shakey came over the intercom saying it was 2:03 and would all the teachers therefore stop whatever they were doing and please water the plants? As Mrs. Harness went for the door, Bethany-Anne reached over from her desk and peeked out under the shutters.

Mr. Shakey? Oh, sorry. Mr. Sheckley, the principal. But we call him "Mr. Shakey," because sometimes his judgment is kind of off. Like, that has to be the lamest code phrase ever. I mean, I ask you: if you're in the school intent on a killing rampage and you hear "drop everything and water the plants" over the PA, wouldn't you at least suspect that that means "go to lockdown?" Because you have to know a lockdown is the logical response to your being there with a rifle; whereas it makes no sense to interrupt class just to water the plants. And Mr. Shakey orders "plant watering" like every other day, because he is totally paranoid.

What? No, no; nobody had a rifle. I'm just saying it's lame, that's all. So Mr. Sheckley says about watering the plants, and right away Bethany-Anne sneaks the bottom of the shutters up—

What? No, the shutters were down already before the announcement, because Mrs. Harness had us doing this frog on the Smartboard. So, anyway, Bethany-Anne is leaning—

What? Okay, okay. Because our class gets the sun in the afternoon, and you can't see a thing on the Smartboard, even if you're right up front with the shutters up. We have one of the old-style boards, where the projector hangs down from the top? It's so old, it just totally washes out in direct sunlight. But Mrs. Harness says it will be like another three years before she can even *apply* for them to do an upgrade for our room, but we'll all be graduated by then, so just too bad for us, eh?

So they were down, right, because of the frog? The shutters, I mean. So Bethany-Anne, reaches over—

Frog. The dissection you have to do in Science 7? Gramps says in his day they did real frogs, which is just barbaric. I can't believe that was ever *legal*, let alone something you *had to do* in school. Where was the SPCA? Where was PETA when this was going on? Now you just do it on your slate. But why even *simulate* a dissection? Sure, somebody—some scientist dude—had to do that the first time once, to find out. But why would you want to keep *re*-doing it? If I want to know what's connected to which, I can just look it up.

But anyway, Mrs. Harness was showing us all on the Smartboard first, before our doing it individual on our slates, and the shutters are down, and Mr. Shakey comes over the PA. Clear?

So when Mrs. Harness goes for the door, Bethany-Anne reaches over and flips the shutters to see if she can see anybody skulking around outside, and right away she spots it.

Sorry? Well, mostly that's true. But the shutter on Bethany-Anne's row is missing the bottom slat, so if you kinda work your hand into the gap and twist the roller, you can get the bottom four or five slats to all rotate, and you can get a pretty good look outside. Of course, Mrs. Harness goes all freaky if she catches you at it, and you have to listen to her go on and on about how someone could get a shot in, but I mean, how realistic is that? That they would happen to be focused on that particular window the exact moment you happened to flip the slats? And then there is still the whole question of getting the shot through the opening. Because four or five slats is okay to see *out*, but you can't really see *in* from more than…I don't know…a couple of feet away, maybe. It could be done I guess, with a good scope, but it would have to be someone who knew what they were doing, deliberate, calm, and that's hardly ever what you're up against with your typical lockdown. I think Mrs. Harness is more worried we'll spot a flasher or something. Like we haven't all seen everything there is to see like a million times before on our slates. Last week, Justin forgot to close a window after break and left it running in the background, and when Mrs. Harness asked him to flip his math to the Smartboard, guess what popped up! I thought Mrs. Harness was going to blow an artery for sure that time. Though, you know,

I was kind of disappointed in Justin. Why do guys always want to watch that kind of stuff? I mean, we get like fifteen minutes for break, and instead of actually *talking* to one of the girls next to him he spends it watching something like—

Oh, right. Sorry. So anyway, Bethany-Anne makes this kind of a sound that is, you know, not quite a scream and not a choke exactly, but the kind of sound where you just *know* something is seriously up. So Todd pushes her aside and sticks *his* head to the glass, and he's just kind of glued there, even though Mrs. Harness is already half way back from the door and shouting at him to "get down this second." So the rest of us start crowding in, in the hopes of a quick glimpse before Mrs. Harness gets there, and the crowding slows her down quite a bit, so most of us are able to get an okay look at it, sitting right out there in the rink.

Then Mrs. Harness orders everyone to the far wall, and she starts tipping tables over and telling everyone to get into crash position behind their desks...only that is so obviously lame! It just makes no sense to me. It's like, well, if it's going to blow, what exactly do you expect a set of shutters and a couple of tipped over student desks to do about it? We looked pathetic. I didn't want people seeing me like that. Because by now half the kids have their cells out and are phoning EMS or their folks, and the other half are uploading video of the first half, who are cowering there like morons.

And we were already way beyond "locked door" as the appropriate response, here. Because if they've got interstellar travel down, a locked door is probably not going to deter them. So either we should all be moving out the opposite exit as fast as our feet could carry us, or we should just relax and go greet our new masters from Megnar 7 or wherever.

So I go over to the fire exit and start leaning on the crash bar. Casual, you know? Not making a production of it? Like I was just thinking maybe of leaning out for a quick look. But I had already figured it as pretty safe.

Well, no, I didn't mean "safe" exactly. Obviously, this was not a normal situation. I understand your point there. I'm just saying that if something were going to explode, it probably would have done that already when it came down. But none us had even heard a thing. And I know for sure I had my earbuds out when it must have come down. Because it certainly hadn't been there at break, and I hadn't exactly been in a hurry to tune into Mrs. Harness putting that poor frog down—simulated or not—so my ears were still naked right up to Mr. Sheckley's announcement. I definitely would have heard *something* if that had been a crash out there. So if there wasn't a crash, then no "kaboom", right?

Oh. I didn't know that. Well, I'm just telling you what I was thinking at the time. Just let me finish here or I'm going to get all jumbled up. So I'm saying, I didn't think we were in any danger from the *ship* aspect of it. I mean, it pretty much looked like it had landed there in one piece as intended.

But on the other hand, if I were flying around the galaxy and I wanted to put down on Earth, the hockey rink of Allan Wilson Middle School would not necessarily be my first choice, you know? So either it was some kind of mistake, or accident, or emergency landing kind of deal, or this was part of like a much larger fleet, and they were landing everywhere with so many ships that there was even one to spare for Prairie Creek. And if that were the case—well, like I said, time to meet our new masters, and here's hoping they aren't into eating our brains.

But I figured, you have interstellar flight, you probably have to be like some kind of way advanced civilization, and that probably implies a certain level of vegetarianism when it comes to intelligent species. Assuming that we qualify.

So, I figured probably they were having some kind of problem, and the polite thing—the civilized thing to do—would be for someone to go and ask, you know, if they needed anything.

So I am starting to lean on the crash bar a little harder, when I hear this clop, clop, clop coming up fast behind me, which I know to be Sarah's clogs without having to turn around, so I wait a second for her to get there and she whispers, "What are you doing?"; only, you know, her tone is more like, "What, *are you crazy*?!" And so I say, "I figure they're probably not here to eat our brains," and she says, "Well, duh. But what about radiation?"

So I ease up on the crash bar again, because this thought has given me pause. This is precisely why Sarah is my best friend. Because more than once she has thought of something that I have maybe missed. "An advanced civilization," I said, working it through with her, but still whispering so as not to attract Mrs. Harness's attention, "would probably include safety regulations. With regard to acceptable levels of radiation."

"Well, yeah," Sara whispers back, "but the number one safety rule would be, 'no landing on Earth' and the second rule would be, 'no landing in school hockey rinks.' So probably something went wrong, already."

I see her point. So I ask, "Okay, maybe radiation. What then?"

And she says, "Shielding or distance. Assuming always we haven't already taken a fatal dose."

I look over at everybody still huddled behind their desks and kind of nod in that direction and ask, "Any good?"

"Maybe if we covered the desks in layers of aluminum foil from the cafeteria," Sarah tells me, "but wood is useless."

"Distance?" I ask her.

"Levels decrease with the square of the distance."

"My basement?"

She nodded. "We could still see okay from there, but would be nearly three times further away. Radiation would be only a tenth whatever it is here. And cement is good."

Well, I don't know; they never said. I'm just telling you what Sarah told me.

So then I looked over to where Mrs. Harness was still under her desk, and there was no way she was going to unlock the door to the hallway. Mrs. Harness is not a half-bad teacher, but she is not one for taking initiative. She sticks pretty much to the curriculum, whether simulated dissections make sense or not. So if Mr. Sheckley had called for a lockdown, we were going to stay locked in until the "all-clear."

"Okay," I said, "we make a run for my house," and slammed my elbow into the crash bar. I saw Mrs. Harness bang her head when the exit alarm went off, but we were out and pelting along the side of the school before she could even crawl out from under her desk. I was pretty much just focused on making it around the corner of the school and could hear the clacking of Sarah's clogs keeping up with me, so I didn't look back at all, and I didn't immediately recognize that the grinding sound was the saucer splitting open, and so neither of us saw the ramp coming out of it until it was nearly on top of us.

So I hit the brakes and pull back, but Sarah plows into me and kind of knocks me, and I'm on the ramp, teetering, and Sarah's all, "What are you *doing*?!" and I'm looking back at her in disbelief because it's not *my* fault I'm on the ramp, *she's* the one who knocked me, but then it penetrates that they've opened up and I'm thinking, "Wait!" and I point at the ramp and say, "No radiation!" and Sarah's looking at me, and I explain that they wouldn't open up if there was a radiation leak or whatever, and Sarah's all, "You don't know that! Maybe they're just not affected by it!" But I figure, they're kind of inviting us in, and that wouldn't make sense if the radiation was going to kill us, so it's gotta be okay.

I look back at the school, and I notice the shutters are like a quarter of the way up in Ms. Rossiter's class, and there are like forty arms sticking cells out the bottom, filming me and Sarah, waiting to see what we do. Or whether something comes out with a death ray or whatever. So I take like maybe half a step up the ramp, when Sarah shouts, "Viruses!" and I pause again, but just for a second this time, because I remember Mrs. Harness telling us how our dogs don't catch our colds and vice versa, and dogs are practically family compared to whatever is in *there*, so I just shake my head and say, "I doubt we're that compatible," and keep going. And Sarah does this exasperated little stomp with her clogs and says, "You don't know that!" So I stop, because she's not wrong. But I tell her, "They've got the ship, so I'm guessing they're brainy enough to have thought it all through." Only she says, "You can't know that!" again. And she's right of course, but I just kind of shrug, because, hey, you can never *know*. Not completely, right?

So we're standing, looking at each other, and Sarah says, kind of quiet, "You can't go in there. It would be crazy." Then I just say, "I have a plan," and start going up the ramp again. So Sarah runs after me with her clogs clanging on the ramp and catches up and asks, "What's the plan?" And I explain, "I'm not going in. I'm stopping half-way up. That way, they'll have to come out and we'll meet half-way." And Sarah says, "That's your plan?" and I say, "Yes," and she says, "That's it? That's not a plan!" And I say, "No, this will work. Because it shows we're willing, and because, you know, meeting half-way is what you do!" And Sarah shouts, "What do you mean, 'That's what you do?' What you *do* is call out the Army and the Air Force!" And I have to stop and give Sarah "The Look" because, come on! She's been here for like her whole life, almost. "Sarah! That's maybe how Americans do it, or maybe your dad when he was an Air Force Captain back in the Bangladesh, but for crying out loud, you're as Canadian as me. Meeting 'half-way' is how Canadians do it!" And then Sarah gives *me* "The Look" back and says, "You're the one who told me Canadians don't change the light bulb, they wait for the government to do it." And I wave my arm at the school where all the teachers are hunkered down and say, "Do you see the government anywhere? Look, if they (I'm pointing up the ramp here)—if they wanted the Army and Air Force and diplomats and world leaders, they would have landed in front of the White House; if they land in back of Allan Wilson Middle School, it's because they just want to do some repairs maybe, or get directions or whatever, but the appropriate response is to be neighborly and offer to help them out without making a huge deal out of it!"

So then I noticed Sarah isn't saying anything and is looking kind of stressed, so I say, "Sarah?" Because now I'm thinking I was maybe out of line implying she wasn't being Canadian enough. Because she can be sensitive about that: like the time Drew said he thought she looked like "a foreign princess" in her blue sari with the diamonds; he just meant she looked exotic, but things never come out quite right when Drew says them, and Sarah had been totally slammed he'd said "foreign." But it wasn't about that this time. She looks at me and says, "So the plan is we only go half-way up, right?" And I say, "That's the plan," and Sarah says, "and we stopped about a third of the way up to have this little chat, right?" And right away I get it, because we're already way past the half-way mark and getting closer to the top every second, even though we've stopped walking, so I just grab her arm and yell, "Run!" and we take off for the bottom of the ramp.

The one thing Sarah and I hate most about school is the Ding Test. You know the one? Where this bell goes "ding" and you have to keep running as many laps as you can before the next "ding." It's so stupid and demeaning. With Sarah's lungs and my ankles, it's just torture. And what's it for, exactly? When do you ever need to run like that and keep running until you actually fall down from exhaustion?

That's what I was thinking as we ran for it and kept running and running as hard as we could, but didn't seem to be making any progress toward the bottom. But instead of a "ding," there was this sort of collective groan from the school windows as Sarah started to flag.

Then the fire exit to Mrs. Harness's room crashes open, and Justin and Drew come pounding out. Todd came out too, but just far enough to grab the door and drag it closed again. I didn't know what they were doing at first and wanted to warn them away, but I didn't have the breath or the nerve to stop running; and frankly, if they were stupid enough to come *out* when they saw us coming *back*, that was their own look out.

But after a second, I realized they were headed for the ramp and for us.

Say what you want, but those guys can *run*. They hit the ramp in a blur and were racing up to meet us fast, faster than any relay race I've ever seen them do, and I was worried for a second that they were going to crash right into us as we were trying to get away—only that never happened. Sarah and I kept running down at best speed, and they were racing up—I mean, really sprinting it!—but somehow the distance between us didn't shrink at all. On the contrary, space started to slowly expand, stretching out between us, until it became obvious that we were never going to reach each other.

Justin must have seen it too, because he started undoing his belt; he almost stumbled yanking it out while still running, head down and coming on like a fullback, and then he flung it at me. I kinda ducked at first, but on his second throw I got what he was doing and I grabbed for it. I caught it on the third throw, by sort of lunging at it like in volleyball, and then I was tumbling past Justin, and Justin was shooting past me up the ramp.

I was still holding the belt with Justin on the other end, so I kind of pivoted to get myself up and standing again, dug in my heels and yanked him back toward me, now that I was closer to the bottom of the ramp than he was; he spun around and crashed into Sarah and Drew, who were both behind me, which left me disoriented because Sarah had been higher up the ramp and Drew lower, so I couldn't figure out how any of that was happening. Then I saw that we were, all of us, very nearly at the top and moving inside, but before I could shout a warning, Justin was pulling me with the belt toward the edge, and shouting, "Jump!"

But it's way too late, and next thing we know, we're all inside.

Justin and I jumping? Yeah, we saw that too. Which was pretty weird for us, but we were already inside by then, so we were kind of preoccupied with that. It was only later that they explained it was just the 4% of us that reacted fast enough that had jumped. But I remember thinking at the time, *man, that must have hurt!* Because we were pretty high up by then, I'm telling you!

So anyway, we're inside and right away it's just like that movie—the original, I mean, not the remake—because everything is this kind of gloomy black and white, and it's kind of hard to make anything out, and I'm like half expecting Gort to step out of the shadows but of course, it wasn't like that at all once we got the goggles.

Sure they gave us goggles. Why wouldn't they? Because, as I'm trying to explain, everything is virtual with them, so without the colors, it's just blank walls. Nothing to see at all. Like trying to watch TV with the picture off. You've got to have the goggles.

To see the colors. Because our eyes don't see in the same range, and the goggles adjust for that.

I'm not sure, exactly. Early that first day, sometime. Within a couple of hours, I guess. Because things only started to make sense once we got the goggles and could see what's going on.

Well, that's a lot harder to judge. I mean, it's not like they had a big clock anywhere. Oh, and our watches didn't work. Sarah and Drew both had watches on, but they were both frozen at 2:19. The watches, I mean, not Sarah and Drew. Same with Justin and my cells. And you can't phone out, though I guess that's obvious. So, I'd have to guess a couple of days. Four, maybe. Though now you come to say it, it's funny, because we never got hungry or had to sleep or anything.

Yeah, yeah! That's it! That's exactly what *they* said: "Subjectivity of time". Something about how you "can't master faster than light travel without first mastering the subjectivity of time". I don't pretend to get all that; Sarah's the science geek.

Well, no, not "said." I know I said "said," but mostly it was writing. On the walls. Texting, you know? Sarah says she thinks they're deaf because they never tried talking to us, so maybe they don't use sound that way? But then *I* said they must be blind too, because they never used pictures either, but Drew said that was really stupid. Anyway, it became obvious pretty early on that they were asking if we wanted to go with them. Like be exchange students. And from the second they said it, I was beside myself with indecision. Because part of me really, *really* wanted to. I mean, you know, the whole "boldly go where none have gone before" thing, right? That's pretty wild! But of course, another part of me wanted to stay right here. Keep my regular life. Go for the theater, instead. Because Mr. Bartain says I have a real shot. A *real* shot. And I've worked hard for that. And I'd miss Kasia, my little sister. And my folks.

But then I'd think, I would not miss Allan Wilson Middle School. Okay, Mr. Bartain, maybe. But seriously, I've got what, another year of middle school and another three of high school and then who knows how many of university? I think my dad lived his whole life practically before he finally graduated. I wouldn't have to do any of that. I could start my life *now*; I could leave with them *now*, and have the adventure of a lifetime, of a hundred lifetimes!

But then I'd realize I didn't have Bear-Bear and Socks with me, and how could I stand to leave them behind? And it would like, *kill* Mom. Dad would get it, sort of: me leaving in a saucer would be cool for him. But he'd probably say that out loud, and then Mom would kill *him!*

I wasn't even clear if we got to say "goodbye" or anything, because when they tried to explain that bit, it wasn't very clear at first. I couldn't imagine what my folks would think, what my little sister would think, if they saw me get in the saucer and the saucer took off, and then not knowing if I was okay. I couldn't do that to them. But then, they said that wouldn't be an issue, and I shouldn't worry about that when I made my final decision, so then I'd flip again.

I kept going back and forth, and every time I did, I'd end up arguing with myself, again. That part was definitely weird. Though also strangely reassuring. You really get to know yourself, to understand what it is you *really* want when you have to work through a decision like that. A life-changing decision.

I think Sarah got it faster than the rest of us. What it would really mean. Because her folks had to make that decision coming to Canada.

And then there was the whole Justin thing. A lot of Justin really wanted to go, but only if I would go with him. That really kind of freaked me. Because, I had just never thought of Justin that way before. So at some point we noticed we were talking about Justin almost as much as about the decision, and I said, "Look, Justin is not the question. Justin stays or goes, but either way, he's going to *be there* so we can worry about that another time; there will be lots of opportunities to sort out how I feel about Justin later. The only question is—what do *I* want to do." I have to say, I was a little proud of myself for saying that, because I could hear my mom always telling me, you should never make a decision based just on what some boy wants. And this was a perfect example of that. So I dug around and found some receipts in my jacket pocket, and a pen, and used the scraps to write down my decision, and I told Justin to write down his, and the others, so that we all made our own decision without worrying about what the others were planning. And that made it a bit scarier, not knowing if anyone was coming with you, or if you stayed behind, whether they would all go off on an adventure without you. But that was the only way to be sure it was our own, independent choice.

Of course, as I sat down to write my answer, I probably flipped flopped a thousand times again. But in the end, I had something written on the paper, and I put it down on the floor in front of me, and the others had too. And then we all sat there for a minute, all of us, thinking about what we had done. And then they said it was time to go, so we all went our separate ways.

And here I am.

I got the impression they were really pleased with the way things turned out, too. That we had all made such thoughtful, deliberate decisions. And of course, because all four of us were so ambivalent about it all, it ties up all the loose ends for them pretty neatly, too!

Sorry? What? Oh, I just meant, that it doesn't look like "Alien Abduction" if the people who go in come out again. Because if we had all chosen to go, like unanimous, then I guess they'd have some explaining to do! Though I gather, that doesn't come up very often.

Sorry? What don't you...? Because a lot of me wanted to go, of course. I was pretty evenly divided on this one. Almost completely down the middle. They told me in the end about 49% went and 51% stayed. With Justin, it was closer to 90/10. I mean, 90% wanting to go. What do you suppose that says about Justin? Do you think that means he's terribly unhappy with his life here? Because that could be a problem if...you know, something were to happen with Justin and me. Or does it just mean he's into adventure? That could be okay.

Sarah came out about 40% going and 60% staying. She told me that after all her parents went through to get her here, she would have felt bad choosing somewhere else; though, of course, the ones that went felt differently. I shouldn't say this, but I think some of them chose to go because I did. Sarah and me make a pretty good team. I can't even guess where Drew comes into it with Sarah, though. For or against, I couldn't begin to tell you.

What are you talking about? No, that's not it at all. Look, you're completely missing it. Let me start again. Every time you make a decision, every time you choose to open the door or not to, the universe splits: in one continuum you opened the door, in the other you didn't. They explained it to us just like that. So, normally, you're just you and you opened the door and go through; or you're the you that didn't, but you still just go on with your life from that point, maybe wondering, maybe not, what your life would have been had you made the other choice. Right? Every decision is like that. Every one.

But what if you were in a place where you could see the split coming? What if every time you had a choice, you had the chance to see both continuums stretching out in front of you, the door open and the door closed, and both of you poised to make the choice? And you could talk to the other you, and debate which was the right choice, discuss the pros and cons? Maybe, switch sides. Choose the other option instead, this time.

But then, as the other you makes a point, part of you decides to go with that option, and part of you sticks with your original choice—so you split again, between the you that was convinced to change, and the one that wasn't. And then there's a friend with you, who offers to go with you if you choose the first option, and you're torn, so suddenly there's two more of you. Except by now your friend is having second thoughts, so there are two of him, and so part of you wonders if your friend will see it through, so you split again. And, well, you see how it works. Pretty soon, there are an awful lot of yous sitting around debating, and some of you wander off topic and start talking about Justin. But in the end, you have to make your decision. And some of you go through the door, and some of you don't.

Some of us—some of me—went with the saucer, and some of us didn't. So they get the exchange students they wanted, and Mom and Dad and Kasia get me back safe and sound. Everybody wins.

Nope. No regrets. None at all. What's to regret? That's the real beauty of it all. Because, of course, that part of me that would have regretted not going, went.

Robert Runté is an Associate Professor in the Faculty of Education at the University of Lethbridge and an editor with *Five River Books*. As an academic, editor, reviewer, and organizer, Robert has been actively promoting Canadian SF for over thirty years. He was a founding Director of NonCon, Context89, and SF Canada, and has served on the Boards of the ESFCAS, *On Spec Magazine, Tesseract Books,* and The Writers Guild of Alberta. In addition to dozens of conference papers, journal articles, book chapters, and a half dozen entries in the *Encyclopedia of Literature in Canada*, Robert has edited over 150 issues of various SF newsletters. In 1996, he co-edited (with Yves Maynard) the *Tesseracts⁵* anthology.

Hide
by Rebecca M. Senese

Billy skidded to a stop beside her. She smelled sweat and Doublemint gum as he opened his mouth.

"The opening to Maple Crescent. After dinner. Be there."

Then he was gone, running away from her, his untucked blue striped shirt flapping in the breeze.

Pauline's heart pounded. They'd invited her! How long had it taken to get that invitation? Weeks of sucking up to twerpy Annie Burton at lunch. Swiping extra chocolate bars from home so she could use them as bribery. Smiling and laughing at Annie's stupid jokes, trying not to be sick as the older girl chewed with her mouth open, exposing gobs of melting chocolate goo in her yellow teeth.

But it had all been worth it! She was invited to the best hide and seek game in the school. Pauline wanted to dance down the sidewalk home but didn't; she kept her steps even and measured. She couldn't look too excited to be invited to the game. That wouldn't be cool.

At dinner, she ate all her vegetables, even the brussels sprouts, in record time. Thankfully no one noticed. Her father was too intent on the paper and her mother was arguing with her younger brother, Jason, who was fussing over his food. He kept pushing the offending brussels sprouts to the edge of his plate, balanced precariously. A glare from Mother would cause a grumble, and he'd pull them back onto the plate for a moment then push them back to the edge. Pauline sighed. He hadn't even figured out how to hide them properly; what kind of a brother was that? She was cursed.

She set her knife and fork down beside her plate. Only a trace of mashed potatoes remained.

"Mom, can I go outside?" she said.

"Once you clean your plate," her mother said without looking.

"I have."

Her mother glanced over, blinking as if she was just waking up. "Oh. All right, then. Put your plate in the sink."

Pauline scrambled from the table, dumped the plate and cutlery in the sink and was out the door before her mother could change her mind.

The early evening was crisp with the scent of cut grass. Pauline's runners thumped hard on the asphalt as she ran toward Maple Crescent. Three blocks down and four streets over. She raced past identical houses with similar lawns cluttered with bikes and children's toys. The sun had shifted since her walk home and she felt like she was chasing her long shadow. Maybe they would even be playing the hide and seek game until dark! The pounding of her heart was not only from running.

She passed a cluster of bushes and emerged at the entrance to Maple Crescent. New houses lined one side of the street; partially constructed shells lined the other. Fresh sawdust on the breeze tickled her nostrils. The front of the second unfinished house was covered with a plastic tarp that had come loose and flapped with a sharp snap in the wind. It looked like a tortured flag.

"You're early."

She turned to see Teddy Williams slouching on the sidewalk. He frowned at her, beefy hands fumbled with a silver yoyo that he stuffed into his back pocket.

"Billy told me after dinner," Pauline said. "I finished dinner."

Teddy kept frowning, shifting on his off-white runners. Behind him, Pauline could see a couple of other kids approaching. Yes, it was Ravi and his brother Jamil, both short with light brown skin. Pauline noticed Bridget and Sandra, cutting across from another street. Bridget had bright red hair cut short which only seemed to accent her height. Sandra, one year older, stood three inches shorter with blonde hair past her shoulders. A gold barrette clipped her hair neatly to the back of her neck.

Pauline turned back to Teddy and raised her eyebrows. He muttered under his breath and shifted again.

Ravi joined them first. "Where's Billy? He late again?"

"Don't know," Teddy said. "Ask her. She was here early."

Bridget and Sandra were within earshot. Pauline felt everyone looking at her. Her face grew hot. Oh no, she couldn't stammer and look stupid. She'd never get another chance!

She shrugged in a way she hoped seemed casual. "I haven't seen him."

For a moment, all the gazes fixed on her, then the kids looked away. Pauline let her breath out. That had been close.

Over the next several minutes, kids drifted in from all directions except from the new houses on Maple Crescent. Pauline glanced back at them. Why did the kids meet here?

Finally the last of the kids trickled up until there was about twenty of them, but still no sign of Billy. Ravi and Jamil consulted with several of the other kids, then called for attention.

"Billy's not here, so we'll just start." Jamil clapped his hands. "Now we got a new player today." He pointed at Pauline.

Pauline froze. Again she felt their gaze, this time magnified twenty times. Her cheeks burned. She hated blushing, but there wasn't any way she could stop it. She forced her mouth to move, cracking her cheeks as her lips tried to curve into a smile. Her hand lifted in a limp wave.

"The rules are this—everyone hides and you have to find them. The first one you find has to help you find another one, the next one you find helps you find the one after that. And it keeps going. Nobody hides together and kids can change their hiding place. We go until an hour after dark."

Pauline sucked in a breath. They played until after dark? She hadn't known that.

Jamil's expression hardened. "You got a problem? You have to go home early, like a baby?"

Pauline clenched her teeth. "No. I don't gotta go home."

Jamil's black eyes glared and then he relaxed. "Good. We'll get started. You count to a hundred and then get started."

"Wait, don't we have to figure who's it?" Pauline said.

"You're it. You're new. New one is always it first game. That's the rules."

Other kids around her nodded, muttering "the rules." Pauline tried to find a sympathetic face but they were all closed to her. She sighed.

"Okay."

Jamil led her to a telephone pole and watched as she faced it, covering her eyes.

"No peeking," his voice hissed in her ear. "Count out loud."

"One, two, three," Pauline counted off. Over the sound of her voice, she heard the shuffle of running shoes on pavement as the kids scattered. She kept counting and soon the sounds faded, leaving just the rustle of the leaves in the evening breeze. She passed forty and kept counting. Would they know if she didn't count all the way to one hundred? She didn't want to take the chance. Probably they had figured out how long it took and they'd never let her play again if she stopped early. She kept counting.

"Ninety-eight, ninety-nine, one hundred." She stepped back from the telephone pole and blinked. Even the fading light seemed brighter now. Her eyes watered. She rubbed them, then turned to look around. Not a sign of any of the kids. It was as if they'd never even been there. A thrill ran through her. She was in the game now. Time to get started.

Her gaze settled on the unfinished houses. Surely, several of the kids were hiding there. Who could resist that? She moved forward. The plastic tarp on the second house snapped in the breeze. She breathed in the scent of freshly cut wood. Clean wood beams peeked out from under the tarp. The sidewalk ended and she was walking on uneven ground, gravel rustling under her feet. She studied the ground. No footprints. The dirt hid any trace of the kids.

Would any of them hide in the house with the flapping tarp? She couldn't imagine hiding there, listening to the plastic snap and crackle. It even drowned out her footsteps as she moved forward. Anyone hiding there wouldn't hear her coming. Still, she had to look, just in case. If she didn't she might miss someone.

She circled around the tarp and found an opening at the side of the house. The inside was just the ground floor with wood beams marking where the walls would go. She could see clear through to the back of the house. Nothing, only dust that made her nose itch. She rubbed it with the back of her hand and retreated.

Pauline headed for the next house. Had she made a mistake looking here? Surely a couple of the kids had hidden in these houses. How could anyone resist? Wasn't that why they met at Maple Crescent, to take advantage of the construction? Sure it was. She nodded to herself. She'd find somebody soon.

The next house didn't have a porch, so she circled around the back. Holes in the walls marked the windows and the back door. Pauline walked in.

Orange sunlight glowed through the rooms. Pauline breathed shallowly as she inched along. Her feet stirred the dust on the floor.

Ahead of her, the dust had already been disturbed. Her heartbeat quickened. Someone else was here! She was going to find them!

She crept forward, following the disturbance. It rounded a corner. She stopped at the edge, listening. Tree branches creaked in the breeze. The plastic tarp from the house several doors down still snapped but it was less like a gunshot and more like a finger snap. Inside, the house was only stillness, a hush as if the house was holding its breath. Was it hiding one of the kids? She would have to turn that corner to find out.

Pauline hunched down to peer from closer to the floor. The kid wouldn't spot her then. For a moment, she hesitated. Her mom would kill her if she got these new salmon-colored pants dirty but wasn't that what pants were for? Dust puffed up as she knelt down. Hands resting on her thighs, she leaned forward and peered around the corner.

A hallway led to the right. Stairs at the far end led to the second floor. A thrill ran through her. The trail led toward the stairs.

Pauline stood up and crept forward. Her runners stirred the dust. It itched at her nose. A cough welled up in her throat. She pursed her lips and blew air out through them. The urge to cough stopped.

She crept up the few stairs then stopped, listening for any creaking. Nothing. She continued climbing. Silence followed her to the top. Plain wooden planks covered the unfinished floor. It had a precarious look that made her nervous but the trail led off around another corner to the left. Someone was definitely here and she could catch them. She couldn't back out now. She'd never live it down. It would get around the school before lunch the next day. She'd have to switch schools, maybe leave town!

She swallowed and rubbed her sweating hands on her pants. Her legs trembled with excitement. Time to find the kid who was hiding here. She followed the trail, moving carefully to avoid raising more dust and alerting the kid. Outside, the plastic tarp snapped in the distance as if urging her to hurry. Was there another way down to the first floor? Maybe that kid was already getting away.

Her heartbeat quickened. She had to find someone, then they had to help her find others. She had to show all of them she was worthy of playing their game. She hurried forward and peered around the corner into an empty room with a pile of debris in the corner. She saw the hole where the closet would be. She started to move away, then stopped. The trail ended. Either the kid had learned to fly over the dust or...

Pauline turned back to the room. The shell of the closet was empty, gaping like a shallow mouth. She studied the debris, a mix of wood, slabs of drywall and wire. She stomped forward, kicking up as much dust as possible in front of her. She reached the debris pile, leaned down and scooped up a pile of dust then blew it toward the debris pile.

Nothing happened. Dust tickled her nose. She pinched her nostrils, stifling the cough that threatened to explode out of her. The cloud of dust hung in the air then drifted down, layering the debris. Anybody would be coughing like crazy by now. Could she have been wrong?

Somebody had to be hiding here. There was no other place in the house to hide. A length of wood stuck out of the bottom. She grabbed it with both hands and gave it a tug. Broken brick, pieces of fabric and wood collapsed. Pauline dropped the wood and covered her mouth and nose with her hands. Her eyes squeezed shut against the cloud of dirt. After a moment she opened her eyes.

Dust coated her hands like fine gloves. Grit scraped along her back, between her T-shirt and her skin. Her new pants were smeared with dirt. Oh, Mom was going to kill her!

And it hadn't even been worth it, she realized. No one hid under the debris pile. How could that be, she wondered. She'd been so sure. The trail had been unmistakable.

A silver glint caught her gaze—something near the edge of the debris. She stepped forward and bent down. A yoyo. Teddy's yoyo. He had been here and faked her out. Her fingers closed around it. It felt wet and the string was frayed, snapped. Probably how he lost it as he'd made the marks and taken off. She looked at her fingers. Dirt smeared the wetness into reddish brown. Strange.

She couldn't see his retreating tracks but he had to be fooling her. Pauline nodded to herself and pushed a strand of brown hair off her forehead. She understood, now. She wiped the reddish wetness on the side of her pants and left.

She searched through three more houses without finding anyone. In one of the houses she found a gold barrette with a broken clasp. Bits of red hair were caught in the tiny screw. It looked familiar—had Bridget been wearing it? She couldn't remember. She left it behind.

Several times she thought she saw traces of someone hiding, a trail of footsteps or even sections of debris moved around, but no kids. Could they all hear her coming and escape before she got there? Maybe one or two of them could do it without her knowing, but all of them? Wouldn't she have heard somebody? She tried to swallow but her mouth was suddenly dry.

Sunlight streaked orange across the sky. Pauline watched it sink below the line of houses in the distance. They played for an hour after dark. How could she be able to find anyone by then? Her cheeks flushed with heat. How embarrassing that she couldn't even find one kid.

So far she'd stayed on one side of the street. Time to vary the routine. She hurried across and searched through four houses. Nothing. How could this be? The sun was slipping away. She had to find someone.

She ran to the next house. It had a real front door and intact windows. She slipped inside and closed the door. Darkness enveloped her. After a moment, her eyes adjusted. The living room entrance stood on her right. She peered in but the room was empty. She headed toward the upstairs. Better check the second floor. She didn't want some kid slipping back down the stairs and out the front door before she found them.

Under her foot, the third stair creaked. She froze. Her breath caught in her lungs. Her hand gripped the railing, grittiness scraped her flesh. No sound. Maybe it had been just a little creak, not enough for anyone else to hear. She crept up the stairs.

At the top, she found a trail in the dust. Someone was hiding up here! Her heart pounded. She rubbed her hands on her pants, trying to dry them of the sudden sweat that beaded on them but she only succeeded in smearing the dirt into the fabric. Oh man, her mom. Could she make Pauline get any deader than dead?

Pauline followed the trail to the back. One of the smaller bedroom doors stood ajar. She flattened herself to the wall and crept forward. Light from the window leaked into the hallway, but not enough to illuminate her. She held her breath, not daring to make a sound. Her feet inched along, silent as she moved. The door was a hand's width away. She couldn't see anything through the crack. She took a breath then lifted her hand to the door and pushed!

The door swung wide. She jumped through the doorway.

"Ha!" she yelled.

The room was empty. They hadn't even put the windows in up here. Pauline's shoulders slumped in disappointment. Another dead end. She started to turn back. Her gaze fell on the open closet.

Something lay at the bottom of the closet. It looked like a piece of fabric. Pauline crouched down for a closer look.

A torn pocket, she thought. She lifted the fabric and a small kid's flashlight rolled across the floor. It stopped against her knee. A Sammy the Shaggy Dog light. They came with different filters that made shadow shapes when you slid them over the end of the light. She turned it over in her hand. The casing looked cracked and dented. She tried the button but the light stayed stubbornly off. She shook it and heard a rattle inside. Had it broken? She tightened the bottom. Dim light sprang out, illuminating the dust floating in the air.

Now she noticed the fabric was soggy, as if dunked in water. She turned the light on it. Reddish smears streaked her palm. She dropped the fabric pocket. Her heart pounded in her chest. She rubbed her palm on her pants. Hadn't the yoyo she'd found been wet, too?

Somebody had been here and dropped the flashlight, but where were they now? What had happened? Nobody would just leave it here for her to find. She swung the light beam around then noticed something funny about the window frame.

Floating dust finally made her sneeze as she struggled to her feet. She walked over to the window and shone the light on the ledge.

Shards of glass stuck up from the ledge like baby teeth. Pauline traced the frame with the light and saw other pieces of glass sticking out. On the right by the top, part of the frame bent inward. She could see where the wood had splintered. Along the bottom, the reddish liquid streaked down the plaster into a small puddle on the floor.

Her fingers whitened around the flashlight. She backed away from the window and almost yelped when her back touched the door.

The flashlight wove crazy patterns along the wall as she ran down the stairs. She burst past the front door and skidded to a stop in the middle of the street. Her heart thudded in her chest like a big man hammering on a door. She felt as if a dozen pairs of eyes were watching her, but when she spun around to look, nothing but empty windows faced her. The sky above her darkened as the sun dipped behind the trees in the distance. Soon it would be completely dark. What would she do then?

Now she wanted to go home. She didn't care about the humiliation, didn't care if her mom would kill her for the stains on her new pants. The light from the flashlight jerked back and forth across the asphalt. She tightened her grip to stop the trembling in her hand. Yes, time to go home.

She retreated back along the streets. The unfinished houses weren't interesting and exciting anymore; they were creepy and sinister. Their very emptiness hid things from her and she no longer wanted to find anything inside them.

As she neared the end of the construction zone, she drew level to the house with the tarp. The wind picked up, pushing at her back and tossing her brown hair in a cloud around her face. The tarp lifted, higher than before, exposing the floor marked with wood beams. Something white glimmered inside, a figure. Was it one of the kids?

Pauline stopped walking and pushed her hair from her face. The tarp floated down, covering the view. The edges ruffled, scrapping across the ground as if calling her forward.

What should she do? She still wanted to go home, could still feel her heart beating rapidly in her chest like a staccato drum beat. But if that was one of the kids and she just walked away, she'd never hear the end of it. She bit her lip, nibbling a loose piece of skin. The sharp edge of the flashlight pinched her palm.

She shuffled forward. The tarp rustled. How long would it take for her to look? Only a few moments. The entire floor was wide open, she could see all the way through. All she needed was to peek under the tarp, see if anybody was there and then go home.

That she could do. Her steps quickened with her resolve. The faster she looked, the sooner she could run home.

The tarp was grimy when she touched it or maybe it was her hand sweating. She lifted the tarp and slipped underneath. As it swung back down behind her, she realized that shadows hid the interior. She could only see a few feet in front of her. She flicked on the flashlight. Its feeble beam only extended her view a few more feet. She would have to walk around the entire floor to see if anyone was there.

Her feet inched forward. She remembered seeing the wood beams marking out the walls. She would have to be careful not to walk into any of them or get tripped up. She didn't want to twist her ankle.

Her feet kicked up small clouds of dust as she moved forward. The dust danced in the beam of her flashlight. She moved deeper toward the back of the house. Still no sign of the white figure. Had she really seen someone?

A noise came from the back of a house. Someone moving, disturbing dust or debris. Her hand tightened on the flashlight. Now the pounding of her heart was also from excitement. Maybe if she found one of the kids her humiliation wouldn't be so complete.

She picked her feet up, trying to move faster and quieter. Her shoulder bumped a wood beam, unsettling dust that rained down on her. Her throat constricted as she tried to hold back a cough. Another few steps, then she couldn't stop herself. She coughed.

The sound floated away in the darkness. She held her hand to her mouth, tasting dirt. Suddenly the darkness seemed heavier, more sinister. Maybe this had been a mistake. No kid was hiding back here. Maybe she'd find some sicko. Wrecking her new pants didn't seem quite so bad any more.

She started to back away. The flashlight beam swung crazily in front of her. She caught a glimpse of something white lying on the floor. It jumped and jerked away. She heard a soft, high-pitched squeal. That didn't sound like a sicko.

Pauline couldn't help herself, she had to know. She swung the flashlight back to the area where the white had appeared and headed toward it. Nothing for a moment, then she caught another glimpse. The tip of something, like a rat tail. It didn't move. She aimed the flashlight off to the side, just enough that she could still see it in the soft glow.

She took a breath, felt the dust tickle her nose, then jumped forward. One foot stomped on the white tail-thing. It squirmed under her foot. Something squealed, this time loud and long. She aimed the flashlight along the tail then almost dropped it.

The body rose out of a hole in the floor. A multiple of white tentacles wrapped around it so she couldn't see the definite shape. In the middle, a slit appeared and the edges of pinkish white flesh pulled back. A watery, pale blue eye blinked at her.

Pauline shuddered. The flashlight shook in her hand. The jerking beam fell across scraps of clothing and discarded running shoes. Blood smeared across the white tentacles. As they wrapped around itself, she saw bones sticking out from the crevices. She recognized Brenda's tank top, Ravi's jacket, Billy's shirt. Now it would never get tucked in.

A squeak immerged from her parched throat. She watched as the tentacles waved closer. Her heart hammered in her chest. It was going to kill her! She ground her foot down on the tentacle.

Another shriek, this time louder. The tentacles withdrew, wrapping around the body. The eye blinked at her.

Pauline wiped sweat from her forehead. In that blinking eye, she thought she saw something. Annoyance? How did she know? The feeling seemed to rise up in her, and she realized it was coming from the thing in front of her. It was upset. Why?

She'd *found* it! When it hid so well.

The eye closed. The tentacles began to tap a rhythm on the dusty floor. Pauline stepped off the tentacle and backed away. She stared at the scraps of fabric dotting the creature. As it tapped, a piece of Sandra's blond hair dislodged and fluttered to the floor. The tentacle kept tapping.

What was it doing?

It tapped again. One-two-three...

Her heart thudded. It was counting. Counting to a hundred!

Her throat clenched. When it reached a hundred that eye would open and it would start seeking her. She had to hide.

Pauline dropped the flashlight and began to run.

Based in Toronto, Canada, **Rebecca M. Senese** writes horror, mystery, and science fiction, often all at once in the same story. She garnered an Honorable Mention in "The Year's Best Science Fiction" and has been nominated for numerous Aurora Awards. Her work has appeared in *TransVersions, Future Syndicate, Deadbolt Magazine, On Spec, The Vampire's Crypt, Storyteller*, and *Into the Darkness*, among others. When not serving up tales of the macabre, she dresses up as a zombie or vampire and volunteers at haunted attractions in October to scare all the unsuspecting innocents. She also tends to her rabbits, Domino and Gunther, to stop them from embarking on their plans for world domination.

Four Against Chaos
by Kurt Kirchmeier

Once upon a time, there were four gifted boys who went to war against chaos and won.

With their mittens full of fingers and their boots stuffed with toes, they set out from the street they all lived on and made their way to the nearest hill. On their heads were snug-fitting toques, like army helmets shrunk in the rain, while wrapped around their hands were the ropes that connected them to their saucer-style sleds, all of which were plastic and therefore much lighter than the wood toboggans of old. Light enough, the boys would soon discover, to be tossed about violently if the wind were to blow in earnest.

"Ten times!" said the first boy, whose name was Gunner Wilson. "Ten times I'll go down the hill!" He stomped vigorously through the snow, kicking up white powder clouds. Gunner Wilson was strong and tall, and had the gift of a "very hard melon" according to his father.

"Twenty!" yelled the second boy and he smiled a one-up smile. This boy's name was Domenic Johnson, but the others just called him Do-Jo. "Twenty times, for sure!" Do-Jo's gift came in the form of paramount peepers, which is to say, eyesight so sharp that should a procedure come along by which to attain it, even the proudest of eagles would surely line up, put beak to inkwell and sign on the dotted line.

The third lad, Lester MacLean, opened his mouth but said nothing, for it occurred to him quite suddenly that thirty trips *down* the hill would necessitate thirty trips *up*, and boy heck, would his legs ever be sore after that! Lester MacLean possessed the gift of thought before action.

"Twenty!" he concurred and nodded in eager agreement with Do-Jo. "Twenty trips down the hill!" He made a whoosh sound, then turned to regard the last of their keen coterie who had fallen a ways behind and was now standing quite still, a single licked finger held up to the wind.

This fourth boy, who thought himself to be gifted differently than his friends and whose mother opined, nay, *insisted*, he was something very special indeed, swallowed hard and sighed. "I think I should maybe stay home," he said and discreetly returned his fingers to his mittens, pretending he hadn't been holding one to the air at all. "I'm not feeling so good, all of a sudden." The wind had begun to blow just a tad.

In a show of pre-teen synchronicity, the three companions tilted their heads at curious angles, eyebrows arching above left eyes. "What's up, Gabe?" they asked as one. The road here was slanted down, so although they stopped, their sleds continued to slide forward like impatient dogs straining at their leashes.

"Stomach's not feeling so hot," said Gabriel Aguirre. He put a hand to his mid-section and doubled over for dramatic effect.

Lester wondered about the licked finger and the wind, and what either had to do with an abrupt case of indigestion. Nothing, so far as he could figure. Probably Gabe was just worried on account of some silly idea his mom had put in his head. All that chaos and order stuff she was always going on about...enough to turn a boy into a basket case. "You'll be fine," Lester said and waved dismissively.

"Ahh, c'mon, Gabe," said the others. "Don't be a whiner! Don't be a dud! Or maybe he's just scared we'll beat him down the hill! Yeah, I'll bet that's what it is, all right! Gotta be!"

"That's not it," said Gabe, and he scowled for he hated being swayed by bravado and hated even more the fact that while his friends were always jolly and gay, he was just cautious and scared.

"Okay, here," said Lester, reaching into his coat pocket. "I got some antacid tablets right here. Couple of these and you'll be bouncing like ole Gunner."

Gunner grinned as though he'd had his name mentioned by a celebrity on television rather than by a friend who was standing right beside him. Gunner liked being referenced.

But what Gunner didn't realize was that Lester didn't have antacids at all. He was bluffing; what his fingers concealed was merely the end of a pack of grape-flavored hard candies. Lester always did have a thing for grape. Fibbing, on the other hand, was new, but delicious in its own right.

Gabe looked Lester in the eye, then stretched a bit from side to side. Not because he believed Lester, but because the wind had just died down again. Perhaps he wouldn't have to be goaded into coming along after all. "Nah," he said. "I think maybe it was just a stitch. Stopped walking a spell and now it's gone away." He skipped ahead, pretending to test his capacity for play.

"Good, then let's *go* already," said Do-Jo with a roll of his eagle eyes. If it wasn't Gunner acting like a doofus or Lester over-analyzing things, it was Gabriel alternating between cowardly and strange. Always with their dilly-dallying. It would surely be nice, Do-Jo thought as he compacted a snowball between his palms, if friends came with wind-up knobs on their backs, because then you could get them going again if they happened to come up short on their approach. Do-Jo wanted to be a pilot when he grew up, but since it was winter he'd been forced to trade in his flight goggles for headwear "better suited for the clime" as Do-Jo's dad had put it.

Setting his sights on a distant road sign, Do-Jo let fly the ball of snow which spun threw the air straight and true—guided as though by a laser—and connected with a resounding *bong!*

The other three shared a look at Do-Jo's impatience but opted to shrug and high-step it rather than comment on the thing. And so off they went in companionable silence.

Gabe continued to monitor the wind at regular intervals along the way, hoping against hope that it would let him alone for the afternoon. He hadn't gone sledding at all yet, hadn't even left the house for those three days when it stormed so bad. His mom had phoned the school and said he was sick that day, but he wasn't really sick at all.

Gabe's mom explained it like this: "The wind is a force of chaos, Son, and you're a force of order, so it's only natural for the wind to try to rub you out from time to time, but only from time to time, because if it did so regularly, then it wouldn't be adhering to its code of chaos, now would it?"

As for the "order" she spoke of, well, that went something like this: Ever since Gabe was a boy, all he had to do was walk into a room and something would change. If there happened to be an out-of-tune piano in the corner, boom, it would be in tune again, and if there happened to be a partially constructed jigsaw puzzle missing one little piece, poof, there was that piece, the puzzle made whole again. And what about socks disappearing in the dryer? No, siree, no such thing ever occurred in house *Aguirre!* Order.

But Gabe never played the piano nor did the laundry, and he didn't much care for puzzles either, so his gift had always seemed somewhat elusive and mysterious to him. Truth be told, there were even times that Gabe thought this gift—which he'd been blessed with since birth according to his mother—was imaginary, and that the reason it remained as invisible as the wind was because it wasn't actually there. But such bursts of doubt were few and far between.

The one thing Gabe knew for certain was that he didn't dare take on the wind, for the wind was everywhere and nowhere all at once, something and nothing at the very same instant, and how was a mere boy to defeat such a thing as that?

"Not possible," said Gabe's mother, "which is why you have to stay home!"

Even now, she didn't realize Gabe was going sledding. He'd told her he was going to Gunner's to play Scrabble, which was funny because Gunner had little in the way of a vocabulary and even less in the way of patience for things like board games, or "bored games" as he preferred to call them. Gabe hated lying to his mom like that, but the guys had been giving him a hard time ever since the first snowfall of the year.

"Ten-Hut!" said Gunner as they neared the base of the hill, at which point they all stopped out of duty and waited for further instruction. As usual, it proved slow in coming for Gunner relished these brief opportunities to play the leader and therefore stretched them out for maximum enjoyment.

Silence. Listening as if for the rumble of distant artillery. Then an air of seriousness, after which Gunner raised a closed fist into the air, pumped it three times, opened it and leveled a karate-chop at the hill. "Charge!" he yelled.

And so they charged, one by one, up the snowy climb, sleds like empty stretchers behind them.

Gabe was the first to the top, but also the last to go down, for he wanted to watch the others have a few runs before committing, wanted to evaluate their chosen paths to the bottom so that he might better be able to determine the least dangerous, most *orderly*, way down.

"Wouldn't do that if I were you," said Lester, who knew a thing or two about pausing for purposes contemplative rather than joining right in. "Can't think about it. Just gotta jump. It's the risk and uncertainty that makes it fun. Trust me, I've analyzed this thing to death." And with that, he hopped on his sled and pushed himself toward the edge.

"I don't know," said Gabe. "My mom always says better safe than sorry." Gunner and Do-Jo had both gone down, and already Do-Jo was making his way back up—eager, it seemed, on getting to the twenty mark he'd set for himself earlier.

Lester halted his forward progress to look back over his shoulder. "Yeah, well, no offence, Gabe, but your mom's got one foot in Looney Town." And with that, Lester disappeared over the edge and was soon descending the hill at the speed of an ice-cube kicked across kitchen linoleum.

"Does not," said Gabe to the empty air. Frustrated and angry and embarrassed all at once, he booted a hunk of snow and glanced down the path the others had been taking to the base of the hill. It was steep and water-slide smooth. Gabe recalled the summer past, thought again of how the others had frequently gone swimming and sliding without him, for a packed pool was no place for an order-gifted boy, what with all that awful bacteria floating around. Gabe's mom filed germs under the same heading as she did the wind—chaos.

But what would have happened, Gabe wondered, if he'd gone with his friends? Would he have been okay? Would he have been able to join in when they talked about all the fun they'd had, instead of just smiling and experiencing thrills vicariously which was never really thrilling at all? Gabe couldn't bear the thought of going through that again, of following the gang to Gunner's house so that they might all drink hot chocolate and relive the hours spent in the snow, imaginary trophies being handed out for the best trip down the hill. And since there was never an award for being careful, Gabe would be left out, yet again.

Or maybe he wouldn't. Maybe this time he'd show them all, and to heck with chaos!

With a glance to the heavens and a silent prayer, Gabe lowered himself to the saucer and threw himself down the hill, skeleton-style, like in the winter Olympics.

"Yeeeaaaiiiii!" he yelled, his arms tucked in at his sides, his face mere inches above the snow and ice disappearing beneath the front of the saucer.

So daring was the headfirst ride that when Gabe finally got to his feet, he found Gunner standing at attention, a hand raised to his forehead in salute. Lester laughed, and then all three of them did, after which Do-Jo came shooting down the hill to scatter them like bowling pins.

It was then the wind began to blow—called forth, Gabe presumed, by the chaotic ride that was the skeleton, summoned by a fellow burst of danger and unpredictability and crazy topsy-turvydom. Gabe felt a prickle deep inside and silently berated himself. He should have known that if one throws caution to the wind that the wind will not only catch it, but that it'll also trace it back to the source.

Gabe thought of his mother; he thought of chaos. "Hey, guys..."

And there it came from around the corner and behind them and in front of them all at once, a thing like laughter but not, a frigid blast of *hello, I'm here, I'm dancing all around you—can you see me, feel me in your hair?*

All four of them fell silent, sleds abandoned.

It began to snow, timidly at first, the clouds insecure in their right to let fire their million flakes but then gradually more confidently, until finally reckless abandon took hold, at which point the white scattered like confetti from the gods. The wind gusted, lifting one of the saucers so that it stood momentarily sideways, balancing on its thin edge, after which it flipped fully twice before disappearing into the swirling storm.

Soon all the boys were running after their sleds, which meant that they were no longer running together. Out of sight, out of earshot, separated by compounded membranes of snow, fast moving layers that whistled and wailed and stung both the eyes and the skin.

Gabe called out for the others to no avail, his every vocalization masked by sudden increases in the volume of the wind, anticipated and swallowed by air. He ran left, right, forward, around, until finally his own footsteps, deep now, tripped him up and left him lying on his back, staring up at a million spots of swirling cotton.

On one level, it seemed to him strange that the wind should have such freedom to do as it pleased when operating so close to an imparter of order—should not opposing forces balance each other out?—and yet on another level it made perfect sense, for Gabe was a mere boy with little experience in matters universal, while the wind was old and surely intimately familiar with such things. Perhaps Gabe was simply too young. Whatever the case, he wanted nothing so much as to find the others and run on home before things got especially bad.

But no sooner did he get to his feet, than an airborne sled came whishing past his ear. Gabe succumbed to a moment's paralysis, felt the prickle grow sharper inside, then sharper still, as the sled made its way back to him a few seconds later, this time grazing the outside edge of his left knee as it passed, after which Gabe came out of his stupor and began running in panicked circles.

Lester stood transfixed as the wind, seemingly sentient in its manipulations, spun his saucer round and about like a coin rotating on the tip of one's finger, then a bounce and a flip, a sudden *smack* as it suctioned against the side of the hill. It was as if the wind were familiarizing itself with this flat chunk of plastic red, this Frisbee grown ten sizes too big.

And what if it were flung like a Frisbee, Lester wondered; what if it were to slice through the air, throwing-star like, and collide with, say, the bridge of one's nose? Boy heck, now there would be a bleed to see the nurse about! Best, perhaps, if someone were to set about rounding all four sleds up just to be on the safe side.

Nodding to himself, Lester jumped forward and pinned the potentially problematic saucer. Holding it flat to the ground with his boot, he began to pile snow on top of it, armful after armful, until finally the sled was so thoroughly weighted down it would have taken the might of a tornado to free it.

One down, three to go.

Do-Jo, unable to see the others—which was odd for one so used to seeing everything—tackled the hill in the hope that higher ground might provide him a better opportunity to spot his friends amidst the cursed snow, which was now racing almost straight sideways, walls of it, dizzying and hypnotic to look at.

Strangely, the weather seemed slightly more accommodating from on high, almost as if the wind were conducting its business only near ground level, which of course was just silly. Do-Jo squinted his superhuman squint, and there near the base of the hill, a wingman amidst the clouds, was Lester, running after a sled. He quickly caught it and buried it beneath the snow, after which he immediately went chasing after another.

Smart, thought Do-Jo, mistakenly assuming his friend was burying the sleds for no other reason than to keep them from being carried off and deposited in some distant field, never to be found again. But then Do-Jo located Gabriel, and saw that two of the sleds were not being carried off at all, but rather flung about like saw-blades, here again, gone, here again, gone, encircling poor Gabriel in an ever-tightening dance of death.

And worse yet, Lester had just put himself directly in the line of fire. "Four o'clock!" yelled Do-Jo, his hands cupped around his mouth. "Hey, Lester! Bogey at four o'clock! Hey, watch out!"

In one fluid motion, Lester dropped to the ground and kicked up, knocking the four o'clock sled right out of the air, freeing it from a manipulative current of wind. It fell to the ground and was immediately picked up again, but Lester was quicker and managed to bury it like he already had the two others, leaving only the one, which Lester would never get to in time, Do-Jo realized, as he turned his attention back to Gabe. All in an instant the world turned slow motion, the sled swish-swish-swishing its way through the air, sure now in its course, bound for an imminent collision.

Do-Jo cupped his hands again. "Dive, Gabe! Dive!"

But Do-Jo might just as well have been yelling "fore" on a golf course, which, as golfers will tell you, does nothing but prompt the person one is yelling at to turn around in an attempt to locate the yeller, leaving the golf ball free to crack him in the face rather than the back of his head.

The slow-mo effect still operational; Do-Jo watched with increasing dread as Gabe twisted back around to look up to the top of the hill, thereby turning his back on the closing sled which had nothing between itself and its target now, but several feet of open space. And Gunner. From seemingly out of nowhere, there was Gunner.

Blundering blindly through the snow, Gunner came upon Gabe quite by accident, but of course it was a happy accident, for Gunner had spent nigh on five minutes negotiating his way over and around drifts so high that they might have been trenches coated with talcum powder. As always, the thought of trenches had propelled Gunner out of reality and into a daydream of war, which carried with it the sudden realization that he, Gunner, soldier extraordinaire, had somehow become separated from his platoon which was very bad indeed.

At that point he began to grow anxious. "Lester?" he yelled. "Gabe? Do-Jo? Anybody?" No answer. And then…yes, something, faint but audible, coming closer, getting louder, mumbling, the wind blowing the words this way and that. Shouted commands from high atop the hill.

And now here was Gabe to the right of him and a big spinning saucer to his left, and all of a sudden the shouted command was crystal clear. "Intercept, Gunner! Intercept!"

And so, like any soldier worth his salt would, Gunner intercepted, and so it was that the saucer struck him full on in the head, sled against skull, plastic against bone. But it might as well have been rickshaw versus tank, for Gunner's dad had been correct in his claim that his son had been gifted with a melon not easily cracked, a noggin not quickly concussed.

With a shake of his enviable head, then a shake of his triumphant fist, Gunner smiled. Then Lester appeared from behind a curtain of snow to wrestle the sled as if it were an alligator on the loose.

"That's four!" Lester stated emphatically. "That's all of them!" Do-Jo arrived to high-five him, after which they danced a goofy jig with Gunner soon joining in.

Absolved of its four-sled arsenal, the wind eased up considerably. Perhaps it needed to regroup, to ponder how it might focus its energies more efficiently, or maybe it was simply confused; indeed, it had good reason to be.

Gabe stood dumbfounded, surrounded by friends who, despite having no power over order whatsoever, had somehow joined forces to beat back chaos itself. He, meanwhile, had done nothing to help them the whole time, just laid down for a while, then got up and moved in hopeless circles, silently cursing himself for not heeding his mother's constant warnings.

But maybe his mother was wrong; maybe the relationship between chaos and order was no different than that between a six-year-old boy and the monster beneath his bed. Maybe chaos only gains power through fear and belief and the unwillingness to stand up and face it down, as Lester and Gunner and Do-Jo had just faced down the storm—as he himself had faced down the hill just a short while before, when he'd dared to do the skeleton.

Perhaps the fury of the wind was just a coincidence, and wasn't life chock right full of things like coincidences? Heck, maybe that puzzle piece was always right there on the table beside all the others, but never was found until Gabe happened to walk in the room and smile at his mother, and maybe every single key on that there piano was out of tune except for the one that got hit the exact moment Gabe came into view. And as for those socks, well, maybe Gabe's mother was simply too orderly a person to let single ones go missing.

All those times Gabe had stayed home on account of chaos when he could have been out walking trails or climbing trees or slip-sliding away without the least bit of notice taken of him by forces malicious and untoward.

But of course, there was still the chance that maybe his mom knew exactly what she was talking about, and that Gabe had better watch out because chaos had a thousand different eyes and a thousand different arms with which to reach out and touch an unwary boy. But if so, then so be it, for Gabe was no longer scared at all and knew that if things ever did get dicey, he'd have Gunner and Lester and Do-Jo to stand shoulder-to-shoulder with, and what force could hold up against that, when not even the wind could?

The cyclone of snow was now a feather-light rain of huge fluffy flakes, white as cotton. Gabe stuck out his tongue and caught one, and the world had never tasted so good.

Kurt Kirchmeier lives in Saskatoon, Saskatchewan, and is currently working on a diabolical plan to make the prairies less flat. He's also working on a Young Adult novel. It remains unclear at this point which project will be finished first. Kurt's fiction has appeared in *Albedo One, Shimmer, Weird Tales, Tales of the Unanticipated,* and elsewhere.

In his free time, Kurt enjoys graphic art, nature photography, reading, and hanging out at his local pool hall.

Ice Pirates
by Claire Eamer

Curled within a huge coil of rope near the main mast, Jem braced himself as the *Otter* wallowed in a slight swell. Frozen shrouds, invisible in the fog, clattered together overhead and a hatch banged somewhere below deck. Sheltered by the rope, Jem was hidden from everyone on deck. Especially the captain. He pulled the ragged scrap of blanket tighter over his shoulders and listened.

The fog muffled sound as well as sight. It even dulled the chock-chock-chock of hatchets on the port side, where half a dozen sailors were attacking the mounded ice that formed on rope and rail and made the ship tilt sluggishly under its weight. Left alone, the ice would build layer upon layer, as droplets of fog settled on sheets, masts and spars, until the burden toppled the little *Otter* and spilled everyone aboard into the icy northern sea.

Other than chip away at the ice, there was little to do until the wind returned and blew the fog away. The rest of the crew shivered below decks, wrapped in every bit of clothing they owned and buried in blankets and bits of torn canvas. They feared the cold, the grey water and the chattering skiffs of floating ice almost more than they feared their pursuers, stalled equally by the frigid calm. Jem wasn't afraid, didn't feel the cold. He wasn't sure why.

Perfectly comfortable, he curled tighter in his nest of rope, hugged his knees and savored the hint of icy sea carried in the cold air. Piercing air with the taste of salt. As long as he could remember, he had breathed salt air, but soft and tropical, heavy with growth and decay. This air smelled sharp-edged, crystalline and glittering. It promised something different and, at the same time, it filled him with a sense of familiarity.

Odd that, because all he knew was the south...warm seas where the *Otter* plied her trade gliding silently between headlands and through narrow straits in the black of a tropical night, sometimes coming right up to a wealthy merchant ship, rail to rail, before the victim realized she was there. The *Otter* was small by pirate standards and her crew scant, but it didn't matter. Surprise was her strength. No one knew when she would strike next or where she might disappear to, leaving the unlucky merchant ship stripped bare and, as often as not, burned to the waterline and still smoldering in her wake.

The *Otter's* captain was uncanny, so said word around the pirate ports. She could read the tides and currents like a seabird and see in the dark like a cat. No one knew how she did it, but it kept a crew of violent, bitter, half-broken men content to follow her. And Jem, who knew how but did not understand, said—and dared say—nothing. As if thinking about her was enough to call her, a gravelly voice over-rode the sound of the hatchets.

"Pup! Where's the pup? I want him!"

Jem shivered, but not from cold. There was a pause in the chock-chock, a sullen silence and then muttering voices. They wouldn't protect him. Never had. Heavy footsteps clumped across the deck. Jem heard her hoarse breathing and smelled her, a mix of stale, unwashed wool, tobacco, and rum. His blanket was whisked away and a strong hand clamped onto his shoulder, dragging him from the shelter of the rope coil.

"Come along, whelp. Now." Long, dirty ringlets dangled from beneath a British officer's battered hat. Jem remembered the officer. The captain had made him strip off his uniform coat before she jammed a sword through his belly and tossed the still-twitching body overboard. She wore the coat now, its blue dulled with years of grime, the gold braid worn and lined with black and the deep pockets full and sagging from use.

Her hand bit into Jem's shoulder, and he squirmed as she turned to snarl an order at the ice detail. They ducked their heads, avoiding her eyes and Jem's, and the sound of the hatchets resumed. Then she hauled Jem, stumbling, to the small vessel's high stern, shoved him against the rail and loomed over him, blocking the sailors' view. Jem knew there was no escape and a beating if he tried. He was small for his twelve years—twelve, he thought but didn't know—and skinny on the portions the cook begrudged him. He didn't think he'd ever grow big enough, strong enough, or brave enough to resist the captain. Only her need for his mysterious talent kept him alive and in one piece.

"Search, pup," she hissed in a voice that carried to his ears alone. "What's out there and where? Find me a current or a wind that will take us away from here, get us back south. With every other captain locked up or worse, we'll have the sea lanes to ourselves." She gave Jem's shoulder a final shake and turned him toward the sea.

Jem closed his eyes on the white fog and reached out with his mind. He had no idea how he did this, just that he had been able to do it as long as he could remember. And as long as he could remember, the captain had demanded it of him. Salt tickled the back of his throat and the *Otter* rocked gently beneath his feet. He sensed the blue-grey sheen of the ocean surface and the depths, where currents blew through the water like wind through the air, and weak, fog-dimmed light faded to darkness. He felt the currents' pull and reach. They curled, embracing, around a small island off to his right. Beyond it was a greater bulk, too big for the currents to embrace. Instead, they skimmed its edge, sending waves lapping toward the shore. The mainland, perhaps, or an island so big that it stretched beyond Jem's reach.

"Land," he said, pointing without opening his eyes. "There. Half a day's sail at most, in a fair wind. And an island, there. Small and rocky. A league or so away."

"The ships. What about those damned ships? Are they still there?" she growled in his ear.

Jem felt for the imprint of hulls on water and the jammering warmth of human souls. There. And there. And there. "At least three. Maybe more, farther away." He pointed, still without opening his eyes. South of their position, spread out, cutting them off from easy escape, herding them toward land. The captain cursed under her breath.

"Find me a way out, pup." She dug her fingers into his shoulder again, a reminder of what could happen if he didn't find what she wanted.

Pushing aside his fear, Jem reached into the ocean again, casting around for a sense of movement, of light, of change. Anything to say the fog and the calm weren't endless. There!

Beyond the pursuing ships, far to starboard, waves stirred in the wind, light glinting off their facets. The calm was breaking. But the wind would reach their pursuers first.

"Well?" She grabbed his ear and twisted. Jem yelped and squirmed in pain. "Wind, Cap'n! There's wind coming from aft. Over beyond them ships." She released Jem and he dropped to the deck cradling his ear.

The captain glared into the swirling fog, muttering curses. "They'll have full sails while we're still collecting ice. Ain't natural, wind from that quarter this time of year. None of it's natural. They shouldn't have kept coming, never should have found us at all."

She was right, Jem thought, lying still and hoping she'd forget him. It was strange. All the sea-faring nations, at war with each other as often as not, had banded together against the pirates. For weeks now, every flag had been their foe. The navies of England, Spain, the Low Countries, France, even America, had chased the *Otter* and every other pirate, freebooter, and self-proclaimed privateer through brilliant blue straits and past reef-rimmed islands. And ship after ship had fallen. The last they'd seen, before turning in desperation to the unfamiliar northern ocean, was Captain Hornby's *Ram*, lying hull-up and gutted on the sugar-white sand of a half-moon bay, wisps of black smoke still drifting among the palm trees. The *Otter* should have been able to slip away even then, guided by Jem's strange knowledge. But the pursuers kept coming, almost as if they had uncanny senses of their own.

"Pup!" She dragged him to his feet again. "Find me a bolt hole. Somewhere out of their sights." Gripping his arms in hands like claws, she turned him back to face the sea and gave him a shake that rattled his teeth. "Now!"

Jem was used to the cuffs and kicks, but not to the shrill undertone of fear in the captain's voice. Desperately, he reached out with the sense that had found the *Otter* rich prizes and safe havens in the past. South and east, the hulls of the pursuing ships denting the water began to stir in the freshening wind. To the northeast, grey swells rolled endlessly, and below them ran a current—he traced it with his mind—a powerful current that would push them into the enemy's embrace.

Westward, he felt something else, a solid presence on the surface. Not a ship. Far too big and somehow different...ice! Not the thin, jittery plates that surrounded the ship, but solid sheets of ice, thick, ponderous, merging and growing, pushing outward from land, closing the gap between the small island and the mainland. Beneath the ice, he sensed the living background of the sea: creatures that crept, crawled, drifted, and swam, the vast warm bulk of a whale, great fish that lurked in the depths and never came near the surface. And something else...

Jem flinched with surprise and pulled his sea sense back. Then he reached out again, carefully, tentatively. A voice had spoken. A voice with no sound, just a sense of warmth and darkness. It spoke again, the words forming in his mind.

Child. Come to me, child.

It seemed to come from where the ice was forming, Jem thought. He touched the current that curled around the island and the one that skirted the larger shore and felt how they came together, pushing the growing blocks of ice into each other so that they fused and then rose up in ridges. There, amid the crushing and crackling, was something else. Something warm and living... and almost familiar. One being. No. More. Perhaps a score or even two score, he realized, as he felt gently around the edges of the floes and beneath them. But one drew him, reached toward him, spoke to him. Again.

Have no fear, my child. You are welcome here.

He'd never heard sounds in his mind before, not even the sound of the sea or of any of its creatures. He tried forming words in the same way, without sound.

Who...are you?

Your kin, the voice said with a curious accent. *I have waited for you, long and long again.*

I don't understand, whispered Jem in his mind, horribly aware of the captain towering over him, waiting for an answer, a direction, an escape.

Come to me. I will explain.

How? What are you?

The voice disappeared in an explosion of pain, and Jem suddenly found himself on the deck, his head ringing. The captain had lost patience. She stood over him, her calloused hand raised for another blow. Jem scrambled to his feet, stammering frantically.

"I'll find something, somewhere...please, Captain, please."

Bring her to me.

Startled by the return of the voice, Jem spoke aloud, "I can't! You don't know."

The captain snarled in fury and lifted Jem off the deck by the fabric of his own worn jacket. "You what?"

"No, I can, I can! I can find us a place to hide."

And in his mind, desperately he said, *You don't know her. She'll kill you, all of you!*

Trust me. She will not win. Not this time. Bring her to me. To the ice.

Not this time? Jem asked, baffled. But the voice only repeated faintly...*To the ice.*

The captain had lowered him back to the deck, her hand still twisted in the collar of his jacket. Jem twisted and pointed toward the small island. "That way," he said. "Behind the island, between it and the mainland. Once the wind comes, we can get out of sight before they reach us."

"There's nowhere else?" She gave him a shake.

"No, nothing. *Just open sea, and a current that will push us into their arms.* Truly, Captain!"

She released him and Jem sagged against the rail in relief. The captain turned to look back over the stern. Already, the fog seemed thinner and there was more movement in the sea beneath them, a hint of the waves the wind would soon bring. She slapped her hands on the rail in decision and turned toward the bow.

"Go stir those lazy sods below decks and get them up here. And then come to me. I want you beside me."

Jem scurried toward the hatch as the captain strode forward. Had he just killed them all or only himself? And who or what was speaking in his mind?

It was hours before the wind reached them, hours during which the crew cleaned ice off every surface and warmed the shrouds and sails gently over small braziers so that they wouldn't snap in the cold. Finally, the fog lifted, softly and slowly, revealing a night sky as black as pitch, the stars still lost in haze. A soft wind plumped the *Otter's* sails enough to set her moving through the fragile ice pans that bumped against her hull. The captain stood a few paces in front of the helmsman, gazing forward into the darkness. Her hands were clamped on Jem's shoulders. He whispered directions to her and she called them out to the helmsman, as they had done night after night on the track of a fat merchantman. The crew thought him a sort of talisman, he knew. She had told him once that if they ever learned the truth, they would toss him overboard as a witch. He believed her.

Jem felt the ship creep slowly past the small island. The pursuing ships were gaining on them but heading roughly north as they veered westward. Soon the island would screen them from view well before dawn lightened the horizon. They were also drawing closer and closer to the ice, the thick floes of ice he had sensed earlier, still building, growing, piling higher as currents converged and pushed them together.

Come to me. The voice he'd been expecting for hours rang out in his mind. *Follow the path.*

And, indeed, Jem could see it, a gleaming path through the floes lit by an impossible shaft of starlight. He closed his eyes and the path grew brighter behind his eyelids. He shuddered and the hands tightened on his shoulders.

"What is it? Pup, if you've led us wrong."

"No, no." He winced at the pain in his shoulders and pointed in the direction of the shining path. "Through there. Truly, Cap'n!"

And he watched in his mind as the *Otter* sailed slowly down a shining corridor of open water, deeper and deeper into the ice. Behind her in the darkness, the floes moved softly closer, narrowing the passage to little more than half her width. And Jem scarcely dared breathe, unsure what he had done or what it would lead to.

When cold, grey light finally crept into the southeastern sky, it revealed a world of white. The *Otter* lay in a pool of open water surrounded by ice. Behind them, small in the distance, was the grey bulk of the small island and a thin lead of open water. Ahead, a line of black along the horizon might have been land. And in every direction was ice, thick broken blocks of ice jammed against each other and forced up into ridges and mounds, shifting, groaning. The growing light revealed a glittery layer of frost and snow, patches of pale grey where the wind had blown the ice clean and flashes of brighter blue where the ice was fresh from the sea.

And shapes. Dark shapes, sprawled on the edges of the floes and bobbing in the water between ice and ship. "Seals," breathed the helmsman. "Dozens of 'em." But the captain's hands gripped Jem's shoulders even more tightly for a moment, then she shoved him aside and shouted, "No!"

Well done, my child, said the voice in Jem's head. Staggering to his feet, he found his eyes drawn to the largest of the seals, propped almost upright on the ice in front of the ship and looking directly at Jem with dark, dark eyes.

The seal, black against the ice, seemed to waver and shimmer as if heat waves rose from the frozen surface. And then it wasn't a seal at all, but a man who stood solid on the frozen surface of the sea, clothed all in black and his hair a sleek, close-cropped dark cap.

A shiver of fear ran through the men on deck and they backed away from the rail. "Selkie," someone whispered, and a soft, hissing chorus took it up, "Selkie...selkie...selkie..."

"Greetings, Mairi," said the selkie-man, speaking aloud in the voice Jem had heard in his head. "You were a maid when last we met, and a pretty one. You've changed."

Jem stared at the captain. Mairi?

The captain gave a bark of laughter, but her weathered face was pale beneath the tan and there was no humor in her laugh. "A maid on the shore. Like many a song and many a maid before me. A maid on a stony shore, with little to look forward to but a life as hard as those stones."

The selkie-man looked up at her from the ice floe. "I meant you no harm. Perhaps, I should have thought more. I'm sorry for that."

"Fool!" she spat at him. "You thought as much as the village boys thought. I did more than enough thinking for both of us."

She leaned over the rail and glared down at him.

"I knew what you were. Are. Magic was the only road out of that place and I meant to have yours, but you slipped away too soon before I could find your skin and seize it, and your sea magic with it."

She grabbed Jem painfully by the arm and hauled him to the rail. "But you left something behind, did you but know."

Glaring down at the selkie-man, she shook Jem until his eyes blurred. "A little mewling babe that lay in his cradle and shifted from human child to seal and back again with no more thought or control than a blind kitten. So one day, as he shifted, I took his skin and tucked it away. And his soul and his power have been mine to command ever since."

Jem's mind reeled and his knees turned to water. Could it be true? He'd heard tales of selkies, of seals that could become men at will. Could this explain his gift?

Believe, said the voice in his head. He looked at the selkie-man and saw nothing in his face, in his eyes, but gentleness and pity.

"Now I have brought you back to my realm and this will end, Mairi. We have come to claim our own," said the selkie-man aloud. Behind him, a few more seals shimmered into human form, and the seals in the water glided closer to the *Otter*, surrounding her.

"Give us the boy and his skin, and we'll release the ice and let your ship go. Deny us, and the ice will hold you until the hunters arrive. Even now they're rounding the island."

Mutterings of alarm came from the crew, crowded together as far from the rails as possible. But the captain simply lifted Jem half off his feet and shook him again. "This? There's no skin to have. I destroyed it long ago. He's mine now."

Jem's confused hope drained away, but the selkie-man simply shook his head.

"If you had destroyed the skin, he would be dead. You have it close at hand. Give it to the boy and let him go."

The captain threw Jem to the deck, her face twisted with rage. "I'd rather kill the brat and have done with both of you!" She dug deep into the bulging pocket of her grimy officer's coat and pulled out a scrap of fur, dark and sleek as a seal but small enough for a babe. With her free hand, she hauled one of the small braziers, still smoking, close to the rail. She held the skin high above the dull red coals, waving it like a banner where all the seal people could see.

"Watch your pup burn and die!" she shrieked.

And the voice came again, urgently, in Jem's mind: *Seize your skin, child. Seize it now!*

Without daring to think, Jem scrambled to his feet and leapt over the brazier, reaching, reaching... His hand brushed the corner of the skin, suddenly warm to his touch, and he closed his fist around it. Suddenly, his mind filled with a chorus of voices: *Jump. Jump. Come to the sea!*

Jem grabbed the rail and tumbled over, falling down and down toward the ice-choked water, cringing already against the burning cold. But it didn't come. As he fell, he felt the change. His body shrugged into the skin, or the skin wrapped itself around him—he wasn't sure—and when he reached the water, he slipped into it like a knife into butter. He sank below the surface and then, with a flip of his tail, he popped back up.

All around him, seals dove and splashed and celebrated. The selkies on the ice floe shimmered back into seal form and slid into the water to join him, all but the selkie-man, who paused for a moment and stared up at the captain. Then he too shimmered, changed and slid into the water beside Jem.

Above them, the captain—his mother—stood on the ice-rimmed, shifting deck of the *Otter*, fierce with hatred, and screamed curses at Jem and the selkie-man—his father. But the curses hit the green and dancing waves of the narrow lane of open water that led back to the sea, and they spread and thinned to a sheen and soon, to nothing.

Beneath the waves, Jem and the selkie-man, sleekly furred, swooped and soared above the blue-green deep, scattering flocks of silver fish with the joy of their flight. And when they broke briefly into the world of air, there was nothing but the blue-grey dome of the sky above and the distant glitter of ice, far behind them.

Claire Eamer lives in the Yukon in Canada's North. She spends a lot of time writing about science and reading about magic. She has never met a selkie, but she'd like to. She has never met a pirate either, and doesn't regret that. Claire's latest book is about flying snakes, diving deer, ice worms, and other real animals that are just as amazing as selkies: *Lizards in the Sky: Animals Where You Least Expect Them* (Annick Press, 2010).

You Always Knew
by Michelle Barker

I'm going to tell you something
about Death,
though you suspect it already.

Death owns a rollercoaster,
the rickety kind—
cotton-candy-pink paint flaked,
colors faded,
wood rotting,
old stereo blaring seventies rock
in a nameless city

but you've been there.

There he is now,
greasy hair hanging stringy
from his black leather cap,
a moustache,
dirty T-shirt stretched
over a heart attack belly,
pants slung low

maybe a finger missing,
maybe the stub of a cigarette dangling
from the corner of his mouth

and he smiles
as he shuffles toward the empty cars

and you get in

and wait for the click
of the protective metal bar
that never seems to reach close enough
to your legs
to protect anything.

One of these days someone
is bound to fall out

and you wonder if today
it will be you.

Michelle Barker lives and writes in Penticton, B. C., with her husband and four children. Her poetry has been published in literary reviews across North America, including *Tesseracts Fourteen*. A chapbook of her poems "Old Growth, Clear Cut" will be published this year by *Leaf Press*. Her non-fiction work has won a National Magazine Award, and she has also published short fiction. The poem "You Always Knew" makes her think particularly of the roller coaster at the PNE in Vancouver. Next time you ride it, look for the man with the heart attack belly and hold on tight.

Michelle is currently working on two fantasy novels for young adults and has been involved in writing workshops for teens.

The Illumination
of Cypher-Space
by Lynne M. MacLean

Dannie woke up stiff and sore. The stone behind which she was hiding—the biggest one in the graveyard—had lost the sun's warmth that made it such an attractive hiding place earlier in the day. Now the ground was cold and the sun was lowering in the sky, shooting out long shadows. Little creatures rustled through the brown leaves blown into rifts around the cemetery. Night came early in late October.

First, though, she stretched out flat, face down, in the shadow of the gravestone. Neither Josh nor her grandmother was buried in this cemetery. But lying with her cheek in the soft grass, her heart pressed against the earth, she felt closer to them than anywhere else in this stupid city. She remembered when she had been by Grandma's gravestone for the last time. Alone in the night, just before she ran away, Dannie had stopped by for a last visit. For reasons she couldn't explain, she wrote "farewell" on the stone in marker. The writing had first glowed, then little sparks shot out that fizzled in the darkness. Fireflies, she had thought then. She wasn't so sure, now.

Grandma was long dead, two years, but Josh's death was fresh and painful. Dannie had spent the last two weeks crying for him. Enough. Now it was time to act.

She sat up slowly, looking around. No one was there, but that didn't surprise her. It was a week since she had escaped and found her way to this private cemetery. It was tucked away behind a hedge wall and creaky gate in the far end of a mansion's property. She couldn't hole up here much longer without being caught, but it had served its purpose. Billie and his crew wouldn't come into this neighborhood by day, and they were too superstitious to come into a graveyard at night. Stupid-stitious was more like it. Idiots.

She leaned against the gravestone again, hidden from the view of the gate and opened her backpack. She removed a half-finished bottle of cola and the remaining portion of the submarine sandwich she had stolen last night from a twenty-four-hour confectionary. Her stomach twisted in hungry knots as she shoveled in the food.

Dannie took out the exacto knife given to her, along with other art supplies, by Josh. She wiped tears away with the back of her hand, bit down hard on her bottom lip and started to hack away at her long dark hair. Billie would pay for Josh's death.

The knife blade was small. This haircut was going to take some time.

Josh had been the only person to really care about her, to really know her since she ran away from home following Grandma's death. Given how life had been before she moved in with Grandma, she sure hadn't stuck around that town to see where she'd end up. When she'd heard that Social Services was on its way, she'd grabbed her small savings, hitchhiked to the next town, bought a ticket on the greyhound bus, and headed to the big city. If she'd known what was waiting here she would've taken her chances with Social Services.

She had been fourteen. She met Billie at the bus depot after she had been panhandling for a couple of weeks. Billie was a friendly adult, hanging around, flashing his money. Real friendly. Before she'd had time to thaw out her brains and fill her stomach, she was stuck bad. Like a fly in a web. Billie had himself an organization based out of a night club and he had a lot of "employees," adult thugs as cruel as he was, and kids as hopeless as she. Pushing drugs, working the streets, stealing cars, running gambling dens and protection rackets, and more, anything awful you could think of—Billie's crew did it all. He wasn't big time yet, far from it, but he had ambitions.

He called her "Danielle," which she loathed. He said it was fancier. He made everyone else call her that, too. After awhile, she didn't mind separating Dannie, her real self, from Danielle.

He forced Dannie to work for him, and he had his guys keep close watch on her so she wouldn't run. Dannie was fast, with nimble fingers and the ability to slip away into the darkness. She was small and pretty, but not too pretty; the kind of girl you wouldn't stop and stare at, but one you wouldn't worry about around your car, your junior high school, your unlocked windows, the kind who, if you were a cop, you wouldn't think was up to trouble. The first year, all she did was work and head back to Billie's for beatings where bruises wouldn't show. She had tried escaping but without success. All it got her were more beatings. The other kids there were just as trapped. Somehow, she managed to stay off the drugs. She was pretty much the exception, though. Still, her spirit was broken and life was a waking hell. During the second year, having proven herself to be an obedient little girl, she was given more freedom. Once she turned in the night's money, she was on her own for a couple of hours.

She had roamed the limits of Billie's territory and beyond into other areas, learning the streets. She talked to other street people. She learned about the two big street gangs, the BluShuz and the Perditions, though she didn't venture into their districts, not yet anyway. Billie was moving in on their turfs and his people would not be welcome. She spent most of her time in the neutral zone, No Man's Land. That's where she'd met the taggers. And Josh.

Damn. She cut her finger hacking off a lock of hair. Blood dripped down, forming a pattern on the ground. The wind gusted, lifting her hair, swirling leaves. She sucked on the wound, bound it with a less than clean bandana and then returned to her task. Hair fell in hanks around her. Some were long, some short. Nice and jagged, the way she planned it.

The taggers. Graffiti artists, young people mostly but not all: girls, guys, all drawn together by their common passion for graffiti. They worked alone most of the time, moving through the dark nights and dawns of the city, through alleys and culverts, under bridges, in a spider web of routes through No Man's Land. Once every few weeks, they met and worked together. A grim few were gang members who did the tagging of their gang's turfs, marking territory as borders shifted or bravado was asserted. They, too, felt called to join in with the others on those nights of sharing fumes and colors and line. BluShuz's tagger, Zack Tattoo, stayed far away from Perditions' Night Hawk. They worked on the far edge of the tagger swarm, occasionally throwing shifty glances in each other's direction. No Man's Land was respected.

The first time Dannie came, she was transfixed, both by the raw emotion on the bridge girder rising above her and the amazing artistry. She watched the spray painters do stuff she had never dreamed possible. Especially that one guy, Toulouse. His work was astounding, bold and abstract. It sang of three dimensions. It gave her goose bumps whenever she saw it, and watching him work had been magical. Her hand itched to hold one of the cans, to see what she could make it do. Josh had been a tagger, too, and helped her join in.

Josh had shown her how to do it, and damn, she was good. Really good. She lost herself in the flow of it, all the burdens of her life lifted and forgotten. She had found something important to her, and she had found people who respected it. That night she became a tagger.

She realized Billie knew what she did in her free time. Not everyone who worked for him was as good as she at blending into backgrounds. At the beginning, she would see a thug she recognized drifting around at the swarm's edge. Then his thugs stopped following her. She didn't know why. Everyone knew she worked for him. Maybe it looked like Billie had his own tagger like the big boys. He would like that, even though he didn't have a tag. Or maybe he just didn't care. She had thought of trying to leave Billie, especially now that she knew more people. Maybe someone would take her in? But that would be too dangerous unless she went to a gang, and that wouldn't have been any better. Out of the frying pan, into the fire, as her grandmother would've said.

Often, she returned to her paintings. Many times, she found others there, taggers and civvies alike, like at an art gallery. She stayed in the background observing them. Once she found an old man breaking down in tears looking up at her stuff. He was probably crazy, she thought to herself. She slunk off, leaving him to his moment. When she turned back for one last look, she thought she saw a faint glow rising from her graffiti. A trick of the light. Still, it was one of her favorite memories, one she hugged to herself when times with Billie were bad.

She gained a reputation among the taggers and proved herself worthy of a name. She chose "Cypher." It seemed to fit because she felt both hidden, like a code, and also like a nothing, a zero. Now, no one called her Dannie except Josh.

Josh had big dreams and shared them with her. She started to dream, too. She would go to the police, escape Billie's clutches, get a scholarship and study art. She had just worked up the courage to take the first step when Billie found out about Josh.

Dannie pulled out her dollar store compact mirror, the one with the built-in light, to check the results of the hair cut. It was a ragged mess. A lot of the hair on the top of her head was now short. She took out her hair gel and spiked it up, hard and fierce. The rest of her hair hung down in randomly varying shards, some ear length, some down to her waist, and the rest everywhere in between. Darkness was falling. Soon she could be on the move. By the light of her compact, she took out her safe passage ribbons—one colored Perditions-green, the other BluShuz-orange. It had been worth taking those gang jobs just to get these. The Perditions had grabbed her one pre-dawn night when Josh wasn't around. They asked her to paint them a victory mural after a big surge into BluShuz's turf, something special. Night Hawk was in jail. There was no one else to do it. They said she was better than Toulouse. If she didn't do it, they'd beat her senseless and leave her for Billie to find and beat some more. But if she did this job, they'd give her a safe passage cord. What choice did she have? Her mural was an eye-popper.

Once word got out, BluShuz wanted their own mural. They wanted one twice as big. Zack Tattoo worked alongside her, grudgingly at first but with growing respect. When they were done, he handed her the fluorescent cord at the edge of the territory, booted her butt across the border and grunted, "Later," as she sprawled on the pavement. He nodded to her at the next swarm, as close as he ever got to acknowledging anyone else's existence. Both her murals had a nice glow to them in the dark, especially the abstract symbols that served as the gangs' tags. She had been pleased with the effect and surprised too, given she wasn't using fluorescent paint.

Dannie made two braids out of a few of the longer hanks of hair falling on either side of her face. She wove in the ribbons, one each per braid, knotting the end around the hair to secure it.

Billie was no fool. She figured he knew someone like Josh would lead away his kids, help them break the control Billie wound tightly around them. When Billie found out, he sent down his second-in-command, Pietro, to put a bullet between Josh's eyes as a warning to Dannie and all the other Dannies who worked for Billie. It was quick and painless for Josh, she heard, but she felt like she'd had her innards scooped out.

She took out her black eyeliner and piled it on, extending it until her eyes looked like a fox's with the predator's cold, clever glare. The rest of her face she muddied with dirt. She looked again. Yes, only Josh had known her as Dannie and now Josh was dead. This face looking back at her certainly wasn't Billie's "Danielle." This was Cypher. And Cypher was ready.

She stood up, watching the rising wind blow away her severed tufts of hair, separating the dark strands, whirling them with eddies of leaves deeper into the shadows. She shrugged on her backpack and headed off through the cemetery gate, through the mansion grounds and into the street beyond.

The night was cold. The stars were sharp and icy diamonds in the deep distant black of the cloudless sky. She had a long way to go, but her anger kept her warm, her blood pumping, her feet moving in quick, silent strides through the city darkness. She eventually made it to the back alleys of BluShuz turf. From her hood, she pulled out the one braid woven with BluShuz's safe passage ribbon, the other kept tucked safe inside, just in case she was seen. But she really didn't want to be seen. It could spoil her whole plan if she was identified in this territory tonight. A few times she had to fade into the shadows, skulking silently past groups of BluShuz warriors, hiding from the patrols. Eventually she found the hidden path off a playground, going down through bush and over a chain link fence to the back of an abandoned shed. It was a known BluShuz hang-out. No one was about. The sides of the building were covered in layer upon layer of graffiti, mostly Night Hawk's work, but some other, less proficient gang members had added their own touches. Still, Night Hawk's tag was at eye level, dominating each wall, the message loud and clear: BluShuz territory. Keep Out.

Moving fast, Cypher dug out her spray paint and wrote all over the tags: "Property of Billie" over top of a skull and cross-bones. As a final touch, she made blood drip out of the skull's eye sockets. The whole thing glowed, especially the words. She stopped only briefly to admire her work. She had more to do. She scooted through BluShuz turf, hitting all their key tagger spots like a new dog in town marking its territory and challenging the others. She managed to stay hidden from both the BluShuz gang and Billie's crew, looking over her shoulder, watching the shadows and listening for footfalls. Still, she felt like someone was watching her the entire night. The hairs on the back of her neck prickled. She put it down to a mix of adrenaline, nerves and anger.

She paused for a break under a bridge where some of her favorite paintings had glowed. The temperature had plummeted. To help herself wind down a bit, she thought she would paint a picture. She found a place near a girder where not too many sleeping bodies were already huddled. She drew a fireplace, so realistically she could almost see the flames dance as they shimmered. Underneath it, she wrote "Heat" with little wiggly lines above and below. She put her hands up to it and thought she felt actual heat emanating from it.

Cypher was spiking up her hair when she noticed a tagger leaning against a girder watching her. It was Toulouse. He was short, stocky, dressed in an oversized army surplus jacket and fingerless gloves. He had pulled a gray toque down over his long brown hair. His work, she had noticed previously, also glowed.

He caught her looking and grinned. He hunkered down on his haunches, picked up two cups of takeout coffee and ambled over.

He held out a coffee to her. "Want one?" he said. "It's hot. Lots of milk and sugar, too."

"Thanks." She took it, warming her stiff and chilly hands around it. The smell was comforting.

"Hey, Cypher. You a free agent now?"

"Yep."

"Billie's been looking for someone named Danielle, I hear."

"Put the word out, would you? Danielle's dead."

"Will do." He winked at her, tugging a corner of his toque as if to tip a hat and moved on, stepping over and around the others. She watched until he vanished from sight, sipping the coffee, the heat seeping into her core.

Next, Cypher crept her stealthy way into the very center of Perditions' turf, this time hiding the orange braided hair, with the Perditions' green one dangling free. She waited until the decrepit house that served as their headquarters was emptied. It took some time, but she wanted to make sure that her message was received loud and clear, and this was the place to do it. She knew it was their leader's birthday, a night to go out and celebrate. She watched until the last lieutenant walked out the front door. He peered around and then brought up the rear of the nasty, festive, boisterous group heading down the street they virtually owned. Her plan? Besides writing "Property of Billie" with the skull and crossbones, she would add Pietro's name written tag-style, as if Pietro were the one leaving it behind.

Cypher moved to the front wall, hidden by a bush in the yard. She started painting, faster than she had ever done before, getting into the flow of it all, losing herself in her anger. She forgot about getting caught until she had that feeling of being watched again. She paused and looked around. She saw no one. She picked up a fresh can, shook it and finished the job. The feeling remained. She headed off around the corner of the house and ran into Toulouse, sitting on the fence. He hopped down, swinging his backpack. He walked backwards away from her, grinning again.

"I won't say anything," he said.

Before she could answer, he bolted off into the darkness, his footsteps echoing down the street after him.

Did she want Billie dead? She thought seriously about that. Lots of times over the last two years she had wished his death and wished that she would be there to see it when it happened. But now it seemed so unlikely. Billie was like a snake, able to slither away from the worst danger. No, she would be happy with less. She wanted Billie's career smashed into pieces with a long jail time and with freedom for all his kid slaves. She wanted Pietro's life to career out of control so badly he never picked up a gun again. Maybe, she thought, she could put so much pressure on Pietro and Billie that recovery was impossible. She decided she would write "Property of Billie" with Pietro's tag, now followed by a vicious crossing out of the Perditions' own tag, and surrounded by rude, crude pictures dancing in the flames of hell. She had saved the best site of all for last. Scar Valley was a hot spot on the border between the two gangs, a piece of turf much battled over. It was a trench filled with empty pipes with diameters as tall as a man, left over from a discontinued sewer line. At either end of the trench was an entrance into the sewer line itself, an underground route through large sections of town. It was fenced off by the City. Since when did that ever stop anybody, thought Cypher. Tonight, the gangs would be too busy with Billie, she hoped, than to be fighting in Scar Valley or even hanging around it.

And she was right. No one was there. She felt calmer now than since she started this whole thing. Cypher settled in to her work with a grim yet ferocious joy, again forgetting who she was and what she was in the middle of. The work was alive with her anger and disdain. She had no need of light, which was good considering the lights over the trench had long been smashed.

Her work glowed more strongly than ever, casting shadows around her. She stopped, almost done, to look closely at the optical illusion of movement she had created, when Toulouse stepped out from one of those shadows.

"You know," he said, lounging against the pipe wall, "there's a better way to put Billie and Pietro out of business."

"What do you know about it?"

He leaned over conspiratorially. "Cypher, it doesn't take a genius to figure out what you're up to. But I've been watching you. You're a special kind of artist. Like me. You glow without fluorescents. Your words, especially. What if I told you that you could kill Pietro and Billie just by writing it a special way?"

"You're crazy."

"No. Haven't you ever heard the pen is mightier than the sword? A pen's nothing compared to a can of spray paint."

"Go away. You'll get us both killed."

"You know you've felt it, that power when it's in your hand. It's like you go someplace else, leave your body but you don't. You go inside and pull that power up from the core of your being, and it flows right out through the paint, doesn't it? Like a trance, like swimming. And when you're done, the painting seems alive. Like this."

He grabbed the can away from her, and wrote "Top Hat". It glowed faintly, but that was all.

"Now watch this," he said, "We take it further." His pupils dilated and his body went still. The change was profound, visible even in the semi-light created by her own mural of rage.

"Elevator going down," he said with a grin, and then his face went blank. He painted the same words again. They blazed on the pipe's wall illuminating a real hat, now sitting on the ground by Toulouse's feet. He shook himself, picked up the hat and put it on her head.

"You try. Words are more powerful with you, I think," he said. He talked her through it, again and again, through the failed attempts until finally she got the knack of it. She felt the power surge through her brain and body and out her arm in waves like he said. She wrote: "There's a rabbit inside it". And so there was, under the top hat on her head. She set the rabbit down on the ground and watched it hop off. She laughed out loud and gave the hat to Toulouse.

"Feels good, doesn't it?" said Toulouse. "But we can do so much more." He took the paint and wrote: "Mad dog appears".

And one did, standing with hackles raised, watching them and growling softly through its spittle-flecked muzzle. Toulouse wrote: "Mad dog dies". It fell over, stone dead.

Toulouse said, "Just like Billie. We could make that happen." He grinned hungrily. "I have my own complaints against Billie. You're not the first kid to break free from him, but together, we could make it so you're the last who has to. We could practice first on Pietro."

Cypher went cold. She had to fight off the sick feeling in her stomach or she would throw up all over her shoes.

"No," she said. It was one thing to set wheels in motion so others would hurt Billie. It was another to kill him and be the one doing it.

"C'mon," he said. "We'll make it fast. He won't feel anything. Like the dog."

She looked over at the dead animal. It looked forlorn and helpless now. Like Josh. It had been quick and painless for him, too. Her anger started to fade, leaving a deep dread behind.

"No. Then I'd be just like Billie."

Toulouse grabbed her arm, pleading. "You're sure about that? Anyway, think of the good we'll do. Think of all the kids. Think of how great it'd feel to stare him in the face and spit on him." She tried to pull her arm away but he held fast.

"Look, I'm not going to. You do it. In fact, why didn't you do it before?"

"Because," he snarled, as he twisted her arm up behind her back, "I can't do it alone. Getting rid of a sick, dying dog is one thing. Wiping a healthy grown man out of existence needs more power than I have yet. And we have two of them to get rid of. You're going to help me whether you want to or not."

He pulled her arm higher behind her back and tried to force her to take the paint in her other hand. He yanked up on the arm and she yelped in pain. He didn't take into account, however, that she had been on the streets for two years. She twisted free of the hold despite the pain and slipped from his grasp. She ran.

She put her head down and ran for all she was worth up the path to the closest fence. Her thudding heart matched the rhythm of her feet. Her heartbeat filled her ears so she was unable to hear much except her own breathing until Toulouse's yell behind her. She turned to see how far away he was and ran into something solid. Arms grabbed her, yanking her head up by her hair to stare into her face.

It was Billie. And Pietro.

"Thought I might find you around here," said Billie. His voice was as cold and as hard as the night.

"Nice makeover," snickered Pietro. "Wouldn't have recognized you."

"Yeah, but we recognized your painting style. Figured you'd show up." Billie picked her up by her hair and shook her above the ground. She grit her teeth, fighting the pain. Her rage and grief surged back. She wished she had gone along with Toulouse's plan. Where was Toulouse, anyway? It seemed Billie and Pietro hadn't seen him.

"You've cost me a lot. Maybe ruined me, in fact. Now you're going to die," said Billie. "And then we're going to paint over everything you've done tonight."

"You won't be able to find it all. You're done for." She tried to fight her way out again but failed. Then Billie suddenly dropped her to her feet and grabbed her again when she staggered. Where the heck was Toulouse? Couldn't he paint her out of this corner? Didn't he hate Billie enough? Or was she going to be tonight's sacrifice so Toulouse could live to devise some other plan?

Pietro took out his knife and cut off her braids with the safe passage ribbons. He twirled them in front of her face and said, "We're going to have a little fun. It's either us or the gangs who'll get you tonight." He put the knife away and got out his small, hateful-looking gun.

Billie put his face down close to hers. His breath stank. "When I let go, you run, little rabbit. Pietro will give you a few seconds and then shoot you. Or, maybe you'll get away and run into BluShuz's or Perditions' patrols. There's a lot of both around tonight. They won't recognize you."

"They're looking for you, Billie. You'd better run, too." She spat the words out.

He released her, propelling her forward so that she stumbled.

"One..." he said. She heard Pietro chuckle.

"Two..." She regained her feet and pushed forward, wishing she was indeed a rabbit. She ran as fast as she could, zigzagging up the slope to the top of the trench, her breath ragged, waiting for the sound of the shot that would signal her end. It never came. Instead, she heard Billie yell in dismay.

She grabbed a tree for cover and looked behind her. Billie was there but not Pietro, just a gun on the ground where Pietro had been standing. Toulouse stood smiling grimly under a street light with a spray paint can in his hand, the word "Pietro" written and crossed out on the pavement at his feet.

"I did it myself!" he called out to her. His glee made the hair on the nape of her neck rise. He gave her the creeps.

Billie grabbed the fallen gun and aimed it at Toulouse, who had begun painting again. A shot rang out. Toulouse dropped the paint can and grabbed his now bleeding arm.

"Run!" Toulouse screamed at Cypher. He took off after Cypher before Billie could make another shot.

She cleared the fence before Toulouse, and because he was injured, helped him over. Billie was not far behind. Before Toulouse could finish saying thanks, Cypher was gone again.

She ran down the street, turning down an alley. BluShuz turf. Not that it mattered. If they found her she would be as dead as if Billie shot her. The alley was littered with garbage, drug paraphernalia, and broken needles. She didn't want to trip and fall here. She slowed down slightly, which unfortunately gave Toulouse time to catch up. Damn. She wanted to shake him as well as Billie.

She heard the sound of Billie's heavier footfalls coming closer. She picked up her speed again and found herself in a blind alley. She looked around and realized it was Zack Tattoo's alley, his personal dead end. She spied a pile of spray cans. She shook each one until she found one that worked. She focused the way that Toulouse had taught her. Toulouse himself was now standing nearby, breathing heavily, clutching his bleeding arm.

"Yeah, go for it," he said. "Here. Maybe this will help." He grabbed her shoulder with his hand, wincing and concentrating. She cringed at his touch. Then she felt a doubled power flow surge through them both.

Billie was rounding the corner.

She wrote "Freedom for…."

A door in the dead end opened, showing a glimpse of blue sky and freedom. There was just one word missing from her sentence. She maintained her painting trance while approaching the door.

As Billie moved toward them, she leapt through the doorway, spray can in hand. She slammed the heavy door shut on both of them and wrote on the back of it,

"…me."

The door vanished, echoes of angry screams lingering in the air. All that remained of the opening was a brick wall running as far as she could see in either direction. She had added the word which shut this world off to Billie and gangs and Toulouse. She was not yet finished. She wrote "Toulouse escapes." She was so glad to be rid of him, she could afford to be generous.

Her painting hand was shaking. The can no longer felt like an extension of her. It felt like lead, even though a quick shake told her it was empty. She let it drop. It made a dull thud. "I'll leave Billie to the gangs."

Finally, she could take a slow, deep breath. Cypher slumped against the wall and sank to the ground on rubbery legs. She leaned her head back, closed and then opened her eyes. She was in a large brick cavern. Off in the distance were large windows showing blue sky and tree tops. It was gentle summer here. Birds sang. A sweet fragrance wafted to her on a soft breeze. She took in the wonder and beauty of this world and said, "Things are looking up."

She stood and wandered down the space toward a window, her hands trailing along the red brick surface. She walked around a marble pillar, enjoying the intricate carvings covering it. She drew up short in front of a line drawing done in black paint, a cartoon really, of a goofy big-nosed man looking over a fence. The words beneath it had originally said, "Toulouse was here." Only now, the "was" was crossed out. Written above it, in bright red letters, was the word "is."

Lynne M. MacLean lives in Ottawa with her busy husband, busier teenagers, and shockingly busy kittens. She, herself, tries to remain un-busy but with limited success. The "Illumination of Cypher-Space" is her first Young Adult story. She has adult stories published in *Melusine, or Women in the 21st Century, The Lorelei Signal, Mystic Signals,* and *MicroHorror.* She won an Honourable Mention in the 2010 Speculative Literature Foundation's Older Writers Grant competition. She also writes and edits academic articles, book chapters, and reports. Lynne has a Ph. D. in Psychology. As well as doing community health research in Ottawa, she has lived and practiced as a mental health practitioner in the Northwest Territories and the prairies. She worked with street kids many years ago. Though they would all be grown up now, she hopes they are somewhere warm and safe tonight. And she hopes you are, too.

The Tremor Road
by Tony Pi

From atop his runestilts, Kulno surveyed the line of devastation before him. As wide as a broad avenue, the strip of broken ground cut southeast through the sweeping moors. But though the stilts raised the smallfellow higher than any tallfolk, even the added height did not show where the tremor road might end.

On the path ahead, the last light of day shone on a fallen standing stone, half-hidden behind the foliage of an uprooted larch. He strode to where the sandstone monolith lay. The stone had broken in two, the great moss-covered rune it bore damaged beyond reconstruction. Could this glyph have caused the tremor road? No, the curved remnants of the symbol suggested a sky-rune. He would bet his thighbones that an earth-rune powered the quakes.

He had stopped in Tockwick the night before in search of rumors of rune-bearing stones when the first quake struck. An ordinary earthquake would have affected the entire town, but the tremors cut a limited path through Tockwick.

Watchmaker Lane took the brunt of it. Prized clock-turrets fell, killing six below and trapping dozens. A crumbling wall had left Kulno bruised and bloodied, but despite his injuries he hastened to help, squeezing into small pockets among the rubble to find and comfort those who lived. The townsfolk worked through the night and into morning to free the trapped, but a second identical quake caught them by surprise, claiming the lives of two more men.

After the third quake, the clockmasters uncovered a disturbing pattern: the interval between tremors halved each time. When he heard of it, Kulno volunteered to track the source of the tremor road.

He unwound his braided white-gold beard from around his neck and checked the timepiece woven into it. Clockmaster Phinge had gifted him with it. "You've less than three hours until the next quake strikes on the cusp between sunset and moonrise," Phinge had said. "Take care, my stiltling friend. Such precision could only mean foul sorcery." If Phinge's calculations were accurate, Kulno had only a pinch of time to prepare. He suspected someone had corrupted a ley line to create the tremor road, but he needed to see the energies underground to confirm his theory.

He sought a patch of dirt not far from the standing stone, dug a navel in the peat-covered earth with his left stilt and vaulted atop the makeshift axis mundi. Balancing there on one big toe, he shook the soreness from his other foot.

Wielding the other runestilt with the toes of his right foot, Kulno sketched a land's eye glyph in the surrounding dirt, drawing the power from the earth into the symbol. Manipulating the earth magic increased his mass and slowed his motions, a side effect he always hated. Once he completed the glyph, he heaved the stilt over his shoulders and closed his eyes.

The land's eye was less visual than an extension of his sense of vibration through his toe. Kulno felt the ley line beneath, but also the motions of all creatures touching the ground within a league. The weave of life rippled around him: ponies ambling, snakes slithering, frogs hopping, night crawlers burrowing. But Kulno focused on the tremor road, waiting.

The earthquake struck at the dreaded hour.

Unlike previous quakes it had burst the bounds of the tremor road. Caught by surprise in the earthquake's zone, Kulno almost fell off his runestilt, but his inborn sense of balance saved him. Before the buckling earth could knock down his stilt or destroy his land's eye, he channeled more earth-energy skyward through the shaft and his body, rooting him as immobile as a world pillar.

His land's eye felt the tickle of animals scurrying away from the tremor road, while the tainted ley line convulsed and sank deeper into the earth. Though the tremors soon subsided, the eye revealed that stray energies in the earth continued to flow into the ley line like creeks into a river. Even odder, the slitherings of snakes had ceased everywhere within his sorcerous sight. Instead, he sensed wheel-like movements spinning toward the tremor road. Two were racing his way.

He slid down the stilt to see with his own eyes.

Two hoops rolled toward him. Vipers biting their tails he thought at first, but no—the hoops were shrinking.

The snakes were swallowing their own tails.

There ought to be a limit to how much of itself a serpent could devour. Half its length, perhaps. But the snakes kept gorging and shrinking. The viper-hoops diminished until they were nothing but head and a snippet of body. They could fit in the palm of his hand with ease.

The closer one hit a clump of grass, bounced into the air and vanished.

Kulno blinked.

The second viper-hoop fell on its side and ate itself out of existence as he watched. Gone, with only swirlings in the dust to prove it was ever there.

Where'd they go?

He knew—hoped—he would see astounding things on his journey around the world, but this chilled him to the bone.

The tremor road and the vanishing serpents had to be related, but how?

His mind raced through all that the Towering Magi taught him about magic. The Rule of Sympathy said "like produces like." What if the ley line was eating its own tail like a world-circling serpent? Then it might sink deeper into the earth as he had observed. But who would force snakes to eat themselves out of existence, and why?

He had only an hour and a half until the next quake, and who knew what new twist that would bring? He did not know if he could stop the tremor road in time. However, he was certain the source lay in the moors since the tremors started in the south-east. The townsfolk said strange stones could be found there, including four called the Fangs of the Earth.

No one knew who had raised the ancient monoliths or carved runes of power into them. The Order of the Towering Magi cata-logued and studied these runes. Every apprentice knew seven key runes, but to earn the rank of Master, they had to build their own repertoire of glyphs. To complete his apprenticeship, Kulno must circle the world in search of these standing stones, etch-ing every glyph he found onto his runestilts. Almost certainly, aspirants would encounter obstacles on the road now and again, but the Order expected them to handle those hurdles as part of their training. The Grand Steeplechase, as some called it.

However, Kulno had hoped for more opportunities to hone his skills on this journey. There had been few challenges in the fifty days since he left Catawampus Canyon. So far, he had only collected three new runes: witchflare, shadow whip, and antlion's spiral. How could he hope to beat his brother's record of ninety-two runes in two hundred days? If he had taken the familiar northern route like the others, he'd have dozens by now. On the other foot, if all glyphs on this untrodden route were as powerful as the one that created the tremor road...

Kulno chastised himself for letting such thoughts distract him. He had promised the people of Tockwick he would undo the tremor road, and that had to take priority.

The gibbous moon began its ascent in the west, bringing sky magic with its light. Kulno mounted the runestilts again, climbing the shafts with vise-like toes. Drawing moonbeams into the hawthorn stilts, he spun them into silvery shafts of solid light that extended from the ends. The moonstilts lifted him skyward until he became as tall as four men.

Kulno's handling of the moonbeams countered the lethargy brought on by earth magic, making him quick and light. Above the stink of peat, he breathed in the exhilarating air, enjoying the cool summer breeze tickling his skin. He strode alongside the tremor road, keeping an eye to the ground illuminated by the moonbeam shafts and hummed a travelsong as he went.

Two leagues further southeast, the fissure's path crossed a moor-land stream, forming a stretch of muddy pool. In the air above the water, Kulno caught sight of an oddity. At first he thought it was a bird, for white-feathered wings bore it aloft. But as he neared it, he realized it was a winged serpent caught in the midst of the tail-devouring spell.

He had read about winged guardians before, enchanted creatures that protected animals of their kind and lived amongst them. Always white as clouds, the grimoires said, and feathered like the Pegasus. This one hadn't vanished like the others...yet. Its wings probably saved it, keeping it away from the ground where the ritual's power was strongest. But flight had tired it, and it plummeted toward the pool.

Kulno cursed and flicked his right foot, threading the moonstilt through the hoop of the winged serpent's body mere moments before it would hit the water. For now, the stilt threading the serpent kept it from vanishing, but for how long?

Another step and he stood on firmer ground. He jabbed the snake-wrapped stilt into the soft soil and balanced on top. Using his other stilt as a stylus, he inscribed a glowing omphalos knot around them, lacing the lines with sky magic. He slid down the moonstilt and leapt off before he reached the serpent ring, careful not to tread on the magical pattern.

The white serpent's head wrapped impossibly around the moonstilt. The only trace of its wings were the tufts of feathers protruding from its mouth.

Kulno saluted with his right foot. "Great winged guardian, I've shielded you from the spell. Please free yourself, but take care not to stray outside the bounds of the omphalos knot."

The white serpent first freed its wings and pulled its body from its jaws. As it revealed its true length, easily as long as his rune-stilts, Kulno wondered how any creature so long could fit down its own gullet. Once the serpent spat out its tail, it immediately coiled up and around the stilt in a helical fashion.

"Thank you, morsssel," it said in a soothing, gentle voice.

"Um, excuse me?" Kulno eyed it suspiciously. He had heard that some snakes could swallow whole pigs.

"I sssaid thank you, mortal." It hissed its sibilants and tried very hard to enunciate the last word. "My name is Sigira. May I ask your name?"

"Kulno at your service...milady?" he guessed.

"Mistress." Sigira scrutinized Kulno. "You're hurt."

Kulno recalled the head wound he sustained in the first quake. It had stopped bleeding but remained still tender to the touch. "This? It's nothing."

"Allow me." Sigira's forked tongue darted out and licked the cut.

Kulno touched his forehead. The pain was gone, and the scab had fallen away to reveal new skin. "Thank you."

"I wish I could do more in repayment, Master Kulno, but I haven't the strength."

"Please—not Master. I've yet to earn that title." He swatted gnats away from his face. "Might you know who's behind this spell, Mistress Sigira?"

Sigira hissed. "Mazheus of the Abominati. He and his hawkish servants have desssecrated the Fangs of the Earth."

Abominati! They were an order of human mages who worshipped the God of Horrors. "What do they intend?"

"The Ourobouros Rite will enslave all serpentkind for their conjurations. If they succeed, who knows what scaly horrors they'll unleash in the name of their god? I, too, would have been captured had you not found me in time, good sir."

Kulno told Sigira what he learned of the tremor road. "These Fangs...do they bear runes?"

"Yesss, one each."

Four! He would love to add them to his runestilts but dreaded what he must face first. "How much further?"

"A league east, but I fear I haven't the strength to fly."

"Neither would it be safe for you without the protection of the omphalos knot." Kulno touched the moonbeam shaft. They would reach the Fangs faster on moonstilts, but the Abominati might see them by their light. But that sky-magic needn't go to waste. He coaxed the moonbeam shaft back into the runestilt, letting Sigira slither onto the original section.

Kulno found the sign of the omphalos knot on the runestilt and lit it with trapped moonlight. "The glyph should bar earth magic from reaching you, so long as you remain in contact with the runestilt. Stay coiled around it, Sigira."

"Again, I'm in your debt."

"Not at all. Shall we?"

Back on runestilt-legs, Kulno continued to follow the tremor road with Sigira wrapped around his left stilt. She had added considerable weight to the stilt-leg. Thankfully, the buoyant effect of sky magic offset some of that, adding only a slight limp to his gait.

"I haven't tasted the likes of you before," Sigira said. "Are you a dwarf?"

"Not dwarf, not gnome, not goblin. I'm a stiltling."

"Ssstiltling? What a delicious word." Her tongue darted out of her mouth repeatedly. "Where do you come from?"

"Just now? Tockwick." Kulno's stomach grumbled. He dug around in his pocket but found only a few sunflower seeds left. He shouldn't have left all his gear and supplies in town with Phinge. "If you mean my homeland, Catawampus Canyon to the west."

"Ah, I haven't passed that way in centuries. You're far from home."

"And much farther to go before I'm there again. I'm on a Grand Steeplechase 'round the world in a hundred and ninety-nine days, you see." Memories of his lush, verdant motherland made him ache to be home already.

"Then I envy you, Kulno. Many marvels await you. Sssavor those moments."

"Dangers as well, I daresay." Kulno tugged on his beardbraid absent-mindedly, troubled by thoughts of the Abominati. When Kulno fought against the hob tribes in the border skirmishes, the most savage foes rode two-headed coywolves, spawns of the God of Horrors.

"And you will conquer them. You handle two staves better than I've seen a wizard wield one."

"These runestilts, you mean?" Kulno blushed. "I suppose I have a little skill with them. But in comparison with my brother, I'm a novice."

They covered the intervening league at a brisk if hobbled pace.

Ahead, four megaliths jutted like serpent's teeth from atop a bump of a hill in a field of bracken. Bonfires burned between each pair of stones. The tremor road cut straight through them. Loinclothed men and women danced in a sinuous circle, droning rounds of incantations.

Kulno checked his timepiece. The next quake would hit very soon. "We go on foot from here."

He dismounted his stilts and hefted each over a shoulder. Taking advantage of bracken for cover, he advanced on the foot of the hill and hoped that none of the Abominati would spot their approach.

As they neared the Fangs of the Earth, Sigira nudged him with her tail. "The closer we are, the weaker I grow," she hissed.

"I can do no more to help without drawing attention. As it is, I must risk using my land's eye," Kulno whispered.

He found the tallest clump of bracken and stuck the stilt without Sigira into the ground. The runestilt was too tall, too noticeable, but he needed it for the land's eye. Quietly, he climbed and balanced on top. Using the stilt bearing Sigira, he sketched the runes for the land's eye; feeling the instrument's heft return, he called on earth magic.

The land's eye told Kulno that twelve Abominati danced a ring around four concentric glyphs dug into the hilltop. A lone figure whirled at the center of the Fangs of the Earth. Mazheus? On every revolution, he struck the ground with a fang-tipped staff, poisoning the ley line beneath with fetid magic. Indeed, the Ourobouros Rite had shaped the ley line into a mystic serpent devouring its own tail, its head beneath the Fangs of the Earth. Myriads of ghostly snakes brooded inside the Ourobouros, slaves to the dark magic.

Thirteen against one. Those might be even odds for a Stilt Knight, but stiltfighting wasn't his forte. Runescrawl battles, on the other foot...

One of the dancers spun to a halt and shouted an alarm.

Fiddlestilt, he'd been spotted!

Mazheus spun to a halt and impaled the staff into the eye of the glyphs.

The fifth quake struck with unforgiving force. Even the Abominati around Mazheus lost their footing and fell. Kulno lifted Sigira and the other stilt above his head and fought the heaving ground, drawing more earth energy again to steady him.

The land's eye revealed that the phantom serpents were streaming out of the ground and into Mazheus, changing him.

Kulno opened his eyes. A great green serpent rose in the maw of the Fangs of the Earth, but in place of a snake's head, it bore Mazheus's naked, scarred torso. The sorcerer towered over the megaliths, letting coral snakes stream out his nostrils and burrow back into his mouth. He had truly become a servant worthy of the God of Horrors.

Mazheus pointed his staff at Kulno. "Slay him and bring me Sigira!"

The tremors subsided. The servants of Mazheus rose to their feet, drawing wavy daggers. They shrieked in delight and licked the steel of their blades, coating them in a film of slick ichor.

Sigira hissed. "Poison."

"Snakes have those extra eyelids, right?" he whispered to Sigira.

"Yesss. Why?"

"Be my eyes."

The Abominati charged down the hill.

Kulno broke the spine of energy holding him upright and retreated with heavy steps. He scrawled witchflares in the soil as he moved, imbuing them with sky energy and regaining speed. He pinched his eyes shut and ignited the runes with blinding light.

The Abominati cried out. Kulno heard bodies tripping over one another.

"Move to your right!" Sigira warned.

Kulno side-stepped as Sigira advised, feeling the disturbance of air where he had been. He counted down from five to zero before opening his eyes.

Most of the Abominati minions had been blinded, save two or three who had closed their eyes in time, but even sightless they slashed with bloodthirsty abandon. Two of their own fell to ally blades.

But they were not the true threat.

Two new giant heads grew from the Mazheus-serpent's body: a cobra's and a pit viper's. The cobra flared its hood, spitting a glob of venom at Kulno. Though he wobbled out of the way, the poison sprayed the left side of his face, half-blinding him.

Kulno cursed and fought the pain. He vaulted over a fanatic, clubbing the fellow's head with a stilt. Another Abominatus lunged for him, but he scribbled an antlion's spiral that sank the man's legs into the ground.

He thought he heard a whistling sound when Sigira flapped her wings hard, pulling him off-balance. But for her intervention, the javelin would have skewered him through the heart, but instead it pierced his right shoulder to the bone. Kulno cursed and pulled the scaly weapon out. No, not a javelin, but a jaculus serpent that hunted by falling out of trees to impale prey.

The viper-head reared back to spit another jaculus, and a python-head already sprouted from the juncture of necks.

Kulno dropped his right stilt. Grabbing the jaculus with his toes, he hurled it with all his might. But his blinded eye spoiled his aim, and his throw went wide.

Mazheus laughed. "Such sweet power, these serpents! Twisted horrors spawn wherever the Ourobouros touches, and I am their master."

Sigira hissed and licked Kulno's closed eye. "Mazheus may control many heads, but they all share a sssingle heart. Aim below where the body sssplits."

His left eye was healing but his vision remained blurred. "Guide my hand, Sigira."

"My pleasure."

Kulno dodged another jaculus. As he climbed the angled slope on stilt-legs, he channeled moonlight into the Sigira-stilt in preparation. The cobra-head spewed more venom at him, but Kulno had regained a lightness that let him evade the attack. The venom hit a bonfire and extinguished it, sending a cloud of noxious smoke into the air.

Kulno kept the Sigira-stilt and dropped the other, tumbling between the serpentine coils of Mazheus' body. Mazheus thrashed to crush the stiltling under his bulk, but Kulno somersaulted into the trench of a glyph.

He braced the stilt upside-down against the ground. "How's my aim?" he whispered.

Sigira tugged the staff to point higher. "Now!"

Kulno forced a moonbeam shaft out of the runestilt, faster and longer than he had ever tried. The silvery shaft lanced forth and impaled the heart of the Mazheus-abomination.

The creature writhed, pulling the moonstilt and Kulno out of the trench, but Kulno held on with both hands and toes, Sigira's wings in his face.

A newborn head budded from the juncture of serpent-necks, this time with diamondback markings.

"Why won't he die?" Sigira hissed.

"Mazheus has another heart in his body, and he's still tapping power from the Ourobouros," Kulno guessed. "We need to divert that energy."

"Can we make the World Serpent release its tail?"

The python-head bit and pulled the moonstilt out of its body. The force of the motion and the growing numbness in his left side made Kulno lose his grasp.

Sigira uncoiled and caught him with her tail moments before the python flung the moonstilt off the hill. She flew him safely into a glyph trench, but without the omphalos knot she twisted and sought her own tail.

Kulno scrabbled for his other stilt and helped Sigira wrap herself around it. But the python-head spewed a shower of snakes on top of them, and one found Kulno's neck. It wrapped itself around his throat and swallowed its own tail, choking him. Kulno dropped the stilt and grabbed the snake with both hands.

Mazheus laughed and twisted all his heads to face Kulno.

Still coiled around the runestilt, Sigira flew before Kulno. "Sssever the flow!"

Kulno fought his instinct to survive and seized the runestilt with one hand, planting it in the earth. With his other hand, he gripped the winged serpent twisted around the shaft. Piping the Ourobouros magic from the earth, he channeled it into Sigira. With his final breath, he managed a single word.

"Heal."

Sigira's eyes flashed open. Brilliant light shone from her every scale.

Kulno's vision cleared as the light granted him renewed strength. The snake around his neck released its hold and fell off him while his jaculus wound closed.

Touched by Sigira's healing light, the serpent heads above him erupted into writhing masses of snakes, restored to their true form and raining down on the hill. Returned to true human shape, Mazheus fell from the air with a scream and smashed into the hilltop. The swell of serpents swarmed over Mazheus and the other Abominati until they were seen and heard no more.

Kulno released his control of the Ourobouros energy, but sensed it continued to stream into Sigira without his aid. "Mistress Sigira?"

Sigira unfurled from the stilt and shed her old skin in the air. She had grown and her new scales shone pearly white. "With Mazheus' death, it seems the Ourobouros has chosen me as its guardian."

"Then it's over." Tockwick would be glad to hear of their success. He pulled a garter snake out of his sleeve and set it down gently.

"Is it?" Sigira asked. "I may have restored serpentkind to the moors, but the Ourobouros Rite had trapped countless of my kind. I must travel the Ourobouros road and ensure that none of them remain thrall to the Abominati. Will you journey with me, O Towering Magusss?"

Raising his eyes to the runes on the Fangs, Kulno considered Sigira's invitation. What of his aim to beat his brother's record and become a Master?

Then again, following the Ourobouros with Sigira would take them around the world. Surely he'd find runes along the way?

Kulno smiled. It sounded like a Grand Steeplechase at last.

Tony was born in Taipei, Taiwan, and once lived behind his grandfather's printing press business. In Mandarin his last name is pronounced "Bee," but when he emigrated to Canada, it was transliterated as "Pi," which sounds much better as "Pie." He studied linguistics at university and knows a thing or two about English dialects in Canada, eh? (He'll crack a smile if you call him Doctor Pi.) But it is because of his love of books, games, and manga, that he now writes fantasy and science fiction.

He's been afraid of heights ever since he fell off an embankment and broke his jaw as a kid, but while visiting the Grand Canyon, he finally decided to conquer his fear and tackled the glass-floored Skywalk. He found his courage by imagining he was walking on mile-high stilts and made it across, eyes open. This story is for those magical stilts.

The Memory Junkies
by Kate Boorman

We stood together in a dark corner of the schoolyard, tucked away from the iciest windblasts. It must have been twenty below even without the wind, and I wondered why Reid would pick an out-door rendezvous point in the dead of winter on the prairies. A 3-D sims café would have at least been warm. Yeah, yeah I know—too dangerous, because Why Would the Four of Us be Hanging out Together and What if Someone Should Overhear and all of that. Far better to risk frostbite and all turn up at J. P. Magnus High School on Monday with purple-blue appendages. *Far* less suspicious.

"That is so *choke*." Sara waved her arms in front of her face, her delicate flat nose scrunched in disgust. She flicked a hand toward Shaun's cigarette, "You do realize those will kill you."

Shaun stood a couple of feet away, savoring a long inhalation, "And you do realize they're made with forty-five percent less tar and nicotine now? And that this little baby comes with an echinacea-coated tip?" He pronounced it wrong "Etch-Ee-Nay-Sha," but Sara didn't seem to notice.

"Whatever. Smoking is so last year. You wanna be 2019, go ahead."

"Right, and you're what? Retro 2007? Hate to break it you but your Goth meets Manga outfit was hype, like fifteen years ago."

They went on like this for a few minutes while we shifted in the cold. It was the first meeting we'd all attended, in person, at the same time. It wasn't the best start.

My toes felt like they were fusing together, becoming ice flippers in my Converse, and Leonard Cohen's *Everybody Knows* was running through my head—if you don't know, he's a singer from my grandparents' time. And yeah, the guy was melodramatic but the lyrics totally fit my situation. Hanging out with my Pretend Friends to plan the biggest terrorist act this side of the BC pipeline bombings was a pretty intense Saturday night.

Everybody knows that the dice are loaded; everybody rolls with their fingers crossed.

"What d'ya care if I smoke?"

"I don't, do what you want. But *my* body is a temple."

"Oh I get it. You're thinking about your own precious lungs."

"Well, *guh*. It's a good thing health care is finally private. Won't have to be paying for your new lungs when you're old and hacking blood."

"Yeah, we really dodged a bullet there," I broke in sarcastically, eager to end it. "Let's all just pay for our own health… what could go wrong? It's not like there'll be a licensed Wellness Facility that destroys your sanity and drains your finances. Oh wait, there is—check my parents' bank account." I was referring to Life Keep, of course, and they knew it. It was, after all, the reason we'd gathered on that balmy evening.

Even so, they glanced at me with passing interest, as though I might be a piece of more-clever-than-usual graffiti on the eTrain. I was used to that look.

"Right, but Life Keep's not technically in health care." Reid was rifling through his courier bag like a man possessed but he was still able to enter the conversation as though he'd been devouring every word, "They're more like…cosmetic surgery, designed to make you feel good about yourself," he looked up and his charismatic grin wobbled slightly, "at any cost." He went back to rummaging, his pale neck and hands dimly reflecting the glow from the schoolyard floodlight.

We'd agreed to dress in dark colors to be less conspicuous. It might have been all a little secret agent but Reid was adamant about Taking No Chances. It was fine by me; I wasn't in the habit of advertising my existence with bright clothing. Shaun had thrown on some dark mechanic's overalls and Reid, of course, looked infinitely more hype in his all-black attire. The three of us were practically invisible.

Sara, on the other hand, had far too many Fashion Sensibilities to fully play along. Her compromise was a shiny, knee-length purple coat, less crimson eye shadow than normal, and some black stuff on her fingernails. It was a bit of overkill but despite what Shaun said, she pulled it off. She looked like a vampiric punk who could end your life with a well-placed karate chop. Or maybe just being Asian lent her the street cred.

Reid looked up from searching his bag and squinted at us in a way I knew girls found Adorable. Everything Reid did created legions of swooning fans, and in the six months we'd been partners it had become apparent to me the guy could club puppies for fun and barely lose points with the ladies. He was J. P. Magnus's version of the brooding rock star: Effortlessly Hype Hair, soulful lyrics and no end of emo torment.

Fortunately, he was also a total clinic when it came to cyber-tech. This was extremely critical to our plan. And truthfully, he was the only reason our group existed. He was more than just the angsty hype guy; he was obviously Paying Attention. How else would he figure out that the four of us, all from distinctly separate corners of the school atrium, were that desperate and miserable we could be united in one common, illegal goal? Four multi-colored, rejected peas in a pod, that's us.

Reid straightened up. "Should we start?"

"I thought we had." Sara eyed him. "I'm not hanging around you guys for funsies."

GargantuShaun (I'd never called him that to his face) let out a large ring of smoke. He shifted his six-foot-three frame. "Let's get this over with before Sara blows a neuron."

"Ease it, Shaun." Reid gave him a cool smile. Looking hype in any given situation was one thing he had down pat. "You alright, Mahone?"

I nodded and frowned, because frowning was one thing *I* had down pat. Mahone: a name you'd expect for a Cage Fighter. Me: thin bones, No Fly List-colored skin, and girlishly long eyelashes. Yes, the Scowl was my defense against the irony of it all.

"Great," Reid said. He'd finally found the tiny SimuGram in his oversized bag and he snapped it open. I couldn't see how the thing would work in the cold and was about to say as much when a familiar muted chime signaled that it was, in fact, booting up.

"Hey, hype." The device registered with GargantuShaun. "Does that Simu have Motion Correct?"

"Yep, but it drains the battery faster."

"How about Sonic Flare? That'd be killer at parties."

Reid grinned. "About the only thing it can't do is make you a sandwich."

"Or make my parents notice that I haven't be home eight freaking nights in a row," Sara muttered.

"Well actually, I'm hoping it *can* help with that." Reid watched the micro-sized screen carefully.

Everybody talking to their pockets, everybody wants a box of chocolates.

"Okay, let's do inventory. Mahone, Nitroxylene?"

I nodded. Scowled.

"Hype. Shaun, fertilizer?"

"A boat load. Literally. Hid it under the tarp of the fishing boat at my uncle's farm. No one even looks at that thing until the ice is off the lake, and it's been so freaking cold—"

Reid cut him off with a nod. "I checked with each of our seven partner orgs and they're all prepared to copycat. All we need to do is broadcast it."

"And the minute it goes viral," Shaun took up the narrative a little too gleefully—it made him look a bit simple in my Unprofessional Opinion, "Life Keep all over the world goes boom."

"I've also got the facility completely mapped: points of entry, places that'll result in residual explosion, all of it. And their security system's a joke; I've hacked in twice, already. I could disable the alarm in my sleep." Reid shook the Simu impatiently.

"Tell me again what she's here for?" Shaun jerked his head toward Sara.

"Sara is our historian." Reid looked up from the sluggish device. "She'll shoot the explosion on her Spec Goggles like any innocent passerby would. As for traces of our actual presence, we'll just have to be really careful."

"And hope it all burns." Sara chipped at her black polish.

The thought of that pristine Life Keep building engulfed in flames sent a quick pang through my chest. It was an excited, Can This Really Happen pang, a Maybe I'll Get my Life Back pang. It was so hopeful it was embarrassing, but I knew that each member of our Unlikely Terrorist Gang was feeling similarly optimistic.

It was going to work. We had no other options.

"Finally." Reid tapped the tiny screen of the Simu and a miniature blue hologram of the Life Keep facility materialized. He tapped it again to keep the projection in its location—hovering chest-height in the middle of our circle, then placed the device carefully in his bag.

He sank a hand into the image. "We'll put a Fertilizer/Nitroxylene cocktail here." He pinpointed a space that looked like a treatment room. "Here. And here."

"So how'd you get your hands on Nitroxylene?" Sara asked me.

"My parents work in a stem cell experimentation lab. I 'borrowed' some the last time I dropped in."

"Hype." She raised her eyebrows.

I shrugged in what I hoped spelled No Big, but secretly I was pleased. Nitroxylene was a new stimulant used for accelerating stem cell growth. It was expensive and extremely hard to source because of its volatility. In large doses it was super unstable around nitrogen-rich substances like fertilizer. It was perfect; it would Blow Up Real Good. And being able to get it meant I was more hype than everyone usually assumed.

"What kind of Specs do you have?" Shaun crossed his arms and addressed Sara. "We can't have a choke broadcast."

Sara pulled them out of her jacket pocket for us to see. They were Witness3—top of the line, able to detect and correct all kinds of optical aberrations. Basically, they'd capture whatever Sara witnessed perfectly and then upload the images to the web almost instantly.

There were murmurs of approval from us guys.

Sara pocketed them and turned to Reid, "So this goes down next week, right?"

"Yeah. Life Keep is celebrating one year in business on the fifteenth of this month. It'll be the perfect anniversary gift."

"Hype."

Reid nodded. "Yeah. We're going to nail Life Keep."

We're going to nail Life Keep. Life Keep: the new "health and wellness facility" that was cropping up in every major center across North America and Europe and also certain parts of Asia. Lucky for us, our Why Halt the Oil Drilling Province was the first to get one. Life Keep wasn't dumb; they knew full well where the bored-to-tears-with-all-their-expendable-income citizens lived. Two ubermalls and a Life Keep—look no further for a reason to Travel Alberta!

Actually, Life Keep had the drop on those crowded, deteriorating megamalls hands down. It boasted the Extreme Tourist Attraction: you.

Ladies and gentlemen, introducing...Memory Dive! Now available to the public, Memory Dive is a perfectly safe medical procedure that allows you to sort through your brain and pinpoint the most exciting memories of your life. Then, folks, you are able to...RELIVE them. Yes, it's true: once a memory or two that really rocks your world is found, it's downloaded and stored in a Virtual Intelligence receptacle at Life Keep, where you are able to experience that memory in virtual 3D, again and again and again.

Now, the procedure does include a general anesthetic so, due to the new Health for All Protection Laws, minors are exempt. BUT it's approved and administered by licensed physicians and nurses! The technology is state-of-the-art; your safety is top priority. It's completely confidential and truly unique. And don't forget: Life Keep offers a money-back guarantee. Can't find any happy memories for storage? You don't pay a cent!

Life Keep: Immersion in Life's Happiest Memories.

I could remember when the only clients were geriatrics with money to burn—eccentric millionaires, ex-celebrities, well-to-do government officials. That lasted about six weeks. And then word got out: it wasn't just unique, it was *amazing*.

Why rely on ordinary luxuries for your Break From it All? There was no *guarantee* they'd erase anxiety or create happiness. A Memory Dive was a sure thing because the memory was *already* perfect. It was a foolproof escape, a harmless way to forget troubles and just Be Happy.

But no one banked on addiction.

No one anticipated hundreds of people, including parents like ours, spending every ounce of their spare time and life savings to re-experience a particular part of their past.

I think my parents started with the intent to Dive whenever fun money and time permitted. Then they were gone more often and for longer periods of time, returning home moony-eyed, listless. Within a day or so *that* would turn into full-blown depression (alternating with Short Bursts of Mania!) that stayed until they were treated. As in, until they went back for another Dive.

Everybody knows you've been discreet...

And it's strange, really, that *nobody* anticipated it—didn't they run control tests on this thing? Maybe there was a margin for error; maybe the test subjects didn't have addictive personalities, maybe they didn't have the money to Dive once the test period was over—I'm not sure.

But I'm also not sure Life Keep was blindsided by it all. Because what're a few addictions and lawsuits compared to the profit margin? At $5000 an extraction and $1500 a session, Life Keep was pretty well guaranteed the Best Lawyers Money Can Buy.

There were dozens of Woe Stories circulating in Cyberland, about parents who'd pawned the family heirlooms, sold the second car, made their kids quit any extra-curric that cost money. Parents who struggled to keep their jobs so they could Dive, parents who were absent, basically 24-7.

But those were tame, completely No Big.

The stories that kept you up at night had nothing to do with depleted life savings.

We'd heard about some kids whose parents had begun speaking to them only in Arabic. The family was second generation, and the parents, for whatever reason, had reverted completely to their language of origin after Diving for several weeks. Thing was, the kids couldn't speak a word, never had. And when they were unable to respond to their parents for days on end, the father had raged so mass he'd ended up locking them outside in thirty below. I think those kids were taken into protective services.

And then there was the rumor about Sadie McElroy's mom being hospitalized for hypothermia after Sadie had found her catatonic in a cold bath. Apparently, Mrs. McElroy hadn't been able to afford to Dive for two weeks, and she just kinda lost the plot one night. People say she'd been in that water all weekend, but since Sadie'd been out capitalizing on her New Found Freedom, she hadn't found her mom until she finally came home on the Monday. And apparently the hypothermia was so severe it caused some mass neuron damage, because Mrs. McElroy now has the social skills of an uninteresting vegetable.

Those were the extreme stories, the cautionary tales but even so, it freaked you out.

"So where do we enter?" Shaun was poking a finger into the hologram of the building. Sara gave him a look that could freeze lava.

"This door." Reid pointed it out. "It should only take thirty seconds to get the cocktails in place. Once we activate them we'll have six minutes to get out. And then, kids, it's 'V' for victory."

'V' for victory. Life Keep's carefully filed gold mine obliterated—Ball of Fire styles.

Everybody knows it's coming apart…

"Freaking *hype*." Shaun was nodding excitedly. "Hey—wonder what withdrawal will be like for our parents?"

"Probably depends on how often they've been Diving, how many memories they have stored," Reid said.

"Well whatever. My dad deserves to come down *hard*."

I'd never publicly agree with GargantuShaun, but I felt the same way. I was pretty sure I knew which memory was draining my RESP. A month ago, Reid had hacked in to Life Keep's records and then e-mailed us our parents' files. We couldn't see the memories themselves, of course—just the names, the descriptions.

My parents had downloaded a shared memory of me from Kindergarten: "Q-tip Snowflake: Mahone". I'd puzzled for weeks about their selection. I'm almost positive it was the day I brought this winter craft thingy home for them. I remembered making it: three Q-tips glued together in the center, each cotton end dipped in glue and then glitter, with my picture in the center. It was an epic monstrosity, and it'd been sitting on my parents' dresser for eleven years. And yet they were willing to spend mass cash to relive the moment I gave it to them. It redefined stupidity.

"I'm not sure how bad it'll be for my parents, it's just one idiotic Kindergarten memory." I realized I was thinking aloud, and I scowled to look casual. "I don't get it."

"Join the club." Reid rolled his eyes. "Could my mom be any more choke? You'd think she'd want to Dive for the days she was a high-powered attorney, but no, there's all this "Reid's birth" and "Reid's first Tooth Fairy visit" and crap like that. Mass crank."

"Check it." Shaun threw the cigarette down, stamped on it. "My dad drafted for the NHL but buggered up his shoulder a couple years in. Then I played hockey because he wanted me to. I was good but I ended up quitting because I like working with my hands and making things run. But now I doubt we can afford the tuition at MechanaTech. It's unfair, y'know?"

Oh, we knew.

"But you know what's really crank? He Dives for *my* games, not his." GargantuShaun looked pensive, which was no small feat.

He noticed Sara shift beside me.

"So what's the story, Gothgirl? What're your parents railing for?"

I half expected her to tell Shaun to Get Bent. It looked as if it was on the tip of her tongue—and then her shoulders softened slightly. "My brother. He died four years ago, just after his four-teenth birthday."

None of us expected that.

"They mostly revisit the last Christmas we had together before we found out about his lymphoma."

Reid cleared his throat. "How often?"

"Well, I have enough practice making meals that I could attempt rack of venison if we could afford anything but canned soup. I mean, I miss my brother, too, but I'm getting sick of Noodle

Oodle." Sara shrugged, but in that moment I could see despair through her indifference. It hovered behind her eyes, threatened to yank her Street Punk façade clear off.

"My mom pawned my Fender," Reid offered. "Said since she bought it, she'd decide what it was good for." He managed to make a grimace look hype. "Good thing she doesn't know about the SimuGram—it's worth a small fortune."

"Whatever—my dad keeps asking his brother to lend him cash. Couldn't even pay the heat this month. Talk about freaking choke," Shaun complained.

"Yeah they're totally spending our inheritance," I agreed. Scowled.

It was a good thing none of our parents made under six figures a year—we'd have all been acquired by Social Services long ago. On the other hand, if our parents had never been able to afford the first Dive, none of us would be freezing to death in the schoolyard on a Saturday night.

"It's not just that." Sara's eyes drifted away from us. Her voice got small, like she was trying to relay the words without having to say them. "It's...that they're no longer *here*. I don't mean physically. I mean..." a slight shudder, "they notice me the way they notice the furniture. I can't remember the last time they asked me how I was doing at school, or if I've painted anything lately. They're here, but they're...*gone*."

"Right. *Gone* to withdraw the last of our post-secondary tuition." I didn't like where this was going and I tried my best to sound off-handed. Leonard Cohen's crooning had ground to a halt.

Sara continued like she hadn't heard. "I guess I get it. Elgin was so...hype to be around. He always made you feel like you were the most important person in the room. Like—he listened well, asked the right questions, stuff like that." She stared at her glittery boots, dug a toe in the snow-crusted grass. Her Tough Girl persona had all but evaporated into the freezing wind.

"That Christmas my parents Dive for? Elgin had organized a dumb joke gift exchange. And we were all crying we were laughing so hard; he'd bought me this self-twirling spaghetti fork and my dad got some spray-on hair." She tilted her head to the side. "It felt impossible that he could ever get sick. But he did. Seeing him half his size, that horrible shade of grey, face distorted from the Prednisone...it destroyed my parents." She paused. "When he died, it took me a long time to stop resenting him for leaving us."

No one spoke.

"But I did," she continued, "I moved on to missing him more than I ever imagined. But now...I just—well, I never thought I'd resent him for taking my parents, too."

We all stared at our shoes for a minute—embarrassed, stripped by her sincerity. A flicker of shame burned in the base of my stomach. If I'd felt Socially Suicidal enough to be honest, I would've agreed with her, admitted that it wasn't the depleted college funds or second-hand clothes that mattered. It was the Absence.

It felt like a massive, gaping wound in my chest—one that grew a bit each day. Hooking up with my As Desperate classmates was my one chance at sealing it shut. And truthfully, the fact that I even noticed the Absence was totally crank. It's not like my family was mass tight; we weren't into Game Night Wednesday or Taco Tuesday or whatever. My sisters and I didn't talk much, and I tried to stay out of my dad's way as much as possible since all we ever agreed on was How Bad the Oilers Sucked Last Night. Mom was annoyingly touchy-feel; we were all forever trying to avoid her heart-to-hearts.

I kept up my grades, made appearances at the family dinner table, deflected questions about my inactive social life, and, when all else failed, retreated to the basement. Basically, I navigated my parents' attentions with as few lectures and Group Hugs as possible.

But...it was different when I had the choice.

I thought again of that Q-tip Snowflake—how that glitter-and-glue disaster had replaced me. It would've been hilarious if it weren't so pathetic.

"So anyway, I'm choosing tough love." Sara laughed but it sounded forced, "Erase some happiness so we can find our way out of misery. Crank, hey?"

We were silent, unable to meet one another's eyes. Grief hung in the air, silent and lethal.

And then Reid realized something we didn't, "Hold up. What do you mean 'tough love'?"

"The memories of that Christmas; it's the happiest we ever were as a family."

"But what do you mean by *erasing* the happiness?"

Sara frowned, "Well those memories are *downloaded*; they're *stored* at Life Keep."

"So?"

"So what do you think will happen to them when you flick the switch?"

I could feel myself staring at Sara, knew that Reid and Shaun were doing the same.

"Hello?" she bunched her hands into fists then flicked them open violently. "Boom?"

"You're saying that once we blow up Life Keep we destroy all of the memories inside. As in, forever?" I knew at this point I wasn't winning awards for connecting the dots, but I couldn't believe this glaring fact had escaped us.

"Well, *guh*." Sara looked at us scornfully.

"Seriously?" Shaun's mouth was agape. "The only decent memories my parents have of me will be wiped out?"

"All. Of. The. Memories. Go. Boom." Sara spoke as though she was addressing a group of children.

We continued to stare at her. That stupid Snowflake edged into my mind.

And then Shaun exploded, "Well this chokes! My dad is *really* going to hate me now—he won't even know I *attempted* that stupid hockey dream!"

"My mom has a TON of memories stored there. A TON." Reid gazed at the hologram, his tone soft.

Shaun was muttering, "Winning Provincials, MVP three years in a row, all of those five in the morning practices to appease my old man—all of it. Gone."

Reid's eyes refocused. "God, she might not even recognize me anymore!"

"Ease it, Rockstar." Sara had folded her arms across her chest. "I find it pretty hard to believe your mom won't know who you are without a Tooth Fairy montage."

"You don't know that. You don't know anything." His tone had a panicked edge.

"Reid, we can't afford not to do it."

"And what makes you think you get to decide?"

"Maybe we should just forget it." It was Shaun, looking sour.

Reid continued, "Seriously. This is *my* plan. If I don't want my mom to lose those memories of me, then it's my call—not yours."

"Think about it, Reid—not doing it is mass crank."

"I want some sort of relationship with my mom—how is that crank?"

Sara shouted, "Why do you think she's Diving for those memories in the first place?"

Whatever I'd planned to add to the argument stuck in my throat. I'd been so caught up in this plan, in how choke my parents were acting, in my own anger, that I'd never stopped to wonder *that*.

Why *did* they go? Why the Snowflake? Why would my parents cling to the memory of that crappy hand-made gift? How could the moment of me bringing it home over ten years ago mean more than me walking through the door today?

That horrible, gaping sensation began worming its way through my core. A tiny seed was unfurling in my mind. Because maybe... maybe my parents were wrapped up in that handmade gift— probably the first and last I ever gave them—because it was a pure, perfect moment when I'd thought they were the Be All, End All. Maybe they'd gone down memory lane to remember what it was like to feel acknowledged, important. Maybe me spending the last ten years avoiding any attempts at a relationship had paved that path. I could feel the anxiety seep up into my chest and I tried to contain it, scared it would burst up into my constricted throat, fill my eyes, ensure "is-a-cry-baby-gleeb" was added to the List of Reasons Mahone Is Un-hype.

"You don't get it, Sara," Reid snapped. "Those memories play a part in our lives *now*."

"I *do* get it," Sara shot back. "We're standing here because they've made your life so very *hype*."

Shaun rounded on her, "Look, I don't know who you think you are, but you can't just stroll in here and act like you know us."

Sara snorted, "Oh, I know you. You're like every other privileged kid in this town; willing to make a scene so long as it's no skin off your own backside." She met Shaun's stare. "Just because you don't want Daddy Dearest to forget your first hat trick doesn't mean you can ditch this plan."

The need to seal shut that ever-widening hole in my chest suddenly consumed me. I had to stop Sara, shut her up, make her sorry she ever started this idiotic Group Therapy Session. "And just because you're psychotic and don't care that you'll destroy the good memories of your dead brother doesn't mean you can tell us what to do."

The words flew from my mouth. They bounced off the surrounding brick walls and flooded our ears, violent, caustic, unthinkable. I didn't need Reid's shocked expression to know I'd gone too far.

A gust of wind billowed around the corner of the school, whipping crystals of snow into our eyes and down the necks of our coats.

I looked at my Cons. "I mean, it's just…well, if you take away all the happy memories…"

Sara turned to me and I felt heat flood my face when I met her eyes. The anguish was back, but her voice was steady, "The happy memories are eating us alive."

I looked back down at my feet. The hole had not sealed shut. It was wide open, and it was tearing at the edges.

"I've lost my parents to those memories. We all have. And I'm not going to sit here while some multi-billion dollar corporation dismantles their minds and takes our life savings for that privilege."

Her next words were spoken with a deadly calm. "Give me the materials and I will blow it up myself."

The wind howled. No one moved.

The materials. She was speaking to me, could only be speaking to me. Any gleeb could find fertilizer, and Cyberland was full of hackers who could dismantle Life Keep's security system. But Nitroxylene—now, that wasn't so easy to come by. For once in my life, I was the fulcrum, the Turning Point. I can't remember how many times I'd wanted to be in this position, the one in the group who got to decide, the person everyone looked to.

I didn't want it now. Not like this.

"Mahone?" It was Sara. "You know we don't have a choice."

I looked at Reid.

"I think we should think about this a bit more," he said. It was the first time I'd ever seen him look uncertain.

"No. Sara's right," Shaun spoke up, surprising us all. "You know why? Because life is for living." We stared at him and he shrugged. "It's something my dad used to say."

That Snowflake hovered in my mind.

I saw us then, our Unlikely Terrorist Group, huddled in a corner of the schoolyard in the dead of winter on the prairies, like a beaten dog gathering the courage to snap at a fatally raised hand.

I couldn't let that hand drop; I needed, we all needed, it severed.

I met Sara's eyes, "Yeah, okay." My smile was only half-scowl, "Happy Anniversary, Life Keep."

I wondered how my parents would view me without that shred of glittery childlike devotion to soften the blow.

I was going to find out.

Kate Boorman is an independent artist and writer with an MA in Dramatic Critical Theory. In the past several years, she has collaborated on a variety of theater productions and arts events in Edmonton and the surrounding area. She now writes Young Adult fiction. Her current projects involve first kisses, past lives, immortal beings with super powers, and things that explode. And scooters. Kate lives with her husband and two small children in Edmonton, Alberta.

About the Editors

Julie Czerneda — Co-editor

Tesseracts Fifteen is, curiously enough, Julie's fifteenth anthology as editor/co-editor. Curiosity has been the mainstay of her life, from being a biologist, to writing science texts, to her present career (which she still finds astonishing) of writing science fiction and fantasy full time. Her novels (thirteen to date, if you like to count, with more on the way) are published by DAW Books, and have garnered awards, international acclaim, and been best-sellers. As editor, Julie gets to read great and imaginative writing, but it's entirely possible, and somewhat curious, that what she most enjoys is to collect new authors and celebrate their success.

Susan MacGregor — Co-editor

Other than a three year hiatus to study stand-up comedy and the occasional break to work on her writing, Susan MacGregor has been a fiction editor with *On Spec* magazine since 1991. Her work has been published in *On Spec, Northern Frights*, and other venues. In 1998, she edited *Divine Realms*, an anthology through Ravenstone Books, an imprint of Turnstone Press. Her non-fiction book *The ABC's of How NOT to Write Speculative Fiction* was published in 2006 and has been the source of many workshops presented by *On Spec*. Currently, she is working on a paranormal romance trilogy set in an alternate medieval Spain where the Inquisition pits itself against gypsy magic. When she isn't writing or editing, she studies Spanish and dances flamenco. She lives with her gypsy-descendent husband, wild children, and laid-back hound dog in Edmonton.

About the Cover Artist

Michael O (Michael Oswald) is an internationally recognized digital artist from California. His iconic style combines photography and digital painting techniques that merge into a unique artistic style that he can call his own. In the age of global business, Michael has been fortunate enough to sustain a freelance career as a digital artist and his hope is to continue to gain recognition throughout a wide range of media types. You can currently find Michael's work on various magazine and book covers, websites, gallery walls and movie posters in India as of late.